Who Killed Una Lynskey?

Mick Clifford is an award-winning columnist and reporter with the *Irish Examiner*, where he also presents a weekly podcast. He has been working in print journalism for thirty years and is a regular contributor to broadcast media. He is the author or co-author of five previous non-fiction books, including (as sole author) the bestselling *A Force for Justice: The Maurice McCabe Story* and, most recently, *Unlocked: An Irish Prison Officer's Story* with David McDonald. He has also written two crime novels. He lives in Dublin.

Who Killed Una Lynskey?

A True Story of Murder, Vigilante Justice
and the Garda 'Heavy Gang'

MICK CLIFFORD

SANDYCOVE

an imprint of

PENGUIN BOOKS

SANDYCOVE

UK | USA | Canada | Ireland | Australia
India | New Zealand | South Africa

Sandycove is part of the Penguin Random House group of companies
whose addresses can be found at global.penguinrandomhouse.com.

First published 2024

001

Copyright © Mick Clifford, 2024

The moral right of the author has been asserted

Set in 13.5/16pt Garamond MT Std
Typeset by Jouve (UK), Milton Keynes
Printed and bound in Great Britain by Clays Ltd, Elcograf S.p.A.

The authorized representative in the EEA is Penguin Random House Ireland,
Morrison Chambers, 32 Nassau Street, Dublin D02 YH68

A CIP catalogue record for this book is available from the British Library

ISBN: 978–1–844–88665–4

www.greenpenguin.co.uk

For Aideen Clifford

Contents

CONTENTS

PART III

The Heavy Gang

Porterstown Lane area, 1971

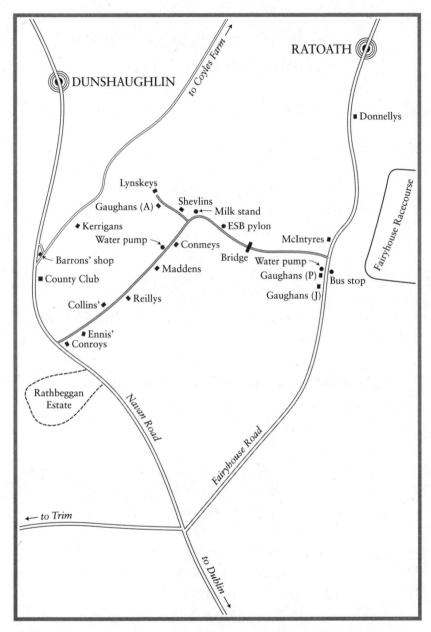

Porterstown Lane is the shaded road between the Navan Road and Fairyhouse Road. It's *c.* 2.4 km long. The map includes the homes of the Lynskey family, of three Gaughan families (cousins of the Lynskeys), and of key witnesses and locations in the investigation into Una Lynskey's disappearance in October 1971. (*Omitted from the map are twelve remaining households on Porterstown Lane in 1971, as well as homes and businesses in the wider area.*)

List of key participants in events of October 1971

Lynskey family, living in the cul-de-sac off Porterstown Lane
- Parents: *Patrick* and *Winnie* (née *Gaughan*)
- Twelve children including *Una* (19), their fifth born, the woman at the heart of this story. On the evening of 12 October, after getting off the bus from Dublin, she disappears on Porterstown Lane. Others who feature in this book include *Sean*, *James*, *Ann* (married to *Seamus Reddin* and living on Porterstown Lane) and *Marita* (8).

Gaughan family, living in the cul-de-sac off Porterstown Lane
- Parents: *Anthony* (brother of *Winnie Lynskey*) and *Mary Kate*
- Eleven children. Those who feature in this book include *Padraic* (19), *Kathleen*, *Danny* and their oldest son, *John* (Canada).

Gaughan family, Fairyhouse Road
- Parents: *Pat* (brother of *Winnie Lynskey*) and *Anne* (sister of *Patrick Lynskey*).
- Four children: *John*, *Seamus*, *Michael* and *Ann* (18). John Gaughan lives near his parents' house with his wife, *Liz*, and their three young

children. Ann is Una's best friend as well as her cousin and is the last person to see Una before she is abducted on Porterstown Lane.

The suspects

- ***Dick Donnelly*** (23), one of six siblings. His family home is on the Fairyhouse Road, near Ratoath.
- ***Martin Conmey*** (20), also one of six siblings, including ***Mary***. The family live on Porterstown Lane, close to the entrance to the cul-de-sac.
- ***Marty Kerrigan*** (19), again, one of six siblings. Lives with his widowed father, ***Martin Senior***, and three sisters – ***Eileen***, ***Ann*** and ***Katie*** – in The Bush, an area off the Navan Road, just north of Porterstown Lane.
  (Subsequent to the tragic events of 1971–2 Ann Kerrigan marries Dick Donnelly. And Martin's sister Mary marries Padraic Gaughan.)

Key witnesses

All but one of those listed here were out and about in the Porterstown Lane area around the time Una Lynskey disappeared. Gardaí return to these witnesses multiple times, as they do to family and friends of the suspects, and to Padraic and Kathleen Gaughan, who were also out of doors that evening, as was their uncle, Pat Gaughan of Fairyhouse Road. After repeated interviews, many witness statements depart from earlier versions in vital details.

- ***Mary Collins***, schoolteacher, wheeling her baby along Porterstown Lane: sees a car going unusually fast and later hears strange shouts.
- ***John Conroy***, farmer: hears strange shouts.

- *Michael McIntyre* (15, a cousin of Martin Conmey): sees an unusual car.
- *James Donnelly*, farmer (no relation to Dick): sees an unfamiliar car with occupants acting strangely.
- *Sean Conmey* (15, Martin's brother): sees an unfamiliar car.
- *Sean Reilly* (23): sees an unusual car while sitting in a parked car with his friend Martin Madden.
- *Martin Madden* (19): initially says he does not see or hear anything, but a statement following a further garda interview proves crucial.
- *John Shevlin* (13): makes four statements, each adding details that align with the garda theory of the case.
- *Thomas Mangan* (20): shares digs with Martin Conmey in Dublin subsequent to Una Lynskey's disappearance; in January 1972 he provides a bombshell statement.

Gardaí

- Sergeant *Seamus McGee*, Dunshaughlin: Una's boyfriend *Paddy Kelly* reports her disappearance to Sergeant McGee around 9 p.m. on 12 October 1971.
- Superintendent *P. J. Keane*, District Officer at Trim garda station.
- Superintendent *Dan Murphy*, head of the Garda Technical Bureau, Dublin.
- Inspector *Hubert Reynolds*, head of the nine-member Investigation Section of the Technical Bureau, more commonly known as 'the Murder Squad'.

- Detective Sergeant *John Courtney*, a member of the Murder Squad.
- Garda *Brian Gildea*, stationed in Balbriggan, North County Dublin, seconded to the investigation into the disappearance of Una Lynskey.
- Detective Garda *Owen Corrigan*, stationed in Drogheda, seconded to the investigation into the disappearance of Una Lynskey.
- Garda *Brian McKeown*, Dunshaughlin: happens to see the suspects at a local shop early in the evening of 12 October; his evidence contradicts the suspects' version of their movements that evening.
- Garda *John Harty*, Ashbourne: garda who tries to keep local factions apart as tensions rise after the discovery of Una Lynskey's body; however, he is unable to prevent a tragedy.

PART I
Missing

1. The Last Day

Una Lynskey's romance had hit a rocky patch around the time she disappeared. She had been going steady with Paddy Kelly for nearly a year. He was her first boyfriend, at least the first that her family or friends knew anything about. She was in love to the point where she couldn't imagine life without him. On the day before she disappeared, Una told her cousin Ann Gaughan that if Paddy broke it off she would never go out with another man again.

Paddy's commitment to the relationship wasn't the problem. What had really come between them was that Una's mother was totally opposed to the union. Winnie Lynskey didn't believe Paddy Kelly was a suitable match for her daughter. And of late she had become more vocal about her feelings. It was all getting to be too much for Paddy, the knowledge that he wasn't welcome in the Lynskey household. How, in a close-knit community, would the young couple have a chance of making things work if Una's mother was determined to ensure they would never walk down the aisle to a life happy ever after?

At times Una wondered what it would be like if she just left, moved into the city, beyond the orbit of her family. She and Ann had talked about getting a flat, but they knew that their parents were dead set against it. One day soon, if the pressure at home didn't ease off, Una was going to make the move.

On the day she disappeared, Tuesday, 12 October 1971,

Una missed the bus into Dublin. Each morning, she and Ann got the Ratoath bus into the city centre, where they both worked. Today, Ratoath is a burgeoning commuter town. In 1971 it was a village in rural Co Meath, sixteen miles from the city centre. Both women lived with their families in a scattering of one-off houses and farms a few miles south of the village, around the Porterstown Lane area. The lane was about a mile and a half long and connected Fairyhouse Road, which led north to Ratoath, to the Navan Road, which led north to Dunshaughlin.

Una was nineteen, Ann a year younger. For the previous ten months Una had been employed as a clerical officer in the Land Commission, based in Upper Merrion Street.

That morning, Una was late arriving at Ann's house so Ann's father, Pat, was called from his bed and he drove them to Dunboyne to catch another bus. The way Ann Gaughan remembered it, Una wasn't herself. But at least she was in better form than she had been the previous day, when she showed up for the bus with red blotches around her eyes.

The Lynskeys were, by the standards of their neighbours and the country at large, pretty well off. Pat Lynskey farmed a holding just shy of one hundred acres. He and most of his neighbours were from the west of Ireland, having been moved across the country in the 1940s by the Land Commission, where coincidentally his daughter was now employed. Winnie worked in the home, as it would be termed today. In reality, she just worked, raising her twelve children, helping out on the farm, engaged in the unseen toil that was the lot of women in general and mothers in particular.

Una enjoyed a steady, rural childhood. She was born on

2 September 1952, the fifth child in the family. Her mother considered her a quiet child, who worked hard and had 'average intelligence'. After primary school in Ratoath she attended the Convent of Mercy in Navan. For the first two years she was a boarder and after that she travelled daily from her home on the school bus. She spent much of her free time studying or helping on the farm, doing jobs like picking peas. In 1970, she sat her Leaving Cert and got one honour. She was five foot two, of slim build with a pale complexion and ash-blonde hair which she wore down over her shoulders.

In November of that year she met Paddy Kelly when she was bridesmaid at her sister Catherine's wedding. Kelly was best man and a cousin of the groom. He was, at twenty-five, a bit older than Una. He worked for a potato merchant's in North County Dublin and lived near Ashbourne, eight miles from Porterstown Lane. The month after the wedding, Una asked him to a dance for past pupils of the Convent of Mercy. Things took off from there.

On most weeks they would meet up three times, Wednesdays, Fridays and Sundays. Kelly would call for her at home in his Austin A40 and they would go to a dance, usually in the Beechmount in Navan, or during the week, to one of the local pubs. Sometimes they just hung out at the Lynskeys' home. Occasionally, it could be a night at the pictures. About three weeks before 12 October, they went to see *Ryan's Daughter*, a big Hollywood movie made in Ireland and set in the revolutionary period after 1916.

At Christmas 1970, while still in the shallows of their relationship, Kelly gave Una a present of a watch. It was heart-shaped with a white face and blue figures and a gold frame. Una was thrilled with it. Then the following Easter, when the couple were really going steady, he bought her a gold-coloured ring with a diamond stone. Una rarely went out without the items affixed to her wrist and finger. She was in love, and before long she was at a point where she couldn't imagine life without him.

Una's mother didn't feel the same. 'Of late I had come to the opinion that this affair was going on too long and of late I started to give Una a hint that I really did not think he was her match,' she would later say.

Winnie Lynskey made various noises about Paddy Kelly's job. She had heard he had had other jobs and he didn't stick at them. That didn't give the impression of a man who was steady and to be trusted. Then there was his motor car. He was paying for it on hire purchase. With a steady job, why wasn't he able to just buy it? Hire purchase, in Winnie's eyes, hinted at straitened financial circumstances.

'I got on to Una about Paddy and said he was a funny class of man not to have his car paid for and not to be keeping his job,' Winnie said. Another aspect of Winnie Lynskey's concern was obvious to Una. In terms of social class, she didn't think Paddy Kelly was good enough for her daughter.

In the first week of October 1971 Una wasn't feeling well. The pressures around her mother's unhappiness with her boyfriend fed into it but she had this pain in her left side that wouldn't leave her alone. She mentioned it frequently but seemed reluctant to have the problem addressed.

All of that was in the background on Sunday, 10 October when Paddy called to the Lynskeys. He stayed for dinner but afterwards probably wished that he hadn't. Una's brother James was going out with Paddy's sister Shelia and the couple had decided they would head off to London together. Mrs Lynskey did not approve and at the dinner table that evening she got stuck into Paddy, as if the whole thing was his fault.

Paddy got the message. The hard words issued to him by Una's mother were more about the woman's unhappiness at him seeing her daughter than anything to do with the other couple striking out for London. After dinner Paddy and Una went out for a quick drink. In the pub he told her that he was breaking it off. He'd had enough of Una's mother constantly onto him. In two weeks' time they were due to attend the annual Convent of Mercy past pupils dinner dance at the Boyne Valley Hotel in Drogheda. This was also the anniversary of their first date. Paddy said he'd hang in for the occasion, but that would be their last evening together. Apart from anything else, he was thinking of getting a flat in the city, and their relationship would be under severe strain if he was living in Dublin and she still at home.

Una was devastated at this bolt from the blue. Her mother's interference got on her nerves too, but she and Paddy were in this together. Now he wanted to break it off. She began crying while they were sitting in the pub. He tried to placate her. He told her that it was time that she had that pain examined. There was a GP in Ratoath, but Paddy didn't rate him. He knew a doctor in Swords in North County Dublin, a Dr Cox, and Paddy would take her to him tomorrow evening. She'd feel better once she found out what it was, and the doctor would hopefully give her something for it. Una was still crying when Paddy dropped her home close to midnight.

She didn't sleep well that night. Her pillow was damp in the morning and her mother noticed that she wasn't herself.

On the bus into the city Ann Gaughan asked what the matter was. Una began crying. 'It's all off,' she said. 'Paddy's breaking it off because he isn't wanted in my home.' Una told her about the previous evening and her mother giving grief to Paddy. 'He was annoyed about it,' Una said. 'He doesn't like fighting.' She told Ann that her mother really wanted her to go out with another local man 'because he had an office job'. But Paddy was not as her mother portrayed him. He had saved £250 and he had intentions of setting up his own business with a lorry. They had plans to get married in the near future, once they could get a house. And now this.

'Are you going to give him back the watch and ring?' Ann wanted to know. Una thought about it. 'I won't wear them once it's all off,' she replied. If Paddy did break it all off on the night of the dance, she said, she would never again go out with another man. The whole thing was having a major impact on her and how she saw her life developing. 'One of these days, I'll be gone,' she told Ann.

Paddy rang her that day at work. He wanted to check in with her as she had been in a bit of a state when they had parted the previous evening. He wasn't feeling too good about the whole thing himself, unable to concentrate on his work, he told her. She was straight up with him, letting him know she was barely able to keep it together. He told her to relax, not to be worrying herself. They'd go to see the doctor that evening and she'd feel a lot better about everything.

He called to the Lynskeys at 8.20 p.m. and the couple headed to Swords, about twelve miles away. At Dr Cox's surgery, Paddy remained in the waiting room while Una went in. Half an hour later she emerged. The doctor believed she had the makings of an ulcer, nothing to be too

worried about, but she should probably get it seen to. He
said he'd organized for her to go into hospital towards the
end of the week. In the meantime, he wrote her a prescription, including something for her nerves. Paddy gave her £3
to cover the doctor's visit and the expected cost of the
medicine. The couple left the surgery and repaired to The
Harp bar in the town, the lingering aftertaste of Paddy's
declaration the previous evening still hanging awkwardly
between them.

Over the course of three pints, Paddy softened a little. He
wasn't going to break it off. He had been annoyed over Una's
mother, but they would keep it going, certainly for now.
He'd ring her tomorrow, just like he always did, and on
Friday they would go dancing in the Beechmount, where the
Royal Showband, one of the top acts in the country, were
due to play.

Una's mood lifted. This was what she had wanted to hear,
what she had been dreaming about all day. She wasn't drinking, sticking to the orange juice, but the turn in fortunes was
leaving her feeling a lot better. On the way home, the couple
encountered a knot of boys on the Fairyhouse Road, whom
they immediately recognized. Una's brothers James and
Sean and their 19-year-old first cousin Padraic Gaughan,
who lived next door to the Lynskeys in a cul-de-sac off Porterstown Lane. The lads hopped into the car, grateful for
the lift.

Later Padraic Gaughan remembered Una as being in fine
form on the journey home. 'She was very jolly and was laughing and joking, which seemed very unusual because you always
had to drag conversation out of her,' Padraic said.

Paddy dropped them off and then the couple turned the
car around and headed out to the Fairyhouse Gates, the

entrance to the Fairyhouse Racecourse, halfway between Porterstown Lane and Ratoath, well known among the racing fraternity throughout the country.

They remained there for forty-five minutes, a little time for the young couple to be themselves, repairing the small fractures that had opened between them over the previous twenty-four hours. It was about 12.45 a.m. when the Austin A40 pulled up outside the Lynskeys' home. As she got out of the car, Paddy told her everything would be all right. 'Mind yourself,' he said, as he habitually did whenever they parted. It was the last time he ever spoke to her, the last time he would ever see her alive.

That night, as she went to bed, Una Lynskey's life was back on track. Two of her sisters were married and, if things worked out with Paddy, she was now en route to the security of a permanent union herself. Paddy was already well into his twenties so he wouldn't be hanging around for ever. They would get married in the coming years, maybe after she, or they both separately, got to move into the city. Once the knot was tied she would have to give up her job, but there was no reason to believe children wouldn't be on the way pretty quickly to keep her busy. They could buy a house in the suburbs, become part of the growing cohort of city dwellers, removed but not too far from her rural upbringing and family.

So much for life opening up in the coming years, her more immediate concern was for the past pupils' dinner dance on Friday week. She hadn't yet got the tickets but would give the school a ring tomorrow. The other thing was her frock. She had a pink bridesmaid's dress from her sister's wedding the previous year, but that would have to be altered. She knew a dressmaker who would do the job and resolved to sort that out after work as well. As for the shoes, she had nothing that was right for the night so she would have to buy a pair.

Winnie Lynskey called her daughter for work at seven fifteen the following morning. Winnie made the breakfast and waited. She had been told the previous evening by another of her daughters, Sally, that Una was going to the doctor in Swords with Paddy Kelly. This had surprised her. Una told her everything, so why was she keeping this a secret? Now, the morning after, she waited for Una to tell her what was happening.

'When she had her breakfast finished she told me she was at the doctor last night, and that his name was Dr Cox, Swords,' Winnie Lynskey remembered of that morning. 'She said that Paddy Kelly had brought her. I said to her wasn't Dr Conway, Ratoath, or Dr McCabe good enough to go to? I also told her that her father would have brought her and anyway that Paddy should not have brought her without our permission. She nodded her head to me that the doctor told her she had an ulcer and gave her a prescription for her stomach and also other tablets to improve her spirits. She then went into the room and said goodbye to Sally and I'll see you in the evening. She came back into the kitchen, blessed herself with holy water and said goodbye to me and went off. That was the last I saw of her.'

On the bus into the city, Una updated Ann with the latest developments. The doctor had told her she was run-down and she needed a colour and there were certain types of food that she shouldn't be eating. Ann was still worried about her. Even though things had been repaired with Paddy, Una still seemed down. That morning when they missed the bus Una told Ann that she didn't care if she was late for work. Yet on the few occasions when they had looked like missing the bus previously, she had been highly anxious at the prospect of being late.

During the day, Una left work to fill the prescription – a medicine to be taken three times daily and mild antidepressant tablets. After clocking off at 5.30 p.m., she walked down through the city centre, crossed the Liffey and headed for Busáras, the main bus terminal in Dublin. She walked with her colleague Anne Finnegan, who travelled up to work every day by bus from her own home in Kildare. Una told Anne she wasn't feeling well. There had been previous mention that her boyfriend didn't meet the approval of her parents, but from what Anne could see it wasn't that big a deal. Anne wondered whether she was pregnant.

They said goodbye and went to their separate buses at the terminal. When Una got on the Ratoath bus, Ann Gaughan was already there, keeping a seat for her. The journey out through the city, into the western suburbs, on to the open countryside, was uneventful. At one point, Una took a medicine bottle from her bag which looked to contain a white substance, but Ann didn't pass any remarks on it.

'Her mind seemed to be wandering, or she seemed to be in a dream,' Ann remembered.

Sometime between 6.50 p.m. and 6.55 p.m., the bus pulled in at the usual stop, the petrol pump on the Fairyhouse Road. The two cousins disembarked. There was a serious chill in the air, the sun disappearing, the signs of dusk closing in. They stood there on the side of the road as the bus pulled away, delaying departure for their respective homes, as they always did, filling a few minutes with chat. Ann lived just up the road, while Una would have to walk about 50 yards to the entrance of Porterstown Lane and over a half a mile to her home in the cul-de-sac. On this day, the chat didn't last as long as normal.

'This was the shortest we ever stopped talking since we began going on the bus,' Ann remembered. 'The reason for this short period of talking was because it was the first evening we felt the cold.' Una went to leave. She put her hand on Ann's arm.

'I better be hurrying on,' she said. 'It's very cold and it will take me a while to get down, and I'll see you in the morning.' In that instant, as they parted, Ann thought Una looked lovely. She paused for a second as Una walked towards the mouth of Porterstown Lane. Ann Gaughan then turned and made off at pace to her own home down the road.

By 7.25 p.m. Una had not arrived home. Her mother wondered what was up. Ordinarily, she would have arrived in by 7.10 p.m. or so – the walk from the bus usually took about fifteen minutes – but there was no sign of her. The most obvious explanation was that after getting off the bus she went back to Ann Gaughan's house for something or other. Winnie Lynskey told her 14-year-old son Andrew to shoot over to Gaughans' on his bike and check whether Una was there.

Andrew set off. He cycled out of the cul-de-sac and on to Porterstown Lane. He went along the lane towards the Fairyhouse Road, past an area known as the Three Acres, where there was also a landmark of a large pylon. After rounding a corner he hit the long straight stretch of the lane that ran all the way to the Fairyhouse Road. He didn't see anybody on the lane as he cycled along.

When he arrived at Fairyhouse Road, he turned right,

towards Dublin, away from Ratoath. He called into Gaughans', but Una wasn't there. Ann said they had parted after getting off the bus. Ann's brother, John, who lived next door, happened to be in the house. He said he'd get his car, take a look around. Ann went with him. They drove up Porterstown Lane to where Una's sister Ann Reddin was living. No, she hadn't called. From there, John Gaughan went to Lynskeys'. After a brief discussion in the house, somebody suggested that maybe she had gone to Paddy Kelly's house. John offered to drive over to the Kellys' in Ashbourne. His sister Ann and Una's father, Pat, and brother James went with him.

Paddy Kelly put in a solid day's work on 12 October. He was up at 7 a.m. and quickly out the door. Over the course of the day he ran deliveries right across the north side of Dublin city, from Finglas to Coolock, Drumcondra to Killester. Then he went southside, delivering a load to Harold's Cross before heading towards Clondalkin later in the afternoon and eventually on to Phibsboro. At Clondalkin, with the time around 4.40 p.m., he stopped to ring Una from a public phone box. As bad luck would have it, the phone was out of order.

He was back at his company's depot in North County Dublin after 6 p.m. and finished up closer to quarter to seven. The depot was about fifteen minutes from his home. 'I had my dinner after going home, hung around for a while and then fixed the exhaust of my car. It was loose,' he would later say. 'I then drove my brother John and sister Sheila to Ballymacadam. Sheila got off to get messages, and John and I went to Ward's service station for petrol. John Ward gave me ten shillings' worth of petrol.'

The brothers collected their sister on the return journey and once home Paddy went straight to his bed. It had been a long day and he had been out late with Una the night before. His head wasn't on the pillow five minutes before he heard a car pulling up outside. One of his siblings came to his room and told him Una Lynskey was missing.

Kelly leaped out of bed, threw on his clothes and went to the front door, where Ann Gaughan, her brother John, and Patrick and James Lynskey were standing.

'They asked me had I seen Una off the bus that evening. I said that I hadn't. They told me that she had alighted off the bus at the top of the road at Ann Gaughan's house but after speaking to Ann Gaughan went on her way home but never arrived there.'

Kelly said he'd come immediately. He hopped in his car and followed the others. They stopped at a pub along the way, where one of the Lynskeys went inside to use the public telephone, to check whether Una had arrived home in the interim. No, there was still no sign of her. Una was still missing.

At the Lynskeys' house there was some discussion as to what to do next, and it was decided that the guards should be called. Kelly offered to go to Dunshaughlin, where the nearest garda barracks was located. He drove to Dunshaughlin, but the barracks was in darkness. He went down the village to the local pub, asked inside what the story was with the guards when an emergency arose. One of the drinkers told him he needed to go around the back of the barracks to the private residence where Sergeant Seamus McGee lived and you'd probably get him there. Kelly went back up the town to the barracks.

By then it was pushing for 9 p.m. This time the previous

evening he and Una had been in Swords, her emerging from the doctor's surgery and the pair of them off for a drink. Now she was gone. It could turn out to be nothing. Maybe she took off. Maybe she was having second thoughts about their relationship, reacting to his change of mood, notwithstanding the better connection between them the previous evening. Maybe she'd turn up in the next few hours, although none of this was like Una.

He knocked on the door of the house behind the barracks and Sergeant McGee appeared. He said he'd phone Trim, where An Garda Síochána's district office for the area was located, and he'd be over to Porterstown immediately after that. A young woman missing from the midst of a settled, stable community in rural Ireland was practically unknown in 1971, but the gardaí were going to do all they could to find out what had happened, where she was and whether anybody had done her any harm.

2. The First Day

Dick Donnelly was the man. The 23-year-old was a popular figure among his peers, nice, easy-going, no big complications. Apart from that, Dick had what most others didn't – wheels. Dick was the owner of a Ford Zephyr, gold in colour but in a precarious condition. For his friends in and around Porterstown Lane, Dick's car was a passport to freedom. Living in rural Ireland, yet in relatively close proximity to the towns and villages in south County Meath and Dublin city, a car could make a huge difference. So it was for those on the cusp of adulthood who hung around with Dick.

Principal among his friends were two other local men, Martin Conmey, who was twenty, and 19-year-old Marty Kerrigan. They were all part of a wider group in the area, but those three were particularly tight, sharing the same interest in cars, the same sense of humour. On 12 October 1971, their lives were about to be altered forever and Dick's car would be central to their fate.

The Ford Zephyr was a large passenger model known as an 'executive car'. It was first introduced by the manufacturer in 1950 and produced in the UK and in Ford's Irish plant in Cork city. It was one of a family of vehicles made by Ford at the time, which also included the Zodiac and the Ford Executive. The model ceased to be manufactured in 1972, when it was replaced by the Ford Consul and Granada. There was nothing executive about Dick Donnelly's

Zephyr, but you could funnel half a dozen or more bodies into it and it got you from A to B. Most of the time.

Dick was on his second Zephyr by October 1971. Previously he had had a black one, but the body was in rag order. So, he organized with a friend, Brian O'Neill in Ratoath, to buy a new body, swapping black for gold. Donnelly told O'Neill he'd give him £20 for the new body, but the money never changed hands. He and a few of the lads towed the new body down to their friend Seamus McIntyre's yard. Seamus lived near the lane and was a cousin of Martin Conmey. While it was there, Seamus and Marty Kerrigan and Christo Ennis, another one of the group, took the engine and gearbox from the black model and transferred it to the gold. They did the same with the registration plates and the latest Zephyr was ready to roll.

Not that there was anything new or smooth about it. The handle worked on the driver's door, but for the other three doors you'd have to lower the window and open it from the outside.

The battery was temperamental. Nearly always the car required a push to get it to cough into life. And then there were the little things that constantly required attention to ensure that the engine would continue to function at a passable level. Over the course of a normal week, it wouldn't be unusual for Dick to, at least a few times, raise the bonnet and dip his head down to closely examine what little adjustments needed to be made to keep the show on the road. On completing his tinkering, Dick would slam down the bonnet in a gesture of triumph. For those in the area, you'd often hear Dick's Zephyr before you'd see it, the sound of an engine chugging along like an old lady struggling for breath as she put down the miles. An examination of the state of the vehicle a few months after 12 October would conclude that it was not roadworthy.

Still, Dick Donnelly or his friends weren't looking to give Formula One driver Jackie Stewart a run for his money. This was all about freedom and convenience, nothing more. The Zephyr allowed for new possibilities. Going out to the pub during the week now became a simple matter. Equally, heading off to the Beechwood in Navan or the dancehall in Kilmoon at the weekends could now be done without having to worry about transport there and back. And the lads even ventured further afield, shooting down to Dublin if anything there took their fancy. Somebody made the discovery that there was a particularly choice chipper at Hart's Corner, on the North Circular Road on the northside of the city. So it was that every so often a voice among them might begin mulling over the appetizing thought of a bag of chips. A few shoulders would get behind the rear lights on the Zephyr, bring it to life, and they'd hop in, all ready to eat up the road right down to the city.

Dick Donnelly was different from nearly all his pals in that his family had not been transplanted from the west. He was one of a family of six, a twin with his brother Christo, living on the Fairyhouse Road, just outside Ratoath. Martin Conmey's father had arrived from the Belmullet area thirty years earlier. Martin was also one of six children and the family lived on the lane, a few hundred yards from the Lynskeys. Marty Kerrigan's family lived on the far side of the lane, in an area off the Navan Road known as The Bush. Marty's father, Martin Snr, was another migrant from Co Mayo, but he had packed in the farming and by 1971 worked in construction. His wife Ann had died in 1967, leaving behind six children. The two eldest

had emigrated to England. Marty was the second youngest, the only male among the four Kerrigan siblings still
living at home.

All three lads had finished in full-time education at fourteen, never completing the Leaving Cert, which was not
unusual for the time. They were unskilled, but work was
plentiful. Early in 1971, Donnelly and Conmey had worked
for a construction firm in the Robin Hood industrial estate
in Clondalkin, but they returned home that summer to work
locally. Both were employed by a farming family, the Coyles,
which was run by father and son Charles and Raymond
Coyle.* Marty Kerrigan was working for another local farming family, the Dunnes.

They were typical of young people at the time, wearing
their hair long and the cut of their jeans flared. They were
getting their heads around coming of age, enjoying life, fig-
uring out what to do next in a country that was going
through some change. The sixties, it is said, arrived in
Ireland in the early seventies. And that was how it felt for
these young men, a sense that they were going to begin
adult life in a country that was very different from the one
that had sprung their parents' generation. Music, fashion,
attitudes to the Church and authority, even economic prospects, all seemed to be about to change.

On Tuesday, 12 October 1971, Donnelly and Conmey
were working but Marty Kerrigan wasn't. It is unclear why
he wasn't toiling away at Dunnes', but the casual nature of
the employment, and the sense that this was just something

* Raymond Coyle would years later gain national prominence as a businessman when he established the amusement park Tayto Park — later renamed
Emerald Park — outside Navan. He died in 2022.

to do until life got really motoring, probably contributed to his day on the doss.

Marty spent much of the day mooching around, in and out of the house. By 5.30 p.m. he was in the kitchen of his home, probably bored, as he waited for Telefís Eireann to begin broadcasting. Television consisted of one channel and broadcasting didn't begin until 6 p.m., kicking off the evening's fare with the booming of the Angelus. Marty was home alone, his sisters and father all out working. He ate his tea and watched the clock crawl. He knew that sometime before seven Dick and Martin Conmey were likely to call and set in train another evening of what passed for adventure during the week.

Donnelly and Conmey were putting in a hard day's work while their friend took it easy. Dick Donnelly was working with another young man, Matthew Reilly, under the supervision of the boss, Charles Coyle. They were sowing winter wheat using a mechanical seeder. At six o'clock, they heard the bells of the Angelus ringing out across the fields from a nearby church. Some minutes later, Donnelly and Reilly drove two tractors back to the Coyles' yard and parked them. Then Matthew watched as Dick raised the bonnet of the Zephyr and did the bit of tinkering that hopefully would allow for many more miles to come. Once that was done, Matthew gave the Zephyr the requisite push and watched the exhaust pipe cough into life. He waved as Dick drove out of the yard. The time was heading for 6.30 p.m.

A few minutes later the Zephyr was pulling in about a mile away, at another area of the Coyles' operation where Martin Conmey was working with Charles's son, Ray. The pair of them were loading Brussels sprouts into a van. Ray

Coyle saw – and heard – the Zephyr arriving up at the main road. 'We'll get this last load on and you can head then,' he said to Martin Conmey.

Within a few minutes, the job was done and the pair drove up to where Dick was waiting. Ray Coyle chatted with the two employees briefly, before he and Conmey put their shoulders to the rear of the Zephyr and got her motoring again. Martin Conmey hopped in and off they went. The time was now heading towards 6.45 p.m.

Up at Kerrigans', the house was coming alive. Marty's sisters Ann and Katie arrived home from work in Dublin. Five minutes or so later, at about 6.50 p.m., the two lads showed up in the Zephyr. Marty went out to them. 'What's the story?' he asked. 'We're off home for the dinner and then heading out,' Dick told him. Marty said he'd shoot along with them. Then his sister Katie came out and asked whether there was any chance of a lift down to Barrons' shop; she had to pick up some briquettes. The shop was down at the entry to The Bush near the junction of the Dublin–Navan Road. 'Hop in,' Dick said. She did, and her brother did the honours at the rear of the vehicle.

They drove down to the shop, Katie went in and got her messages and they dropped her back up, kept the engine running while she was getting out because the less pushing the car required, the better. From there, the three of them, Conmey in the front passenger seat, Kerrigan in the back, drove down to the Navan Road from Kerrigans' and then left into Porterstown Lane. The precise time the gold-coloured Zephyr entered the lane and what occurred over the following minutes would be the subject of speculation, allegation and tragedy. At some point over the preceding twenty minutes or so – how many minutes exactly is

unclear – Una Lynskey had entered the far side of Porterstown Lane, a mile and a half away, on foot.

According to Martin Conmey, the car went straight to his
home, where he was dropped off at around 7.15 p.m. The
two lads told him they'd be back within a half-hour. 'I'll see
ya later,' Conmey said, slamming the car door shut. Inside
his house, Conmey's mother Eileen heard a version of this
exchange. Marty Kerrigan got out of the back seat and into
the front passenger seat.

On the pair drove, past the cul-de-sac where the Lynskeys lived, around the slow bend at the centre of the lane
and on to the Three Acres with its distinctive large pylon.
At that point, they passed a parked car, a black model which
they recognized as being similar to the one they were in.

'Look at the Zephyr,' Kerrigan said.

'It's a Zodiac, there's twin headlamps on it,' Donnelly
replied. The Zephyr and Zodiac had many similar features.
Donnelly had to slow down as he passed the car on the lane.
They paid it no further heed. At the end of the lane, Donnelly turned the car left and drove up the Fairyhouse Road,
in the direction of Ratoath, to his home. He went inside for
his dinner while Marty stayed in the car.

That was how they all remembered that time between
6.45 p.m. and around 7.25 p.m. Later, the gardaí would come
to the conclusion that during that period the Zephyr
encountered Una Lynskey along the lane, walking home,
sparking off something that quickly went out of control.

Meanwhile, back at Conmeys', Martin was getting stuck
into his dinner. The rest of the family had already eaten.
Eileen usually served up the evening meal around 6.30 p.m.
and when Martin was working she kept his warm on the
range for him. Martin came in and wolfed down the meal at

the kitchen table. He did his usual trick, lowering the sound on the TV and tuning into Radio Luxembourg so he could listen to some music. His mother left him at it; sure wasn't he entitled to it after a day's work out in the fields.

Afterwards, he put on a clean jumper and a pair of shoes. He was meeting up with his girlfriend, Patricia Carey, that night and was mad for the road. Over at Dick Donnelly's house, Dick finished his dinner and came outside to Marty. He said he'd be a minute as he had to fix a headlight to his brother's car, which was also in the yard. The task took him a few minutes and they were off out again, back on the road.

Around 7.45 p.m., freshly scrubbed, Martin Conmey heard Dick's car pull up outside. He said goodbye to his family and went out to meet him and off they went again, into the night, young fellas tasting freedom, their world opening up. The three then took off for Patricia Carey's house, about a mile and a half outside Dunshaughlin. Patricia came out and Martin Conmey swapped places with Marty Kerrigan, Conmey getting into the back seat with his girlfriend. They drove to Ryan's public house in Ratoath. There, Donnelly and Kerrigan went inside for a drink, leaving the lovebirds in the car for a little time on their own. Not that they'd be getting up to much parked outside a pub in Ratoath.

After a half-hour or so, the two lads came out and they took off again. The time was now heading for 9.30 p.m. Dick said they were going to call for Irene Ennis and go to another pub, this one in Batterstown. Irene lived on Porterstown Lane. They also had to swing by Martin Conmey's house again on the way because cash was in short supply and Martin had a few pounds put away at home that he could raid for the sake of another pint. Off they went,

24

leaving Ratoath and driving down the Fairyhouse Road, past Dick's house and onward until they came to the mouth of Porterstown Lane. They hadn't gone far along the lane when they came upon a group of people walking with flashlights.

'They must be out looking for cattle,' somebody said, as Dick slowed down. It wasn't unusual for cattle to stray from their fields and for neighbours to lend a hand in rounding them up. Except it wasn't cattle that had brought these people with their flashlights out into the October night.

Dick drove past the scattering of people with their flashlights, but further along the lane it became obvious that something bigger than stray cattle was afoot. Up ahead a garda was waving a flashlight at approaching traffic. Donnelly slowed down and came to a stop beside the garda, whom they recognized as John Morgan, from Dunshaughlin. He stuck his head in the front passenger window.

'Have any of you seen Una Lynskey?'

'No, what's the story?' Marty Kerrigan asked. The garda told them that she was missing and a search was being conducted. Dick could see ahead that the road was blocked by a car, which he recognized as that of Paddy Kelly, whom he knew to be Una Lynskey's boyfriend. Then Winnie Lynskey came over to the Zephyr, looking worried. She told them that her Una was missing.

'He [the guard] asked us did we see any cars stopped on the lane, and we told him about the Zodiac,' Dick Donnelly later recalled. After a few minutes they drove on. There was, as far as they were concerned, no reason to panic just yet. Besides, Irene Ennis was expecting them to call and the night was not yet done. At Conmeys', Martin went in to get the money. He ran in through the kitchen, where his sister Mary was watching TV. She had already heard about Una.

They picked up Irene Ennis. She slipped into the front seat beside Marty Kerrigan, with Dick still behind the wheel. Somebody asked Irene had she heard that Una Lynskey had gone missing. Irene hadn't heard that.

At Batterstown all five went into Caffreys' and had a few drinks. Afterwards, they drove home. Patricia Carey was dropped to her house. Martin Conmey got out and saw her to the door. It was just another weeknight date, driving around in Dick's car, a few drinks, everything operating at half speed in anticipation for the weekend, when they could give it a proper lash, a bit of dancing, no work in the morning. Conmey got back in the car and they took off again, this time bound for Marty Kerrigan's home.

At Kerrigans' Marty got out and next they swung by to drop off Irene Ennis. Outside Ennises' a few other lads were congregated, and between them they thought it might be best to head down to the pylon and see what the story was with this search. Within an hour Marty Kerrigan also went down to join the search with his sisters. Something big had happened that very evening. Later, Patricia Carey and Irene Ennis would both recall the night as just your average Tuesday, driving around with the lads, a few drinks, a few laughs. There was nothing unusual about their behaviour. There was nothing that might suggest they had possession of a dark and terrible secret, as the gardaí would come to believe. If they knew exactly why the community was out walking the roads, and crossing fields that night, searching for a young woman plucked from their community, the three lads were hiding it very well.

3. Another Country

The young people living around the Porterstown Lane area grew up in a different country from today's Ireland. In the early 1970s Ireland was by the standards of western Europe an underdeveloped backwater. Fifty years after achieving independence, the state was still waiting to take off.

Education was more a privilege than a right. Most of those who would get caught up in the aftermath of Una Lynskey's disappearance did not sit the Leaving Certificate. Four years previously, the Minister for Education, Donogh O'Malley, had introduced free second-level education, a transformative move that would change the country. For huge swathes, including those in the heartlands of Co Meath, its full impact had not yet kicked in.

Immigration had long been a staple of life, particularly, but by no means exclusively, in rural Ireland. By 1971, Marty Kerrigan's older brother and sister had taken the boat to England, but in earlier times the attrition rate was even higher. In *Ireland 1912–85* historian J. J. Lee pointed out that most of the twenty-six counties in the state gained population between 1966 and 1971, some for the first time in a century. 'The changes were not spectacular in absolute terms,' he wrote. 'But they assumed historical significance in that they reversed the trend of more than a century.'

'The "vanishing Irish" were no longer vanishing,' Lee wrote. 'But the battle had to be unceasing. The advance on the unemployment front was painfully slow.' In 1970, income per head in the Republic of Ireland was half what it was for the nearest neighbour, the UK.

Marty Kerrigan, Martin Conmey and Dick Donnelly were working in agriculture on a casual basis. That was typical of the times, but this reliance on casual agricultural labour was a disappearing world for most young, unskilled workers near any of the big towns or cities, as those men were. There was a lot of hope that living standards would be raised when the country joined, as was expected, the European Economic Community (EEC), the forerunner to the EU (Ireland and the UK joined in 1973).

The Catholic Archbishop of Dublin, John Charles McQuaid, died in January 1971. Through his office and personality he had occupied one of the main power centres of the country over the preceding thirty years. Nothing happened without his say-so if he considered it to come within the Church's sphere of influence.

Over 95 per cent of people declared themselves Catholic in the 1971 census, with just 0.3 per cent ticking 'no religion'. Weekly Mass attendance was running at 91 per cent of the population. Going to Mass on a Sunday wasn't just a way of life but central to the week. In small towns, there would be talk about the person who hadn't been seen at Mass for a while. Local businesspeople who had no religious instinct still attended, lest anybody in the community might think they had gone wrong or fallen foul of the parish priest. The writ of the parish priest ran far and wide. He was the sage, the arbiter of morality, the exemplar of good living, the agent who had a direct connection to the Man Above and was therefore well on the road to deification himself.

Nowhere was the power of the Church more obvious than in the matter of sexual mores. There was a constitutional ban on divorce, which would remain in place until 1995. Homosexual activity was illegal, punishable by imprisonment. It would be 1993 before that changed. Contraceptives were only available through prescription from a doctor, and only for married couples. In May 1971, women from the Irish Women's Liberation Movement stepped off a train in Dublin's Connolly station wielding condoms bought in Belfast which were illegal in the Republic. Some saw this as a sign that the country was going to pot. Others smiled to themselves but were careful to keep a straight face in public. What was important was that the appearance of piousness was maintained.

The lot of Irish women was particularly oppressive. Thirty-four years earlier, the 1937 constitution had set out a vision for the place of women in society, and not much had changed in the interim. Article 41.2 stated that 'the state recognizes that by her life within the home woman gives to the state a support without which the common good cannot be achieved. The state shall, therefore, endeavour to ensure that mothers shall not be obliged by economic necessity to engage in labour to the neglect of their duties in the home.'

By the early seventies the state was still treating women as if the evolution of western society had stalled back when the constitution was written. A marriage ban, which decreed that married women could not occupy state jobs, was in place. Those like Una Lynskey who worked in the public sector would have to resign once married, as all were expected to retreat to the home for the exclusive duty of raising children. (The 'marriage ban' would finally end in July 1973.)

Within the Catholic Church women were regarded equally as a threat to morals and the bedrock of the family, the nuclear family on which Irish Catholic society was based. A line in a garda report compiled after Una's disappearance noted: 'From enquiries made, and facts disclosed, it appears that Una Lynskey was not a girl of loose morals.' The phrase 'loose morals' was rarely if ever applied to Irishmen.

Much of this was in early stages of change at the time of Una Lynskey's disappearance. The youths living around Porterstown Lane were part of a generation in Ireland who were inhaling the currents of freedom drifting in from abroad, particularly the UK and the USA. By 1971, the fashion and music of the swinging sixties were at last putting in an appearance. Progressive music was where it was at for the youth, but there was still life in the old dog of conservative Ireland. In April 1971, the whole country was agog as Ireland hosted the Eurovision Song Contest, following the win the previous year by Derry singer Dana with the gentle pop song 'All Kinds of Everything'.

For the greater part, particularly out beyond the main conurbations, the showbands still held sway. The Royal Showband, which was due to play in the Beechwood in Navan the week that Una disappeared, were among the top acts, both in terms of popularity and longevity. First formed in 1957, they remained a staple on the Irish circuit all the way to early 1971, when three of the main members, including Brendan Bowyer, left to seek fame in Las Vegas. But the Royal continued to play, as if their future, and symbolically that of the showband era, could hold back the tides of change.

Music was also changing on the wireless, as the radio was still known. The national broadcaster, RTÉ, had just one station, and that was dominated by speech, a little pop music, only occasionally late at night breaking out into the wild and dangerous world of rock 'n' roll. Most young people who had an interest knew where to find Radio

Luxembourg on the dial, as Martin Conmey did at the dinner table on the day his life was about to change for ever. The station was the only commercial outlet in Ireland or the UK at the time, broadcasting what its audience wanted to hear rather than what was deemed appropriate and acceptable by the powers that were.

Television for the greater part in Ireland also consisted of just one station, RTÉ's Telefís Eireann. And, as Marty Kerrigan experienced on 12 October 1971, it didn't begin broadcasting until 6 p.m. each day, kicking off with an image of the Virgin Mary and a recording of the Angelus bell to remind people of the traditional Catholic devotion.* In the greater Dublin area, all the way out to parts of Ratoath in Co Meath, it was possible to also tune into the BBC. The biggest draw on RTÉ was a drama series *The Riordans*, which ran from 1965 to 1979 and centred on an eponymous farming family in the fictional townland of Leestown, somewhere in Co Kilkenny.

Overall, the country was still a backwater, clinging to the edge of Europe. Beneath the surface, there were oceans of darkness that would not come to light for decades. In such a milieu, deference was an overweening feature of society. There was deference to authority, born out of a relatively poor, uneducated population cowed down by the power of the Catholic Church. Everybody knew that the deference was not earned, but few were willing or even able to challenge it. Change was coming, but organically, with the literal

---

* Most Irish readers will know that the Angelus is still broadcast on RTÉ Radio One at noon and 6 p.m. and on RTÉ One TV at 6 p.m., though the latter is now accompanied by secular imagery, the thinking being that if you're not a person of faith, it can be regarded as a moment for reflection.

dying off of those who had held sway in the post-revolution state.

One official body that had a major impact on rural Ireland in the decades leading up to the 1970s was the Land Commission, the agency where Una Lynskey was working on the day she disappeared. The commission was created by the British in 1842 to 'inquire into the occupation of land in Ireland'. During the 1880s it took on the role of rent-fixing body. Following that, it was the vehicle that facilitated the transfer of farmland from landlords to tenants in response to the agitation over appalling conditions for tenant farmers. By 1920 it had overseen the transfer of 13.5 million acres.

Under the Free State government from 1922, a series of new laws were passed giving the commission further powers. One of these related to sorting out 'congested' holdings, particularly in the west of the country. These holdings dated from the land wars that commenced in the late nineteenth century and were, for the greater part, too small to be economically viable. The solution arrived at by the commission was to offer these small farmers the opportunity to relocate to the east of the state, principally counties Meath and Kildare. Applicants would surrender their land in the west and be given smallholdings of typically around 20 to 25 acres. Everybody was aware that land in the east was more viable, even rich, compared to much of the stony grey soil in large tracts of counties Mayo and Galway. Those who migrated east were often known in their new homes as 'the westies' or 'the Gaeltachts', or 'the colonists'. The first Free State government, under W. T. Cosgrave, instigated the laws designed to lead to more land distribution, but it wasn't until Éamon de Valera came to power with Fianna

Fáil in 1932 that the commission made a push to ramp up the programmes.

One of the Land Commission developments was a large tract of land in and around Porterstown Lane, which it bought in 1939. It was divided among families who agreed to leave their homes in the hinterland of Belmullet in Co Mayo and relocate (though at least one of the families who relocated to Porterstown Lane originated in Galway, not Mayo). Most of the extended families that got caught up in the aftermath of Una Lynskey's disappearance came from Co Mayo.

Mary Conmey, Martin's sister, remembers growing up in a close-knit community that was sure of its roots yet perfectly at home in Co Meath. 'When I first went to primary school I was amazed that not all of the other children's parents had come from Co Mayo,' she said. 'I had thought that that was just the way things were. Your parents came from there.'

The migrants who came east weren't always welcomed and were often treated with suspicion. One legend that took flight was that the westerners were taking land from local people and being given preferential treatment. This was wholly untrue. Those native to Meath and Kildare who were farming similar smallholdings were given first refusal on the commission's land. Some of the resentment was channelled to local politicians, who gave it voice on the floor of the Dáil. In 1927, just over a decade before Porterstown Lane was divided among 'the westies', David Hall, a Labour Party TD for Co Meath, told the Dáil that his county people 'have no objection to the migrants, but at the same time they do not want them coming in such numbers as to scrooge out the people of Meath'.

He went on: 'I do not think it is fair to have people hawked in and thrown in on the people of Meath this way.

I would like to know if it is the intention of the Land Commission to plant all Meath with migrants. They are coming in such numbers that they are scrooging out the people of Meath who have just claims for allotments of land, evicted tenants and others of that kind. The Meath people are being shoved out and the others are getting allotments of land.'

Such a speech in the national parliament today would likely be condemned, both inside and outside the chamber. Yet there was little reaction. The deputy's tone reflected feelings among some of his constituents. It was informed by the sight of new arrivals setting up home in the eastern counties with what appeared to some to be free land. Mixed in with this was resentment and fear that they were relatively primitive, bringing their alien mores over from the untamed west.

The kind of tensions that often existed between 'the colonists' and the native local people were evident in a flashpoint that could have turned very ugly. A migrant community in Allenstown, about 32 kilometres north-east of Porterstown Lane, had arrived in 1940 to begin anew. They had been under the impression that a local area was reserved as part of their resettlement for recreational needs. However, some in the native local community believed they were entitled to the lands for use for the local GAA club.

Two sides lined up to literally do battle in early August 1940, resulting in the arrest of four of the migrants. Recounting the incident in his book *The Lost Gaeltacht*, published in 2020, Martin O'Halloran writes that 'there were no arrests of the locals, even though evidence adduced showed they were in possession of sticks, pitchforks and guns, for legal and perhaps not legal purposes. There were between 20 and 25 people in each of the groups who confronted each other and took part in the ensuing melee.'

The handling of the matter, O'Halloran posits, 'prompts questions of police bias against the migrants'. However, the judge hearing the case against the four migrants ultimately dismissed the charges. 'The colonists had been put to a great amount of expense and that being so he suggested that the whole matter should cease. The judge described it as a comedy of errors, a tragedy of errors and much ado about nothing.'

There is little doubt, however, that with tensions and emotion high on both sides, and an array of weapons present, things could have turned ugly very easily. Such incidents were not unknown during the early years of the migration, but over the long term those who came from the west merely integrated into their new homes.

A retrospective view of the Land Commission programme was offered to the Dáil over sixty years after the fulminations of David Hall in the same forum. Fine Gael TD Ted Nealon, who said his people had come from the west under the programme, spoke during a debate on the dissolution of the commission in 1989.

'The biggest migration was to County Meath and those who came were known as colonists,' he said. 'They got 24 acres of land, a house and a bank of turf. The Land Commission looked after them very well. Many people from the west are extremely grateful to them for their help. The colonists were a great asset to their new areas and they brought with them a new culture, one that has survived to the enrichment of the areas they settled in. Their children have turned out extremely well and many of them subsequently became public figures. However, it should be said that the migrants from the west were not universally welcomed in their new homes.'

In time, some around Porterstown Lane would claim that the fact that most of the families were originally displaced from the west resulted in prejudicial attitudes towards them from certain members of the gardaí in the investigation into the disappearance of Una Lynskey.

The Lynskey family's experience, both in terms of relocation and integration, was an example of how the displaced communities evolved. Una's grandfather James Lynskey was provided with 28 acres when he relocated. 'We came here as migrants with seven other families from Co Mayo, the Belmullet area,' Patrick Lynskey, James's son and Una's father, would recall. In 1945 Patrick married Winnie Gaughan, a neighbour whose family had also come east. Patrick's sister Anne married Pat Gaughan, Winnie's brother, in a double wedding. 'The both of us married on the same day, 21 August 1945,' Lynskey remembered. 'Patrick Gaughan is one of the migrants referred to already. I got a farm, 28 acres, from my father.' Pat and Anne Gaughan moved to a house on the Fairyhouse Road. Among their children was Ann, Una's double first cousin, who accompanied her home on the bus on 12 October. Next door to the Lynskeys down the cul-de-sac on Porterstown Lane was the home of Winnie's other brother, Anthony Gaughan, his wife Mary Kate and their family.

Patrick Lynskey had done very well since he arrived in Porterstown Lane with his father and siblings. He made a good living growing and selling vegetables, to the point that he harboured ambitions to expand. He had his eye on a neighbouring holding of 66 acres. The close family ties came in handy at this point. Patrick managed to buy the farm privately through a solicitor who was married to a niece of Winnie's.

'I paid £5,300, plus fees for the farm. This came as a big surprise to my neighbours. They thought that I wasn't in a position to buy a farm, and they expected that the Land Commission would divide it between the local tenants. It would have made a few thousand more if it had gone by public auction.'

Patrick Lynskey's origins, connected to his success, led to what he perceived to be resentment among some neighbours. He had a couple of minor disputes, one of which concerned a neighbouring farmer whose cattle trespassed on to Patrick's holding. On one occasion a field of peas was destroyed. Patrick Lynskey took the neighbour to court and was awarded £39. However, when this farmer passed the business on to his son, the old animosity disappeared.

'We are getting on very well,' Lynskey would recall of the son. 'He often bought potatoes from us and I would call him a good neighbour. If he saw an animal of mine straying he would ring me, but he never objected to my sons shooting on his lands. His father is now dead.'

Lynskey was not a man to hold grudges. He was remembered locally as quiet but diligent, an astute businessman. He got on with things, made a success of his business, but he knew that he would always be regarded as an outsider. 'While the local people, the Co Meath people, never accepted us, they never did us any harm,' he said. However, some local people believed that he thought everybody was jealous of him.

This theme also appeared in a garda file compiled after Una's disappearance. 'It is known that the other inhabitants of Porterstown Lane, fellow migrants of the Lynskeys, and many of them related through marriage, are jealous of the progress made by the Lynskeys and are not very sympathetic towards them in their trouble.'

Locals who saw or heard this analysis took exception to it, suggesting it was driven by unconscious prejudice by the author or other members of An Garda Síochána against the migrant community rather than rooted in fact.

One incident in the Lynskeys' lives may indicate how as migrants they were considered different from the natives but is also an example of the deference to authority that existed at the time.

Their son, Michael, who was attending a local national school, received a beating from a teacher that left him bleeding. His parents were so upset they approached the local parish priest, Fr John Cogan. As a result, the teacher came to the Lynskeys and explained why he had felt it necessary to administer such a brutal punishment, but that was the end of the matter. No other action was taken against the teacher and, as far as Pat Lynskey could see, the only long-lasting effect was that his children had been marked out because of he and his wife pursuing the matter at all.

'After this incident with Michael, he [the teacher] didn't like my children, so we decided to change to another school. We called the Department of Education and made the necessary arrangements to have them changed. Michael and the others transferred. I was very hurt with what was done to Michael.'

Overall, despite such incidents, the Lynskey family were getting on well with life, working hard, embedded in the local community. All of that would be shattered, never to be repaired, after Una disappeared somewhere nearby, in the heart of the countryside where they had made their home.

4. A Grey Dawn

AN GARDA SÍOCHÁNA
METROPOLITAN AREA
Communications Centre
13 October 1971

Commissioner,

Report for the period between 5pm 12th and 9.30am 13th October 1971

At 8.55pm, 12.10.1971 it was reported to the Gardaí that Una Lynskey, 19 years, Porterstown, Ratoath, Co Meath had not arrived home from her employment at land commission offices, Merrion St, Dublin.

On investigation it was established that the missing girl travelled from Dublin by bus as usual and was seen leaving the bus at 6.45pm. She would then have to walk about ¾ of a mile along Porterstown Lane to her home. There is no further information about her movements, but two people have stated that a car resembling a Ford Zepher [*sic*], greyish colour, was seen parked on the roadway to her home. It is also stated that two other people allege that they heard a scream from a field adjoining this roadway.

Supt Keane, Trim, organised an exhaustive search of the area, assisted by Gardaí and local people, as well as gardaí from Dublin and a dog team.

So far the girl has not been located. The search continues and any useful information will be promptly reported.

D Kenny

Inspr.

Some stayed out all night. They moved through the fields using torches and flashlamps. They crossed over ditches and poked around the bases of groves of trees. They pulled back thickets of briars with scythes and spades. Every so often somebody would call out her name, as if there was a chance she might be lying injured somewhere, like a fallen mountain climber, and would respond.

'Una, Una,' they called against the night. No response came back.

In the morning, the search continued. Before midday, word had spread to the daily newspapers and the national broadcaster, RTÉ. Reporters began turning up, and the man in charge, Superintendent P. J. Keane, briefed them.

'We've been searching through the night but can't find any sign of the girl or any clues,' he said. 'We've covered a radius of twenty miles. Now we're going to have to start looking for people who would have been walking down the lane at around the same time as the girl.'

Many of the locals skipped work that first day to help with the search. Dick Donnelly, Martin Conmey and Marty Kerrigan did so. The Lynskeys' first cousin Padraic Gaughan took the day off from his job as an apprentice cabinet maker. He had last seen Una on the night before she disappeared when Paddy Kelly and Una had stopped to give him and her brothers James and Sean a lift home.

'The night we went out was really dark and there must

have been fifteen or twenty of us going around those fields and even further on,' he remembers. 'Next day we just kept going, spreading the search out further. It wasn't all totally organized. Some of us just went off to places where we thought there was the chance she may have been. There were a few bridges in Dunboyne that we checked to see if she could be under any of them. There was an old railway that we went looking along. We'd tell the gardaí about some of these places and they'd say, "Yeah, check it out." We weren't looking for a body or anything. Nobody thought at that stage that she could have been killed.'

Already, the gardaí had been informed about the car which Donnelly and Kerrigan said they saw parked near the pylon on the lane after they had dropped off Martin Conmey and were en route to Donnelly's house. Word spread quickly about this sighting. Others mentioned a strange car they had seen in the general area that evening. With each morsel about the disappearance hungrily consumed, speculation turned to whether the car was a Zephyr, like Dick's, or a Zodiac, a similar model made by Ford.

Ann Kerrigan, Marty's sister, had been out with members of her family searching on the first night. She went to work the following day at a drapers in the city centre, but that evening when she returned she joined the search again.

'A lot of the talk was around the strange car that was seen at the Three Acres,' she said. 'Marty and Dick were the first ones to spot it, but then others came forward. There was a lot of worry around that car, but even so nobody was thinking that she had been killed or anything. We all still had a lot of hope at that point.'

Pretty soon, the first clue was discovered. In a field about two hundred yards from the Lynskeys' home a small medicine bottle was retrieved from a drain. When it was produced Ann Gaughan remembered Una taking a bottle from her bag on the bus home on the day in question. The gardaí were told. Speculation ran riot. An opinion formed locally that the bottle must have fallen from Una's handbag as she swung to ward off her attacker or attackers. The area immediately around where the bottle was found was gone over again, this time slowly, meticulously, hoping the foliage would yield further clues. Some locals came across the fields just to stand there, as if to get a sense of what might have occurred, of how Una may have fought off her attacker and what happened thereafter. Later, the bottle would be discounted from the investigation.

Apart from the search locally, gardaí made inquiries at the state's ports and airports. Word was also sent to the police in Britain, with Una Lynskey's details supplied in case she came to their attention for one reason or another.

The Lynskey family, the gardaí and locals were grateful for the attention the story was being given by the media. There was a belief that if Una were alive she would read of their concerns in the newspapers. Or maybe somebody saw something and the coverage might jog a memory or prompt them to come forward.

On that first day, a number of the Lynskeys and the two Gaughan families spoke to reporters. Winnie Lynskey described her daughter as 'a real home lover'. Una's uncle, Pat Gaughan, told the *Cork Examiner* that he had heard a scream the previous evening shortly after 7 p.m., 'but when myself and others went to investigate we could find nothing amiss'.

Ann Gaughan, the last known person to see Una, had her own theory about what had happened. 'I definitely think she was forced into a car and taken away,' Ann said. 'She was a very attractive girl.' The quote was reported as Ann speaking of Una in the past tense, but it is unclear whether this was intentional on her part. Certainly, in those first days, Ann Gaughan was fervently hoping to see her cousin and close friend alive again.

Paddy Kelly was equally pessimistic about his girlfriend's fate. 'I think everything points in one direction,' he said. 'The possibility that she was taken away by someone.' There was also fear that whatever befell Una could occur again. On 15 October, two days into the search, the *Evening Herald* reported that doors in some homes were now being locked for the first time. 'Girls returning from school and elsewhere are being escorted home by parents and older brothers,' the report read.

One local woman, who didn't want to be identified, spoke of her fear. 'I have three children attending the local school, and when they are away I have both doors locked,' she told the newspaper. 'My husband was thinking of leaving his work and staying at home until this mystery is cleared up, but we can't afford to do that.'

Among the local people who were canvassed by the media was 24-year-old Carmel Conroy, who lived in a cottage outside Dunshaughlin, about 6 kilometres from Porterstown Lane. It is unclear whether she was approached or whether she activated contact with the media or gardaí. She told the *Sunday Independent* of a startling incident five months previously when she had been pregnant with her second child and was given a lift by a stranger. 'I'm convinced I was attacked by the same man who is involved in this mystery,' she said. She was so terrified by her ordeal that she never went to the gardaí about it at the time.

'I'll never forget it as long as I live. When I heard the girl was missing the whole incident came back to me in vivid detail. And I think that if I had reported the attack to the police at the time I could have saved this girl. I'm shocked to think it might have happened to me.'

'He was small and tough-looking with a raw scar on his left arm. His hair was black and combed back and he was driving a black Zephyr or Zodiac,' she said. The newspaper reported that this was the same make of car seen on Porterstown Lane on the previous Tuesday around the time Una disappeared.

Ms Conroy was able to provide the reporter with a detailed account of what had occurred. It had been a warm May morning. She was seven months pregnant and was going to get a blood pressure injection at a Dublin hospital. She had hoped to catch a bus into the city at lunchtime. But as she stood at a bus stop on the Navan Road, the car approached. The driver stopped and Ms Conroy asked was he going towards Dunshaughlin, which he said he was. On the outskirts of Dunshaughlin, the car suddenly came to a halt and the man attempted to attack Ms Conroy.

'I told him I was pregnant, but he kept mauling me and then I started screaming. I pleaded with him to let me go, and he just kept staring,' she told the reporter.

'Eventually he took a handle from the glove compartment and opened my door. It was only then I realized I couldn't have got out.' Once she was out of the car, the driver took off. Ms Conroy went on to say she was shaking from the shock and ran out in the road to flag down another passing motorist. In her distressed state she told this man what had happened and this man said he would pursue the assailant, but Ms Conroy just wanted to be taken home.

'I'm frightened,' she said. 'Every Zephyr or Zodiac I see I look at it and the driver. I know that if I ever saw him again I'd recognize him straight away.'

The account was shocking, and any such random attempted assault would receive major news coverage even today. The gardaí interviewed her, but little more came of her account.

In those early days, some seriously considered the possibility that Una had taken off of her own volition. Some of this speculation might be explained by a sense of disbelief that she could have been abducted, or a hope that she was alive and well.

Could Una have, by arrangement, or on an impulse, simply left home? She could have organized to meet somebody on the lane by prior appointment and gone in the first instance to Dublin to consider her next move. Such a plan was not unheard of in the Ireland of the times. Young women took off, some of them never to return. This was usually attributable to a pregnancy in a country that looked savagely on birth outside of marriage. Early on, speculation gathered around the possibility that Una had gone to England for an abortion. This gained some currency, but before long it was dismissed by the gardaí. In the absence of any body or any clue pointing towards violence or abduction, there was always the chance that she had, for some reason, decided to just leave. There were questions around such a theory though, not least, why would she do so having alighted from the bus rather than simply not coming home from work, melting into the throng of the city and making her next move from there?

By the weekend, the search was ramped up and appeals went out for more personnel. The Meath senior hurling semi-final between Ratoath and Kilmessan was postponed to allow the players and supporters to join the search. Una's brothers Sean and James and their cousin Padraic Gaughan all played for Ratoath.

In Masses right across the south of the county and the western suburbs of Dublin, priests appealed for help. By Sunday there were over six hundred people combing the fields, roads and ditches and lanes all around the area. Local groups such as the Dunshaughlin Development Associ-ation mobilized and organized the provision of tea and sandwiches for all searchers. Yet as the sun went down on the weekend, there was still no sign of Una Lynskey.

The following Tuesday, gardaí set up checkpoints along the roads from Dublin to Ratoath and Dunshaughlin and along Porterstown Lane, just to see if anybody on their weekly routine might have been in the area on the day in question. Nothing of evidential value came from that exercise.

By then a few clues had emerged. The first of these was the fact that not just one but a whole range of people in and around Porterstown Lane may have heard Una calling out in distress.

Porterstown Lane is 2.4 kilometres long or, as was meas-ured at the time, one and a half miles. From the Fairyhouse Road end the lane continues more or less straight for around 500 metres to a small bridge over a stream. From the bridge it curves slowly to the right. Another 100 metres on it passes by the large pylon that is a local landmark, in the area known as the Three Acres. This was where everybody gathered on the night Una went missing.

From there the road continues again, mainly straight for

300 metres to a sharp end. This bend is at the point of an upturned 'V' in the overall shape of the lane. About 50 metres from the point is the entrance to the cul-de-sac where four families lived: the Lynskeys, their cousins, the Gaughans and two other families.

Whatever befell Una occurred along that stretch of the lane from the Fairyhouse Road to the cul-de-sac, which measures roughly 1 kilometre. In 1971, there were no houses along that stretch. The nineteen homes on the lane, all but two originally Land Commission properties, were on the other half that led out to the Navan Road or on the cul-de-sac. Practically everybody on the lane who travelled by bus walked to the Navan Road end where there was a greater number of bus routes than via the Fairyhouse Road on the other end. The only reason Una went in the opposite direction was because Ann Gaughan lived on the Fairyhouse Road, which was served by the Ratoath bus. Ann was not only her cousin but a close friend. Prior to Ann getting a job in Dublin in the summer of 1971 Una travelled to work on buses serving the Navan Road end of the lane, like everyone else. But when Ann started getting the Ratoath bus to Dublin, Una changed her commute so they could travel together.

There were no witnesses to Una being abducted, or even voluntarily getting into a vehicle. Searches revealed no forensic evidence, no fingerprints, nothing that might have pointed towards an explanation or suspect. There were, however, plenty of people about the vicinity at the time in question.

Some were outside their homes, bringing in or milking cows, or doing general farm chores. Others were en route home from work, having disembarked from a bus on the

Navan Road end of the lane. While most of the activity was on the populated part of the lane, running from the cul-de-sac to the Navan Road, there were a few people who travelled along the side where Una was walking home.

One person who travelled the length of Porterstown Lane on the evening of 12 October was Mary Collins. She was a national schoolteacher living close to the Navan Road end of the lane with her family. Each evening she walked for exercise, sometimes pushing her youngest in a pram. Her usual route took her the full length of the lane to the Fairyhouse Road. Then she would turn around and retrace her steps. When she walked alone, it took her fifty minutes. With the pram it was an extra ten minutes.

On the day in question, she set off, pushing the pram, just before the Angelus. She met a couple of people as she walked. Around halfway along the lane a light blue Anglia car passed her. She didn't pay it much heed. She kept going as the shades of light on the horizon began to darken. About ten feet shy of the junction with the Fairyhouse Road she turned back. That junction was where, about twenty minutes later, the Dublin–Ratoath bus would stop to drop off Una Lynskey and Ann Gaughan.

When she was more than halfway back, past the end of the cul-de-sac, she met Kathleen Gaughan, Padraic's sister, who lived down the cul-de-sac beside the Lynskeys. Kathleen was on her way home, having got off a bus on the Navan Road. The two women stopped to talk. Within a few minutes a car came around the corner, travelling fast from the Navan Road end. The car flew by, a big, dark car. They both noticed that it was an unfamiliar car and travelling very fast. The time was pushing for 7 p.m. The two women parted and went their opposite ways.

Further along the lane, now within a few minutes of her home, Mary Collins heard something. 'After walking about a quarter of a mile I heard a shout,' she said. 'It sounded like a shout coming from a frightened person. I only heard one shout and it came from the Fairyhouse direction. The shout appeared to me to come from a grown-up person, and I couldn't say whether it was a man or a woman. It was not a very deep shout and lasted five seconds or less.' She kept walking.

Kathleen Gaughan heard something similar after she left Mary Collins. 'When I was turning into my own lane [the cul-de-sac] I heard a scream and it was lasting for about ten seconds and it sounded as if somebody was very frightened. After about a minute I heard two more screams of shorter duration. I looked in the direction that I heard the screams and I could see nothing. The last two screams were softer than the first one and I barely heard them at all. At the time I thought it may have been a child getting a good slapping.'

The most poignant-sounding of what was apparently a cry of distress came from Pat Gaughan, Ann's father and Una's uncle. That morning he had been called from his bed to give the two girls a lift to Dunboyne to catch a bus to Dublin after they missed their usual bus. 'I didn't notice anything unusual about Una,' he said later. He spent the day working on his farm. That evening he rounded up the cows and brought them to the milking shed near his home, did the business and took them back down to the field afterwards.

When he came into the house, Ann had arrived fresh from the bus, a few minutes after she had left Una. 'Ann was home with her dinner in front of her, but she had not started to eat it,' Pat Gaughan remembered of the sight that greeted him when he came in.

Pat Gaughan then went out to fetch some water from a pump that was around twenty yards from his house. 'I let down the first bucket into the well, and as I was letting it down I heard a shout which was loud, I heard a second shout which was louder, a little time elapsed and I heard two more shouts, which were more croaking or muffled, and they didn't last as long as the first two. I did not pass any remarks on the shout as I often heard shouting in the evenings. The time I heard the first shout it could be around 7.05 p.m.'

He got the water and went back towards home. He might later have reflected that his day had begun ferrying his niece to the bus, and then, as the sun went down, had he heard the same young woman across the fields crying out as she was subjected to an assault?

The land around the lane lies flat and the lane's 'V' shape means that though it is over a mile and a half long, no point along it is far from another as the crow flies, as would be the case if it ran straight from one end to the other. So it was that John Conroy, who lived near the Navan Road end of the lane, the opposite end from Pat Gaughan, heard something at the same time as Pat Gaughan.

He was bringing cows from a field for milking soon after 7 p.m. 'It was semi-dark at this stage, the sounds I heard were like the cries of a child and did not sound to me to be the shouts of a grown-up person,' he said. 'I saw no car or saw no signs of any car lights on the Porterstown Lane.'

Kathleen Gaughan's brother Padraic was also on the lane at this time. Padraic was serving his time as an apprentice cabinet maker in Dublin's Thomas Street and his bus home dropped him near the Navan Road entrance to the lane. As he remembered it, he disembarked at around 6.50 p.m. and began walking home along the lane in the company of three other locals, siblings Michael and Jenny Reilly, and Mary Madden. All lived on Porterstown Lane. As they were walking, something rang out from across the fields.

'I heard a scream and it seemed to be very long,' Padraic recalled. 'This scream seemed to me to be a rabbit caught in a trap or being killed. I only heard one scream. I am nearly sure I made some remark to Michael [about it], but I don't know what I said.'

Collectively, these screams were heard across the lane and even over as far as the Fairyhouse Road. Could this be a central clue? At some point, either on the lane or in one of the adjoining fields, was Una crying out for help in the course of an assault? It is particularly tragic to think of a young woman in a small community crying out for help, and many who knew her, either personally or through her family, hearing her cries and not realizing what was going on.

One possible alternative explanation for the cries was stumbled on in the course of collecting statements. Michael McIntyre was fifteen years old and lived with his family on Fairyhouse Road, about twenty yards or so from the junction with Porterstown Lane. He was a first cousin of Martin Conmey. At around 7 p.m. he and his sister Christina, who was twelve, went down the fields to collect the cows.

'We had a dog with us, and every time we called the dog it started barking,' Michael remembered. 'The dog had a funny bark. He barks as if he was crying. I remember that particular evening Christina and I were imitating the dog as we were gathering the cows. Christina's imitation of the dog was sharper than the imitation of the bark I was doing. We were doing this barking as we started gathering the cows at about 7.10 p.m. We were just imitating the dog. We weren't laughing. We were doing this about ten times until the cows were gathered.'

Did this explain the cries that were heard? It was certainly plausible, although the timing was slightly later than that mentioned by some of those who heard the cries.

In time, the gardaí would examine the evidence in relation to these sounds that were heard through the dusk around Porterstown Lane on that October evening. These would provide a strand of evidence suggesting Una was abducted. The main thrust of the evidence, however, would ultimately consist of details gathered by detectives around supposed sightings in the lane and their alleged timings. That would be the job of the gardaí from a special unit that had an excellent record in solving cases of violent deaths, informally known as the Murder Squad.

5. The Murder Squad

Ireland was a very safe place in 1971. Crime rates in the largely agrarian society were extremely low. This was reflected in the garda commissioner's report for the year ending 30 September 1971, just twelve days before Una Lynskey's disappearance. For instance, illegal drugs play a major role in crime at all levels today, but at that time drugs were something of a novelty. Commissioner Michael Wymes's report related that the 'drug squad' had been in existence for the last three years.

'The present strength of the squad is 1 Detective Sergeant, 5 Detective Gardaí and 1 Ban Garda,'* the report stated.

'The members of the drug squad have received special training in relation to their duties,' the commissioner assured readers.

Then the incidence of drug-related crime was outlined.

'During the year 113 persons were charged under the Dangerous Drugs Act, 1934, and the Health Act, 1970. Of this number 87 were charged with offences in the Dublin Metropolitan Area, 3 with offences committed in Drogheda, 18 with offences committed in Sligo, (during a pop festival which was attended by three members of the Drug Squad), one with an offence committed in Arklow, 1 with an offence committed in Ballina, 1 with an offence committed in Cork City

* A 'ban garda' was a female officer.

and 2 with offences committed in Ballyvaughan, Co Clare (during a pop festival which was attended by members of the Drug Squad).'

. There were a handful of murders and manslaughters also recorded but, apart from that, the rest of the criminal activity outlined was of a relatively petty nature. Policing, as might be expected, reflected the peaceful nature of society. It was largely basic, not having evolved hugely since An Garda Síochána (AGS) was formed nearly fifty years previously. There were only a few special units, the most notable being the Technical Bureau. One element within the bureau was the Investigation Section. Colloquially, it was called the Murder Squad.

The Garda Technical Bureau was based in a dilapidated, 100-year-old building on Military Road, near Heuston Station in Dublin. The bureau was the sophisticated front of Irish crime fighting in the early 1970s, though its sophistication was relative. Those who observed the workings of AGS at the time reckoned that the bureau was at least ten years behind the force's equivalent organizations in the UK and on the continent.

Work such as biological analysis, or what was called spectrographic analysis – the detailed examination of minute particles – had to be farmed out to external agents, often working in industry. Certain blood samples had to be sent to the London Metropolitan Forensic Science Laboratory for analysis. Other work had to be seconded to the Institute for Industrial Research and Standards in Dublin, a body primarily engaged with industry. At the time, there was a nascent lobby calling for the establishment of a forensic science laboratory within the force, but it would be some years yet before that would receive serious consideration.

The bureau of seventy personnel was headed up by Superintendent Dan Murphy. One newspaper profile at the time described Murphy as a man 'seldom seen at his desk without a phone in his hand'. His domain included five sections: fingerprinting, ballistics, photography, mapping and investigation. As might be expected, most who worked in the bureau required specialist technical knowledge. The exception to this was the Investigation Section. The men – and they were all men at the time – who staffed the Investigation Section had acquired, some through training and others not, the skills of interrogation. Their brief, to the greatest extent, was to talk to the suspect and get them to come around to 'fessing up for what they had done.

There were nine members of the Investigation Section, which was headed up by Inspector Hubert Reynolds. Among the brighter lights of his staff was a detective sergeant, John Courtney, who had joined the force in 1947. Five of the section were practised in interrogation and the other four members were drawn from one each of the technical areas.

The bureau was on call round the clock. A serious crime that occurred anywhere in the country would immediately require technical assistance. The bureau would be called in and put to work, its specialists gathering all physical evidence while the Investigation Section went about interviewing witnesses and, ultimately, suspects. A feature of the work of the Investigation Section was that it often interacted with and recruited for a case detectives based in a separate unit of the force or a district completely removed from the Technical Bureau. Sometimes these detectives would be in the district or division where an incident occurred. Other times they might be called in from elsewhere. These were members of

AGS whom the Investigation Section knew were reliable and had a good nose for detecting. Much later there would be suggestions that outsiders brought in were there primarily because of their willingness to intimidate and assault suspects.

The Murder Squad had an excellent success rate in solving crime. According to one newspaper report in 1971, there had been only one unsolved killing in the previous five years. With an average of around ten murders a year, this was notable.

Not that the solving of homicides at the time in Ireland required difficult police work. In most cases the culprit could be identified almost immediately, and the motive become apparent pretty quickly also. For the greater part, suspects tended to confess after interview or, as some would have it, interrogation, by members of the Murder Squad. Often there would be supporting forensic evidence, but the main thrust of crime-solving by the gardaí was down to confession.

In the commissioner's annual report for 1971 there were just thirteen violent killings, nine classified as murder and four as manslaughter. These figures compare favourably with what was to unfold over the coming decades. In 2007, when violent death was at a peak in the Republic of Ireland, 152 homicides were recorded. By 2020, this had fallen to 78.

The circumstances around the violent deaths were listed in the 1971 report. For the nine murder cases, two each occurred in Dublin, Kildare, Cork and Limerick, and the final one in Wicklow. Identifying the suspect in these types of killings was relatively straightforward. The suspects were rarely hardened criminals and the killings were often matters of regret not long after occurring. In such a milieu, the high detection and conviction rate for homicides in the state makes perfect sense. Take this case from early June:

'A 37 years old man received a fatal stab wound when he was involved in a fight with another man on the roadway outside his home. The incident is alleged to be the outcome of a row which had taken place in a public house earlier that evening. The assailant, aged 20 years is alleged to have followed the deceased to his home and resumed the fight in the course of which he stabbed the deceased in the stomach with a butcher's knife. A man was arrested and charged with murder. He is awaiting trial.'

Family or domestic tragedy featured in a few cases, such as the following, which occurred in Cork, also in June: 'The dead body of a 27 years old farmer was found in a field near his home. The body bore severe head and facial injuries. A post-mortem examination revealed that death was due to skull fractures and brain laceration caused by a blow from a heavy instrument. The 31 years old brother of the deceased was arrested and charged with murder. The tragedy is alleged to be the outcome of a row between the two brothers in the course of which the accused allegedly struck the deceased a number of blows on the head and face with an iron bar. The accused is alleged to have suffered from a mental illness. He is awaiting trial.'

Then there was the kind of gender-based homicide that remains a feature of violent death to this day. 'On 3rd April, 1971, the dead body of a 26 years old female was found in a laneway off the Dock Road, Limerick. The body bore marks of injury. A post-mortem examination revealed that death was due to asphyxia the result of the obstruction of the airway by compression of the neck with a hand, or forearm. A 36 years old electrician was arrested and charged with murder. He is awaiting trial.'

While the vast bulk of policing in the Republic reflected society at large in the early 1970s, in one respect the work of the gardaí was highly unusual. Unlike most countries, the task of ensuring the security of the state was, and remains, in the hands of An Garda Síochána. The trend in other jurisdictions is for a separate body to be in charge of this sensitive – and by its nature, secretive – function. Not so in Ireland. And in the early 1970s there was a major issue around the security of the state.

This arose from the implosion of Northern Ireland as it had been governed since its foundation in 1920. In the late 1960s violence had broken out in the North following attempts by the minority Catholic population to attain civil rights. Northern Ireland had been functioning as 'a Protestant state for a Protestant people'* for nearly fifty years by then. Discrimination was a way of life. Allocation of housing and jobs was weaponized by the unionist establishment and successive governments so that people from the unionist tradition got preferential treatment. The boundaries of electoral districts were manipulated to ensure that the nationalists' writ would be squeezed. By the mid-1960s, inspired by the rise of the civil rights movement in the United States, the Catholic minority started to demand fair

* Variations of this common phrase can be widely sourced, but it originates with utterances of Northern Ireland's first prime minister, Sir James Craig, in the 1930s, who spoke of presiding over 'a Protestant parliament for a Protestant people'.

treatment. The resulting civil rights marches prompted a violent response from unionists, which in turn prompted a violent retort from a minority of nationalists, initially in an attempt to defend their communities. The violence grew and spread, leading to British army troops being drafted in to keep the peace in 1969.

At first, the troops were welcomed in places like Belfast by a Catholic or nationalist population under siege, but this soon changed. By 1971 a full-blown conflict was underway between the security services, including the British Army, and a resurgent IRA, which had the bigger goal of reuniting the island. Bombs were going off, shootings occurring, innocent people who weren't directly involved were being blown up or shot dead. The structures of a sectarian state were falling apart and it was having a huge impact on the social, political and economic life of large swathes of the population.

All of this was happening in a statelet whose border was just an hour up the road from Dublin. At government level there were fears that the violence could spill over. The IRA began fundraising through robbing banks both north and south of the border. There was also an issue with offshoots of the IRA, which itself had split into two factions, Official and Provisional wings. Further fragmentation saw several tiny breakaway groups, such as Saor Éire, engaged in criminal activities in the South.

On 3 April 1970, three armed men, members of Saor Éire, robbed the Royal Bank of Ireland on Dublin's Arran Quay. A garda who arrived on the scene, Richard Fallon, was shot dead by one of the raiders. He was the first garda to die on duty in over thirty years. His death created major shock among the public, his colleagues and the government. From a policing point of view, it demonstrated the threat posed by the political violence north of the border.

John Courtney, the detective who was making a name for himself in the Murder Squad, later recalled the killing and its impact, which had implications for his career.

'The murder of Garda Richard Fallon in the early 1970s, following a Dublin bank raid, marked the start of a major escalation in crime for which neither the government nor the gardaí were prepared. The violence in the North spread quickly across the border, with bank robberies, murders and shootings of all kinds. I was put in charge of many of the investigations.'*

So it was that Courtney and the Murder Squad found themselves effectively operating on two levels. On one hand they were investigating serious crime, including homicides, committed by a ruthless, organized paramilitary outfit like the Provisional IRA and smaller outfits of a similar bent. These kinds of crimes were usually well planned and executed, with considerable emphasis on eliminating forensic or physical clues that might produce leads. In addition, witnesses of such crimes were susceptible to intimidation and highly unlikely to cooperate in an investigation or testify in a trial. On the other hand, there was the Murder Squad's ostensible primary function – investigating what one might call 'ordinary' serious crime. By contrast with the work to combat the paramilitaries, this was relatively straightforward, as reflected in the Garda Commissioner's 1971 report.

On 14 October, forty-eight hours after Una Lynskey disappeared, the Murder Squad showed up in Porterstown Lane. This was a quick reaction, given that whether Una

* Courtney's memoir, *It Was Murder*, was published in 1996.

might have left of her own volition hadn't been established, nor indeed were her family or neighbours yet of the belief that she was dead, whatever their imaginings or fears. How the squad went about its business would now drive everything. Within days of its arrival the number of statements taken from local people began to stack up. And one of these offered a concrete clue about what might have happened to the missing woman.

6. Sightings

James Donnelly was a farmer living on the Fairyhouse Road. He was no relation of Dick Donnelly, but he knew Dick's father. James Donnelly and his family lived about half a mile south of Porterstown Lane, while Dick's home was about half a mile north of the lane.

Around 6.50 p.m. on 12 October James Donnelly left to go up to a farm he owned near Ratoath to milk the cows. He drove up Fairyhouse Road and as he approached the mouth of Porterstown Lane a large car, a Zephyr or Zodiac, suddenly came out of the lane.

'I had to slow down or I would have hit this car,' he told gardaí. 'This was a dark green or black car. When I reached the lane it would have been about two minutes to seven. The driver of the car was between forty-five and fifty years, reddish complexion, heavy build. His hair was going light in the front and going grey at the sides and back and it was short on the side and back.

'He stopped his car when he saw me coming and he was very far out on the road. He turned around in the car, and when he was turning he turned right to face me. I got a full view of his face. This man had high cheekbones, a long thin nose. His ears were normal. He was wearing a grey-coloured jacket. I think he was wearing a light blue shirt. The car was an old type car but was well-kept.'

Then James Donnelly revealed the most startling aspect to his sighting. 'I saw a girl standing up in the back with her back to the driver and I took it to be the man in the back seat was kissing her. She had shoulder-length hair and it seemed to be a little bit wavy on the bottom. I could not be definite of the colour of her hair. I saw the length of her body down to her knees, and the coat did not seem to be very long. It might have been three-quarters length and it was darkish in colour. She seemed to be a light build of a girl. The first impression I got was the car was turning for Ratoath and the last few seconds it turned towards the Navan Road. I went on towards Fairyhouse and there was no sign of the car in my mirror.' In other words, the car was neither following Donnelly nor going in the opposite direction but instead must have re-entered Porterstown Lane.

James Donnelly's statement was given to a local guard on 17 October. The description was amazingly detailed. This, after all, was a sighting that lasted a matter of seconds. Such detail could be attributed to the dramatic vista that the sighting represented. On the face of it, this was a major breakthrough. The possibility immediately hove into view that Una was the woman in the back of the car and had encountered this car in the lane as she walked home. She either got into the car or was forced in and the car then proceeded to the end of the lane. Did it turn back because the driver panicked on seeing James Donnelly?

That was the most dramatic but by no means the only sighting of a strange car in the lane in the crucial time between 6.55 p.m. and 7.15 p.m. On the night of Una's disappearance, Dick Donnelly and Marty Kerrigan had revealed that they had seen a car parked at the pylon after they had dropped off Martin Conmey at around 7.15 p.m. and were en route to Dick's house, travelling along the lane towards the Fairyhouse Road. The pylon was about three hundred yards from the cul-de-sac where the Lynskeys lived. Within days both men had provided the gardaí with statements of what they had seen.

This is what Donnelly related. 'Near the [Fairyhouse Road] end of the lane on a straight part of it, I saw a car parked on the lane. This car was on its correct side of the road and facing towards me. It was a light-coloured grey Ford Zodiac. I know it was a Zodiac as it had twin head-lamps. It was of the same type as the models made with square back and long tail lamps. As the lane is narrow, I had a tight squeeze to get past this car. I noticed when passing that there was nobody in the front of the car as I just glimpsed in when passing. I noticed that there was papers and a briefcase on the front seat on the passenger side. The case appeared black in colour. The car was in a good clean condition. As we came up to the car Kerrigan said, "Look at the Zephyr." I said, "It's a Zodiac, there's a twin head-lamp on it."

'I had a look at the number plates and there were two noughts on it. I can remember that plain. I'm nearly sure there was a J on it at the beginning, middle or end of the letters and three figures on the number plate. I would place the time of passing the car at about quarter past seven.'

Kerrigan's version of what he saw was similar. 'As we were passing the car I noted the word "Zodiac" was in let-ters right across the boot door in silver. I travelled the road with Donnelly nearly every evening and I never noticed this car on the road before. I thought it unusual to see a car stopped where it was. We forgot about the car when we passed it.'

Donnelly and Kerrigan weren't the only ones to report a sighting of the car parked at the pylon. Sean Conmey was

Martin Conmey's 15-year-old brother. He was working around his family's home on the lane, located near the entrance to the cul-de-sac where the Lynskeys lived. He told gardaí that around 7 p.m. he noticed a car stopped on the lane, 'about one hundred yards from the bridge'. He could see this across the fields.

'It looked a sort of blackish colour to me and a fairly big one [car],' he said. 'It was facing in the direction of our house, or in the Navan Road direction. I have no idea what make it was. It was parked three or four hundred yards away from me when I saw it. It was just starting to get dark and I passed no more remarks on it. After that I did not see any sign of life about this car and cannot say when it stopped there or when it left.'

He also heard what he thought might have been somebody in distress. 'I think I heard a noise like a child shouting. I went over to the side of the shed and looked in the direction where I thought I heard this noise. I saw no sign of anybody.'

Mary Collins, the schoolteacher with the pram, passed by the pylon about twenty minutes earlier than that, shortly before she stopped to chat to Kathleen Gaughan at the top of the cul-de-sac, and didn't see anything. If a car was parked there it was for a short time only. Within ten minutes of Donnelly and Kerrigan passing, a local market gardener, Thomas Lowthe, drove along Porterstown Lane, passing by the pylon. He was en route to see the Lynskeys, with whom he did business. He entered the lane from the Fairyhouse Road end.

'I left home at 7.15 p.m. It takes about six minutes [to get from his home to Porterstown Lane]. I definitely did not meet anyone between the Porterstown Lane/Fairyhouse

Road junction and the Lynskey house,' he said. 'There was definitely no car parked on the lane. I am aware this parked car was supposed to have been seen, but it wasn't there when I passed.'

That time would have been between 7.20 p.m. and 7.25 p.m. If there was a strange car parked at the pylon, along the road that Una would have travelled, it wasn't there for very long and any occupants were either hiding behind it when Donnelly and Kerrigan passed or were in the adjoining fields somewhere.

In addition to sightings of the parked car, several witnesses saw a car coming along the lane from the Navan Road end around the time in question. Mary Collins, the schoolteacher, gave details of the fast car that passed while she and Kathleen Gaughan were chatting on the lane, at nearly 7 p.m.

'During the time we were having our conversation a car passed us and came from the Navan Road direction,' she told gardaí. 'As the road is quiet [sic] narrow at this point I pulled in the pram on the grass margin. It was travelling fairly fast, about forty miles or more. It did not slow down when passing us. When it passed by I noticed it was brown in colour and I'd say it was a Zephyr. I did not get any number or part of numbers. I was unable to see in the window and cannot say how many people were in the car. I was surprised I was unable to see through the windows and I tried to see whose the car was. I think the glass in the windows must have been tinted.' It was minutes after this that Mary Collins heard the cry she described as sounding like 'a shout coming from a frightened person . . . one shout and it came from the Fairyhouse direction'.

Kathleen Gaughan gave a similar version of what she saw.

'While I was talking to her (Mary Collins) a car passed by from the Navan Road direction and travelling about 50mph. I thought at the time of seeing it it was a Zephyr or something similar. I didn't notice the driver or the number.'

Just before that, as he made his way along the lane, having got off a bus on the Navan Road end, Kathleen's brother Padraic also saw a car pass by. 'About ten yards before we came to Collinses' house a car passed us from the Navan Road direction,' Padraic remembered. 'This car was travelling at about 35 or 40mph and it was chocolate brown or darker in colour, Ford Zephyr make with a long bonnet and sort of ox type booth, and there was only the driver in the car. I thought the driver was well built, between 40 and 50 years, red face, round, black hair with a high forehead and he seemed to be leaning heavily on the wheel. The driving of this car was normal.' Padraic was about 200 to 300 yards further on when he heard the scream as described in Chapter 4.

So it would appear that a strange car, possibly either a Zephyr or Zodiac, was seen in the lane around 7 p.m., either some minutes before or up to fifteen minutes after the hour.

Not only that, but there was also a sighting of a car matching the witnesses' description of a Zephyr- or Zodiac-like car from about a half-hour earlier. At about 6.35 p.m. Michael McIntyre (the 15-year-old who was out herding cattle with his sister shortly after 7 p.m.) was driving towards Ratoath to collect his brother Tony and a neighbour, Sean Reilly, when he encountered a car coming towards him.

'I met a Black Zephyr at the school between Ratoath and Fairyhouse at 6.35 p.m.,' he said. 'I remember the car because it was well over the white line on the wrong side. I could only see the driver in the car. I had a fairly good look at the driver, he was between 45 and 50 years. He looked small behind the wheel I would say he was stout, his hair was starting to go grey, the hair seemed to be light at the front of his head. He had a fat face and it was red. I think I would be able to identify the man again. On my way to and from Ratoath I can't see any car parked along the way.'

There was one other sighting, or probably more a sounding, of a car in the lane. Having collected his bicycle at the McIntyres', where he left it every day before cycling home along Porterstown Lane, Sean Reilly was at home a few minutes when his friend from up the road, Martin Madden, called up in his car and the pair sat into the vehicle outside Reilly's home.

'While I was sitting in the car with Martin Madden a car passed,' Reilly said. 'It was travelling from Fairyhouse towards the Navan Road. This car passed at about 7.10 p.m.' Reilly told the guards that the way Madden's vehicle was parked, he didn't get a good look at the passing car. This sighting of a car going towards the Navan Road would turn out to be a crucial element of the case that would develop.

Taken collectively, the sightings in and around Porterstown Lane on the evening of 12 October could present a plausible scenario as to what may have befallen Una Lynskey. There were sightings of what could be described as a strange car from a time before Una disembarked the bus until soon after. Michael McIntyre's sighting at around 6.35 p.m. on the Fairyhouse Road was fifteen to twenty minutes before Una would get off the bus, further down the same road. If the driver of that car had anything to do with Una's disappearance, he would have had to be driving around rather than passing through, or parked for some time somewhere in the vicinity.

Michael McIntyre's description of the driver matched sightings of a similar car over the following twenty minutes or so. James Donnelly's sighting at the Porterstown Lane junction with the Fairyhouse Road at around 6.55 p.m. included a driver who roughly matched the description given by McIntyre. Padraic Gaughan's recollection of the driver he saw at the Navan Road end of Porterstown Lane in and around the same time was also similar. That makes three sightings in which both the car and the driver sound remarkably similar.

Then there were the sightings of the car parked on the lane near the pylon. Separately, Dick Donnelly and Marty Kerrigan passed by the vehicle, and Sean Conmey saw it from across fields. The time of these sightings was sometime between 7 p.m. and soon after 7.15 p.m. or so. But when the market gardener Thomas Lowthe passed at around 7.20 p.m.–7.25 p.m. he saw no parked car. Neither was there a parked car when Mary Collins walked past the Three Acres before 7 p.m., or maybe 6.45 p.m., pushing her pram.

So, what could have happened? Here is one theory. The driver in the Ford Zephyr or Zodiac was driving around the general area from at least fifteen minutes before Una and Ann Gaughan disembarked from the bus on the Fairyhouse Road. There may have been a second man in the car with him. At around 7 p.m., he entered Porterstown Lane from the Navan Road end. He was seen driving past by Padraic Gaughan and the other young people who were going home through the lane after getting off their bus. Further on, his vehicle was seen by Mary Collins and Kathleen Gaughan as they stopped to chat.

Somewhere between there and the Fairyhouse Road end of the lane, the man or men encountered Una Lynskey walking home. Remember, there were no houses on this stretch. Una ended up in the car, voluntarily, or far more likely, against her will. The screams heard around this time were Una's. The car continued in the same direction. Within minutes, it came to the end of the lane, the junction with the Fairyhouse Road. Here, James Donnelly was driving along the Fairyhouse Road when he encountered it. Whoever was in the car saw Donnelly pass. The driver had intended going towards Ratoath but after the very brief exchange of glances with Donnelly, decided to turn the car around and re-enter the lane rather than follow Donnelly's vehicle.

The car retraced its route along the lane. On the way back it stopped at the pylon. After moving off again, it passed the Reillys' house, where Sean Reilly was sitting with his friend in the car and heard, or fleetingly saw, the vehicle passing. The car then exited Porterstown Lane on to the Navan Road.

There are some inconsistencies with this scenario. James Donnelly's sighting included two men, while Padraic Gaughan only saw a driver. Mary Collins couldn't see into the car that passed her, yet Padraic Gaughan saw enough to give a detailed description of the driver. And what of the parked car at the pylon? If this was the vehicle used to spirit Una away, as seems entirely possible, then it was parked there, according to Dick Donnelly and Marty Kerrigan, at around 7.15 p.m. This timing would not fit exactly into the other sightings if, for instance, it was parked there on the way back along the lane and Una was taken from the car into a nearby field for whatever reason. One possible explanation for it could be that this was the car returning to the scene of the crime to retrieve something, a shoe or some personal effect of Una's that had been left behind.

The problems that arise in such a scenario are ones of detail. And it is well known that witnesses to an event, particularly involving crime, often retrospectively get details wrong. It is not unusual for two people having witnessed the same event to give accounts that differ.

Notwithstanding that, the gardaí had some major leads in the case. These pointed towards an unknown middle-aged man being in the vicinity at the time, possibly acting suspiciously, driving along the quiet half of Porterstown Lane where Una was walking home. With no word from Una, and no body located, it might be expected that the gardaí would embark on doing everything possible to locate this individual, to at least eliminate him or any associates from inquiries.

On 14 October, two days after Una's disappearance, a memo was sent out to all garda stations to be on the alert for a Ford Zodiac. The memo directed that any such car should be stopped and the driver asked to account for his, or her, movements between 6 p.m. and 7 p.m. on the day in question. Nothing came of this alert.

Within days, however, it became apparent that the Murder Squad were not concentrating on locating any such car. Instead, their instincts told them that the answers were, as was nearly always the case with violent deaths, far closer to home.

7. A Definite Line of Inquiry

With little advance in identifying who might have been driving the strange car, the detectives began to examine who else might have been on the deserted half of Porterstown Lane as Una Lynskey was walking home. Sean Reilly had cycled along the lane sometime before 7 p.m. Mary Collins had walked it with her pram around the same time. Then there was Dick Donnelly and Marty Kerrigan in the Zephyr sometime after 7 p.m. Reilly and Collins were quickly discounted from any possible involvement. But what about the two young men in the car?

The statements from Donnelly and Kerrigan had them entering from the Navan Road end, dropping off Martin Conmey at his home, which was near the cul-de-sac, and continuing along the lane. They pulled into Donnelly's house on the Fairyhouse Road and Dick went inside for his dinner, while Marty waited in the car. Afterwards, Dick came out and fixed a light on his brother's car before the pair took off again, back along the lane to pick up Conmey. A key aspect to the statements given by Donnelly and Kerrigan was the sighting of the Zephyr or Zodiac at the pylon.

But what if the sighting of a Zodiac or Zephyr at the pylon was invented? What if these lads had something to hide and as part of their ruse they wanted to point the finger towards another vehicle being in the lane? What if they weren't alone? Maybe Conmey was with them too. Conmey's mother had put the time of his arrival home at 7.15 p.m., but what if that was after he had been out with the other two and possibly encountered Una Lynskey? What if they had entered the lane up to ten or possibly fifteen minutes earlier than they said?

By the second week of Una's disappearance, there were a few straws in the wind as to the gardaí's thinking on the matter. Padraic Gaughan was one of those who saw a strange car in the lane in and around 7 p.m., when he was walking home after getting off the bus on the Navan Road. Having taken his statement, gardaí later called to his house with a dedicated sketch expert in order to develop a photo-fit of the man he had seen.

'It was done in the bedroom at home,' he says. 'There were five or six of them there, this man had a briefcase and all the equipment to draw out a face. As I was describing the man in the car, they kept saying doesn't this look like Dick Donnelly. I didn't even cop it at the time. One of them in particular said it a few times and I kept saying no, it doesn't. It wasn't Dick Donnelly I saw in that car. Then one of them said that I was probably colour blind [Gaughan was describing a car that was brown in colour; Donnelly's was gold]. They caught me by surprise with the colour blind thing. As far as I was concerned the car was chocolate brown.'

Gaughan soon began to notice that word was getting around about the three men. He knew all three of them but wasn't particularly friendly with them. He was into sport; they were into cars. On the football and hurling teams, he played with his cousins Sean and James Lynskey and also with Martin Conmey's brother, Tony.

'One of the problems with the way the guards appeared to be directing things was that word got around that they were focusing on the three lads,' he says. 'I was at training one evening in Ratoath and we went for a drink afterwards. One of the team asked me was there any word on Una and I said no. Then he says to me that it was most likely those lads, meaning the three. I was fairly taken aback.'

James Donnelly, the farmer who said he saw the two men in the car with a young woman, was also shown a photograph, believed to have been Dick Donnelly. The farmer couldn't see a connection. 'The photo shown me by the guard was too young looking and too fat in the face for the man I saw,' he told the gardaí.

So, what was the emerging garda hypothesis about what had happened in Porterstown Lane in the minutes before or after 7 p.m., when, they seemed to believe, Dick Donnelly's Zephyr came across Una Lynskey walking home?

The first question was who exactly was in the car. Subsequent events would suggest that the gardaí came to the belief that Martin Conmey had not been dropped off home, as all three claimed, but was still in the car when they encountered Una. And what happened then? The first possibility was that the car stopped and Una was forcibly dragged in. One motive for such action could have been to sexually assault her. This seemed an implausible scenario. There was no history of violence of any kind among the men. They knew Una Lynskey; Martin Conmey more or less grew up with her. Why would they ever do such a thing, unless all three had suddenly been overcome with some violent and irrational impulse?

Far more likely was that they encountered Una and something went wrong. Donnelly may have accidentally hit her on the road, either entirely innocently or as a prank that turned into tragedy. Thereafter they could have panicked, lifted her into the car and taken off. If she was dead by that stage, they would have been in an overwhelming state of despair, envisaging what awaited them.

Equally, they might have simply offered her a lift home when passing on the road. Donnelly could have swung the car around and off they went, except she never made it, for one reason or another.

Or, just as possible, he could have driven on to the end of the lane at Fairyhouse Road with Una in the car. Was the car sighted by James Donnelly actually Dick Donnelly's? James Donnelly gave a detailed description of a middle-aged man and was clear it couldn't have been long-haired 23-year-old Dick; but maybe the gardaí didn't accept that description.

Apart from the issues around the details given by James Donnelly, there were problems with the general hypothesis. Timing was the first issue. According to all three, and with supporting evidence from others, Conmey was dropped home around 7.15 p.m. This was twenty minutes at least after Una disembarked from the bus on Fairyhouse Road. If nobody else had encountered her on the lane, she would have been home by then. So, if Donnelly and Kerrigan – and possibly Conmey – were responsible for her disappearance, all of their movements would have had to have happened earlier than the timings in the statements.

According to Donnelly, Conmey and Kerrigan, they entered the lane from the Navan Road end at around 7.10 p.m. This estimate was backed up by Katie Kerrigan, whom Donnelly had driven down to Barrons' shop for briquettes when he called for her brother Marty. Katie said that she was at the shop around 7.05 p.m. Anastasia Barron, who served her, also told gardaí that the time was around 7.05 p.m. Such a timeline would have Donnelly dropping Katie back home up the road and heading down to the lane at more or less the time he estimated.

The gardaí, however, soon had a different timeline, one that suited their developing theory. A local garda, Brian McKeown, was sitting in a car outside Barrons' around 7 p.m., waiting for a phone call. He provided a statement in which he said Donnelly's car drove up with Katie Kerrigan around 6.50 p.m. Katie, he says, went inside for a few minutes before emerging again and getting back into Donnelly's car. Such a timeline would plausibly allow for Donnelly's car meeting Una along the lane sometime between 7 p.m. and 7.10 p.m. While there was an obvious conflict in timing between the locals and Garda McKeown, the Murder Squad went with believing their colleague.

Another problem with the emerging garda theory was how the three young men had spent the rest of the evening. They had met up with girlfriends and had a casual time visiting a couple of pubs, even calling back to Conmeys' along the way to get some cash. Would they have been so casual if they had earlier that evening committed an awful crime against a young woman in their own community? Would they have been able to disguise any anxiety, or regret, or fear, from the girlfriends and others with whom they had socialized?

Then there was the body, on the assumption that Una was dead. How and when could they have disposed of it? There would have been precious little time to do anything before Donnelly and Kerrigan showed up at the Donnelly family home before 7.30 p.m., and possibly ten minutes earlier. After Donnelly had had his dinner – and fixed the light on his brother's car – there was very little time again before they picked up Conmey and, within minutes, Patricia Carey. If a body was disposed of, it must have been done quickly and its location couldn't be far away. Issues around what may have been done with Una's body led the guards to pay particular attention to another young man living on Porterstown Lane.

Christo Ennis was tight with the three whom the gardaí now believed to be central to Una's disappearance. Christo was one of a family of four living on the lane, close to the Navan Road end. His sister Irene had been in the car with the three on the night of Una's disappearance when they all went for drinks. Like his close pal Marty Kerrigan, Christo's mother had died, in his case when he was just eleven. Unlike all the others, bar Dick Donnelly, Christo's family was not from the west. They lived in what he describes as a labourer's cottage and the family didn't have any holding, apart from an acre attached to their home.

Christo's education ended on completion of primary school. He worked locally through his teens, went to England for a while and returned home after a few years. In October 1971, he was working for farmer Eddie Dunne, who also employed Marty Kerrigan.

'We were like a family really, the crowd of us, like brothers and sisters, we all hung around together,' Christo Ennis says. 'Marty was a bit younger than me, he was good fun and he was small though, physically looked like a *garsún*, a lot younger than his years, a lovely lad.'

Like everybody else on the lane, Ennis was interviewed by the guards. But they seemed to be paying particular attention to him. At the time he was engaged to Vera Kavanagh, a young woman from Ashbourne. The couple had met at a

dance in Ratoath soon after Christo returned from England. Their wedding was scheduled for late November.
During those early weeks of the investigation, two guards
showed up at Vera's home, but she was out at work in
Dublin. They came back in the evening and her father
invited them in.

'They were asking me about Christo in the days after Una
Lynskey went missing,' she says. 'I told them there was
nothing unusual about it apart from Christo told me that
the girl had lived on the lane. I didn't know Una Lynskey, I
didn't know anybody in the Porterstown Lane area at the
time apart from Christo and Marty Kerrigan's sister, Ann.
But they kept at it, asking me did Christo say who was
involved and how he was the day after she went missing
when he came over to my house. In the end my father asked
them to leave, it was getting to be a bit much.'

One of the theories that the gardaí had developed at that
point concerned what had happened immediately after Dick
Donnelly's Zephyr encountered Una on the lane. On the
assumption that Una was dead soon after the encounter, or
at the least incapacitated and unconscious, Donnelly and
Kerrigan – and possibly Conmey – couldn't have gone far,
as Dick soon went home for his dinner. One strand of
inquiry concerned whether they had, presumably with the
consent of Christo, deposited the body temporarily in the
vicinity of the Ennis home. Such a scenario immediately
dragged Christo Ennis into suspicion of involvement in a
serious crime.

According to Christo, one day in those weeks after Una
went missing several gardaí showed up at his home. In the
adjoining field, Christo's father had saved hay and gathered
it into a few cocks. 'They came in and scattered the lot of

them,' Christo says. 'They wanted to see whether anything was buried in there but sure they found nothing. They left the hay all over the place too when they were done.'

The Murder Squad clearly believed that Christo Ennis, at the very least, knew more than he was telling.

The gardaí kept digging. They returned to witnesses again and again. Martin Conmey was visited in his home for a second time. 'They brought me out to the shed and inter- viewed me,' he says. 'I didn't notice anything much about it. I thought they were doing the same with everybody else. There was nothing in it that made me think they thought I had been involved in Una's disappearance.'

They went back to the Kerrigans. Ann Kerrigan remem- bers one of the occasions when a couple of guards called to see Marty. 'It was strange. They kept calling around. And one of them would say something like "keep the curtains closed", as if we should be afraid that whoever took Una might be out and around the place.

'One time they called into my workplace, Harper's dra- pery, in Dublin. The boss came over and said to me, 'Ann, there's two detectives here investigating a murder, do you want to talk to them?' I said I would, because if I didn't I knew they would be waiting for me when I got home.'

Over the weekend of 23–4 October, the garda theory about Donnelly's Zephyr driving back along Porterstown Lane towards the Navan Road, with Una in the car, received further support. Mary Collins, who had been out walking with the pram that evening, provided a second statement. It sug- gested that she had neglected a detail in her original account: a possible sighting of another car, coming from the Fairy- house Road end of the lane, when she was closer to home.

'I cannot recall a car passing near Maddens or Reillys on that evening going in the direction of Navan Road,' she said. 'I recall a car passing near that point but cannot say for certain if it was on the evening of 12th October 1971 or on the previous evening. In this particular car were at least two men. They appeared to have long hair, and I'd say they were in their working clothes. This was a big old car. I cannot say what colour it was.' The statement did not give any explanation as to why she had omitted these details in her original statement.

This was an unusual development. Why would Mary Collins suddenly come forward to say that she had seen a car passing in the direction of the Navan Road possibly, but not definitely, on the evening in question? If she had seen such a car, surely she would have mentioned it in her original statement, taken ten days previously. Now she was referencing not just a possible car, but that in it she saw two long-haired men in their working clothes. Such a description could plausibly fit Dick Donnelly and Marty Kerrigan. And the real kicker to her statement was that she couldn't remember whether it was the day in question or the previous day.

There is absolutely no reason to suspect that Mary Collins was inventing details. But the fact that she came up with this, at a time when the gardaí were pursuing a particular line, leaves open the possibility that the gardaí somehow steered her towards these details which would fit nicely into their theory.

The statement added to the developing jigsaw. If Mary Collins might have seen Donnelly's Zephyr travelling back along the lane at that time, she probably wasn't the only one. What about Reilly and Madden, the pair who were sitting in Madden's car outside Reilly's home? They had already stated that they heard a car pass them going towards the Navan Road at about 7.10 p.m. but didn't see it due to how Madden's car was parked. What if they were mistaken? Or what if they simply needed to have their memory jogged? There was also the possibility that, like the other Westies, this pair thought it best to keep their mouths shut when the force of law and order came calling. A decision was taken by the gardaí to interview the pair again. This time, though, the interview would take place not at their homes but in the controlled environment of a garda station.

Sean Reilly was the eldest of a family of ten who lived with their parents on the lane. The family was originally from Co Mayo. Sean worked in Swords as a labourer. He was twenty-three.

Naturally, he was of interest to the gardaí in the early days of the investigation as he had cycled along the lane on his racing bike after work. He was quickly discounted as having met Una at that time, as he also met others, Mary Collins and Kathleen Gaughan, before he arrived home. This put him out of the timeframe. Soon after he arrived home, his pal Martin Madden showed up in his car.

'We would have been close at the time, myself and Martin Madden,' he says. 'We were neighbours and we hung around together.'

Reilly gave his statement about the car which he and Madden heard passing on the lane as they sat in Madden's vehicle. Over fifty years later, he still remembers it.

'I gave the first statement to two guards from Dunshaughlin,' he says. 'They did it in the bedroom at home and there was no problem about that. I was one of the chief men on the road [Porterstown Lane] that evening as I'd come across it on the bike, so of course they were going to want to talk to me. Anyway, I told them about that and then later that we heard a car when we were sitting in Martin's outside my house, that I hadn't a clue who it was and couldn't see anyway because Madden's car was facing in off the road and it was getting dark. You'd want to have had eyes in the back of your head to know who had been passing.'

That statement, Reilly believed, was all he had to contribute to the investigation. Then, on Monday, 25 October, he was at work when the foreman on the job approached him.

'It was about half two that afternoon and he came down and said there were two men here who wanted to talk to me. I went out and they introduced themselves. It was Gildea [Garda Brian Gildea] and another fella who was from Drogheda. They said they wanted to bring me to Porterstown to show me a few sketches on the map, and I said no problem. I was only in the car a short time when I knew I was in trouble.'

Reilly remembers Gildea driving the garda car, banging his hand on the steering wheel in a fit of rage. 'He started in to saying I knew everything; I knew a lot more than I was saying and I wasn't telling them. Then I realized we weren't going to Porterstown when we went through Ratoath and on to Dunshaughlin. I was in Trim before I knew it. We went into the station, and they brought me upstairs to a room, big room with a table in it. And that's when all hell broke loose.'

Reilly was subjected to over seven hours' interrogation. The whole thrust of the questioning was that he had not told the truth in his original statement, that he knew the car which had passed outside his home was Dick Donnelly's. They kept coming back to this point.

'They were taking turns at it,' he says. 'There was a load of them, maybe six or seven. They would come in and out of the room, always with one or two questioning me. It was the same thing over and over.'

Brian Gildea, he claims, was the most aggressive garda present. 'He was thumping me on the shoulder, effing and blinding at me, saying speak up, speak up, we know you know. All of that. They sat around the table, taking turns with me. I didn't get as much as a cup of tea while I was there. By the end of it, I was brainwashed from it all, what I would call torture. I went along with whatever they wanted me to say.'

By Monday evening, Sean Reilly had signed a statement that differed greatly from his original one. That first, taken on 20 October, noted that Madden's car was not parked facing the road. The crucial line was: 'While I was sitting in the car with Martin Madden a car passed. It was travelling from Fairyhouse towards the Navan Road. This car passed at about 7.10 p.m.'

Now, after hours of interrogation, under what he describes as intimidating and at times violent questioning, he expanded greatly on this.

'Madden was seated behind the driving wheel, and the way his car was parked he had a good view of Porterstown Lane. I sat in along with him and I was seated with him for about five minutes when I heard the noise of a car approach from the Fairyhouse Road direction. What attracted me was that it was being driven at a very fast speed. It had its full headlights on. This car was "Didi" or Dick Donnelly's car.

He lives on the Fairyhouse Road. I had a good look at it. I am sure there was no one in the back seat. I am sure it was "Didi" that was driving it, and I am almost sure Martin Kerrigan was sitting beside him, but I am not sure if there was a third person with Donnelly and Kerrigan. As the car passed my gate I saw it, and it had its rear lights on and it continued on towards the Dublin–Navan road.'

In the statement, as in his original one, Reilly detailed the journey he and Madden took soon after. They dropped Madden's brother to the County Club on the Navan Road, a popular pub in the area, and returned home via Ratoath and down the Fairyhouse Road, past Dick Donnelly's home. This time he had an added element, now that Dick Donnelly had been introduced to his narrative: 'I remember passing Dick Donnelly's house, and there I saw his car, a brown-coloured Zephyr parked outside his front gate. It has its parking lights on and I distinctly saw Martin Kerrigan seated in the front passenger seat.' Reilly went on to say that he arrived home, back in Porterstown Lane, at 7.30 p.m. That detail, ironically, backed up the version of events given by Donnelly and Kerrigan. However, the gardaí weren't interested in that. What they wanted was Reilly admitting he saw Donnelly's car sometime earlier on the lane, heading for the Navan Road.

'I told them about seeing Dick's car outside his house when we were coming back,' Reilly says. 'They didn't seem to care about that, even though it showed that the two lads were at his house exactly when they said they were and we were passing it around 7.25 p.m. All they were interested in was that the car was in the lane earlier.'

The statement was witnessed by Garda Brian Gildea.

Unbeknownst to Reilly, his friend Martin Madden was

being questioned elsewhere in Trim garda station at the same time. 'When they finally brought me out of the room, I was standing there and up the hallway was Martin. One of the guards turned to me and said, "Do you know this man?" I realized afterwards that the reason they were in and out of the room with me was they had Martin in the other room and were doing the same with him, swapping between us.'

Martin Madden, who was nineteen and worked as a barman in the County Club, also gave his original statement on 20 October, five days before he was taken to Trim garda station. His recollection was that no car at all passed while he and Sean Reilly were sitting in his car. After five hours of interrogation in Trim, Madden's version of events had changed to the extent he not only remembered a car but had some detail about its occupants. 'Sean Reilly sat into my car. Just as he got into the car [my car], a car passed going towards the Navan Road. As soon as this car passed I said to Sean Reilly that must be Dick, meaning Dick Donnelly. I said that because I know Dick Donnelly's car very well, it's a silvery-coloured Zephyr. I think JZE are the letters [on the registration plate]. I also know it by the sound, there is a rattle in it. This would be around 7.05 p.m. or 7.10 p.m.'

This was a huge leap from his original statement. The first time, he didn't even mention a passing car, and now, after intense questioning from the Murder Squad, he not only remembered a car but could describe it in detail and say it was Dick Donnelly's. Leaving aside the detail that Donnelly's car was gold rather than 'silvery', the change in Madden's version of events is startling. Either he was afraid to give this version initially, even though he did not mention any such issue in his statement made in custody, or he was so afraid in Trim that he told the gardaí exactly what they wanted to hear.

In any event, the gardaí now had the prima facie evidence necessary to put some serious questions to those whom they believed were not telling the truth. Mary Collins's second statement had suggested the possibility that Donnelly's Zephyr had been on the lane, heading in the opposite direction to which Donnelly and the others claimed they had travelled, around the time that Una disappeared. The new statements from Reilly and Madden confirmed the trajectory of the guards' general theory. It was time to bring in those whom the gardaí believed knew the answers, Dick Donnelly, Martin Conmey, Marty Kerrigan and Christo Ennis.

8. 'You're a murderer'

On Sunday, 24 October, Martin Conmey went to a dance in Kilmoon with Marty Kerrigan and Dick Donnelly. He didn't get to bed until nearly 4 a.m. The following day he went to work as usual in Coyles, but it was a drag of a day. He wasn't operating at full speed, tiredness in his bones from the late night. That evening he resolved to make up for lost sleep. At around 9.30 p.m., just as Martin was about to hit the hay, three guards arrived at his home. Detective Sergeant John Courtney from the Murder Squad and gardaí Michael Fanning and Brian Gildea asked would he come with them to the station. Martin remembers the station mentioned was Dunshaughlin.

It is, and was, general practice for gardaí to arrest, or seek to detain, a suspect in the morning. Most of this is done early, around 6 a.m. or 7 a.m. Bringing suspects to a station late at night, unless it is in the immediate aftermath of an event, is highly unusual. Subsequently, the gardaí would say that it was necessary in this case, following the statements that had been acquired that evening from Sean Reilly and Martin Madden. The gardaí didn't want a scenario in which Reilly and Madden could consult with Conmey, Donnelly, Kerrigan and Christo Ennis ahead of questioning the latter four. This implies that the gardaí believed there was collusion between those whom they suspected to be involved in Una's disappearance and their wider circle in Porterstown Lane.

After they left his home, they drove along the lane. Martin was in the back seat of the car. At the pylon, they slowed down. One of the gardaí blessed himself. That's according to Conmey. The gardaí denied any such blessing, or even the slowing down of the vehicle. On they drove, except they didn't go to Dunshaughlin but to Trim, the district office of the Meath garda division, from where, a short time earlier, Sean Reilly and Martin Madden had been released.

Trim garda station was a detached, two-storey building on Castle Street. It had been constructed in 1948 and two single-storey extensions had been added on in the interim. The front door was accessed by stone steps from the street. On arrival at the station, the car carrying Martin Conmey parked in a yard around the back of the building. Martin was brought into a downstairs room. What occurred over the following forty-four hours is in dispute. All the gardaí who were present subsequently swore that they conducted themselves in a proper and fair manner. Martin Conmey's account differs dramatically from that version.

There was a table and two chairs next to a window in the room into which he was brought. Martin was told to sit himself down. Courtney and Gildea came in to conduct the interview. They stood beside the table. According to Martin, once the door was closed, Gildea's demeanour turned ugly.

'The game is up, you murderer,' Gildea said. 'You thought you had us fooled.' The garda began banging on the table.

'We have witnesses,' he said. He kept banging the table.

'Every time I told Garda Gildea that my first statement was the truth he would bang on the table and say he had witnesses to say – to prove – that it was not the truth, and I asked him at one stage to bring the witnesses into the room,' Conmey said later. Gildea denied that he ever banged the table. He may have, he would say, 'tapped' it a few times.

Martin Conmey had never been in a garda station interview room before in his life. He was now the subject of intense questioning from these two gardaí. At least one of them, Gildea, was acting in an extremely intimidating manner, at times lapsing into violence. Gildea would later say that there was nothing intimidating about how he conducted the interview, and certainly nothing violent. Garda Brian Gildea was not a member of the Murder Squad. He had been brought in to assist and, although he was a central figure in the interrogations, he had no specialist knowledge or training in that area.

This form of interrogation went on for several hours, Gildea asking the same questions, demanding the answers that he believed to be true, Martin Conmey sticking to his guns, pointing out that he had told the truth. They kept returning to the car that Donnelly and Marty Kerrigan said they had seen on the lane. The gardaí didn't believe there was any car on the lane; they thought that this was an invention to divert from the three's involvement in Una Lynskey's disappearance.

'They seemed to be frightening me,' Martin remembered. 'Garda Gildea started getting rised and banging the table and shouting at me. I was frightened by Gildea, his appearance and the way he was carrying on in the room. The whole lot upset me. I felt like I was going to get hammered to death inside in the barracks,' he would later tell a court.

At one point, Gildea left. Detective Sergeant Courtney played the good cop, asking Martin to come clean, to accept that there were witnesses and it would be in his interests to tell the truth. 'He told me we will give you a reference for a job and you can go anywhere you want,' Martin said. Consistently, Martin Conmey and others who were questioned all stated that the main interrogators, Courtney and Gildea, operated

WHO KILLED UNA LYNSKEY?

entirely differently, Courtney the good, concerned cop, Gildea the violent one.

Gildea re-entered the room and the temperature went up once more. Later, around 2 a.m., Inspector Hubert Reynolds, head of the Murder Squad, came in and the two principal interrogators left. It was more of the same from Reynolds, but no shouting or roaring, no banging the table. The inspector told him he had a chance to come clean, to tell the truth. He sat down in the chair opposite Martin. He told Martin that he had the two witnesses who saw the car coming back along the lane. He kept repeating the same things, and Martin kept replying that he had told the truth. After a while Reynolds appeared to be getting fed up with this rigmarole.

According to Martin, Reynolds eventually put it bluntly. 'Are you going to tell me, or will I let the other two back in to you again.' Martin Conmey took this as a threat. The implied message was: *You can deal with me, a reasonable friendly guard, or we can revert to what has been going on for the last few hours.* Reynolds denied that he had made any threat.

According to Reynolds, Martin Conmey put his hands to his head and said, 'I want to tell the truth, but I can't, I can't. What would happen if I told you?'

Reynolds says he replied, 'I don't know what would happen until I hear what you have to tell. Did you see Una Lynskey on Porterstown Lane?'

Conmey started to cry. 'I did, we met her at the bridge.'

'Was there an accident, was she struck by the car?'

At this point, Reynolds says Conmey began to tear out his own hair. Later, this would be provided as an explanation for why hair was missing from Conmey's head. His own version of what happened to his hair differed greatly.

'No.'

'Was she in the car?'

'She was. She got into the car.'

This, if Inspector Reynolds's version is to be believed, was a major breakthrough, a confirmation of the bones of the Murder Squad's evolving theory on what had happened to Una Lynskey.

Afterwards, the other two, Courtney and Gildea, returned, but Martin Conmey would not repeat or expand on what he had allegedly said to Reynolds. Gildea looked to be in foul form. 'He was even rougher looking and [had] a more of a vicious look on his face than the first time I met him,' Martin said.

There was a sheet of paper on the table, so that a written confession could be taken. Gildea came over to the table, his eyes on the sheet of paper. 'He dragged me up out of the chair, pushed the table out of the way and pulled me out in the middle of the floor and said, are you going to tell me, are you going to tell me? I said my first statement was right and he got vicious and he hit my right eye. I fell to the ground. I couldn't get up and he lifted me up by the hair and pulled me up by my left side-lock hair.' This was denied by Gildea. The damage done to Conmey's hair was, the gardaí would claim, self-inflicted.

'I was never in a barracks before, I never knew what guards could do, that they could treat people like that. They upset me and frightened me.'

Martin Conmey says that he received another blow to the head after the first one.

Later, Courtney left the room. Gildea took off his jacket. Slowly, he rolled up his sleeves, his eyes all the time on Martin, conveying the threat of violence.

WHO KILLED UNA LYNSKEY?

'He said nothing, just kept staring at me,' Conmey remembered. 'I felt even more frightened when he done that.'

Brian Gildea remembered very differently what happened when the pair of them, garda and suspect, were left alone in the room. 'Detective Sergeant Courtney left the room and I had a conversation with Conmey, in which I told him that if he met, saw or knew anything about Una Lynskey on that evening he should say so, and that if he did it didn't necessarily mean that he had anything to do with her disappearance. At that stage he was quite calm and composed and he stared at me, didn't speak for a few minutes. He then said, "Fair enough, I will tell you what I know." At that stage D. Sergeant Courtney entered the room, the time was 4 a.m.' This version suggests a civilized conversation, in which Martin Conmey's conscience got the better of him and he agreed to come clean to a garda who was presenting himself as friendly and concerned.

A statement was put before Martin, which he signed. Martin says the statement was effectively dictated by the gardaí. The gardaí say that they faithfully transferred to paper the admissions which Martin was making. The statement was made at 4 a.m. on Tuesday, 25 October, two weeks after Una Lynskey went missing, six hours after Martin Conmey had been brought into Trim garda station. It began:

> On Tuesday 12/10/71 I was working at Charlie Coyle's with Richard Donnelly, Fairyhouse Ratoath. We finished work at 6.40 p.m. After work we drove to Ratoath in Donnelly's car, a Zephyr, gold colour. We stopped outside Maher's public house, Ratoath. We met Martin Kerrigan, he was sitting on his motorbike outside Maher's public house.

Kerrigan got into Donnelly's car. We left Maher's public house and drove towards Fairyhouse. We turned down Porterstown Lane, we met Una Lynskey below the bridge.

The narrative that Donnelly and Conmey went to Ratoath rather than collecting Marty Kerrigan before continuing along Porterstown Lane from the Navan Road end was significant. It also implied that Donnelly, Conmey and Kerrigan had been telling a major lie about their movements.

Martin Conmey agreed that he had made the statement, but he says it was all manufactured by the gardaí.

'The state of mind I was in at that time, I didn't realize what I was doing, what I said. All of these [points] were put to me and I just had to answer it. When they came to a point – didn't you stop outside Maher's public house, Martin Kerrigan was seen there, didn't you collect Martin Kerrigan. I just answered that question. They were writing it down.'

The whole narrative now being suggested by the gardaí was contrary to what the three had said in their initial statements – which was, in summary, that Dick Donnelly left work at 6.30 p.m., picked up Martin Conmey around 6.45 p.m., arrived at the home of their friend Marty Kerrigan at about 6.50 p.m., ran Marty's sister up to a shop on the Navan Road and left her home again, after which Dick's car entered Porterstown Lane from the Navan Road end. Around 7.15 p.m. they dropped Martin off at his house about halfway along the lane, and then Dick and Marty headed for the Kerrigan home on the Fairyhouse Road so Dick could have his dinner. On the way, as they passed the pylon near the end of the lane, Dick and Marty noticed a distinctive car – a Ford Zephyr or Zodiac – parked on the side of the road. When they got to Kerrigans', Marty remained in the car, waiting for

Dick. And by 7.45 p.m. the two men were back at Martin's to pick him up for a night out.

But in the version Martin had just signed Donnelly and Conmey had not gone to Kerrigan's house and directly to Porterstown Lane but gone the long way around via Ratoath. There, they had met Kerrigan outside a pub, he jumped into the car, and they headed for the lane, approaching from the Fairyhouse Road direction. This narrative came about due to a witness statement from Una's cousin John Gaughan* saying that he had seen Kerrigan on the outskirts of Ratoath. This would subsequently turn out to have been a false sighting. But for whatever reason, it was included in Conmey's statement in Trim. Had Dick Donnelly's car come from the Fairyhouse Road direction, it would tie in with the three men going along the lane in the same direction as Una, whom they, the guards were convinced, had encountered on their journey. This theory of the journey Donnelly's Zephyr took from his place of work to Porterstown Lane would soon disappear and is examined in greater detail in Chapter 10. Another significant aspect to this statement was that Conmey said that after they abducted Una he got out of the car at the Navan Road end of the lane at about 7.15 p.m. and walked up to his own house. Previously his mother had told the gardaí she heard him getting out of the car outside their home at around 7.15 p.m. So how could he now be saying that he exited the car over half a mile away at the end of the lane at the same time? However, the timings in Conmey's new statement fit the garda theory neatly. How Martin

* John was from the Fairyhouse Road Gaughans, a family of four children which also included Ann. They were Una's double first cousins, being the children of Winnie Lynskey's brother Pat and Patrick Lynskey's sister Anne.

Conmey made a statement that even the gardaí would later
that day accept was false has never been explained.

The statement taken, Courtney and Gildea retreated.
Martin was brought into another room, an office. Over
the following hours, guards were coming and going. Some
came over to him, asked him to tell all, but there was nothing like the pressure he had experienced through the night.
One guard asked him did he want food. He returned with
something to eat and a glass of water to wash it down.

At lunchtime on the Tuesday, Martin's parents, David
and Eileen, arrived at the station. Martin was brought to an
upstairs room. His father came in first. Superintendent P. J.
Keane, who was the district officer nominally in charge at
Trim, was present, smoking a pipe. David Conmey asked
him what had happened to his son's face. The superintendent, according to David Conmey, replied that 'no hand was
placed on the boy until he went back on his statement, or
on his admission'. Keane has no recollection of this being
the content of the conversation between the two men.

A few minutes later, Eileen Conmey came into the room.
Martin spoke to his parents for about twenty minutes, and
then they left.

On Tuesday afternoon there was a bizarre development.
Una Lynskey's parents arrived at the station and were
brought in, effectively to interview Martin Conmey. It is
unclear who informed the Lynskeys that the local men were
being held in the station and why exactly they decided to
travel to Trim. In any event, they arrived in the company of
the local parish priest, Fr John Cogan. Several gardaí subsequently questioned on the matter said that they did not
contact the Lynskeys or invite them to the station.

What is not disputed is that over the preceding two weeks members of the Murder Squad were a constant presence in the Lynskey home. This was highly unusual. It is understandable that they would have liaised on some level with the family of the missing woman, but their relationship had appeared to develop way beyond that.

Winnie Lynskey would later say that her husband had heard the previous evening that the men were being held in Trim garda station over Una's disappearance. Another version she related was that her daughter Marita, who was aged eight, came home at 11.30 p.m. on the Monday and said, 'Mummy, there are three men after being taken to the garda barracks in Trim tonight.' This was not quite accurate. On Monday evening, four men, including Christo Ennis, had been taken to Trim. Given the low probability of an eight-year-old child being out so late on a school night, particularly when her older sister was missing, this seems dubious. Marita Lynskey was never asked about it, and legally couldn't have been because of her young age.

'My husband and I had a discussion, and my husband suggested to me in the morning that we should go and interview Martin Conmey,' Winnie said. 'He was our neighbour, he grew up with Una, he went to school with her, and we expected he would help us. Martin Conmey was our nearest neighbour and we were very friendly.'

Martin Conmey was informed that Una's parents were in the station. Garda Gildea told him that he was to tell the parents what he had told them. Martin asked Superintendent Keane could he talk to him privately. Keane accompanied him out of the interview room and they spoke in the corridor.

'I cannot tell Mrs Lynskey these lies,' Martin said. 'I cannot tell that poor woman these things, that's not right.'

Superintendent Keane replied: 'Get back in there like a good lad.'

He went back into the room and the Lynskeys and Fr Cogan came in. Pat and Winnie Lynskey walked over to Martin and shook hands.

'Would you tell us what you told the guards?' Mrs Lynskey said.

'I can't because it's lies,' Martin replied.

Mrs Lynskey appealed to her neighbour to help them find their daughter, dead or alive. She said she would protect Martin.

Then the priest spoke. 'Martin, if it is only to administer the last rites to her, and, you know, Martin, we will all have to appear before our creator one day and render an account for everything.' After speaking, the priest broke down and cried.

'Don't cry, Father,' Mrs Lynskey counselled. She turned again to Conmey. 'Martin, supposing your sister, Mary, was missing. How would your mother feel?'

She went on: 'Martin, I will appreciate everything you tell me and I'm sure you will be treated very well, if you tell me the truth.'

She put her arm around the young man. 'Martin, please tell me where Una is.'

'Mrs Lynskey, can I see you on my own?' Martin said.

'Certainly you can, Martin.'

Fr Cogan and Pat Lynskey left the room, as did Superintendent Keane. According to Winnie Lynskey, Martin spoke about the day in question, how he and Donnelly had finished work and called for Kerrigan at his home. Then they entered Porterstown Lane, from the Navan Road end. This was contrary to the initial garda theory, as outlined in Martin

Conmey's statement made at four o'clock that morning, which had them coming at the lane from the Fairyhouse end after picking up Kerrigan in Ratoath.

According to Winnie Lynskey, the conversation between the two of them over the following minutes went like this:

'Did you pass your own house?' Winnie Lynskey asked.

'Yes, I did.'

'Did you continue up to the Fairyhouse Road?'

'Yes, we did.'

'Did you see Una?'

'I did.'

'Where did you see Una?'

'Near the well.' (The well was located near the bridge.)

'Martin, what happened then?'

'She got into the car.'

'Martin, Una would not get into that car. Then what happened next, Martin?'

'We turned the car and we continued. She tried to get out of the car then, and we continued down the Porterstown Lane and on down to the Navan Road.'

'When you got to the Navan Road what happened, Martin?'

'I will have to leave the country now.'

'Go on and tell me what happened.'

'They put me out of the car. They turned towards Dublin. They drove on to Dublin.'

'Martin, can you tell me where she is, where they took her to?'

Conmey made some noises about a flat in Ballymun. This was the first time that a flat in Ballymun or anywhere else was mentioned.

'I begged of him to tell me what was the number of the

flat in Ballymun and I would go out and find her, and if she was in need of medical aid that I would see to her,' Winnie Lynskey said.

'I don't know, I can't tell you, I can't tell you, I can't, I can't,' Conmey replied.

Winnie Lynskey said that during their conversation Martin Conmey never mentioned the police, or any ill treatment to which he had been subjected, or any lies he had told.

Martin remembers telling her that what he told the guards was lies. 'I was in the room alone with her for a short while and I told her that what I'd told the guards was lies and I was afraid of them.'

According to him, Gildea and Courtney re-entered the room at one point while Mrs Lynskey was asking him questions. They stood behind Mrs Lynskey. 'Garda Gildea started raising his fist at me and grinding his teeth, and he kept repeating, "Tell her, tell her." At this stage I thought Mrs Lynskey, I thought she was fainting or collapsing, and she had a hold of my hands. The first thing that came to my mind was a flat or something like that and I said . . . I said, first in a flat or something in Ballymun.'

Mrs Lynskey related that at that point Martin appeared to be afraid, that he couldn't say what he wanted to say. The implication here was not that he was afraid of the gardaí but of those the gardaí suspected to be his accomplices. 'I asked him about the flat number and he said he didn't know. I didn't pursue it any longer,' she said. Afterwards, Martin had a conversation with Fr Cogan alone. And then the priest and the Lynskeys left the station.

Martin Conmey was held throughout the afternoon. That evening, around 10 p.m., his parents turned up again at the station. They were asked to come to witness their son giving a statement. Martin gave a statement in their presence, his second in eighteen hours. Contrary to the first written statement, the route that the three took in this statement was as they had claimed, going directly from Kerrigan's to Porterstown Lane and not around by Ratoath. There has never been an explanation about the crucial difference in these statements. This new statement still had Martin saying he was dropped at the end of Porterstown Lane after he and his two friends had picked up Una and driven her along the lane, and when he came to this point in his account Eileen Conmey looked up at Keane and said, 'But Superintendent, I heard the car.' Keane bent down to where she was seated. 'Now, Mrs Conmey,' he said. Eileen Conmey was relating exactly what she had told gardaí in an earlier, routine statement she had given. On the evening in question, around 7.15 p.m. or so, Martin had arrived home. His mother heard Dick's car pulling up and her son telling his friends he'd see them later before they took off again. And now, here was Martin relating that he had got out of the car at the top of the lane, well over half a mile away. She couldn't understand it.

When the statement was concluded, Martin got up, as if he intended leaving with his parents. The three of them moved towards the door. and one of the gardaí intervened. Martin was staying put for the moment, they were told.

The Conmeys didn't know it, but under the law as it stood in 1971 the gardaí had no right to detain Martin. In fact, the legal status of the detention of Conmey and his friends was highly suspect. Officially, the men had been invited to go into the station. They were not under arrest. If they had been, they would also have been automatically entitled to speak to a solicitor. There would have been no interrogation.

A commission appointed in 1977 to examine issues around garda custody would point out that among gardaí a 'practice has grown over the years to secure "voluntary" attendance at stations by refraining from advising the "invitees" of the legal realities of the situation'. The commission, chaired by judge Barra Ó Briain, found that most people who went to garda stations to assist with inquiries did so 'under the misapprehension that they have no other choices than to do so. This practice has been condoned and as a result has become the established norm.'

So, any of the four could have refused to go to Trim. And certainly, when Martin Conmey attempted to leave with his parents, nothing could have been done to stop him. While the gardaí were well aware of the law, the vast majority of the population believed that they had no rights in this respect.

Within an hour of Conmey's second statement being taken, Garda Brian Gildea was leaving to go home for a rest. Later, he would claim that as he was departing he asked Martin Conmey how he felt about coming clean. 'I feel much better,' Conmey said, according to Gildea. 'Will Dick and Kerrigan know what I have said?'

Around midnight on Tuesday, Conmey was brought downstairs to another room. He had already had engagements with Una's parents and his own parents. When he was brought into the room downstairs, Marty Kerrigan was sitting in a chair in the presence of Detective Sergeant Courtney and another garda. According to Conmey, he was told by Sergeant Courtney to tell Kerrigan what he had said in his statement. Instead, according to the gardaí, a conversation ensued and went like this.

'Do you remember the evening we were searching the fields for Una?' Conmey asked.

'Yes,' Kerrigan replied.

'Do you remember Donnelly telling us that he put her under a bridge near Lucan and he told us not to say anything about it?'

'Yes,' Kerrigan replied.

Then Kerrigan said that he took the body out of the car and put it in some bushes near the bridge. 'Donnelly got out and stood beside the car, but he did not help me to shift the body,' Kerrigan said.

Everything about the exchange is strange. Why would Conmey ask Kerrigan if he remembered something from the night they were out searching for Una? If these men were aware of exactly what happened, this was an unusual thing to focus on and a strange way to raise it. But gardaí would later consider the alleged interaction significant, treating it as admissions from both men that they had been involved in Una's disappearance. Martin Conmey has always maintained that the conversation was prompted by the gardaí and he was going along with whatever he thought they wanted him to say.

Early on Wednesday morning, Martin Conmey was brought to a cell. He lay down on a bunk and fell to sleep almost immediately. His world since the last time he had gone to bed, early on Monday morning, had tilted on its axis. Now he was walking through a nightmare. He couldn't believe what he was being subjected to. He had heard about life behind the Iron Curtain, where the communists dictated the extent and franchise of human rights. But Ireland was a democracy. The gardaí were an arm of the state, charged with pursuing criminals. What had happened to him was completely outside his frame of reference.

Some time later, his eyes opened and he saw Marty Kerrigan sitting on the floor in front of him. Marty had blood on his face, around his nose. He was still wearing his leather jacket, as he had been in the pub on Monday night when he was lifted. The two friends shared stories of what they had been through, but none of it seemed real. There were two cells in Trim. It was against good practice for two prisoners to be placed in a single cell. For instance, Dick Donnelly, who was brought in at the same time as Conmey and Kerrigan, was allowed to sleep in a camp bed in the main office in the station. Yet the two friends were in the same cell. One explanation for this is that it could be subsequently claimed that any injuries either man sustained could be attributed to them fighting each other.

Some hours later, Superintendent Keane came in with food: a rasher, egg and slice of toast for each of them. After he left, Martin Conmey ate his, but Marty Kerrigan couldn't.

'While he was eating the egg he vomited the whole lot up again in the plate,' Conmey said. 'He tried to [eat] and he was complaining about pains in his stomach and his face. There was blood around his nose.'

At around 7 p.m. on Wednesday Martin Conmey was released. His mother, father and uncle were at the station to bring him home. Back in Porterstown Lane, a large crowd of relatives and friends had gathered at the Conmey home. For the second time in two weeks there was a major sense of shock pervading the community.

9. 'We need to clear up a few points'

Dick Donnelly was having a jar in Ryan's of Ratoath on the evening of 25 October. Unlike Martin Conmey, he was still up for a little socializing the night after they had been to the dance in Kilmoon. Around 9.30 p.m., he was approached in the bar by Garda Brian Gildea. 'Is that your car outside?' Gildea asked. Donnelly confirmed that it was. Gildea said a few members of the Murder Squad wanted to talk to him. Outside, Superintendent Dan Murphy and Sergeant Francis Browne were waiting. They told him to follow them in his car to Trim garda station for a chat.

'What's it about?' Donnelly wanted to know.

'We just need to clear up a few points,' Murphy said. Reluctantly, Donnelly agreed to go along. Just like Martin Conmey, he believed he had no choice. He got into his Zephyr and followed the unmarked garda car the eighteen miles to Trim. As with Martin Conmey, there are irreconcilable versions of what happened during Donnelly's time in the garda station.

Once they arrived, he was brought to an upstairs room. According to Donnelly, Murphy and Browne left the room, with Gildea remaining.

Just then, according to Donnelly, Garda Brian Gildea reached forward and slapped him across the face. Gildea denies this, says he was interviewing Conmey at the time. This may well be true. Having said that, both Donnelly and

Conmey have said that various gardaí came in and out of the respective interviewing rooms at various times.

'Where is Una Lynskey?' Gildea said. This question was repeated time and again over the following hours. *Where is Una Lynskey? Where is the body?*

Dick was resolute in his responses. He did not know. He did not meet her on the evening she disappeared. He knew nothing about what had happened to her. The interrogators changed over the following hours. John Courtney came in; so did another guard, Owen Corrigan. Corrigan, like Brian Gildea, was not a member of the Murder Squad, although unlike Gildea he was a detective rather than a ranking garda. Like Gildea, he had no specialist knowledge of interview techniques. Similar to Gildea, there would be allegations that he was violent towards the young men in custody.

Donnelly was questioned through the night, the same questions repeated ad nauseam. *Where is Una? Where is the body?* According to Donnelly, John Courtney was playing the good cop, Corrigan the bad. At one point during the interrogation, Donnelly would later claim, Corrigan approached him and wrapped his hands around his throat, as if Corrigan was about to strangle him. Corrigan denied exercising any aggression or threats, not to mind violence.

The interrogation went on right through Tuesday. They kept telling him that they had information that did not tally with what he had said previously. They had witnesses that saw his car travelling back along Porterstown Lane, after initially entering from the Navan Road end. They had reason to believe that Una was in the car with them.

Tuesday evening turned into night and the early hours of Wednesday. As the clock approached 1 a.m. he was brought into another room. Marty Kerrigan was sitting in a chair. The room filled up with gardaí. 'We took her to a bridge between Clonee and Lucan,' Kerrigan said. 'We dumped her body near a bridge. There was two bends on the road.'

'Who was with you?' one of the gardaí asked. Kerrigan pointed at Donnelly. 'He was.'

'Do you remember, we took her out to Wilkinstown Wood?' Kerrigan said, looking at Donnelly.

'Is that true?' one of the gardaí asked.

'It's not true,' Donnelly replied. 'He must be mad.' As far as Donnelly was concerned, the gardaí had terrified Marty Kerrigan into saying these things in an attempt to get him, Donnelly, to confess to something, anything, that would show that they had encountered Una Lynskey on the lane. As with the alleged exchange between Conmey and Kerrigan the previous afternoon, this one was peculiar. If Kerrigan was attempting to draw Donnelly into admitting something to which he had already confessed, the obvious approach would have been to say straight out what he had confessed to the guards and tell Dick that the game was up. Instead, there was this disjointed interaction that made little sense. If it was a ruse by the gardaí, it didn't work. Donnelly was taken back to the room upstairs soon after that.

Some time later, Corrigan told him that the gardaí now knew where Una's body was, that Marty Kerrigan had told them it was out in Wilkinstown Wood. Wilkinstown Wood was just off the Navan Road, a short drive from the mouth of Porterstown Lane. Dick replied: 'You needn't bother your head going out there. You won't find it. It's not there.' This would later be used against Donnelly, suggesting that because he knew they wouldn't find the body there, he must have known where it actually was.

He was questioned throughout Wednesday. He was tired, hungry, dazed; sore, he would say, from being beaten. On Wednesday afternoon Brian Gildea struck him several times. At one stage, the garda got a poker which was sitting by the fire and used it to hit Donnelly across his back. That's Dick Donnelly's recollection. Gildea denied that it ever happened. None of the gardaí who subsequently gave statements or provided evidence under oath saw any assaults or mistreatment of the young men.

On Wednesday around 6 p.m., Donnelly was told he could go home. He could not, however, take his vehicle with him. That was being kept as evidence in the case of Una Lynskey.

Marty Kerrigan gave the gardaí a number of statements on what allegedly happened to Una Lynskey. Much of it made no sense, and Martin Conmey would say that when he saw Kerrigan in the cell on the Wednesday he had a bloody face, complained of pains and was unable to hold down his food. There is no reason to believe that his experience in Trim garda station was any different to that of his two friends.

Marty was questioned throughout the Monday night into Tuesday. At around 8.30 p.m., Winnie Lynskey was brought into the room in which he was being held. She asked him what he had done with Una, and he replied that he knew nothing about what had happened to Una. She stayed with him for about fifteen minutes, but nothing more emerged from their conversation.

Later that evening, according to Garda John Harty, who was stationed locally, Marty asked to talk to him alone. Harty later stated that Marty told him that they had left Una's body in Wilkinstown Wood. The garda would claim that Marty said there was a specific tree at the wood where the body had been left.

A decision was taken by the gardaí to go to the wood almost immediately, despite the late hour and complete darkness. They left Trim, led by Inspector Reynolds of the Murder Squad and accompanied by Marty Kerrigan, to drive the eighteen miles to the wood. One of the gardaí in the car with Kerrigan would later claim that during the journey, he 'mentioned on at least two occasions that he felt happier now that he had told us about the incident'.

One of those on the search, Garda John Mollahan, related what occurred once they arrived: 'We got out of the car and Kerrigan said to look for a cutting in the ditch, that Donnelly went into the wood through a small cutting or hollow in the ditch. We found the hollow and Kerrigan took us to a big tree and showed us where Donnelly and himself had left Una Lynskey. Kerrigan appeared surprised when she was not there and he took us to another tree a short distance away in case he had gone to the wrong one the first time.

'After going to the second tree Kerrigan said that it was the first tree they had left her at as he was satisfied it was a very big tree. I then asked Kerrigan where would Una Lynskey be and he said, "She must have been moved."'

The garda asked him who would have moved her.

'Dick Donnelly,' Kerrigan allegedly replied.

'Where would he have left her?'

'He might have put her in the pond.'

A torchlight was cast across the dark waters of the pond, but nothing could be seen. Soon after that, everybody got back in the cars and returned to Trim. The excursion was a complete waste of time. If taken at face value, it would imply that Kerrigan and Donnelly left Una's body in the wood and something happened thereafter of which Kerrigan was ignorant. Would it have been plausible that Donnelly subsequently moved the body on his own, or with others, and said nothing about it to Marty?

On the way back to the station, Kerrigan said that he would make a statement about all that he knew. That's the garda version of how the statement came about.

'I have already made a statement to the garda about the missing girl Una Lynskey,' the statement opens. 'I want to make this statement to tell the truth about what happened.'

The first part was a rerun of his original statement, outlining how Donnelly and Conmey called to his home, that they brought his sister Katie to the shop, and dropped her back home. Then the three left, went down the Navan Road and entered Porterstown Lane.

'It was 7.10 p.m. when we entered the lane. We then drove on to Conmey's house . . . we stopped at Conmey's house at 7.15 p.m. We left off Martin Conmey there.' This line, which is in complete contrast to aspects of the statements given by Conmey, effectively absolves Conmey of what occurred thereafter.

And then: 'When we approached the bridge we met Una Lynskey. She was walking on the left-hand side of the road. We stopped just beside Una Lynskey and Dick Donnelly screwed down his window and I asked Una did she want a lift. I leaned across Donnelly when I was asking her if she wanted a lift. She said, "Yes," and she came around the front of the car and I opened the door. She got into the car and sat in the front seat between me and the door. The time was then about 7.20 p.m.' This does not correlate with Una getting off the bus around 6.55 p.m. and walking along the lane.

'I pulled the door and she got in. We then turned the car at the bridge and we drove back towards the Navan Road. When we were turning the car at the bridge I did not see anybody. When we turned the car I put my left arm over on Una Lynskey's right shoulder. When I put my arm on her shoulder she lay back against the door with the back of her head against the glass. I saw her eyes starting to blink and she turned pale. I thought she was going to get sick.

'We then drove on as far as Lynskeys' lane [the cul-de-sac] and I saw Kathleen Gaughan a little bit past Shevlins' [the first house along the cul-de-sac]. She was walking with her back to us. We did not stop at Lynskeys' lane but drove on towards the Navan Road. We did not see any person or motor car from Lynskeys' lane until we reached the Navan Road. We turned left at the end of Porterstown Lane and travelled in the Dublin direction.

'We drove on the Dublin Road for about half a mile. I did not see anyone I knew. We then turned right into Wilkinstown Lane. We drove up Wilkinstown Lane to within about ten yards of the bridge. We did not go as far as the bridge. We stopped the car but left the engine running beside the bank on the left-hand side. I would say it was then about 7.40 p.m.' Again, timing is a problem with this line from Kerrigan's statement. According to Sean Reilly, Kerrigan was sitting in Dick Donnelly's car outside the Donnelly house at around 7.25 p.m. Yet now Kerrigan's statement was saying that not only had they not arrived at Donnelly's by 7.40 p.m., but they were miles away in Wilkinstown Wood.

The statement went on: 'Dick Donnelly then got out of the car and went around the front to the passenger door and opened it. He then took Una Lynskey up in his arms and walked across the ditch into a dip and up at the far side and left her down at that big tree that I showed D/garda Mollahan and Garda Harty tonight. Her eyes were open but they were not moving. Her hands were lying by her side.

'Una Lynskey was wearing a bag on her right shoulder when we met her and it was still on her shoulder when she was lying at the tree. It was a brown shoulder bag. She was wearing a short blue skirt and a bright-coloured coat. Her coat was closed. I am not sure about the kind of blouse she was wearing. She was wearing brown nylon stockings. She had a silver ring on her left little finger. She had light blonde hair down to her shoulder. She had nothing on her hair. I know Una Lynskey for about two years. I worked with her father once.

'I walked in after Donnelly when he was going in to put her down in the ground at the trees. When Donnelly stopped on Wilkinstown Lane I heard him saying I will leave her here. Una Lynskey seemed to be in a faint all the way down to where we left her. We then went back to the car and Donnelly reversed all the way back out to the road. We drove back into Porterstown Lane and on to the Fairyhouse Road to Donnelly's house. Donnelly reversed the car into his own house and he went into the house. I stayed in the car.

'We got back to Donnellys' at about 7.50 p.m. or 7.55 p.m. Donnelly stayed about fifteen minutes in his house and then he came out and we drove to Martin Conmey's house in Porterstown Lane. We picked up Martin Conmey and drove to Dunshaughlin, arriving there at 8.20 p.m. When we were leaving Dick Donnelly's house that evening he said, "Don't say anything about what happened." On this night, the 26 October 1971, I brought these two gardaí to where the body was left but she was not there.'

The statement is full of holes, particularly in relation to timing. The idea that all of what Kerrigan said occurred could have happened within such a very tight timeline stretches credulity. That does not mean it couldn't have happened, but a lot of other people would have to have been inaccurate about times they gave, such as Marty's sisters, Anastasia Barron in her family shop, Dick Donnelly's family, Martin Conmey's mother, and Irene Ennis, who was picked up by the three lads before 8 p.m. on the way out for the night. All of that was apart from how Una was rendered unconscious or even killed. Marty Kerrigan's description of putting his arm around her didn't suggest any violence.

Some hours later Kerrigan made a further statement in the garda station that differed from the first in a few crucial elements. As before, he described the run-up to encountering Una, asking if she wanted a lift, and Una getting into the car. Then: 'As we went down Porterstown Lane again Una tried to get out of the car. I caught her and I hit her and then she put her head on the window. I thought she fainted.' From there the narrative returns to that of the previous statement until the point Una is dragged out to the base of a tree in Wilkinstown Wood. Then, there's a further change from his original statement. Now Marty was claiming that in the wood Dick Donnelly said to him, 'We won't leave her here.'

So, this further statement included the use of violence against Una, in the form of a single strike or punch, and also accounted for why the body was not located in Wilkinstown Wood.

On the Wednesday of his detention, Marty Kerrigan

gave yet another statement, explaining his earlier claim that he and Donnelly had seen a car at the bridge on Porterstown Lane after they had dropped off Martin Conmey.

'Further to my statement already made, I further wish to state there was no Zodiac car parked in Porterstown Lane near the bridge on the night of the 12 October 1971 at approximately 7.15 p.m. to 7.20 p.m. I said to Dick Donnelly I will tell the guards there was a Zodiac car parked near the little bridge on Porterstown Lane on the 12 October 1971, if the guards ask me anything I will say it was a grey Zephyr. Dick Donnelly then said, "I will say it was a grey Zephyr." Dick Donnelly then said I will say it was a Zodiac with twin lights and the letter J and the letters [numbers] 00 is part of the registration of the car.

'We did this to cover for ourselves and to keep the guards away from Donnelly's car. When Garda John Morgan who is in Dunshaughlin asked me did I see any car in Porterstown Lane on the night of the 12 October 1971, I first told him it was then a Zephyr. He then asked me was it a car like Donnelly's. I told him it was a Zodiac as Donnelly had told me to say that.'

This suggests a degree of sophistication in crafting a story to tell the gardaí. Why, if the two men were inventing the story, would they have one of them initially suggesting the car was a Zodiac and the other identifying a Zephyr? If it was all made up, surely the obvious thing to do would be for both to be emphatic about what make of car they were claiming it to be?

In the round, Marty Kerrigan's various statements were confused, disjointed and did not form a plausible narrative.

Martin Kerrigan's father, Martin Snr, showed up at Trim on Tuesday but was not allowed to see his son. He went to a local solicitor, Marie Noonan, who said they would apply to the High Court for a writ of habeas corpus, an application to literally produce a body, meaning that the gardaí would have to release Marty or bring him to court. A judge heard the application and said that if he had not been released by the following day, he would grant the application. Events overtook the process when Marty was released on Wednesday evening with Dick Donnelly.

In contrast to his three friends, Christo Ennis's time in Trim was brief. He also was drinking in Ryan's in Ratoath when Garda John Harty came in and said they wanted to have a chat with him outside the pub.

'Next thing, outside they're telling me that they're bringing me to Dunshaughlin to clear up a few things. Once we were in the car they said they were bringing me to my mates in Trim,' Christo Ennis remembers. 'I wasn't afraid of them really. I'd had a few run-ins with them before. Whenever anything happened, somebody like me would get blamed for it. I came from a labourer's cottage, not a farm like most of the rest of the lads. When you came from a labourer's cottage you were blamed for everything.'

In fact, the gardaí believed that Ennis might have facilitated his friends by allowing Una's body to be left somewhere around his home on the evening in question. There wasn't a scintilla of evidence that this occurred, but it fitted into the garda theory. The only evidence that Donnelly had in fact driven towards the Navan Road end of the lane was that acquired in the statements of Sean Reilly and Martin Madden, which, it would be claimed, were changed only after hours of intimidation in Trim.

Ennis was brought to the station and placed in a cell. The

cell door, he says, was left open. He was then taken into a room. A number of gardaí came and went. 'The room was full of guards, growling and snarling at me, one trying to outdo the other. They were shouting that I knew where the body was, nearly eating me.'

Christo Ennis says that he could hear screaming from elsewhere in the station. He recognized the voices of Martin Conmey and Marty Kerrigan. 'I could hear them. It sounded like they were being tortured. I could hear what sounded like a lump of Wavin* hitting a table.'

At one point, one of the gardaí had him jammed up against the wall of the cell. 'I thought I was going to get a doing,' he says. 'After listening to the boys and what they were going through, I said to myself I'm not going to be put through that. The guard looked at me. He knew damn well that if I got it, I was going to hit him back. A part of me was hoping they'd give me a clatter.' The gardaí backed off.

Later that evening, Christo's father and uncle showed up at Trim garda station, demanding to know where he was and what was going on. Soon after, Christo Ennis was released.

* A reference to Wavin pipes, hard plastic pipes used in plumbing and drainage.

10. Stating the Obvious

By the evening of 27 October, fifteen days after Una Lynskey had gone missing, the gardaí had assembled what they considered a firm case. The evidence consisted of witness statements as well as statements and admissions acquired from suspects in custody. Supposed sightings of Dick Donnelly's car could be fitted in with the timeline of when Una would have been walking along the Porterstown Lane. Donnelly and Marty Kerrigan had been identified as being in the car with, possibly, Martin Conmey. Mary Collins suddenly remembered seeing men with long hair in working clothes in a big old car, near the end of Porterstown Lane, which sounded like their prime suspects. And Conmey and Kerrigan had both provided statements and made verbal admissions about encountering Una in the lane and what occurred thereafter. Donnelly hadn't, but he had said a few things that indicated he knew where Una's body was – or, specifically, where it was not.

With all of this 'evidence', the case was well on the way to being solved. Such a scenario would have had the Murder Squad very confident that serious charges, including murder, would follow. However, the garda narrative – or, more accurately, theory, as it has been referred to already – was full of holes.

The nature of police work is that statements are assembled to provide a possible narrative of what happened leading up to and in the commission of a crime. Any forensic or physical evidence is also thrown into the mix. From that narrative, the police hope to identify suspects. From there, they focus on the suspects and see what other pieces of information can be gathered to make a case. During the process it may well emerge that despite initial indications there is no longer a case against these suspects. The focus then switches to other lines of inquiry.

Where there is a case, all the evidence is collated and the suspects are questioned on that basis. The questioning may adduce a confession or at least further evidence through admissions of one sort or another. Following that, a file is assembled which provides the basis for a criminal charge. This is basic police work and standard practice.

All the indications in the Lynskey case are that the Murder Squad put the cart before the horse. In other words, instead of fashioning a narrative from the emerging evidence, primarily witness statements, they decided on the narrative and then went on to build the evidence around that. In this regard they set about creating rather than collecting evidence.

It is likely that they believed their narrative to be a true version of what actually happened. They most likely came upon it because of personal suspicions or a hunch. But whatever the reason, they mangled a basic approach to police work. Instead of following the evidence, they sought out evidence to follow their hunch. Apart from anything else, the danger of focusing on the wrong suspect by pursuing such a strategy are obvious. All of that would be bad enough, but there is circumstantial evidence that from early in this investigation the gardaí misused their power to create their preferred narrative, including by means of violence and intimidation.

The garda theory had it that Dick Donnelly, accompanied by Marty Kerrigan and most likely Martin Conmey, were responsible for Una's disappearance. (Later, when circumstances changed, they would suggest that it was Donnelly and Conmey alone in the car when it encountered Una.) The only other outstanding possibility was the involvement of the middle-aged man who had been sighted by several witnesses. For whatever reason, the squad quickly discounted him and decided to focus on the three local lads.

For the garda theory to work, a few details needed to be established. First, Donnelly's car needed to enter the lane – coming from the Navan Road end – at least ten minutes earlier than the time Donnelly and the others claimed that it did. In the garda theory, this fence could be jumped by referring to the evidence of their colleague, Garda Brian McKeown, who claimed that Donnelly's car appeared at Barrons' shop ten minutes earlier than the time the three men, Katie Kerrigan and Anastasia Barron had said.

The Zephyr would also need to have come back along the lane after encountering Una in order to explain the sighting of the car by James Donnelly, the farmer who encountered a large car at the junction of Porterstown Lane and Fairyhouse Road that then turned back into the lane instead of turning out on to the road. The garda theory had it that this was Dick Donnelly's car, despite James Donnelly saying he saw a middle-aged man behind the wheel.

One strand of the theory had it that in driving back along the lane, the men stopped at Christo Ennis's house, where Una's body was deposited, temporarily, somewhere on the property.

The problem with such a theory was that the collection of witness statements – with the exception of Garda

McKeown's – simply did not back it up. So the gardaí, led by the Murder Squad, went back again and again to some witnesses to check whether they had not mentioned a detail, or forgotten something, that could provide a building block to the theory.

For instance, the schoolteacher Mary Collins saw a fast car passing on the lane from the Navan Road end while she was chatting with Kathleen Gaughan. This was the only car she mentioned in her statement. She did not identify the car or the driver. In her second statement she thought she may have seen a car heading in the opposite direction some minutes later when she resumed her walk towards home as it was getting close to 7 p.m. The occupants of this car could have been two young men in working clothes with long hair, she told the gardaí. That would fit a description of Donnelly and Kerrigan. Crucially, she said she wasn't sure whether she had seen this car on the day Una disappeared, or the day before.

Why would Mary Collins make such suggestions in her second statement? The only plausible explanation is that she was prompted or repeatedly asked about the possibility of such a sighting. She was being interviewed by gardaí, a force of authority in a submissive state. These gardaí, dispatched from Dublin, were trying hard to find a missing neighbour. They appeared to know what they were doing. Any local person would be only too willing to assist in any way they could. And if she was repeatedly asked about it, well, maybe it occurred to her that she saw something like that one day. Was it the day in question? If she didn't think so, maybe it was another day. What about the day before? It could have been the day before, but it could have been 12 October. Suddenly the possibility of the sighting of a car going in the direction that fits in with the garda theory enters the picture.

On 28 October, the day after the three were released from Trim garda station, Mary Collins gave a third statement. Now she was no longer unsure which day it was that she saw this other car with the long-haired men. Now it was definitely 12 October, and she was able to give some specific details about it. Soon after she left Kathleen Gaughan, according to her third statement, 'a large car, very broad and well down on its springs passed me. I was walking and pushing the pram on my right-hand side. As it passed me I looked to my left and saw what I thought to be three hairy-looking youths in the front seat of this car. I didn't take note of the colour of this car. I couldn't be certain if there was anyone in the back seat. I am certain of at least two being in front and nearly certain there were three in it. This car appears to be the same car that I have seen since in Porterstown Lane, and being driven by a Donnelly chap, Fairyhouse Road. It is a gold-coloured Zephyr.'

This third statement from Mary Collins was taken by the two gardaí at the very centre of the investigation, John Courtney and Brian Gildea. Over the course of three statements, Mrs Collins went from no mention of seeing a car going towards the Navan Road end of the lane, to a possible sighting of a car with a few long-haired individuals on either 12 October or the preceding day, to a definitive sighting on the 12th, which had further crucial detail, including the similarity of the car to Dick Donnelly's. As with the multiple statements taken from various witnesses which changed in key respects, there was no explanation in the statements as to why new details had been recalled or others changed or dropped.

Another example of a series of statements somehow crystallizing the garda theory was that of witness John Shevlin, a 13-year-old local boy. John lived with his family on the cul-de-sac off Porterstown Lane, a neighbour of the Lynskeys and one of the Gaughan families. On the evening of 12 October, he was out and about on the lane, so he provided a statement to the gardaí. On 17 October he related how he brought his dog out on to Porterstown Lane. He went down to a milk stand which was at the point of the V shape on the lane, around thirty metres from the mouth of the cul-de-sac. 'I stayed at the milk stand until I saw Kathleen Gaughan coming walking at Conmeys',' he said. This fitted in with Kathleen Gaughan's version of events. She had walked from the Navan Road end of the lane after getting off the bus. 'During the time I was at the milk stand I saw no car passing in either direction,' his statement read. Nothing controversial in any of that.

Eight days later, on 25 October, the same day the six local men were taken into Trim garda station, John gave another statement. 'During the time I was there [at the milk stand] I do not remember seeing any car passing up or down Porterstown Lane. They could have passed but I do not remember. I was down at the milk stand for about ten minutes before Kathleen Gaughan arrived.' Now the possibility that a car had passed has entered his version of events. From being definitive there was no car, it was now a matter of he couldn't remember one, and there might well have been a passing car.

Briefly roll it forward another three weeks to 18 November. Now John Shevlin remembers that when he was on his way home, 'I heard a car coming from Fairyhouse towards the Navan Road. It appeared grey in colour ... I have no

idea how many were in the car and cannot give any description as to who was driving it. I think it would be about 7.10
p.m. or 7.15 p.m. when this car passed.' Now the scenario
had evolved to be much closer to the garda theory. A car
going in the direction the gardaí believed Dick Donnelly's
Zephyr to have been travelling had been spotted at a time that
would fit with it having encountered Una minutes earlier.

A fourth statement was provided by John Shevlin on 20
December, which will be seen further on to have been a
crucial date. In this version, John was earlier out in the fields
behind his home where the family kept some livestock. The
field backed on to Porterstown Lane.

'While I was with the calves, I heard a car coming from
the Navan Road and going towards the Fairyhouse end of
the lane. I heard this car slacken its speed and from the
sound of this car I knew it was Dick Donnelly's car. Dick
Donnelly's car is a Zephyr and is golden coloured. The
reason I knew the sound of this car is because it passes up
and down the lane nearly every day and it mostly calls to
Conmey's house.'

John Shevlin went on to say that five minutes later he got
his bicycle and cycled out on to the lane to the milk stand.
'I had just turned my bicycle at the milk stand and I was
facing towards the Navan Road when I saw Kathleen
Gaughan.' This statement now provided a positive identification of Donnelly's Zephyr coming from the Navan Road
end ten minutes or so earlier than Donnelly claimed to be
the case. The timeline was verified by the detail that after
hearing the car he saw Kathleen Gaughan, who, it has
already been established, was getting home around 7 p.m.

So, the trail of evidence leading through young John's
four statements led from nothing of any value all the way

through to sightings – or soundings – of a car going down the lane in time to encounter Una a few hundred yards further on. This car was positively identified as Donnelly's. And then another car – although not identified – was seen by John coming back up some minutes later. As with Mary Collins's series of statements, those of John Shevlin went from no sighting of a car all the way to effectively putting Donnelly and his friends in the frame to have easily encountered Una on the lane.

However, there are many issues around John Shevlin's various statements, principally to do with timing. And nowhere in any of his statements does he mention that he saw Kathleen Gaughan talking to Mary Collins, a conversation that happened close to the mouth of the cul-de-sac where he lived. John Shevlin's parents were present while he was being interviewed. There is no suggestion that coercion was used in questioning the teenager, but equally, if the gardaí kept coming back to the teenager and asking about details that they believed to be the case, if they led him to going some way towards what they wanted to hear and took that down in writing, was he, or his parents, going to object? In this scenario the gardaí are effectively creating evidence through the mouths of witnesses.

Acquiring a few building blocks by returning again and again to peripheral witnesses for further convenient details could only go so far. Something more was needed. This was where Sean Reilly and Martin Madden came in. The pair were sitting in Madden's car outside Reilly's home on the lane around 7 p.m. on the day in question. Initially, Reilly remembered a car passing, en route to the Navan Road end. Madden didn't remember any car.

Yet, after hours of interrogation in Trim, their stories changed to positively identify the car as Dick Donnelly's. In the initial statements Madden's car is parked facing away from the lane. In the statements acquired in Trim, they can see the lane clearly. This fits neatly into the garda theory.

The statements provided by Reilly and Madden are vital because they presented the gardaí with enough evidence to ask the suspects to come into the station for interview. As described in Chapter 7 Sean Reilly maintained he had provided the false statement after sustained intimidation and violence from some gardaí, principally Brian Gildea. Martin Madden's account of how he was treated in custody has never been examined, as he died tragically in an accident in the USA in the 1980s.

Once this other building block had been added to the theory, the gardaí were able to drive home their advantage by bringing in the suspects. Interrogation was the meat and drink of police work for the Murder Squad, and nobody was more skilled at this than Detective Sergeant John Courtney. All other evidence, even changing statements, will fade into the background if confessions to fit the theory can be obtained from the suspects. Of course, if the confessions could also include a crucial piece of incriminating evidence, like the location of a body, that would be it – job done, case closed, call the Attorney General's office.

It didn't work out like that. Some of the suspects did make admissions, but there was no clear narrative and absolutely nothing that would have led to the discovery of Una's body. Crucially, those who were held in Trim have always maintained that they were intimidated and assaulted in custody and any incriminating statements were effectively beaten out of them. Even without any use of force, the power differential between the gardaí and the young men they were interviewing cannot be discounted. One of the suspects, Marty, was a teenager; another, Martin, just out of his teens; Dick was twenty-three. All had left school in their early teens, did casual labouring work to make a crust and were at a carefree stage in life where they lived for the craic – cars, girls and socializing. In their world, middle-aged gardaí were authority figures, akin to priests, doctors and solicitors. That these imposing men, so aggressively sure of themselves, would put these young lads under relentless pressure over nearly two days, the gardaí insisting that they were telling lies, would have been a head-spinning experience in itself, even if no one ever laid a hand on them.

A baffling contradiction between Martin Conmey's two statements that strongly suggests he was not recalling things freely is in his account of how Dick Donnelly's car got to Porterstown Lane on 12 October. In the early days of the investigation he said that the two men left work, called over to Kerrigans', and from there drove to the lane, via the Navan Road. However, in his 4 a.m. statement in Trim he said they drove into Ratoath, where they ran into Kerrigan, drove along the Fairyhouse Road and entered Porterstown Lane from that end. Now, this account of their route conveniently fitted into the garda theory about the three men coming upon Una Lynskey travelling in the same direction, picking her up and something unfortunate happening thereafter.

The supporting evidence for the men taking that journey was a statement from Una's cousin John Gaughan, Ann's brother, one of the Fairyhouse Road Gaughans. Early in the investigation Gaughan gave the gardaí two statements. On 25 October, the day six of his neighbours were taken into Trim garda station, he gave a further statement. In it he laid out his journey home from work on 12 October. Gaughan said he got a lift from a workmate via Ratoath village and 'about 100 yards on the Ratoath side of the national school [on the Fairyhouse Road] we met Martin Kerrigan of "The Bush". He was riding a blue scooter. He was on his own and driving towards Ratoath village.' Gaughan added that he arrived home a few minutes later at around 6.45 p.m.

Martin Conmey's 4 a.m. statement dovetailed with this detail in John Gaughan's statement. And Gaughan's account would fit with Donnelly and Conmey meeting Kerrigan in the village around 6.50 p.m.–6.55 p.m. and it allowed enough time for them to drive down the Fairyhouse Road, on to Porterstown Lane and encounter Una Lynskey walking in the same direction. (What Kerrigan did with his scooter wasn't accounted for.)

But eighteen hours later, Martin's narrative flipped. There was no suggestion of Kerrigan being in Ratoath before 7 p.m., nothing about Conmey and Donnelly somehow deciding to drive to Ratoath, and nothing about the Zephyr then travelling out of Ratoath via Fairyhouse Road and entering the lane from that end.

How Conmey could produce a statement, allegedly of his own volition, that suited the garda theory, which happened to be supported by a statement from one of the Lynskey extended family, and then simply change it eighteen hours later without explanation or probing, is question-begging. And there are just two explanations: either Conmey lied in the 4 a.m. statement, and his lies happened to coincide with a version obtained by the gardaí that very day which suited their theory. Or else he simply, as he alleges, was so frightened and bewildered he went along with whatever the gardaí dictated. So when the gardaí no longer considered one version of events plausible or useful, it disappeared.

As well as the accounts of the interrogations of Conmey and Donnelly in the previous two chapters, there are other details that point towards the pair telling the truth about what happened in Trim. For instance, none of the men suggested that Detective Sergeant Courtney was aggressive or assaulted anyone. Courtney was a central figure in the interrogations, effectively leading the operation on the ground. If Donnelly and Conmey were inventing the allegations of brutality, why did they leave Courtney out of it? He would have been an obvious candidate to fit up with any false allegation of assault in custody.

The two gardaí whom the young men said were intimidating and committed assaults were Brian Gildea and Owen Corrigan. These two were not members of the Murder Squad but drafted in to assist. Much later it would emerge that allegations of brutality against the Murder Squad often centred on gardaí who were brought in from outside the unit for that purpose. Donnelly and Conmey hadn't a clue about any of this and wouldn't have attached any significance to the operational background of any of those interrogating them. So for them both to have identified Gildea and Corrigan as the main aggressors would have to have been uncannily insightful and a major coincidence if they were inventing stories of garda brutality.

What occurred in Trim garda station over forty-four hours would be central to everything that was about to unfold in the local community. There are three possible scenarios as to what exactly did happen when those men were in custody.

First: from the garda perspective, the admissions made in custody were proof that their theory was correct. The fact that they didn't achieve a definitive outcome, most particularly a confession that included the location of Una's body, was merely because these Westies were hardy and devious, holding out on giving the full truth. The notion that the theory was wrong simply was not countenanced.

All the gardaí who were present in Trim, and particularly Superintendent P. J. Keane, Inspector Hubert Reynolds, Courtney, Gildea and Corrigan, claimed that the men were treated properly, that the interrogations were carried out according to proper police procedure. They denied either engaging in or witnessing any intimidation, coercion or violence. They claimed that they witnessed the young men coming clean after sustained but proper interrogation, and that the results were obvious as the men appeared to be relieved to get it all off their chests. This version would subsequently be sworn under oath in court. If it did not accord with the facts, then a whole range of gardaí had committed organized perjury.

Second: another possible scenario is that the truth, or at least the partial truth, was beaten out of the suspects. In this scenario the gardaí are lying about what occurred but the results achieved confirmed their theory. In this scenario a decision was taken to use violence and intimidation to access the truth because that was deemed the only way to do so. If this were the case, then the gardaí broke the law and abused their power, but did so, as they would have seen it, for a greater good.

The third scenario is that they beat untruths out of the suspects to make the evidence fit their theory. This is nothing short of an appalling vista. It would point to shocking police procedure, a propensity to act as if the gardaí were above the law and a refusal to change tack even if the evidence began to suggest that they had the wrong men. It would also involve the effective framing of three young men in a tight-knit community for the killing of a female neighbour.

Whichever scenario represents the facts of what occurred in Trim, of one thing there is no doubt. What followed directly from the detentions in the garda station over those forty-four hours would lead to further tragedy and trauma that would reverberate down through generations.

11. A Community Ripped Apart

There was confusion outside Trim garda station when the three men were being released on the evening of 27 October. Martin Conmey emerged from the station first, walking out into the darkness of a late-autumn evening. His father was waiting for him with the family car. Dick Donnelly and Marty Kerrigan were let out around the same time, but a garda approached them and engaged in further conversation in the yard attached to the station. Dick asked for the keys of his car but was told it was being held as evidence.

While they were talking, Martin Conmey's father drove past, not having seen Martin's friends. Donnelly and Kerrigan now had no way home, and the gardaí weren't offering a lift.

'You'll get a lift yourself,' one of the gardaí said, and walked back into the station.

'They were told to go home through the fields,' Ann Kerrigan remembers. 'They were told the Lynskeys were on the way with a gun and somebody was going to get shot.'

Dick and Marty set out on the 18-mile journey home, initially through the streets of Trim, which had closed down for the evening. They had barely slept during their time in custody. They were exhausted, sore and hungry as they made their way through the outskirts of Trim and on to the dark roads beyond the town. They were also well aware that their lives had changed utterly. In everything but name they were the prime suspects in the missing persons case of their neighbour, Una Lynskey. As members of the gardaí had intimated, and as they knew well themselves, Una's family would not take well to the notion that neighbours were responsible for her disappearance. Their detention in Trim had made the three friends marked men.

Donnelly and Kerrigan kept walking, tensing each time the headlights of a car and the low hum of an approaching motor appeared out of the darkness. They stood in against the ditches. A couple of times instinct prompted them to climb over a ditch into a field out of sight in case the approaching car was bringing violence. Around halfway along their journey, a neighbour, Tommy O'Neill, spotted them on the road and stopped. At first, they advanced cautiously towards the red rear lights, the exhaust pipe's idling fumes. Then Dick spotted O'Neill behind the wheel. At last, this epilogue to their nightmare was coming to an end.

Back at Kerrigans', the two men were duly fussed over. According to Ann Kerrigan, Marty took off his shirt and showed bruises on his back. A sense of shock pervaded the house.

'A neighbour came in and Marty got up and bent over. The neighbour asked what's wrong and Marty said his back was killing him,' Ann remembers. Then, as the neighbour was getting into his car, there was a sudden loud bang and it took a second for everybody to realize that it was the sound of a gun. 'It scared the living daylights out of us,' Ann says. 'The shot appeared to have come from a field next to our home. We knew it was them. It had to have been them. Who else could it have been?'

The incident was reported to the gardaí the next day. 'Them', as far as Ann Kerrigan and her family and friends were concerned, was somebody associated with the Lynskey family. Nobody was ever charged over the incident. The shot was the opening salvo in the events that would tear asunder the close-knit community around Porterstown Lane.

The following morning, when the Kerrigan sisters were leaving to go to work, there was spray paint on the road outside. 'Murderers', it read, and was accompanied by an arrow pointing towards the Kerrigan home.

Later that day, the *Evening Herald* reported that the gardaí now believed that Una was dead and that her body could have been moved on a couple of occasions by her killers. A major search was to be launched, which would include the garda sub-aqua unit and soldiers seconded from the armed forces. As with the great bulk of media reports at the time, the coverage was sourced from within the garda investigation.

The piece mentioned that three men who had been helping the gardaí with their inquiries had been released the previous evening. 'Following information received Gardaí yesterday searched ponds and ditches at Rathbeggan on the Dublin–Navan Road but in each case drew a blank. It is thought the search will be successful in the next few days.' The implication was obvious – these searches were being conducted because of what had been revealed during the interrogations in Trim.

The spokesman was quoted: 'This is going to be a big search. We feel we are close to finding the body.'

Patrick Lynskey told the paper, 'We are still praying that Una is alive. It is a terrible strain on the family.'

The day after he was released from Trim, Dick Donnelly's father brought him to the doctor. John Clarke had a good reputation and practised in the village of Dunsany, 14 kilometres from Ratoath.

His examination found that Donnelly had some serious bruising, consistent with receiving a number of blows. There were four abrasions on the inside of his left arm, measuring one inch square. On the outside of that arm there was a linear red mark measuring three inches and another beneath it two inches long.

Beneath the left shoulder blade there was an area of bruising fourteen inches long and two inches wide, and there was further bruising in the ribs area, three inches by an inch in area. There was also bruising on the right shoulder, as well as swelling in both ears. Donnelly's jaw joint was swollen.

The doctor referred him to Navan Hospital for X-rays on the skull, chest and jaw. Asked later in court for his opinion on how the injuries could have come about, he said, 'As a result of blows or probably by means of fists, and probably the long red marks on his chest were caused by some long, blunt instrument.' This would accord with Donnelly's allegation that Garda Gildea had struck him on the chest with a poker.

On the same day, Martin Conmey's father, David, brought him to a local doctor and then visited Dunshaughlin garda station to complain about the detention in Trim of his son and to insist that his son had absolutely nothing to do with Una Lynskey's disappearance. Marty Kerrigan's father Martin did likewise.

In those early days after the detentions in Trim, a sense of foreboding permeated Porterstown Lane. The close-knit nature of the community, the preponderance of young males in the affected families, meant that confrontation was almost inevitable. What followed was a constant, low level of intimidation and threats, with the odd outbreak of violence. There was aggro when the menfolk on either side met on the lane. There were various skirmishes at dances in the area. Paintings, which included a depiction of gallows, appeared not just at Marty Kerrigan's home but also Martin Conmey's.

Naturally, those on the opposite side from the Lynskeys didn't take things lying down. One night, one of those supporting the Lynskeys was stopped on the lane. A group of youths surrounded his car, conveying threats by their presence as much as anything that was said. The battle lines were drawn repeatedly, with violence always lurking just behind the latest threat.

Some in the community just wanted to keep out of it. Sean Reilly, whose statement had given the gardaí the premise they required to bring the men to Trim, didn't want to get involved. His father went up the lane to the Lynskeys and told them that Sean had nothing to do with anything that was going on. The Reillys believed the three young men were innocent, but at the same time they didn't want to fall out with anyone. Others locally felt the same.

Among the older generation, there were attempts at some form of reconciliation. Martin Kerrigan Snr got word from a sister in England that there was talk in her neighbourhood about a young girl having arrived from Ireland. 'My father got that letter and he went up to the Lynskeys to tell them,' Ann Kerrigan says. 'He was thinking it might be of some help, that it could be followed up to see if it was Una. He was only in the house a few minutes when a guard showed up and brought him to Dunshaughlin garda station. The Lynskeys just didn't want to know about it. As far as they were concerned, they knew what had happened to Una and who was responsible.'

Dick Donnelly and Martin Conmey both decided that they would return to working in the city. Both managed to get work on building sites in the western suburbs. Marty Kerrigan continued to work locally in Dunnes farm. Very quickly, it became obvious that Marty Kerrigan was the focus of particular ire from the Lynskey side. Marty was the youngest of the three whom the gardaí had fingered, and circumstances dictated that he was the most vulnerable. His family lived away from the lane, in the area known as The Bush. He was physically small, described by his friend Christo Ennis as 'a *garsún*'. At home, he was the only young male in his family, his older brother John having emigrated to Manchester. By contrast, there were three or four young males in both the Conmey and Donnelly households. If either of their homes ever came under attack, or if there were sustained attempts to intimidate, either family would have plenty of male hands ready to defend. By contrast, Marty Kerrigan was an easy target.

'They tortured us,' Ann Kerrigan remembers. 'They absolutely tortured us, but it was the men in the family on both sides who were really at it. They would be up outside our house, the engine in a car gunning, and they would be shouting out insults, threats,' she says. 'The Lynskey boys didn't have a car. So, it was John Gaughan who used to drive them up here in his Mini. Nearly every night of the week they would be outside the house, open the windows of the car and shout "Murderers!" We reported that all the time, but it never stopped.

'Marty was afraid of his life. We were at home one day, me and him, and I was going over to a neighbour, Mrs Lynch, who I used to call into. Marty asked me not to go, said he didn't want to be left on his own. I felt obliged to go at the time so off I went. When I came back he was under the bed.'

His family pleaded with him to leave the area, go across to John in Manchester at least until the whole thing blew over, whenever that might be. 'He said no way,' Ann remembered. 'He said if he left it would look like he was running, that he had done something wrong. He hadn't done anything so he was staying put.'

The threat, as his family saw it, was constant. Ann and Katie were working in the city centre. Most days, Ann would ring Barrons' shop down the road to check that Marty had been seen passing on his scooter on the way to work. 'We were all worried, all the time,' Ann says. 'I'd ring the shop just to check that he'd gone to work. Mrs Barron, who was behind the counter there, would tell me, yes that she had seen, or heard, him passing by on this little scooter he had. We just didn't know what was going to happen next.'

The rising tensions and various incidents prompted the gardaí to assign an officer to keep an eye on the Kerrigans. Garda John Harty was a regular visitor to the house and often attended at the home, usually sitting outside in a patrol car.

On 8 November the *Irish Independent* reported again the garda theory about Una's body being moved.

'Gardaí believe that the body of 19-year-old civil servant Una Lynskey, who has been missing from her Dunshaughlin home for more than three weeks, was moved twice after her death. Information that the body of the girl whom the gardaí are convinced was murdered, first taken to a wood and hidden and then removed and dumped in a pond, has come to Dunshaughlin garda station.' This report, obviously sourced from the gardaí, was lies. The information about the wood and the pond had originated in the interrogation of Marty Kerrigan in Trim. It had been shown to be without any foundation.

The news report went on: 'Gardaí are paying particular attention to reports that shots were fired and slogans painted near the homes of certain Co Meath men. A spokesman said at the weekend: "We are keeping an open mind on the matter. Members of the public have been very helpful and information is still coming in."'

As the community around Porterstown Lane fractured irretrievably, one family found itself in a terrible conundrum. Winnie Lynskey's brother Anthony Gaughan lived next door to the Lynskeys on the cul-de-sac. The siblings' other brother Pat, father of Una's cousin, friend and travelling companion, Ann, lived on the Fairyhouse Road. The three of them were, like most of their generation on the lane, from the Erris Peninsula in North Mayo.

There were eleven offspring in Anthony and Mary Kate Gaughan's family, including Padraic, who had seen the strange car on the lane on the day in question, and Kathleen, who had been talking to Mary Collins further down the lane when a vehicle, probably the same one, passed by coming up to 7 p.m.

Padraic was particularly close to his cousins Sean and James Lynskey, as all played GAA for the local Ratoath club, usually on the same team. He was also good friends with Tony Conmey, Martin's brother and their near neighbour, again through a shared interest in hurling and football. Padraic's brother Danny was the same age as his cousin James Lynskey and they also were very close friends.

'We all got on,' Padraic says. 'I got on well with the whole family of Lynskeys. There were rumours about people being jealous of their farm because Pat had done so well for himself. I don't know where that came from, but I didn't see it like that. We got on very well with all of them.'

Similarly, Padraic and his other cousins, the Gaughans on Fairyhouse Road, were pretty close. 'Michael Gaughan was around my age. We went to dances with him and had a few drinks. There was a lot of work around the countryside at that time picking potatoes and strawberries, and me and Michael would have done a bit of that together. Seamus was a bit older and I would have known Ann.'

In the early phase of the garda investigation Padraic had provided the photofit of the man he saw driving the car that evening as he walked home from work. During that time he also observed the comings and goings next door as the investigation was ramped up.

'There was always cars outside the Lynskeys' at that time,' he says. 'The guards were in that house the whole time. Once my father was over there, as he often was, and [Garda] Brian Gildea was in the house. The investigation wasn't going well, something or other was up, but according to my father, Gildea was so mad that he broke a chair. As far as I could see the guards were telling the family that the three lads were responsible and that was getting through to them.'

In the days before Trim, Padraic noticed that he was drifting away from his cousins. They weren't turning up as much for the club and he felt that they were harbouring suspicions about some in the community over Una's disappearance. 'We kind of fell apart,' he says. 'Me and Sean and James. Sean in particular was a big loss to the club; he was a good footballer. But as that was going on they began drifting apart from the rest of the neighbours.'

Then Trim happened. 'We were all shocked when the lads were arrested,' Padraic Gaughan says. 'The whole thing had changed from what had been thought locally in the days straight after Una went missing. It was all about the three lads. There was nothing being said about the car that I and others had seen. That was gone off the radar completely.'

In the immediate aftermath of Trim, Anthony and Mary Kate Gaughan found themselves torn. Anthony went over in the Lynskeys', attempting to offer support to a family consumed with both anger and despair. Then the couple went up to Conmey's to see what was going on. Their visit that evening convinced Anthony and Mary Kate that Martin Conmey, and by extension Conmey's friends, had nothing to do with the disappearance of his niece.

'Mam and Dad were good friends with all the neighbours, including the Conmeys. So when they heard that Martin had been in Trim and was home they went up to the house, because that's the sort of thing that neighbours did, certainly in those days. Anyway, over there they saw the state of Martin after coming home. My dad asked Martin straight out had he anything to do with it, and Martin said no. That, and how Martin was after those two days in the station, was enough for my father. After that he didn't believe they had anything to do with it. And yet the Lynskeys, Dad's sister Winnie, and all her family, they were full sure those lads were guilty.'

Anthony Gaughan's rejection of the theory that the three young local men were responsible for Una's disappearance

was to cost him dearly. He was close to his siblings, Winnie
Lynskey and Pat Gaughan. Among the displaced west of
Ireland people those bonds had always been tight. Physically, the Lynskeys' front door and that of Anthony Gaughan
literally faced each other. Their respective families had
grown up together, and now that the Lynskeys were going
through a form of hell, Anthony obviously wanted to assist
in any way he could. And yet, he simply did not believe that
the guards had the right men.

'When Dad started taking the Conmeys' side he got the
cold shoulder from the Lynskeys. We all got it. I remember
once around that time my sister Kathleen went over to the
house and nobody would talk to her there. We were grad-
ually drifting apart.'

It would have been easy for Anthony Gaughan to keep
his counsel, avoiding the awful dilemma of effectively taking
opposite sides to his siblings, but his conscience wouldn't
allow him to do so. His oldest son, John, had emigrated to
Canada and offered some advice across the Atlantic. He
told his father that he needed to get a hold of Padraic and
Danny in particular and tell them to steer clear.

'My father sat Danny and myself down at the kitchen
table,' Padraic says. 'We were helping with the search and
close to the whole thing. He told us to go back to work and
leave it to the guards. John had been on to him too. John
knew the temperament of the Lynskeys and what might
happen. He told my father to keep me and Danny out of it.
Much later my dad told John that he had saved us, me and
Danny, with his advice.

'The strange thing was, if Dad didn't intervene, I might
have gone on the Lynskey side. We were that close, or at
least had been until very soon before that. But my father

kept control of us. He did all he could to steer us clear of the kind of trouble that was inevitable.'

Despite the tension and threats, life had to go on. Christo Ennis was getting married, the first of his group of friends to take the plunge. The guards, apparently, were so well across events in the community at the time that even they knew that Christo's big day was coming. According to Christo, one of the investigation team showed up at the family home with a proposal.

'He came to the door and offered me money,' Christo says. 'He said you're getting married soon, you could do with it. He obviously thought I was holding back on what I knew and that I could help them pin it to the lads. But there was nothing to know. The old lad [Christo's father] knew the guard, and he was there in the house listening to this. He came out and told him to get the hell up the road to the Lynskeys', he could get all the information he wanted up there.'

According to Christo, the guard, whom he names, was offering £12,000, a considerable sum for the time, which could equate to well over €100,000 today. It is inconceivable that any garda unit, including the Murder Squad, would have access to that level of money, but that does not preclude the possibility that such an offer could have been made under false pretences.

In the build-up to the wedding, Christo was once again asked to help the gardaí with their inquiries.

'They were around all the time,' he says. 'They followed me a few times. Then one day I was doing a bit of work in Maynooth and two of them came and wanted me to go with them. They brought me to the barracks in Dunboyne and it was the same questions they were asking, and I told them what I knew, which was nothing. They were all right that time, they didn't give me any hassle.'

For Vera, the forthcoming life she was entering on Porterstown Lane had some early shocks. One day, she and Christo's sister Evelyn were walking down the lane.

'This fella came along in a tractor and swore at us and he swerved the tractor in off the road to give us a fright, as if he was going to run us over. I asked Evelyn who it was. "That's them," she said. I knew pretty quickly that "them" was the Lynskeys. None of it was nice, what was going on at that time.'

Christo Ennis's experience at Dunboyne garda station chimes with that of Dick Donnelly when he was brought to Dunshaughlin around the same time. There was none of the threats, intimidation or violence that the men said they had experienced in Trim.

On 26 November, Martin Conmey was brought to Kilmessan garda station. He was interviewed by Garda Brian Gildea and Inspector Hubert Reynolds. He told them that the statements he made in Trim were incorrect. 'I had nothing to do whatsoever with that girl,' he said. 'I never saw her on that evening. How could I, as I didn't get home until 7.20 p.m., when Dick Donnelly let me off on my way home from work.' Conmey does not allege any ill treatment or threats occurring in Kilmessan.

The following day, Christo and Vera got married. Dick Donnelly was the best man and the reception was held in the Sunnybank Hotel in Glasnevin on the Northside of Dublin. The Sunnybank, since closed down, was a familiar hostelry to generations of GAA fans due to its proximity to Croke Park.

Four of those who were at the reception confirm separately that two unknown guests turned up in the function room. As the bride and groom came from different communities, and their families were largely unknown to each other, there was some confusion between the bride and groom as to which side of the wedding party these two men were from. 'I thought they were Christo's uncles and he thought they were related to me,' Vera says.

The two men drifted into company before long, making conversation with various guests. One asked Ann Kerrigan out to dance. 'He wanted to know did I know Dick Donnelly and Martin Conmey, and I thought he must be somebody from Vera's side of the family,' she said.

Presently, a suspicion went around that these men were guards acting undercover. Given that many of those at the reception felt alienated from or targeted by the guards, and a good number of these young guests would have consumed large quantities of alcohol over the course of the day, there was potential for serious conflict. Ann Kerrigan spotted something was up when her brother Marty swiped a hand across a pile of glasses in anger, toppling them on to the floor, where they smashed. Pretty quickly, the manager arrived and was told what appeared to be the issue. The unknown men left almost immediately, before things got ugly.

'They were obviously there to see if somebody might start talking once they had some drink inside them,' Vera Ennis says. 'That's what it was, as far as we were concerned.'

It's impossible to establish if the two men were gardaí, detailed to attend the wedding reception undercover to see if they could gather any intelligence for the murder investigation. If it was the case, it could indicate that the members

of the investigation team were dedicated to their task, determined to solve a crime and bring some closure to the
victim's family. Going undercover at a gathering of a large
group of young people who might be hostile to them suggests that these officers were prepared to go beyond the call
of duty.

It could also illustrate the mentality that appears to have
pervaded the investigation team. Not only were the guards
convinced that they had the right men in their sights, they
seemed to believe that others in the community knew more
than they were saying and were actively covering up for the
suspects. This suspicion – that there was a widespread conspiracy among many in Porterstown Lane – fed off the old
concept of the Westies being a law unto themselves, with
their own mores and attitude to the law. This type of thinking was certainly present in previous generations, as seen in
the incendiary Dáil statements of the Meath politician
David Hall in the late 1920s and clashes between native-
born people and migrants in the 1940s. That such a trope
might influence the Murder Squad in 1971 may seem a bit
of a stretch. Yet, it would explain the gardaí appearing to
believe that forces beyond their reach were preventing them
from accessing the full truth of what had happened to Una.

Vera Ennis settled into married life in Porterstown Lane,
initially moving in with Christo's family. One day while she
was at work, two gardaí showed up at the house, came in
and conducted a search. They took away a wig which
belonged to Christo's sister, a pair of Vera's shoes and a
handbag. The purpose was to show the items to the Lynskeys to check whether they had belonged to Una. 'I didn't
know a thing about it until I got home,' Vera says. 'Of
course, we didn't know anything about warrants in those

days. They just arrived and took the stuff. They did drop it back later once they knew none of it had anything to do with Una Lynskey.'

On another evening, she was introduced to what was becoming routine in the area. 'We were out for a drink and Dick dropped us home in his car,' she says. 'As we were getting out, stopped there chatting for a minute, a car pulled up and somebody shouted out, "Are you going to the morgue?" Christo and Dick brushed it off; they were used to it at that stage. But it was unsettling.'

Through this period, the garda investigation continued. More statements were taken, including the third from Mary Collins and the third from John Shevlin, both progressing from having seen little of consequence to advancing towards the possibility that they saw Dick Donnelly's car in the lane at a crucial time. The gardaí also went back to James Donnelly, the farmer who had encountered the large car at the junction of Porterstown and Fairyhouse Road on the evening in question. Donnelly was brought to Phoenix Park on three different occasions to see if he could identify the vehicle. It is unclear why he was repeatedly asked to attend. He was shown several cars, including Dick Donnelly's, which had been confiscated in Trim. On the third visit he finally gave a statement.

'I looked at a large number of cars parked on the Garda Depot Square, Phoenix Park. Those cars were of different colours, make and sizes. Out of all the cars seen by me I picked out a Zephyr car registered number JZE 842 as being similar in colour, make and size as the car which I saw coming to a sudden halt at the junction of Porterstown/ Fairyhouse.' This was Dick Donnelly's car. Further down the statement he elaborated: 'Having again looked at this car JZE 842 from the seat of your car and at the same distance at 4.50 p.m. [he wanted to see it in the same light] as seen by me on that evening, I am positive it is the same car as seen by me on the evening of the 12th October 1971, the sort of shine off its colour makes me that positive.' The statement was taken by Garda Brian Gildea. Later, in court testimony, James Donnelly would dispute elements of the statement.

Through all this period the search for Una continued. In the days after Trim the operation was greatly expanded. Fifty soldiers from Cathal Brugha barracks in Dublin joined around sixty gardaí on the search, which also included the ongoing involvement of the garda sub-aqua unit. Later, the garda dog unit was deployed for three days to assist.

They searched right across south Meath, through bogs, under every bridge in the area, across potato fields which were ploughed up. They searched Coyles' farm, where Donnelly and Conmey were working on the day Una disappeared, and they searched Dunnes' farm, where Marty Kerrigan and Christo Ennis were employed. An old workhouse surrounded by heavy growth was searched, as was the route of an old railway line running between Navan and Drumree.

Nothing was found. Not a clue, not a lead, absolutely nothing. If Una Lynskey had been killed, it was looking increasingly unlikely that her body had been disposed of anywhere within a radius of twenty miles from Porterstown Lane. The failure to locate her body was obviously distressing for her family, but it also perplexed the gardaí. If, as they believed, the three young local men were involved, where did they get rid of the body?

Diviners were retained and went to work as far away as

Cork and Kerry. One diviner did extensive work in Bray, Co Wicklow, and claimed to have found leads, but the gardaí dismissed this. Another claimed that a body was located in the parochial house in Ratoath, home of the local parish priest. Again, this was quickly dismissed.

On 13 November, the *Meath Chronicle* reported that an anonymous group of people were offering a 'substantial reward' for information leading to the finding of Una Lynskey. The paper reported that 'gardaí say any such information will be treated in utmost confidence'. The news was unusual. It was also around this time that Christo Ennis alleges he was approached by a garda with the offer of money.

In late November, the *Evening Herald* interviewed the Lynskey parents. Patrick told the newspaper that he doubted the theory that Una was first abducted in a Zephyr or Zodiac car. This was a reference to Donnelly and Kerrigan's account of seeing either model of car at the pylon around the time Una disappeared, which had been mentioned in media reports of what witnesses saw.

'I believe there are some people holding back evidence,' he said.

Winnie Lynskey was solely concerned with where her daughter's body might be. 'I pray to St Anthony night and day that Una will be found. What else can I do?'

On 4 December the *Meath Chronicle* reported that gardaí were now rechecking on earlier inquiries. 'Murder Squad detectives and local gardaí under the supervision of Inspector Hubert Reynolds of the Technical Bureau are without any clues in the case. They have exhausted all avenues of investigation and are now double-checking enquiries made since the girl vanished.' The news piece ended with a focus on Una's bereft parents. 'Resigned to the possibility that their daughter has been murdered, Mr Lynskey, a 53-year-old farmer with 94 acres, and his wife Winifred are hoping that at least the body of their daughter will be found.'

Within days of the publication going on sale, that hope would be met.

PART II

Two Bodies

12. A Body without Answers

James Williams and Bob Kavanagh were cleaning out a drain in the Dublin Mountains when Williams noticed a smell. Kavanagh was behind the controls of a JCB, Williams accompanying him with a shovel. The two men were employed by Dublin County Council and were part of a detail working on the road in the Dublin Mountains, in the townland of Glendoo, outside the village of Kilternan. It was a Friday morning, 20 December 1971.

Williams crossed to the far side of the road where a wire fence was planted in front of a large forest. He followed the line of the fence some yards, his eyes fixed on the undergrowth that lay just a yard or so from the road. He arrived at a clump of rhododendrons and something caught his eye. Just behind the clump there was a loose bed of fir bushes. This was unusual. Williams knew there were no fir bushes growing in the area. Had they been placed there to hide something? He suspected that there could be a dead sheep beneath the bushes, left there perhaps by a dog owner wanting to cover up a fatal attack.

He pulled at the bushes, but there was more than he had thought. He went back across the road and retrieved his shovel. Beneath the bushes there was some rotten felt, which again had to have been placed there on purpose. There was also an old fire grate, left there most likely to ensure the wind wouldn't lift anything. Williams picked up the grate and got a severe shock when he saw beneath it a human skull. He ran back across the road and told Kavanagh. They left the scene and went to Williams's home, which was just down the road, to phone the gardaí in the nearest station, Rathfarnham.

The guards arrived soon after midday. Inspector Bernard Kelly took in the scene and noticed that the bushes had been cut at their stems and placed there, indicating that it was a primitive attempt to hide the body. The body was in a bad state, with areas like the rib cage exposed, all flesh and tissue gone. There was some clothing, but the only personal effects retrieved were a wristwatch and a gold ring with a stone which had been on the ring finger of the right hand. A few inquiries quickly established that the body was likely that of Una Lynskey who had gone missing fifty-nine days earlier.

Word was conveyed to the gardaí investigating Una's disappearance. She was identified by dental records. A garda car was seen entering the cul-de-sac where the Lynskeys lived that Friday afternoon en route to bear the bad tidings. After nearly two months of uncertainty, Una's family could at least start to grieve. Yet, this was just the end of the beginning. From this point forward and forever more, they would have to live with the knowledge that she had been snatched from their midst and died violently.

Word quickly filtered out that Una's body had been found. Ann Kerrigan heard the news on the radio in her place of work, Harper's drapery in North Earl Street. Her sister Katie was standing at a bus stop on her way home from work in Ballymun when she saw a headline in a newspaper. 'It was sad, but there was also a sense of relief,' Katie says. 'When I got home, I told Marty, I can't remember whether he had heard already. But he said it's great from one point of view, and that was that now at least they should be able to find out what happened to her.'

If such was the hope among the Kerrigans and the wider community, it would quickly be dashed.

The following day, Marty's sister Eileen drove him into Ratoath. They left home around 8.30 p.m. They wanted to talk to Dick Donnelly, to see whether he had heard any more about the finding of Una's body, whether the guards now had another lead. Eileen parked outside Ryan's pub and went inside. Marty remained in the car. Inside, the pub was doing a lively Saturday-night trade, the air thick with cigarette smoke and the din of conversation. She spotted some of the Lynskeys but tried to keep her eyes away from them. She went to the bar and leaned across towards a young fella who was serving, whom she recognized.

'Have you seen Dick Donnelly in here tonight?' she asked.

'No,' came the reply.

She turned to leave, but as she did so, James Lynskey pushed past her. 'Come on, boys,' he said to those in his company. A procession of men followed him towards the door, including his brother Sean, cousin John Gaughan, brother-in-law Seamus Reddin and Una's boyfriend, Paddy Kelly. Eileen knew where they were headed, and she hurried after them.

Outside, the men spotted Eileen's parked car and Marty inside it. Paddy Kelly went over and rapped on the window. 'You're dead,' he shouted in to Marty Kerrigan.

'No, I'm not,' Kerrigan replied.

'If you're not, you're as good as dead,' Kelly said. Eileen moved forward to the driver's door. She had to get in, get the car started and get her brother away from here fast. But then James Lynskey pushed her aside and reached for the handle on the driver's door himself. He got into the car, leaned across and grabbed Marty Kerrigan by the shoulder, pulling him, trying to get him out of the car. Eileen grabbed Lynskey and pulled him away. She got him out of the car and she slammed closed the door. Inside, Marty lifted his legs and hopped across to the driver's seat. He started the car. One of the men got on the roof. James Lynskey sat on the bonnet. Marty Kerrigan started the car and pulled away, the two men sliding off and on to the road. Marty drove off in the direction of Ashbourne, the quickest way out of the village.

When Eileen turned around she saw John Gaughan starting up his green Mini. Reddin got in alongside him and they took off after Marty Kerrigan. By then, Eileen was crying. This was not who she was, who her family were. This was not the community in which she grew up. She knew these men who were intent on doing harm to her brother. Their whole community had been shattered, and now that Una's body had been found, instead of turning down the temperature, it was being turned up.

As she stood there in the darkened street, she looked up and saw another Lynskey, Andy, who lived in Dublin and was Una's uncle, standing in the roadway, a barstool clutched in his right hand. He had followed his nephews out, armed with the barstool, ready for whatever was coming. He turned to Eileen.

'We won't touch you,' he said. 'But your brother murdered Una.'

'I don't know anything about that,' Eileen said, still crying. 'I don't know what's happening.'

'You do know. You know more than we do. We won't touch you, but if we get him again we'll kill him.'

Then, as if the clock could suddenly be turned back two months, Andy Lynskey asked Eileen to come back into the pub, he'd buy her a drink. With her car gone, her nerves shattered, Eileen complied and went inside. Later, she remembered that Ryan, the proprietor, put a drink on the counter in front of her, but she has no recollection of drinking it. The surreal situation wasn't lost on her. A man whom she had known since she was a young girl, a neighbour, one of their shared community of Westerners displaced here to Co Meath, had just told her he wanted her brother violently killed, and now she was having a drink with him.

Somebody drove her home. When she got there, Marty hadn't yet arrived. Her boyfriend drove her to Dunshaughlin, where Marty was drinking in the Royal Tavern, making sure to stay clear of Ratoath for the evening.

The discovery of Una Lynskey's body on a lonely road in the Dublin Mountains, about 40 kilometres from where she went missing, sent the case off in different directions. For the gardaí, the discovery of a body, and the circumstances in which it was found, officially elevated the investigation into one of murder. However, a post-mortem was not definitive on how Una had died. Professor Maurice Hickey, a pathologist working out of UCD's city centre campus in Earlsfort Terrace, couldn't determine a cause of death.

'I examined the skull, the bones of the spine, the ribs, pelvis and all the long bones on both arms and legs. There were no fractures on any of these bones,' he reported.

'I am unable to express an opinion as to the cause of

death. The stage of decomposition would be consistent with the body being two or three months dead.'

Gardaí searched the area around where the body was discovered but found nothing of evidential value. The most likely scenario was that the body had been brought to Glencullen, probably under the cover of darkness. Possibly the whole operation was conducted with a minimum amount of planning. It seemed likely that whoever was responsible didn't know the area that well and had just concluded that the Dublin Mountains were secluded enough for the concealment.

After the weekend, on Monday, 13 December the *Cork Examiner* reported that the finding of the body was expected to lead to a breakthrough in the case. 'Murder Squad detectives believe it will be only a matter of days before an arrest will be made in the case of missing Co Meath girl Una Lynskey, whose badly decomposed body was found in the Dublin Mountains last Friday.'

The paper quoted Patrick Lynskey, who said the discovery of his daughter's body was 'a great relief after all these weeks of waiting'. He went on to say that now that they knew their daughter was dead, 'with God's help, justice will prevail'.

Una's removal was from Stafford's morgue on Dublin's North Strand on Tuesday, 14 December. The condition of the body meant there had been no open-coffin wake, robbing the family of one of the traditional stages in the process of saying goodbye to a loved one. The funeral procession passed along Porterstown Lane. Mary Conmey, Martin's 16-year-old sister, watched it pass, the silence interrupted only by the soft chugging of car engines. The hearse

stopped briefly up the road at the pylon, the spot where it
was widely believed she met her killer or killers. Mary made
a record of the scene at the time.

> Una's body passed up at 6.15 p.m. It was followed by a long
> line of cars. As I stood at the corner of the shed all I could
> see was the road lit up by the red lights of the cars, and
> each one slowed down at the spot where she was believed
> to be picked up. I know what people are thinking, but I
> know the truth. It hurt so much to think that hatred could
> be so strong and I wanted so much to follow those cars. A
> long time ago Una was a good friend. But now she is dead
> and they say we killed her.

On Wednesday morning, the Church of the Holy Trinity
in Ratoath was overflowing for the funeral. Mass was cele-
brated by the parish priest, John Cogan, the man who had
gone to Trim garda station when the three men were being
detained. Padraic Gaughan, by now estranged from the
Lynskey family, attended. 'I went to the funeral and I went
to the removal, but I kept out of the way of the Lynskeys,'
he said. 'It was just a very sad occasion.'

The crowd spilled outside the church on to the grounds.
Among those in attendance were some of the Murder
Squad detectives. The young Meath TD John Bruton* from
nearby Dunboyne was also present. After the requiem Mass,
the coffin was carried the short distance to the cemetery by
her six brothers, who were assisted by Una's uncles and
Paddy Kelly. Also there was Una's grandfather, James Lynskey, the man who had brought his family east as part of the

---

* Bruton would become Fine Gael leader in 1990 and served as Taoiseach
from 1994 to 1997.

Land Commission resettlement programme thirty years previously. As the coffin was lowered, Una's sisters and brothers stood at the lip of the grave offering their final farewell. They were two months into a nightmare that had begun with Una's disappearance, shattering their family. Now the community was also shattered, and there was no knowing where it was going to end.

13. 'They've taken Marty'

The week after Una's body was found, Eileen Kerrigan drove Marty to work in the Dunnes' farm every day. Whatever threat existed for her brother had just gone through the roof. Every evening, by arrangement, a member of the Dunne family drove him home. The Kerrigans didn't want Marty anywhere on his own. He was still refusing to leave the country, to go across to his brother in Manchester.

On the morning of Sunday, 19 December, four days after Una's funeral, the Kerrigan sisters, Eileen, Ann and Katie, went to Mass in Dunshaughlin. When they arrived home, Marty was still in bed. He rose soon after and joined his siblings and father for some Sunday dinner. Afterwards, Eileen and Katie left with Eileen's boyfriend, Syl McAuley, and drove into Ballymun, where Katie worked. After dropping off Katie and doing a bit of shopping, Syl and Eileen drove back towards Co Meath. As they were coming out through Blanchardstown in the western suburbs, around 2.30 p.m., Eileen spotted John Gaughan's green Mini passing them, heading in the opposite direction. Eileen recognized John's sister, Ann, in the passenger seat but couldn't make out the other occupants of the car.

Unbeknownst to Eileen, the Gaughans were en route to the Dublin Mountains, to the area where Una's body had been found a week previously. Whether they were intent on looking for clues that might assist in the investigation into their cousin's death or merely to grieve at the spot where her body was found is unknown. Later in the day John Gaughan would claim that the cars passed up in the Dublin Mountains, suggesting that the Kerrigan sisters had gone up there for some purpose associated with the finding of Una's body the previous week.

When Eileen Kerrigan got back home, Marty had gone out. Christo Ennis had called for him along with their friend, Brian O'Neill. The three had gone to Ryan's pub in Ratoath for a few pints.

Around 2 p.m. Winnie and Patrick Lynskey left their home in the cul-de-sac off Porterstown Lane and drove into Ratoath to visit Una's grave. This was to be a new, sorrowful feature of their lives, regular visits to the grave of their daughter. The grieving process, suspended in the weeks that Una was missing, was settling in for the long, painful haul. The Lynskeys travelled to Ratoath with two friends of Winnie's, a Mrs Sheeran and a Mrs Geraghty, who lived together in a house in Kildare. They all travelled in Mrs Sheeran's Mini.

Mrs Sheeran drove to the graveyard in the village and they stayed at Una's grave for twenty minutes. Afterwards, they got back into the car, Patrick Lynskey in the passenger seat, and drove up through the village, past the Marian grotto, and turned right into Main Street. As they passed Foley's shop they spotted a group of young men, up to half a dozen, on the pavement, walking in the same direction they were travelling. 'There's Ennis,' Winnie said, referencing Christo Ennis. For the Lynskeys, Christo Ennis was tainted with the same suspicion they had of the other three who had been detained by the gardaí. Brian O'Neill and Dick Donnelly were also there.

'Kerrigan is there too,' Patrick Lynskey said, having spotted the man who, in the garda theory, may well have been central to his daughter's violent death. The knot of young men were killing time, having been put out of Ryan's public house up the road, which, under licensing law, was obliged to close between 2 p.m. and 4 p.m. on a Sunday. After her husband identified Marty Kerrigan in their midst, Winnie Lynskey focused in on him.

'I saw Kerrigan; he was laughing and shaking his head at the same time. He had two fingers up like a V sign and kept shaking them at me,' she later said. 'I was disgusted and really upset and I turned my head away. At that stage I did not know what that sign meant.'

Others confirmed that Marty Kerrigan had made the gesture in the direction of the passing car.

On one level, Marty's behaviour reflected poorly on his character. The Lynskey parents were obviously grieving. Ordinarily, the whole community would be huddling in around them, attempting, however clumsily, to alleviate their pain. And yet here was a young local man, making a gesture telling them to fuck off in their time of bereavement.

Flipping the picture, Marty's behaviour is understandable, if not excusable. He had a few pints on him when he spotted the Lynskeys. Over the previous six weeks, members of the Lynskey family had made his life hell, implying that they blamed him for the violent death of their sister and cousin. Regularly, one or more of Una's immediate or extended family would show up outside his home, revving engines, shouting insults, letting him know what they would do to him, given half a chance. He had to conduct himself with caution in his everyday life to ensure he would never be alone when encountering members of the Lynskey family because God knew what they were capable of doing. His safety, his life indeed, seemed under constant threat.

And now, here he was in the village, fortified by drink and the company of friends, and there went the Lynskey parents. *Well, fuck them!* He wasn't going to let that family push him around and blame him for what had befallen Una. He wasn't going to be their scapegoat.

Later that evening, Patrick Lynskey called over to his nephew, John Gaughan, on the Fairyhouse Road. Just as Marty Kerrigan and his friends believed the discovery of the body would lead to the real killers, so the Lynskeys believed the discovery was all the gardaí needed to charge the men they believed to be responsible. But it was now nine days since Una's body had been found and nothing seemed to be happening with the investigation. Patrick Lynskey and John Gaughan discussed what had occurred during the day with Marty Kerrigan. Patrick Lynskey said he didn't want any violence happening over the incident. Instead, they would report it to the gardaí.

They drove over to Dunshaughlin garda station, but the station was closed, as might be expected on a Sunday evening. Patrick Lynskey then told Gaughan he was going into Dublin to visit his brother Andy. 'I advised John Gaughan that if he wanted to take a drink to go to the County Club and not Ratoath,' Lynskey said. The County Club was located on the Navan Road, well out of the village.

But Gaughan wasn't going to let it go. He called over to Lynskeys' and picked up Sean and James. From there they travelled to Dunshaughlin to the home of Garda Brian McKeown. The garda had come off duty at 6 p.m., brought his kids to Dublin for a spin and was now back home, watching *The Riordans*. His wife answered a knock on the door.

'John Gaughan walked into the room,' Garda McKeown

remembered. 'I said to sit down, and he said no, that Sean and James Lynskey were in the car outside. I said to bring them in, and they all sat down while the kids went to bed and my wife went out to bingo.'

John Gaughan told Garda McKeown that he had seen Eileen Kerrigan in a car up in Glencullen, near where Una's body had been found, that afternoon. This was untrue. The encounter had been in Blanchardstown, and Eileen was returning home. What the men really wanted to know was when would arrests be made for Una's murder.

'Sean Lynskey asked when would the three boys [Donnelly, Conmey and Kerrigan] be brought in, that they were still at large,' Garda McKeown said. 'He [Lynskey] said I think the guards are making a laugh at us.' They told the garda that if the three weren't brought in that week there could be trouble.

'They also said there was a number of west of Ireland men coming from England and they would fix these fellows,' Garda McKeown said. They left soon after, en route to the County Club.

At the County Club, the men had two rounds of pints. Before leaving, they all went into the toilets for a routine call of nature. As they were exiting, a local man, Willie Morgan, went in to relieve himself. He noticed on the black tiles in the bathroom that two words had been drawn out in the condensation: 'Kerrigan murderer'. The time was pushing for 10 p.m.

Garda John Harty knew how tense and dangerous things were between the two factions. He had been in Trim when Donnelly, Conmey and Kerrigan were being questioned. He was stationed locally, in Ashbourne, had been there for three years. He had engaged Marty Kerrigan in conversation in the day room in Trim and would claim that Kerrigan told him Una's body was in Wilkinstown Wood. This was what led the gardaí to go out and search the wood in the early hours of the morning, accompanied by Kerrigan.

Since Trim, he had been regularly instructed to keep an eye on the Kerrigans' safety. On occasion, Garda Harty took up position outside the Kerrigan home, effectively to protect a family under siege. On the night of Sunday, 19 December he had another duty to perform – supervision at the weekly dance in Kilmoon. That could turn out to be another flashpoint, particularly as the tensions had ramped up since the discovery of Una's body.

En route to Kilmoon, Garda Harty drove into Ratoath around 10 p.m. The dance wouldn't get underway until the pubs had been emptied. He pulled up outside the Parochial Hall a little earlier. Molly Talty's shop next door was still open, as it had served the crowd who had soon earlier emerged from the hall after an evening of bingo. Across the road, a chip van was lit up, doing some trade.

The garda noticed a few local youths in the doorway of Talty's, including Marty Kerrigan. Across the road, next to the chip van, Paddy Kelly's Austin A40 was parked up. Kelly had been a constant at the side of the Lynskeys since his girlfriend had disappeared. Harty didn't like the look of things. As he got out of his car, Kelly rolled down the window in his own vehicle and called the garda over.

The garda went over and noticed that the car was full of the Lynskey faction, including two of the Gaughan brothers from the Fairyhouse Road. The men in the car complained to the garda about Kerrigan's earlier rude gesture to Mrs Lynskey as she was being driven home after visiting Una's grave. As they were talking, Garda Harty was acutely aware of the other faction gathering across the road, including not just Marty Kerrigan but Padraic and Danny Gaughan. Padraic and Danny had broken with their cousins, both next-door neighbours the Lynskeys and the Gaughans of Fairyhouse Road. Now the brothers were firmly in the opposition camp, certain in the belief that Donnelly, Conmey and Kerrigan were being set up and blamed for a murder they didn't commit.

Garda Harty pleaded with Paddy Kelly.

'Lads, would ye go home, please,' Harty asked them. 'There's two sides in this thing and if ye stick around here there could well be trouble.' He got the impression they paid him due heed as Kelly started the car and they drove off. Harty went back across the road and into Molly Talty's. When he came out a few minutes later he immediately saw Marty Kerrigan and his friends now standing outside the chip van. Kerrigan shouted something across, something that sounded like an insult. John Harty decided to let it go. The tensions that had built up were getting to everybody, and what would be the point in making a big deal out of a stray few words from one of the lads at the centre of it who was obviously the worse for wear from drink.

He had just got into the car when Kerrigan appeared beside it. Harty rolled down the window. 'Any chance of a lift to Kilmoon?' Kerrigan asked. They engaged in casual chat in which the garda noticed that Kerrigan wasn't as drunk as he might have previously thought. Within minutes, more of Kerrigan's friends came across the street, including Padraic and Danny Gaughan. Garda Harty, in the better tradition of the rural police in Ireland, decided to do his bit.

'If anyone else wants a lift, get in, because I'm going,' he said. Four youths piled into the back, with Kerrigan sitting in the front passenger seat. Just then, one of the McIntyres, the Conmeys' cousins, pulled up, and Danny Gaughan got out and into his car. Harty took off, driving down through Ratoath, the McIntyres following.

At the crossroad, just outside the village, they came upon two cars on the side of the road in the aftermath of what had obviously been a collision. Harty told his passengers he had to see what the story was here. 'I can't leave ye here in the car, but if ye still want a lift when I'm done I'll bring ye to Kilmoon.' Everybody got out and Harty went into a house opposite, where he was told that one of the drivers had been taken. Inside, he met some of the occupants of the two vehicles. Nobody appeared to be seriously injured. He took out his notebook and began writing notes.

While Marty Kerrigan and his friends had organized a lift to Kilmoon, the other side was fuming. As Paddy Kelly drove out of Ratoath, after taking Garda Harty's advice, the air in the car was tense. 'That's two nice bastards of cousins hanging around with that gang,' Seamus Gaughan said, referring to his first cousins Padraic and Danny. Kelly drove to John Gaughan's home on the Fairyhouse Road. Gaughan and Sean and James Lynskey were inside, having returned from the County Club. John's wife Liz was serving them tea and apple tart.

Anger built up in the kitchen as the men raged over what had occurred at the chip van, how Kerrigan had insulted the Lynskey parents earlier that day, why the gardaí had not lifted the three despite the discovery of Una's body.

'To hell with it,' Sean Lynskey said. 'That carry-on is

going on too long. We'll go down and see if they sneer at us when there is a gang of us there.' All of the men began to leave the house. Liz Gaughan asked her husband not to take his shotgun with him, but he ignored her. After they had left, she noticed that one of them had taken the breadknife she had used to cut the apple tart. Outside, the men piled into two cars, Paddy Kelly's Austin and John Gaughan's Mini, and took the road to Ratoath.

On the outskirts to the town, they came upon the crowd gathered around the two vehicles that had been involved in the accident. Fairly quickly, they recognized Marty Kerrigan and Padraic and Danny Gaughan. Everybody got out. Circumstance, the consumption of alcohol, building frustration and the late hour all combined to threaten that this was going to be serious.

The two sides got stuck into each other on the street with fists and boots, anger and insults flying. James Lynskey ran straight for Marty Kerrigan, caught him by the hair and pushed him to the ground. Padraic Gaughan ran to Marty's help, swung wildly at his cousin James but missed. Until recent months these cousins were close friends, living next door to each other, playing on the same hurling and football teams, and now this.

James grabbed Padraic and threw him to the ground. He looked around and saw that his brother Sean had grabbed Marty Kerrigan and dragged him towards John Gaughan's Mini.

'I ran up to where John Gaughan's car was and he was sitting behind the steering wheel,' James Lynskey said. 'My brother Sean was pushing Martin Kerrigan into the back seat. I caught Kerrigan's legs and just as I did John Gaughan drove off and left me standing on the road. I think one of

Kerrigan's shoes fell off. John Gaughan pulled up his car and I ran up to it and went into the front passenger seat.' The car took off in the direction of the Fairyhouse Road.

Inside in the house, taking the particulars about the collision that he had come upon, Garda John Harty had no idea what was now unfolding outside. Then Danny Gaughan came running through the front door.

'They've got Marty Kerrigan,' he said. 'There's a crowd of them out there.'

'Will you hold on a minute, I have to sort this out,' Harty said. Gaughan appeared to be in a right state of anxiety, so Harty abandoned his investigation of the accident and followed Danny back out on to the street.

Up the road he saw that a running battle was in progress. 'I saw Michael Gaughan with a starter handle in his hand,' Harty later related. Michael was Ann's brother and he was being confronted by two other youths, including his first cousin.

'Padraic Gaughan and Tony Conmey were trying to get near him. It appeared to be for the purpose of fighting him. Michael Gaughan had his hands raised with the starting handle in it. He was shouting at them, "Come on, come on, ye murdered my cousin." I stood between them and I took the starting handle off him. He did not try to resist me taking it from him,' Garda Harty related.

At this point, Danny Gaughan grabbed the garda. 'They've taken him in John Gaughan's car. They've taken Marty.'

Garda Harty knew immediately that this was serious. There was no knowing how it could end up. When he turned around, he saw Michael Gaughan once more wielding a weapon. 'I had already taken a starting handle from him and now he had a car jack in his hand. He was shouting something, but I was unable to say what it was. I ran over towards him and shouted at him to go home.'

Gaughan walked to Paddy Kelly's car and got in. Garda Harty followed over to the car, which was full of youths from the Lynskey faction. 'Where have they gone with Kerrigan?' Harty asked. The men in the car pleaded ignorance.

Harty went back into the house where those injured in the traffic accident were still recovering. He rang Balbriggan garda station, alerted the member in charge as to what had occurred. Harty asked his colleague did he realize how serious this now was.

He went back outside, got into his car and took off south, down towards Porterstown Lane. On arriving at the Lyns-key home, he was met by Maureen Lynskey. Harty told her that her brothers and cousin had taken Marty Kerrigan. Maureen hadn't seen any of them. From there, he drove to Dunshaughlin and parked outside the garda station, which was in darkness.

Just over two months earlier, on the night of 12 October, Paddy Kelly had called to the same station shrouded in darkness to inform the gardaí that his girlfriend Una was missing. That was in a different world.

The garda drove back to Porterstown Lane, called to Lynskeys' again, but there was no sign of John Gaughan or James Lynskey. It was becoming clear that Sean Lynskey was also with the two of them and Marty Kerrigan. From there, he crossed the lane again, out on to Fairyhouse Road, and arrived at John Gaughan's house. The house was in darkness. He knocked on the door and discovered that the remnants of the Lynskey faction were inside and had turned off the lights because they expected Marty Kerrigan's friends to show up at any minute. And they were right.

Among Marty's friends word quickly got around. Brian O'Neill went over to Christo Ennis's house to tell him. Christo and Vera were in bed. O'Neill rapped on the window. 'They've taken Marty,' he said. Christo got up and the two men drove over to John Gaughan's house, where a crowd was now gathering.

Over at Kerrigans', Ann was arriving home from the pub. As she approached the front door Katie came running out. 'They've taken Marty,' Katie said. At first, Ann thought her sister was referring to the guards, that he had once again been brought to a garda station. 'Then Katie told me that it was the Lynskeys. Somebody had shown up at our house earlier with Marty's shoe, which had been left on the road after they bundled him into the car.'

The sisters drove over to John Gaughan's, where there was a sense of foreboding in the air. Something was happening, something that had been coming for a while, and now it was beginning to look like it might end in tragedy.

John Gaughan knew where he was going. He drove in towards the city, past Blanchardstown, and headed for the Dublin Mountains. What transpired in the car, and on arrival at a spot in Glencullen, near where Una Lynskey's body had been found ten days earlier, is the version proffered by the three men who kidnapped Marty Kerrigan. All that is known as an established fact is that the car stopped along the way for petrol at Rathfarnham.

According to James Lynskey, he and his brother Sean questioned Marty Kerrigan as John Gaughan drove.

'You killed her,' they said to Kerrigan again and again.

'I didn't kill her,' he replied.

'Listen to him, saying he didn't kill her,' Sean Lynskey said.

They shook him by the hair a few times. When they were driving through Clondalkin, Kerrigan, still kept lying on the floor, asked to be let up.

'The three of us said you will stay there until you tell us the truth.'

Sean Lynskey would later say that Kerrigan told them that his two friends had been responsible for Una's death but he had nothing to do with it.

Marty Kerrigan's terror can only be guessed at. A crumb of comfort for his relatives is that perhaps the drinking he had engaged in for most of the day was numbing him against what was unfolding. Six weeks previously, he had been kept, as he would have seen it, captive in a garda station, repeatedly told that he must confess. There is evidence that he had been assaulted, and certainly he had been terrified while he was in custody. Yet in the end, any admissions or confessions he made were simply not rooted in fact and didn't add up.

Now here he was, once more detained. Did he believe his life was in peril? Did he plead with his captors to let him live? Was he, as was apparently the case in Trim garda station, willing to say anything to make it stop? He didn't know where they were headed from where he lay on the floor of the rear seat of the Mini. Was he told that they were bringing him up to where Una's body had been found, a life for a life? The other three men in the car would all claim that they never had any intention of killing him. There is no independent evidence of what was said or done on that journey to the Dublin Mountains in the dead of night.

At Rathfarnham they stopped for petrol. Sean Lynskey held his hand over Kerrigan's mouth to prevent him crying out for help. Lynskey tore at Kerrigan's mouth with his finger. The tank filled, they took off again.

The three captors all claimed that they did not assault Marty Kerrigan severely enough that it would have resulted in his death. Here is Sean Lynskey's version of what occurred when they arrived at their destination.

'When we reached the spot where my sister Una's body was found on the Dublin Mountains we pulled up. I think John Gaughan said something to him, but I can't remember rightly what it was. I then saw Kerrigan was keeping quiet. I was sure he was putting it on. When the car stopped I got out by the passenger door and I lifted Kerrigan out. I caught him under the arms; he was very loose. I still thought he was putting it on. I left him on the grass margin just out where Una's body was found. He just lay there. Sean, my brother, or John Gaughan didn't get out of the car. After I left Kerrigan lying on the grass margin I got back into the car, and I said to the two lads, "He is only putting it on."'

Whatever happened en route to, or at the destination to which John Gaughan drove, what is known as fact is that the car showed up back at the Gaughan house sometime after 2 a.m.

Over the following hour, four squad cars were sent to the Glencullen area in the Dublin Mountains. They didn't have to search for long. Marty Kerrigan's body was found at 2.55 a.m. and an ambulance called. Sergeant J. J. Callinan, who was among the gardaí at the scene, described what he saw. 'The body was motionless and life appeared extinct. The left leg of the trousers was badly torn and the right leg of the trousers was covered in dirt and some form of mud.

There was blood on the fingers of the left hand and about the nose.'

For the second time in ten days, the state pathologist, Maurice Hickey, was called to the scene. 'The body was lying on its back. The front of the chest and abdomen were exposed. The inner seam of the trousers and the thighs were exposed.' There were no shoes on the feet of the body and the underside of the socks were not soiled by mud or dirt. He found evidence of bruising and concluded that death occurred due to asphyxia. 'The injuries to the lips and to the front of the neck indicate that pressure was applied to these regions,' he stated.

He also noted a jagged cut, three inches long, 'in the skin of the left groin extending through the full thickness of the skin'. Afterwards, there would be a credible allegation that the wound suggested an attempt to disembowel Marty Kerrigan. The pathologist said the wound had been 'produced after death'. The medical evidence was thus in conflict with the versions from the three kidnappers of the ending of Marty Kerrigan's life. If they had simply thrown him out of the car and driven off, unaware that he was dead, how could a serious wound have been inflicted after death?

The three gave no account of how that wound had occurred.

14. 'Is It That Easy to Kill a Man?'

The Mini pulled up outside John Gaughan's house soon after 2 a.m. The crowd that had assembled gathered round, both hostile and inquisitive. Immediately it was obvious that Marty Kerrigan was not in the car with them. The three occupants got out and tried to make their way into the house. A number of gardaí elbowed through the crowd, determined that there would be no more violence.

'We were sitting in the car when the Mini came speeding in,' Ann Kerrigan remembers. 'When they got out of it, Dick Donnelly went over and grabbed James Lynskey, starting shouting, "What did you do with him? Where is he?"' Danny Gaughan, Lynskey's first cousin and until recent weeks friend, pulled him away from Donnelly, put his arm around James Lynskey and walked with him towards the house. There was an exchange of words between the cousins who had taken opposite sides in this dispute. Danny asked him where Marty was. James wouldn't reply until finally breaking away and telling Danny to ask his brother Sean and John Gaughan.

One of the guards came over to the Kerrigans, spoke to Martin Snr. 'Why don't you go home?' he said. 'We'll get this sorted out and your son will be at home not long after you.'

They left and went home, but there would be no sleeping in the Kerrigan household that night. 'A few came with us, I suppose for comfort. Padraic Gaughan came to the house.

174

But my father was demented with the dread. We kept giving him whiskey just to calm him down, and with it all he eventually fell asleep,' says Ann Kerrigan. 'At about 5.30 a.m. there was a knock on the door. Eileen went out and there were two guards there. One of them asked how soon we could identify the body. That was when we knew for a fact what we had really known ourselves up to that point. Marty was dead.'

The killing of Marty Kerrigan presented the gardaí with a major headache. No doubt, those among the members who had encountered the teenager during their investigations were shocked. Even if some among them, or all of them, believed that he had been involved in Una Lynskey's disappearance, they knew he was not a hardened or callous criminal. They also knew that, irrespective of any belief they had, his killing was an outrage.

There were, however, other considerations. It was the gardaí who had fingered Kerrigan as a suspect. They had made known to the Lynskeys that they believed he was one of the men responsible for Una's murder. The gardaí at the centre of the investigation may have hoped that if pressure was brought on the suspects internally within the community then there might be the possibility of a full confession. But instead, things had spun out of control. The Lynskeys had gone further than anybody would have imagined. In such a scenario, the instinct for self-preservation must have been a high priority among the gardaí at the centre of the investigation.

The actions of the gardaí in both the immediate aftermath and over the longer term after Marty Kerrigan's killing need to be seen in that light. Those among the members of the force who were closest to the investigation into the killing of Una Lynskey were no longer acting entirely as police. Arguably, they were now players in the tragic drama. From their perspective, the three suspects – as they saw them – had to be guilty of Una's murder. The alternative was that they, the force of law and order, had led the Lynskeys down a dark alley which culminated in the violent death of Marty Kerrigan. Terrible as it was that a man had been killed, it would be unthinkable from the garda perspective if Marty Kerrigan had been an innocent man. What would that say about the gardaí and how they conducted themselves?

Another consideration now was the relationship that had been formed with the Lynskeys during the investigation. For weeks, some of the investigating gardaí had attempted to comfort and reassure extended family. Now three of the family were prime suspects in a revenge killing. The gardaí had to collate evidence and present a file to have the men prosecuted for murder.

Could those who were closest to the investigation really be capable of doing so without fear or favour?

Soon after arriving back from the Dublin Mountains, John Gaughan and Sean and James Lynskey were arrested in Gaughan's house and brought to Dunshaughlin garda station. Within hours, Detective Sergeant John Courtney and Garda Brian Gildea, the two who had led the investigation in the Una Lynskey disappearance, showed up at the station. They were key figures in taking the statements of the two brothers and their cousin in the hours after they returned from the Dublin Mountains, statements that would be central to any future prosecution.

Courtney and Gildea should have had nothing to do with the investigation into Marty Kerrigan's death. Arguably these two gardaí had a vested interest in ensuring that the statements minimized the culpability of the three suspects in Marty Kerrigan's death. But instead of stepping back, both ran straight into this new investigation. Presumably they would have claimed they were simply doing their jobs, taking statements in the standard manner, letting the evidence lead them rather than leading the evidence where they wanted it to go.

At about 3.20 a.m. Garda Brian Gildea arrived in Dunshaughlin. His interaction, by his own account, with Gaughan and the Lynskeys differed hugely from how he was alleged to have dealt with Donnelly, Conmey and Kerrigan at Trim. He walked into an upstairs office in the station first, where John Gaughan was sitting in a chair.

'Hello, John,' he said.

'Well, Brian, what do you think now?'

'Is Kerrigan all right?' the garda asked.

'I hope so. Anyway, when we left him he was all right.'

Gildea exited from the room and went into an adjoining room, where Sean Lynskey was being held.

'Hello, Sean.'

'Well, Brian.'

'How're things?'

'All right. I suppose you heard about Kerrigan.'

'I did,' the garda said.

'Kerrigan is all right. He put on a great act. All he told us was that the others done it.'

In his brief, separate encounters with both men, Gildea remembered them as 'laughing and in a jovial mood'. This is not the demeanour one might expect from three men who had just killed a neighbour, notwithstanding the bitterness that had infected the area over the preceding weeks.

Gildea then went into another room, where James Lynskey was being held. He told James that he was investigating the abduction of Martin Kerrigan.

'I was with them,' James Lynskey replied, referencing his brother and cousin. 'We left him [Kerrigan] up in the mountains, but he will get home.'

'Will you make a written statement?' Gildea asked him.

'Yeah, sure,' Lynskey replied. Gildea set about taking the statement and the two of them got into it. Little over an hour later, Superintendent J. J. Moore, the local district officer, came into the room and told Garda Gildea and James Lynskey that Marty Kerrigan's dead body had been found.

'James Lynskey grew visibly pale and shocked,' Gildea remembered. 'After the superintendent left the room, he buried his head in his clasped hands and then lifted his head and said, "Ah Lord, I don't know how he could have died."'

Those interactions were later committed to paper by Gildea. They portray three men who were under the impression that they had given Marty Kerrigan a right good fright but certainly had not killed him. The reaction of James Lynskey suggests that news of Kerrigan's death came as a complete shock. None of the three statements referred to the jagged wound found near Kerrigan's groin, which had been inflicted after death, in the view of the pathologist. All the statements related in similar detail how they had questioned Kerrigan in the car, given him a few belts, and thrown him out of the car at the spot where he was found, in the belief that he was still alive.

Around 5 a.m., Detective Sergeant John Courtney arrived at Dunshaughlin. He was told that the three men had already made statements about what they did to Marty Kerrigan.

Courtney later related that he went into one of the inter-view rooms, where John Gaughan was being held.

According to Courtney, after greeting each other, Gaughan then said: 'The last thing we intended to do was to kill him. We only intended to frighten him. I never thought he was dead. I was sure he was just putting it on. Jesus Christ, is it that easy to kill a man?'

Once again, the evidence of gardaí about what was said in the confines of a station would be crucial to any subse-quent criminal proceedings. Unlike the gardaí evidence about what Donnelly, Conmey and Kerrigan said in Trim, the declarations of Gaughan and the Lynskeys in Dun-shaughlin were benign in terms of any potential guilt of a crime. John Gaughan's reaction to the news of Kerrigan's death, as related by Detective Sergeant Courtney, was very similar to that of James Lynskey as related by Garda Gildea. Both Gaughan and Lynskey clearly implied that there was no intention to kill Marty Kerrigan. This absence of intent left open the possibility that the men had a case for defend-ing their actions on the basis that they had never intended to kill the deceased man.

Later that morning, there were developments in the investi-gation into the death of Una Lynskey. John Shevlin, the 13-year-old boy who had been on Porterstown Lane around the time Una disappeared, gave a fourth statement. As described in Chapter 10, his chain of statements had pro-gressed from little of note to a sighting of a car going along the lane from the Navan Road end and a few minutes later one returning in the opposite direction. This fitted in with the garda theory of the case. In his fourth statement, taken on 20 December, as the community came to terms with a second violent death, he identified Dick Donnelly's car as the one he saw going along the lane. This was further ballast to the garda theory. One might well wonder why this statement, adding crucial detail to his earlier ones, was taken hours after the death of Marty Kerrigan.

Early that morning also, Dick Donnelly was visited at home. He was taken to Dunshaughlin garda station and questioned once again. This time, the head of the Murder Squad, Hubert Reynolds, was leading the questioning. Nothing came of it. There were no admissions and Donnelly didn't make any allegations against the gardaí, but why had he been dragged in that morning? Later, the gardaí would say that the reason for bringing him in was that further information had come to hand overnight. That information was conveyed by James Lynskey, who told gardaí that Kerrigan had said that he had nothing to do with Una's disappearance, but it was the case that his two friends were responsible.

So, the garda premise for bringing in Donnelly – and, within hours, Martin Conmey – was that their friend, en route to his death, possibly pleading for his life, told his captors that these two had been responsible for killing Una Lynskey. It stretched credulity.

An alternative view is that the death of Marty Kerrigan made the investigating gardaí even more anxious to prove their theory because the alternative, that an innocent man had been killed in a misplaced act of revenge, didn't bear thinking about.

Martin Conmey was unaware of what had occurred in the early hours of 20 December. The previous evening, he had returned to his digs in Dublin and gone to work in the Robinhood Industrial Estate that morning, oblivious to the shock that was once again permeating his community. Around noon, three gardaí showed up at the site. They asked him to go with them to Rathfarnham. By then, Conmey was used to this kind of thing, considered it harassment with which he had little choice but to go along. Leading the gardaí was Brian Gildea, fresh from Dunshaughlin, where the Lynskeys and John Gaughan had given statements.

According to Martin Conmey, the tone of what was to follow was set in the car en route to Rathfarnham.

'Did you read the papers this morning or listen to the radio?' Gildea asked. Conmey shook his head.

'Your pal, Martin Kerrigan, your friend, is dead.'

Conmey didn't believe him.

'You're a black bastard and you're going to get it today,' Gildea said. 'We'll knock it out of you.'

Later, Gildea and his colleagues would tell a court that nothing of this nature passed between them. Similarly, their respective versions of what occurred in Rathfarnham differed greatly from that of Conmey.

According to Conmey he was, over the course of his detention through the afternoon, subjected to repeated intimidation, pushing, shoving and slaps. At one o'clock a radio was brought into the interview room and turned on. The headlines reported that a man had been kidnapped in Ratoath, Co Meath. The main news a half-hour later confirmed that a body had been found in the Dublin Mountains. This was the first time that Martin Conmey accepted that his friend had been killed.

'They continued on shoving me, pushing me, slapping me,' Conmey later related. 'They weren't asking me much questions, just *come on, come on, tell us what you know.*'

Not long after the news bulletin two photographs of Marty Kerrigan's body were put in front of Conmey. 'His face was all black, he was lying on his back. It seemed like a shallow ditch or something of that sort. One of the guards said, "This could be you up there. You're next."'

They brought him through his original statement, the one the gardaí didn't accept, in which he related how the three lads had come along Porterstown Lane and he was dropped off at home.

'When I got to the point where I was left off at my house, Garda Gildea hit me with his open hand across the face. They seemed to be getting annoyed again.'

They put before him the statement that he had given in Trim, which he now disowned.

'Didn't you say this?'

'I did, I did, but it's all lies.'

One of the gardaí demonstrated with his head snapping back, showing what he claimed that Conmey had said in Trim had happened to Una. 'Didn't you do this, didn't you show us?' Gildea reminded him.

'Yes, yes, but it was all lies. It never happened.'

Just then, Conmey says that the guard who had driven the car to the station, whom he had never met before, hit him 'an awful blow and I fell to the ground'.

Gildea and the other gardaí denied that any such assaults occurred. The only outcome from the interview, according to Gildea, was a further admission from Martin Conmey. The garda would claim that when it was put to Conmey that he struck Una, the suspect replied: 'I did not. I was in the back of the car; she was in the front beside Kerrigan. Donnelly was driving. Kerrigan held her when she tried to get out at her own place and her head fell back.' The garda would say that despite making this verbal admission, Conmey refused to make a written statement.

This admission, Gildea would claim, was made entirely without any intimidation or violence and was the result of concerted but entirely appropriate questioning as per standard police procedure. Conmey is adamant that just as was the case in Trim, the sustained intimidation and violence prompted him once more to tell the gardaí exactly what they wanted to hear. One difference from Trim was that when the gardaí were finished with him he was given a lift back to his digs.

It had been a long day for Gildea and some of the other gardaí who had been working on Una Lynskey's disappearance for the previous two months or so. One of their prime suspects was now dead. However, new evidence had been garnered to further the case against the other two. The latest statement elicited from 13-year-old John Shevlin had put Dick Donnelly firmly into the picture in terms of the garda theory as to what had occurred. And Martin Conmey had made another alleged admission that he and his friends had encountered Una Lynskey. As with many of the other building blocks in the garda theory, major questions arise as to how these two new strands of evidence were assembled. But as far as the investigating gardaí were concerned, they added to the file being prepared against the men for the murder of Una Lynskey. Yet still, the case was not as secure as the gardaí would have liked. Something more would be required to bring it home.

15. Picking Up the Pieces

Eileen Kerrigan identified the body of her brother in the Dublin city morgue. On the following day, there were prayers for the deceased in the morgue. A procession of family and friends came in and stood around the open coffin. Martin Conmey went in with his brother Tony. Later, their sister Mary attended with her parents. Mary remembered the crying, the alien sight, and particularly the sound, of young men in a state of helplessness.

'You didn't see that then,' she said. 'Men didn't cry. It was awful. That was one of the things that stayed with me, the sight of that. They didn't hug then, and nobody could do anything because everybody was simply in bits. One of the lads was in the corner and you could hear him wailing. It was awful; his head in his hands and then he would look back over at the coffin and start again. Nobody could believe what they were seeing.

'You just didn't see a young person dead. You might have seen grandparents, even though I don't have much memory of that. But here was a young lad who was not supposed to be dead. He was lying there because somebody hated him for something he didn't do.'

On the Wednesday morning, Marty Kerrigan was taken from the morgue for his funeral at the Church of the Holy Trinity in Ratoath. The funeral cortège rumbled through the busy Dublin traffic and some following the procession got split off from it. The hearse pulled in at Dunshaughlin to allow everybody to assemble again. It was as if this was the beginning of the journey that would really be taking Marty Kerrigan home, back through the roads and past the townlands that he knew so well in his short life.

The church was full for the funeral Mass, just as it had been little over a week earlier for that of Una Lynskey. At the conclusion of the rite, the coffin was lifted from its stand and taken down through the central aisle, Marty's father and siblings leading the procession in its wake. As they came towards the back of the church Ann Kerrigan could see Patrick and Winnie Lynskey standing to the side. 'They came to the funeral, to be fair to them. But they never approached any of the family.'

Their reluctance to sympathize with the Kerrigans is entirely understandable. Who knew what kind of a reception they would get, as their two sons and their nephew were the ones who took Marty's life? But the presence of Una Lynskey's parents at the church was notable, a gesture to show that they knew exactly the pain which the Kerrigans were enduring.

Marty was buried in Christmas week. The warm glow that wraps around communities at the festive time of year was displaced by a black pall, a sense of shock that something irreparable had been broken.

'Everybody was devastated,' Padraic Gaughan remembers of that Christmas. 'People just could not believe what was after happening. The mood wasn't anger; it was just total shock at what had gone on over the last few months.'

The Kerrigan household was simply bereft. 'It was a nightmare. We never really had a proper Christmas again,' Katie Kerrigan says. 'Our brother John and sister Mary came home for the funeral and stayed, but they had others to see, in-laws around the country. On Christmas Day it was just the three sisters and Dad. A few neighbours came by.'

The guards didn't call around. There was no liaising with the family, no updating them on the progress towards trial. Later, one evening when the sisters were out for a drink in Dunshaughlin, Garda John Harty, who had been giving Marty a lift on the night he was taken, approached with an envelope, saying it was a Mass card. Ann Kerrigan told him it wasn't wanted. There was too much hurt. The Kerrigans, and the other families, believed that the guards had set out to frame their sons and brothers. The entire episode was to colour their attitudes towards the force for a long time to come.

Martin Kerrigan Snr never got over his son's death. He had already lost his wife at a young age four years previously. He had had a particular bond with his younger son, with whom he shared a room in their small home. Grief trailed him through the rest of his life. Apart from that, the divisions that had been opened up in those final months of 1971 remained beyond his ken. Mary Conmey remembered one night when her brother Tony came home after spending a few hours in Ryan's of Ratoath following a football match.

'Marty's dad was in there and he'd a few drinks taken. He was talking to Tony and he started crying, saying, "Why didn't you save him?" When Tony came home he was in bits himself after it. There was that shock that so many who were close to it simply couldn't get past for an awful long time.'

In the weeks after Marty's death, as the New Year dawned, Dick Donnelly was spending more time at the Kerrigan household, trying to bring comfort and deal with his own grief. After a time, he began staying over at the house, sleeping in his dead friend's bed. One evening he asked out Ann Kerrigan. So began a romance that was to blossom into a marriage that was to produce two children and a long life together.

As the community around Porterstown Lane attempted to come to terms with the new, harsh reality, the wheels of justice ground on. Normality was on hold until the conclusion of the criminal justice processes.

In early January, Sean and James Lynskey and John Gaughan were charged with murder. The charges were inevitable, given the copious evidence of their involvement in Marty Kerrigan's death along with the statements they provided after returning from the Dublin Mountains.

The case for prosecuting Dick Donnelly and Martin Conmey for Una Lynskey's death was nowhere near as straightforward. Conmey had made several admissions in Trim, all of which were highly contentious and none of which provided a sustainable narrative as to what exactly had happened. Donnelly made no admissions.

The only other evidence was circumstantial, relying on whether or not Donnelly's car had entered the lane at least ten minutes earlier than he claimed and whether he had subsequently driven back towards the Navan Road.

On 11 January, just over a month after Una Lynskey's body was found, a file was submitted to the Attorney General* recommending the prosecution of Dick Donnelly and

* In 1971 decisions on whether to prosecute indictable offences rested in the AG's office. The attorney was a political appointment, but successive governments insisted that he (and it was all men up to that point) was entirely

Martin Conmey for murder. The file submitted, it appeared that the gardaí had done their job. Then, one week later, a stunning development. Another witness came forward with some devastating testimony.

Thomas Mangan was a 20-year-old labourer who worked in Dublin. He was from west Mayo, the area from which the families in Porterstown Lane had originated. He shared digs with Martin Conmey, who had moved into the city in November. On 19 January, Mangan provided a statement to the gardaí. Why he came forward, and whether or not he was approached by the gardaí, is unclear. He has never spoken about the matter. But his statement was a dramatic addition to the case being assembled against Martin Conmey. Mangan's statement described a night the pair had been out drinking. When they returned to the digs that night Conmey was alleged to have, unprompted, poured out details of what had occurred on 12 October.

Here is the relevant section:

> One night when we were in the bedroom he was talking about Una Lynskey. It was before her body was found. He told me that he was in Dick's car and they were driving

independent in dealings with the criminal justice system. Still, there was a perception that political influence could be brought to bear on decisions to prosecute. This was acknowledged by the junior minister (then known as a parliamentary secretary) John Kelly when introducing a bill to set up a new, independent prosecutorial body in 1974. 'I do not accept any such [political] considerations have, in practice, exercised any such influence,' he told the Dáil. 'However, the fact that the office of Attorney General has a political aspect gives rise to a danger that members of the public may harbour suspicions, however misconceived, on this score.' The Director of Public Prosecutions took up office in January 1975.

along a bend on the road on their way home. He said that Una Lynskey was walking a bit too far out on the road on the bend. He said that she was walking in the same direction that Dick was driving. He said that Dick was driving fairly fast, about 45mph. He said that it was a narrow road. He said that the front of the car struck her and knocked her down on the road. He said that she fell out on the road. He said that Dick stopped the car. He said that the two of them got out of the car. He said they lifted her into the back of the car. He said that she was knocked out. He said that Dick and himself got into the car. He said that they drove away in the car and drove to a field. He said that Dick and himself lifted her out of the car and into a field. He said that she did not speak to them. They said that they left her in the field and went home in Dick's car.

The statement went on to add a crucial detail.

When Martin Conmey told me about how Una Lynskey was killed he said that the body was up in the Dublin Mountains. He said that he did not know how the body was brought up there or who brought it up. He told me that the field where they first left the body was a long distance away from his house. When Martin Conmey first told me about the body of Una Lynskey in the Dublin Mountains he said that the body was lying under bushes. He told me this sometime before the body of Una Lynskey was found.

There was also another element to add to the intrigue. On 20 December, the day that Marty Kerrigan was killed and Conmey was taken to Rathfarnham garda station, Conmey left the lodgings in which he had been staying.

Soon after, Mangan followed him and the pair rented a flat together. Mangan mentioned this in another part of the statement. 'One week after we went to the flat we were talking about Martin Kerrigan's death and Martin Conmey said that he [Martin Kerrigan] had got nothing to do with the death of Una Lynskey.'

On initial examination, the statement is a major boost to the gardaí's theory. Conmey was under no pressure to make these admissions. He did so apparently after a night of drink, a time when tongues can loosen, truths held back can tumble out. On the face of it, Mangan had no incentive to lie and was actually in good stead with Martin Conmey.

Closer examination, however, throws up major questions. All of the admissions made in Trim by Conmey and Kerrigan suggested that Una had got into the car and something happened thereafter. Now a version was emerging which suggested that there had been an accident and everything that followed was designed to cover that up. Such evidence conflicted with that of the pathologist, Dr Hickey, who asserted that the body had no signs that it could have been struck by a vehicle.

According to Mangan's statement, the car, Donnelly's Zephyr, was heading in the same direction as Una. Even within the framework of the garda theory, all the admissions in custody, and some of the supporting evidence from sightings, pointed towards the car initially going along Porterstown Lane in the opposite direction.

Una's body, according to Mangan, was taken to a field 'a long distance away from his house'. So how did Martin Conmey make it home for his dinner by 7.20 p.m. at the latest? How was Marty Kerrigan seen by Sean Reilly sitting in the car outside Dick Donnelly's house at 7.25 p.m.?

Then there is the matter of where the body was eventually found. According to Mangan, Conmey said he didn't know how it was brought to the Dublin Mountains or who was involved. Even within the confines of the statement itself, is that credible? Yet, at the same time, Conmey supposedly said that the body was lying under bushes, and he said this before the body was found, indicating knowledge of its location.

Finally, there was the role of Marty Kerrigan in this apparent escapade. Mangan claims that Conmey said Kerrigan had nothing to do with it. So where was he? All the previous accounts, assembled before Kerrigan's death, had him as a central figure. His own admissions in Trim did so. Now it was emerging that he wasn't even there when all of this happened. So where could he have been? None of it made sense.

That wasn't how the gardaí viewed Mangan's statement. On the day after the statement was recorded, Superintendent Michael Flynn of Rathfarnham wrote to the chief state solicitor about this new thread of evidence.

The statement of Mangan goes to show that Una Lynskey was knocked down by a car driven by Dick Donnelly on a bend of a road where Donnelly was driving at about 45 miles per hour. He further states that Conmey told him that Una Lynskey was walking a bit out on the road and that when she was struck her body fell out on the road.

He makes no mention of Martin Kerrigan having been in the car. In this respect it can be seen from statements made by James Lynskey and John Gaughan, who stand charged with the murder of Martin Kerrigan, that before Kerrigan died on his way to the Dublin Mountains he said he didn't kill Una Lynskey, it was the others.

The corroboration being signalled by Superintendent Flynn is highly dubious. He is suggesting that Thomas Mangan's version of events, which is full of inconsistencies, corroborates the Lynskeys' and John Gaughan's version of what Kerrigan said to them on the way to his death in the Dublin Mountains – namely, that he wasn't there when Una was killed. This has about it all the signs of grasping at loose threads of fabric, attempting to fashion a rope.

Superintendent Flynn went on to link Mangan's statement to other aspects of the case. 'This information from the statement of Thomas Mangan corroborates to some extent the statements both oral and written made by the suspects that Donnelly's car was used in the commission of a crime and that both Donnelly and Conmey were in the car at the time.'

Again, this is highly fanciful. The only corroboration is the suggestion that the car met Una on the lane. Everything else is largely contradictory.

There was more in the super's letter. 'Apparently Conmey told Mangan that Una Lynskey's body was buried under bushes in the Dublin Mountains. This information was given by Conmey to Mangan prior to the finding of the body.' Again, this is highly convenient to the garda case.

Superintendent Flynn then gave some background about this new, important witness. 'Mangan is 20 years of age, appears to have a low standard of education. He is a native of Belmullet, Co Mayo, not far removed from where the Lynskey and Conmey families originally come from. If required in court Mangan will not be an impressive witness.'

Mangan returned to live in the Belmullet area around the time he made the statement. The following month he was to give a deposition in Trim court to put legal standing on

PICKING UP THE PIECES

his statement. He was collected in Mayo by gardaí and accompanied across the country to Trim. He was accompanied by the officers for the entire time he was in the courthouse and then brought back home. He subsequently gave evidence in court but apart from that has never elaborated on his highly unusual rememberings of what he claimed Conmey had admitted.

The garda file on Donnelly and Conmey was passed from the AG's office to an experienced senior counsel for an opinion on whether to proceed with charges. John Lovatt-Dolan was one of the leading barristers practising criminal law at the time. On 22 February he provided his opinion. The case against Conmey was to the greatest extent based on what he was alleged to have admitted in Trim and the late evidence from Thomas Mangan.

> As Regards the suspect Conmey: The evidence of his conversation with Mrs Lynskey at Trim Garda station on 26th October 1971 is of importance. It can be established he was in the car and in my view there is a *prima facie* case against him which warrants a charge of murder being brought against him. The evidence contained in his two statements are of course evidence against him and coupled with the evidence of the conversation with Mrs Lynskey there is a strong *prima facie* case of murder against him.

In the case of Dick Donnelly, the admissions, to the extent there were any, were much less central to the case.

> As Regards the suspect Donnelly: There is evidence of his car having been seen and of his driving it down the lane at

the crucial time and the inference must be drawn it was his own car that conveyed the body of Una Lynskey to where it was buried. This inference arises from the fact that the person or persons who caused such death were also the same persons or person who buried the body. It can also be inferred that whatever was done was done as a joint venture between himself, Martin Kerrigan, now deceased, and Conmey, which renders him liable to prosecution for murder. I am bound to point out that the evidence against Donnelly is less strong than that as against Conmey.

On 5 March 1972 Donnelly and Conmey were brought to Trim garda station for the purpose of charging them with murder. The following day, in Howth district court, both men were charged. The stage was now set for a trial in which the evidence gathered would be tested and the culpability or otherwise of the pair would be decided. First, though, another murder trial was about to take place. Ten days after Donnelly and Conmey were charged with Una's murder, James and Sean Lynskey and John Gaughan went on trial for the murder of Marty Kerrigan.

16. The First Trial

The Lynskey brothers, Sean and James, as well as their cousin John Gaughan remained in custody after they were arrested in Dunshaughlin on 20 December. Their trial for the murder of Martin Kerrigan opened on 5 March 1972 in the Four Courts. The case was to be heard in the building's Round Hall, where four separate courtrooms are located. Each reeks of the past, with high ceilings, stiff wooden benches and witness box and the judge presiding from an exaggerated height on the judicial bench. The trial was to be heard by Judge Frank Griffin, who had been appointed to the bench the previous year. John Lovatt-Dolan was main prosecution barrister, while Anthony Hederman appeared for the defence. The jury was all male, as Irish juries had been since 1927. In that year the Minister for Justice Kevin O'Higgins brought in a law that exempted women from serving on juries on the presumptive basis that they did not wish to do so.*

The case for the prosecution was straightforward. The

---

* The minister was reflecting the conservative nature of Irish society, embodied in the provision of the constitution ten years later setting the aspiration that women should not be obliged to neglect their 'duties' in the home by having to work outside it. The general view was that the women should not be exposed to the horrors that might spill out of the criminal courts. This situation pertained until 1976 when, following a successful Supreme Court challenge to the constitutionality of the 1927 act, the government introduced an updated juries act.

three defendants had kidnapped Kerrigan, brought him to the Dublin Mountains and at some point killed him. The first significant piece of prosecution evidence was the statements made by the three early on the morning on 20 December in Dunshaughlin station. There was also testimony from Eileen Kerrigan about the incident the previous week outside Ryan's of Ratoath, where a group of the Lynskey faction attempted to assault Marty but he managed to drive off. This demonstrated intent on the part of the defendants.

Marty's father testified about how he heard that his son had been taken. He was walking home along Porterstown Lane that night and David Conmey, Martin Conmey's father, pulled up in a car. He had a pair of shoes and asked were they Marty's, which Martin Snr confirmed. The shoes had been recovered from the scene of the fight where Marty had been taken. The pair then drove to Dunshaughlin and handed the shoes into the garda station.

The depth of division that had opened up in the community was writ large through the calling of Padraic and Danny Gaughan. These two young men were there to give evidence against their first cousins and close neighbours. Padraic told the court about the hostilities that had blown up. He admitted he had 'a certain attitude' to the accused. This was, he said, because they had been persecuting Marty Kerrigan by driving around his home, and it was also because his own father had been called a murderer by James Lynskey. 'It was because they did not believe us when we told the truth,' Padraic Gaughan said.

Danny Gaughan testified about the fight that had occurred that culminated in Marty Kerrigan being taken away in John Gaughan's Mini 1000. Then he was asked about the scene outside John Gaughan's in the early hours as the crowd waited for word on what had happened. Danny told of the three men arriving back. Dick Donnelly pushed forward and grabbed James Lynskey, asking where Marty was, but Danny intervened and pulled Lynskey aside. Apart from their blood connection, these two had been very good friends, grown up together next door to each other. Danny asked his cousin where Marty was.

'He didn't say anything and I asked again, and when I asked for the fourth time he said, "John and Sean will explain."

'I asked him again and he said, "We left him up where Una's body was found in Glencullen. I asked was he [Kerrigan] dead and he didn't answer me but he looked very frightened,' Danny Gaughan told the court. He added that he told a garda what James Lynskey had said to him.

Under cross-examination, Danny Gaughan admitted he was now unfriendly with the Lynskeys but said that was their own fault; he did not agree with their actions towards Marty Kerrigan and the other two fellas.

Brian Gildea was the main prosecution garda witness. He testified to taking the incriminating statements. In cross-examination he agreed that about two weeks after Una Lynskey disappeared, the goodwill felt towards the family in the area seemed to have evaporated. He said that on 25 October three men, including Marty Kerrigan, were taken into custody and from that time a change in attitude towards the Lynskeys became apparent. This evidence suggested that the feelings of animus originated with others and that the Lynskeys' hostility was merely a response. That would be a highly contentious proposition among the community in Porterstown Lane.

Garda John Harty gave evidence of meeting the men at Dunshaughlin garda station after they had been informed that Marty Kerrigan was dead. He told the court that John Gaughan said to him, 'Jesus Christ Almighty we will have to face it,' while Sean Lynskey said, 'I don't care if I'm strung up in the morning.' James Lynskey made no reply, the garda said, but he was quite obviously shocked when he heard the news.

Detective Sergeant Philip Jordan from the Garda Technical Bureau told the court he had received a breadknife and a penknife and articles of clothing which were retrieved from Sean Lynskey.

He also examined clothing from the deceased man and a square of carpet he had cut from the rear floor portion of the Mini which seemed to have blood on it. He said that the trousers of the deceased man had been ripped along the seams from the crotch to almost the end of the left leg and for a short distance on the right leg. He examined a jacket worn by John Gaughan and there appeared to be a blood-stain under the left pocket.

Under cross-examination, Sergeant Jordan agreed that he had carried out a preliminary test for blood on the bread-knife but that it had been negative. There had been, he said, a substance on both sides of the knife, leading upwards from the serrated edges, but it had not responded to the benzidine test for blood. If there had been blood on the knife, tests should have shown it.

The chief state pathologist Maurice Hickey gave evidence about examining the body on the morning of 20 December. The front chest and abdomen were exposed and the trousers had been torn or ripped along the seams down to the knees. His post-mortem found numerous minute haemorrhages in the skin of both upper eyes; the surface of the nose skin had been rubbed away; inner surfaces of both lips were extensively bruised; and there were bruises under the chin and bleeding into the muscle in the neck. There was also bruising on the scalp, on the back and sides of the left shoulder, on the front of the left arm and the front of the right side of the chest and on the right loin.

Dr Hickey told the court there was a considerable amount of 'frothy fluid' in the air tubes of the lungs. Death was due to asphyxia. He said that the bruising under the lips could have been produced by the pressure of a person's hand applied over the mouth and nose or from the mouth being pressed against some surface or object, or by some impact on the mouth and lips. But the fact that no marks were found on the outside of the lips indicated that the inner bruises were probably not caused by a blow.

Asked by Lovatt-Dolan if, as one of the men's statements had related, one of the accused had stuck his fingers up under the upper lip of the deceased, would this explain the injuries found: 'If it had been done forcibly it could explain the bruising and tearing,' the witness replied. This would fit into the account given by Sean Lynskey that when they stopped for petrol he said he put his hand over Marty Kerrigan's mouth to stop him shouting out.

Then the pathologist dealt with the wound along the leg, which was three inches long in the left groin, extending through the skin. This wound was different to the other wounds in that it was produced after death, he told the court. The cut ran downwards along the left side of the scrotum and was caused by an implement with a sharp cutting edge. He said he examined a breadknife and a penknife shown to him by the gardaí. It was unlikely that the breadknife produced the wound in the groin, unless the knife had been carefully cleaned afterwards.

Under cross-examination, the men's barrister, Hederman, asked Dr Hickey how long after death had the wound been inflicted.

'It's unlikely the wound was produced in the immediate proximity of death,' he replied. 'Further than that I would not go as to a very strong opinion, but as a matter of probability I would think that the wound was produced at least ten or fifteen minutes after death and it could be much later than that period.'

The question and answers opened up the possibility, however remote, that somebody other than the three accused could have been responsible for inflicting the wound. On the other hand, it suggested that if the three accused had been responsible, then Marty Kerrigan may have been dead for ten or fifteen minutes before one of them took the knife to his leg.

The prosecution case rested.

Opening the case for the defence, Anthony Hederman told the court that on his advice the three defendants were going to give evidence. This was, and is, highly unusual in a murder trial. The defence was likely gambling that the jury would have sympathy with the three men. John Gaughan was a family man. The two Lynskeys were hard-working men and, like their cousin, they would never have been involved in serious crime if it hadn't been for their emotional reaction to Una's killing. There was every possibility that the jury would view their plight with sympathy.

Sean Lynskey was first up. He told of travelling in the car to the Dublin Mountains. Marty Kerrigan had refused to answer their questions for a while, Lynskey told the court.

And then Kerrigan admitted it. 'He said they had picked her up, but he wasn't the one who killed Una, it was the other two. I asked him why he did it and he would not answer. John Gaughan turned round and said to me: "Don't kill him in the car. We will push him over a cliff instead." This was to frighten him.' Sean Lynskey got the impression that Kerrigan was very drunk; the heater was on and the atmosphere was very warm. They had travelled 'pretty fast' on the way up to the mountains because they believed that some car from Ratoath would follow them.

When they stopped for petrol, Kerrigan started to shout. Sean Lynskey told the court he put his hand across Kerrigan's mouth and his fingers slipped across the top of the gum and seemed to tear a portion of his flesh there. He had no intention of causing injury.

Then he went through what happened when they arrived at Glencullen. He put his arms around Kerrigan's shoulders, dragged him from the car and laid him on the margin of the road. His brother James put his hand inside Kerrigan's shirt and said, 'His heart is beating, he is only foxing.' Gaughan said to James to roll him, Kerrigan, out of the car.

'Did you believe yourself and were you satisfied that when you got to that place, the Dublin Mountains, that Kerrigan was still alive?' Hederman asked him.

'Yes.'

'When you left Kerrigan in the mountains did it occur to you that he might be there all night?'

'I believed Kerrigan's friends would pick him up.'

The lawyer then asked him about the injury to Marty Kerrigan's groin.

'There was nothing whatsoever used on Martin Kerrigan,' Lynskey replied.

'The breadknife?'

'It was never taken out of my pocket. The penknife never left my pocket either.'

'I put it to you that you, with the others, abducted Martin Kerrigan?'

'Yes.'

'I put it to you that you planned to do so.'

'No.'

'Your purpose in taking him into the Dublin Mountains was to get information out of him?'

'Yes.'

'You planned that so as to kill him?'

'Never.'

'You wanted to be revenged on him for the death of your sister?'

'No, My Lord.'

'I put it to you that you, or another one of the group, inflicted the injury on Martin Kerrigan.'

'Never.'

When Sean Lynskey's evidence was completed, Hederman surprisingly announced that that was the defence case. He had revised his plan for the court to hear all three defendants. It was left then to both sides to sum up their respective cases.

Prosecution barrister Lovatt-Dolan began his speech by explaining the concept of joint enterprise. 'Each is fully involved in this incident from start to finish. And in a common venture such as this you do not have to decide which of them killed Martin Kerrigan. All you have to decide is whether Martin Kerrigan was killed by one of the three.'

The knife, the lawyer said, was an important part of the

case. The fact that Sean Lynskey had taken the knife when he and the others left John Gaughan's house to go into Ratoath showed the intent. Then he turned to the wound that the pathologist said had been inflicted after death.

'The groin injury was of such a nature that it can reasonably be inferred that it was inflicted with a particular purpose in view,' Lovatt-Dolan told the jury. 'What was the purpose of inflicting the wound? It's a comment, but I would suggest it was an attempt to castrate Martin Kerrigan.' He dismissed the suggestion from the defence counsel that somebody else could have caused the death of Marty Kerrigan, saying this was not supported by the evidence.

'The evidence is overwhelmingly one way, in that it shows that the unfortunate Martin Kerrigan was dead when left on the mountain and dead to the knowledge of the three accused. If you come to the conclusion that Kerrigan was dead when he was dumped on the roadside you can come to the conclusion that the post-mortem wound was caused by one of the three,' he said. 'And that the killing of Kerrigan was the execution of the sentence they had passed on him.'

Anthony Hederman rose to give the case for the defence. He referred to the wound in Marty Kerrigan's groin. He pointed out to the jury that the breadknife and penknife had been taken from Sean Lynskey. Did they not think that if either of these knives was used to inflict the wound that they would have been got rid of somewhere between Glencullen and Ratoath on the journey back?

He told the jury that when Sean Lynskey was not cross-examined and challenged on certain things he expected him to be challenged on, he, Hederman, took it on himself that there was no need for the other two to give evidence. He was not, he said, afraid of any further cross-examination, and neither were his clients. He pointed out, for instance, that Sean Lynskey was not asked whether he put his hand over Kerrigan's mouth to keep him quiet.

Apart from the wound to his leg, there was no evidence that when Marty Kerrigan was alive there had been any violence of sufficient force to render him unconscious.

'How did Martin Kerrigan die?' Hederman asked the jury rhetorically. 'Did he die as a result of any force inflicted by the accused or anybody else or did he die by being semi-conscious, drunk, by falling, getting up and falling back again?' With that, the lawyer concluded his speech.

Following the judge's charge the jury retired at 2.27 p.m. on 29 March. After two and a half hours, they returned to ask for the definition of manslaughter. When they came in with a verdict soon after midnight, it was guilty of manslaughter for all three defendants.

The sentencing hearing took place the following week. The first witness was Superintendent Michael Flynn, who told the court that the Lynskeys worked on the family farm and John Gaughan had three children, all under the age of four. He had served his time as carpenter and had gone into business with another man building houses. The garda said the three had 'spent as much physical time as a human being could in searching for Una. That continued until her body was found on 10 December.' The garda was asked was he aware that shortly after Una Lynskey disappeared it was alleged that she was gone to London to have an abortion.

'From hearsay, yes I was,' he replied.

Another witness called was Dermot Collins, from the Irish Agriculture Institute. He told the court that he knew both families, that Patrick Lynskey had started with 29 acres but industry and hard work had increased his holding to 95 acres.

'It would not be possible for Mr Lynskey Senior to maintain the present farm and work it efficiently,' Mr Collins told the court. 'The future of the farm depends on the future of John [Sean] and James.'

The local parish priest, John Cogan, was then called.

'At all times after Una disappeared there was a general air of tension in the locality, with considerable anxiety and nervousness on all sides,' he said. 'The tension increased after three people had been taken into custody and questioned by the gardaí.'

The convicted men's lawyer, Hederman, made one final plea to the judge for leniency.

'I can't unduly stress the circumstances and background of this ghastly tragedy,' he said. 'The mental violence and the violence of the tongue which one could not find any reason for. The allegations about this girl had created a situation in which the finding of the body – and of the truth – were what these young men were looking for. The truth.'

Judge Griffin laid out the reasoning behind his decision.

'Unfortunately, in almost all of these cases the victims are not the accused persons but very frequently their immediate families,' he said. 'In your case, in the case of John and James Lynskey, your father and mother and your brothers and sisters are certainly the victims. In John Gaughan's case, your young wife and young children are seriously affected by what took place on the night of December 19.' For whatever reason, the judge had highlighted the defendants' families as the victims rather than the deceased or his family.

He sentenced John Gaughan and Sean Lynskey to three years' penal servitude and James Lynskey to two years in St Patrick's Institution as he was only eighteen years of age.

Second-guessing a jury in any case, and particularly one involving murder, is a risky business. The members of the jury have a unique function, but they also have unique knowledge. In most cases, only they and the judge have heard every scrap of evidence. Lawyers often miss a part of a trial, usually because they are required elsewhere at some point. This is usually unavoidable and a junior colleague substitutes in their absence. Court reporters are also in situ for most of the trial but may also miss some part of it. So members of a jury take in absolutely everything and come to their conclusion based on a complete picture of all that the trial has heard. That does not mean that verdicts are beyond question. They are not, and in the trial for the murder of Marty Kerrigan there are serious questions about how the jury reached its verdicts.

By any standards, the three defendants could count themselves lucky in the outcome. In the first instance, they were lucky that they had not been charged with kidnapping, a crime Sean Lynskey admitted in the witness box. The reason they were not charged with kidnapping was never explained.

As far as the murder charge was concerned, manslaughter was the best possible outcome. There was no way that they could have expected an acquittal. The evidence that they were responsible for Marty Kerrigan's death was overwhelming. The main plank of their defence was the set of statements given in the hours after they had returned from the Dublin Mountains. These statements all maintained that Kerrigan had been alive when they left him and that they never intended to kill him. There was nothing in these statements about the wound inflicted on Kerrigan after death.

The statements were all taken in the presence of Garda Brian Gildea. All three were on first-name terms with Gildea. It seems likely that Gildea and the other gardaí had told the Lynskey brothers and their cousin informally that Marty Kerrigan was guilty of involvement in Una's death. Under the circumstances, the brothers and cousin could not have asked for a more amenable or friendly policeman to be present in Dunshaughlin when they were under arrest. The jury, it would appear, took these statements at face value.

The jury also apparently ignored the overwhelming evidence that after Marty Kerrigan's death one of the three had inflicted a wound that the prosecution counsel characterized as an attempt to castrate him. It was a wound that could not have occurred casually, in the course of the men grappling with each other. Indeed, nobody challenged the pathologist's opinion that this wound was inflicted after death, suggesting an action that involved deliberation and was designed to show contempt. Even at the furthest reaches of possibility, could anybody genuinely suggest that the wound was inflicted by unknown parties sometime after the three had departed, en route back to Ratoath? There was no plausible alternative explanation as to how the wound could have occurred other than being inflicted by one of the three men. Yet, it seemed that as far as the jury was concerned, that evidence, combined with all the largely accepted circumstances, was not enough to convict of murder.

A jury is asked to consider the evidence that is placed before it over the course of a trial, and nothing else. One might well ask whether this is always humanly possible, particularly in high-profile cases, and the disappearance and the killing of Una Lynskey would have been fresh in everyone's mind. As yet, there had been no trial or conviction in connection with her death. So, in the trial of the Lynskey brothers and John Gaughan there may have been another element that touched on something primal in jurors' minds, something far more powerful than the recitation of evidence in a courtroom.

None of the defendants had a history of violence. They had acted in the belief that they were meting out justice to somebody who had murdered their loved one. There was nothing else at play. So it could be supposed that despite the evidence of intent to do serious harm to Marty Kerrigan, and despite the evidence that a savage wound designed to castrate or disembowel him was inflicted after death, the jury sympathized with the three men's motives and came to their verdict based on that emotion. They may well have been acting based on their perception of what was just, rather than the law.

All of that would be understandable, if questionable, in terms of achieving justice for the deceased man. But it leaves a horrifying question: What if the man who had been violently killed was entirely innocent of the crime for which he had paid with his life?

17. The Second Trial

The trial of Martin Conmey and Dick Donnelly got underway on 28 June 1972. The pair had spent over three weeks on remand after being charged and were released on 30 March. The case for the prosecution was straightforward. Circumstantial evidence would put Dick Donnelly's car in Porterstown Lane around the time Una was walking home. This was largely the case against Donnelly. The case against Conmey was based to the greatest extent on his admissions in Trim garda station and the statements of Thomas Mangan, his former flatmate.

Once more, people from the community around Porterstown Lane assembled in the Four Courts. Roles occupied by everybody attending the trial a few weeks previously were reversed. The Lynskeys and the Fairyhouse Road Gaughans were present to see justice being done for their deceased loved one. But most were there to support the two defendants.

The trial judge was Seamus Henchy, one of Ireland's most prominent judges. Two years previously he had overseen the Arms Trial, in which former government minister Charles Haughey along with three others was charged with conspiracy to import arms in connection with the violence unfolding in Northern Ireland. A few months after the Lynskey murder trial he would be promoted to the Supreme Court, where he went on to have a major influence.

The prosecution side was led, as it was in the Marty Kerrigan murder trial, by John Lovatt-Dolan. The senior counsel for Martin Conmey was another high-profile lawyer, Seamus Sorohan, and for Dick Donnelly, the leading advocate was senior counsel Pádraig Boyd.

The first days of the trial were uncontroversial. There was medical evidence about the discovery of Una's body, the failure to determine cause of death and the absence of any injuries that might suggest she was hit by a car. Witnesses gave evidence of Una's last journey home from work. Ann Gaughan described how they had parted on Fairyhouse Road. All of that established the facts around the rough timing and probable location of where Una went missing. Then there was evidence from people who were in and around Porterstown Lane at the time, including the screams that were heard.

The first hitch for the prosecution came when Sean Reilly was in the witness box. His evidence and that of his friend Martin Madden was crucial. If, as per the statements they gave in Trim garda station, they identified Dick Donnelly's car coming back along the lane, that would go a long way to putting Donnelly, and most likely Conmey, in the frame for the murder.

John Lovatt-Dolan brought Reilly through the early stages of his statement until the point where he said he saw the car.

'Do you know whose car it was?'

'I thought it might have been Dick Donnelly's, but I'm not going to swear.'

'Apart from the driver in the car, was there anybody else in the car?'

'I thought there was someone in the passenger seat.'

'Can you say who that person was?'

'No.'

'Can you say whether it was a man or a woman?'

'No.'

This was a major pullback from the statement he gave in Trim, in which he identified the car as Donnelly's and said he was 'almost sure' Marty Kerrigan was a passenger.

Lovatt-Dolan asked for the jury to be sent out. In their absence he applied to have Reilly treated as a hostile witness. This would allow the lawyer to cross-examine him on his evidence, which now appeared in conflict with his statement. This is a relatively rare occurrence in criminal courts. When a witness has second thoughts about a statement the usual explanation would be direct or indirect pressure from the defendant to get them to retract it. Another explanation might be if the statement had been provided reluctantly or even under duress – say, in an intimidating environment such as a garda station.

In the absence of the jury, Judge Henchy questioned Reilly. He asked about a deposition that Reilly had given in the district court. The deposition gave legal weight to his statement to gardaí and was sworn under oath.

The judge asked did he identify Donnelly's car and Donnelly himself.

'I could have,' Reilly replied.

'Is it correct?'

'I won't swear?'

'You did swear to it in the district court. In the district court did you not swear the following – Dick Donnelly was driving the car.'

'I don't remember swearing it, My Lord.'

'Do you see there [the judge was pointing to the deposition document] Dick Donnelly was driving the car?'

'I do, yes.'

'Is that correct?'

'It's correct, but I'm not going to take an oath on it.'

'You did take an oath. This is something you swore in the district court?'

'I don't remember.'

'You don't want to swear that again?'

'I'm not going to swear that he was driving when I wouldn't be sure.'

On balance, the judge decided, he wouldn't declare Reilly a hostile witness. The jury returned, and the examination of the witness continued. One might well ask why Reilly didn't explain the circumstance in which he had given his statement in Trim. That would explain why he was now changing his story, and call into question how the gardaí were conducting themselves. Such testimony would also support Martin Conmey's case that he made admissions after being intimidated and assaulted.

Expecting Reilly to reveal all that would have, however, been asking a lot. He was a 23-year-old unskilled worker from a rural outpost in a hierarchical society. Would anybody believe him? What would the lawyers subject him to? How would the gardaí react to him when the case was over? Would the judge believe him over the words of a whole platoon of respectable gardaí? So Reilly did what he could under the circumstances. He refused to go along with what had, by his account, been intimidated out of him. But he wasn't going to go looking for trouble. Crucially, the defence lawyers did not have possession of Reilly's first statement, which was completely at odds with the incriminating one he gave in Trim. It is unclear why earlier statements from Reilly – and indeed Martin Madden and other witnesses – were not in the hands of the defence. The onus would be on the prosecution to provide these statements. It may have been an oversight, as over a hundred witness statements were gathered. But it is the case that the failure to provide the earlier statements managed to avoid awkward, or even crucial, questions being raised about why the statements had changed over time.

A few witnesses later it was Martin Madden's turn. He also had a different version from that proffered in his statement.

'Did you see who was in the car?'

'I just saw the heads, I don't know.'

'You just saw the heads?'

'Could you say how many heads?'

'I think there were three in it.'

The prosecution barrister again applied to have the witness treated as hostile. This time Judge Henchy agreed.

Lovatt-Dolan read out the statement identifying Donnelly behind the wheel in his own car and Kerrigan as passenger.

'Mr Madden, perhaps you will explain why today you were unable to identify any of the persons in the car, or even the car itself?'

'Well, I'm not able to identify them.'

'Why?'

'I just thought it was them.'

Again, the defence did not have Madden's original statement in which he said he didn't see or hear any car passing while he and Reilly were sitting in his own vehicle. That would have raised further questions about the statements given in Trim.

A crucial witness was James Donnelly, the farmer who encountered the car coming out of Porterstown Lane on to Fairyhouse Road at around 7 p.m. on the day in question.

He had been brought up to the garda depot three times the previous November and shown a range of cars. On the third occasion, he identified Dick Donnelly's car as the one he saw: 'I am positive it is the same car as seen by me on the evening of 12th October, the sort of shine off its colour makes me that positive.'

In the witness box he was nowhere near as clear.

Asked about viewing the cars in the depot, he said, 'Well, there was one particular car – I went through them all, but there was one particular car, it was the size of the car I saw coming out of Porterstown Lane.'

'There was one particular car the size of it?'

'Yes . . . but when I saw it the car coming off Porterstown Lane looked darker than this.'

Once again, a statement taken from a witness conflicted with the evidence given in court. What was the same, how-ever, was the description that James Donnelly had given of the driver he saw on the evening in question.

'He was not a young fellow,' Donnelly said under cross-examination.

'He could be anything from around forty-five to a young sixty-five?'

'Could be, yes. He was not a young fellow when I was looking at him.'

'Because you got such a good look at him?'

'Actually, he turned round like that to say something and I saw his face.'

The evidence was quite obvious. Whoever was driving a car, the specific features of which James Donnelly was unsure, it was not the defendant, 23-year-old Dick Donnelly.

On day five, the trial entered a crucial stage. The next phase of evidence was to come from gardaí who had interrogated or been present in Trim garda station over the forty-four hours the three suspects were held. Admissions made during that period were central to the prosecution case. Defence counsel Seamus Sorohan objected to the proposed evidence. This opened up the way for a *voir dire*, a trial within a trial, in which the judge hears evidence in the absence of the jury in order to determine whether it should be heard by the jury.

In the *voir dire*, Donnelly and Conmey gave evidence of what they claimed had occurred in Trim and, in Conmey's case, in Rathfarnham garda station, where he was taken hours after the discovery of Marty Kerrigan's body. As far as the defence was concerned, these admissions had all occurred under duress, including intimidation and assault. From the garda's perspective, all the allegations of assault were a smokescreen to backtrack on the admissions.

The crucial evidence during the *voir dire* came from the gardaí most closely associated with the interrogations. If the gardaí were deemed to be telling the truth, there should be little objection to the admissibility of the admissions in custody.

In this respect, it is worth noting the context for how perjury was considered in 1972. Then, as now, perjury is a serious criminal offence, but in the devoutly Catholic Ireland of fifty years ago it was also deeply sinful and something that would put your immortal soul in peril. Every witness in court swore on the Bible that they were telling the truth, the whole truth and nothing but. For devout Catholics, the moral and spiritual force attached to such an oath was heartfelt.

That didn't mean that everyone in a courtroom – judge, lawyers, police, jurors, media – was naïve enough to believe all evidence given under oath. However, it did create an understanding about people's motivations. Witnesses were assumed to weigh whether any lie they were about to tell was worth the price of their soul. This context also created the conditions in which people would be inclined to believe that gardaí would not lie in the witness box. Not only had gardaí got standing in the community, but this was just their work and, ultimately, they didn't have any skin in the game, so why would they perjure themselves in court and risk committing a grievous sin?

Detective Sergeant John Courtney was one of the first guards to give evidence. He was cross-examined by Seamus Sorohan for Conmey. The lawyer explored the atmosphere that existed in the interview room in Trim with Martin Conmey in the hours after Conmey was brought in.

'If Martin Conmey says in evidence that you were on the whole courteous and decent to him, would you agree?'

'I thought I was very fair with him.'

'And if he says in evidence that Sergeant* Gildea was the opposite, that he was rough and brutalizing in his manner, what would you say?'

'I would not agree with that, My Lord.'

Sorohan then dealt with Martin Conmey's allegation that Gildea was intimidating him from early on in Trim.

'Did Sergeant Gildea in the course of the three and a half hours repeatedly bang the table to emphasize his points?'

'No, My Lord.'

'Did he at any time bang the table?'

'No, it was never banged.'

'Did he at any time bang the table?'

---

* Gildea was a ranking garda, not a sergeant. At various points in the court exchanges lawyers entirely understandably mixed up the rank of gardaí either giving evidence or being referred to during evidence.

'No, My Lord, I was sitting on the table practically all the time.'

'Could you be wrong about this?'

'He might have banged it once or twice.'

Then they came to the allegation that Garda Gildea had hit Martin Conmey twice, knocked him to the ground and pulled him to his feet by the hair.

'Did you see Garda Gildea strike a blow to the face of Martin Conmey?'

'No.'

'Did you see Garda Gildea strike a significant blow in the face of Martin Conmey that felled him to the floor?'

'No.'

'Did you see Garda Gildea drag up young Conmey?'

'No.'

'Among other things by the hair of the head?'

'No, My Lord.'

Courtney was then asked about Martin Conmey's demeanour at various times.

'Did you see the appearance and demeanour of Martin Conmey at the time Inspector Reynolds entered the room?'

'I thought he had come . . . sorry . . . in his mind that he wanted to get something off his mind. And that whatever it was, I didn't know, but I thought it was something there on his mind he wanted to tell.'

'He was distressed, can you agree with that?'

'Yes, I would.'

'Worried?'

'Yes, he was worried.'

'Frightened?'

'Well, I wouldn't say frightened. He appeared worried or had something on his mind. I was just thinking what it was.

He appeared to want to say something and was holding back.'

'I have to put it to you that he did appear frightened of Garda Gildea?'

'No.'

Sorohan then moved on to when Conmey gave his first written statement. This was at 4 a.m., six hours after Conmey was brought to Trim. He had been interrogated by Gildea and Courtney first, then Inspector Reynolds spoke to him alone. Conmey says that Reynolds advised him to tell the truth or he would have to let the other two back in. Reynolds denies this. In any event, the other two did come back in and this was when Conmey says he was assaulted, knocked to the ground and dragged up. Sometime after that he agreed to give a statement.

'Was Garda Gildea shouting at him?'

'He wasn't, no.'

'At this stage did you notice any marks on Mr Conmey's face?'

'I did not.'

'Did you notice that any hair was missing in the region of his side locks, leaving a bald patch?'

'I didn't examine him, like.'

'You didn't notice it?'

'No.'

'While he was making the statement did Martin Conmey continue to look frightened and emotionally upset all through?'

'No, he was happy because making the statement released . . .'

'Did it make him happy?'

'He appeared to be happy.'

When Sorohan finished with examining Courtney, Dick Donnelly's lawyer, Boyd, got to his feet and addressed the witness.

'Tell me, Inspector, have you ever had a person in a garda station for approximately forty-eight hours assisting you tracing a missing person?'

'No, I have not.'

'Rather unusual, wasn't it?'

'Yes.'

'Do you still maintain, Inspector, that the reason why you had these four young men in Trim garda station was to merely assist you in tracing a missing person?'

'Yes, because she was still a missing person as far as we were concerned at the time.'

'Inspector, even after all the effort you had taken, the vast expanse of manpower, were you any closer to finding Una Lynskey at the end of this than you were at the beginning?'

'Well, we were told she was in two different places and we were told she was near a pond off the Navan Road, and she wasn't there, and then she was supposed to be underneath a bridge near Clonee. We did not find her.'

'Even at the end of it, you were still no wiser than when you started it?'

The witness did not reply.

Boyd then asked the witness had he seen Dick Donnelly in the hours before Donnelly left Trim on the Wednesday evening. Courtney replied that he had seen him at about four o'clock that day.

'Did you notice anything unusual about him?'

'No, I did not, My Lord.'

'He had, Inspector, four puncture marks, long puncture

marks on his outer arm below the shoulder after leaving the station?'

'Yes.'

'Can you explain how he got those?'

'I would not know.'

'Did you notice anything about the marks on his back?'

'I do not know any of the injuries at all, Judge. I treated him all right. I questioned him all right, and I treated him all right.'

'Inspector, I am making no allegations against you or anything else though at the moment. I am merely asking you if you know anything about injuries which he had when he left the station?'

'I don't know, My Lord.'

'Is there any way he could have sustained the injuries in the station otherwise than by personal physical violence? Was it a dangerous stairway, a broken floorboard, a dangerous chair or anything else?'

'I didn't examine the station. The station was new to me in Trim. I travel all over Ireland investigating murders. We do not go into details about the general set-up of the station.'

'Did there appear to you to be unusual hazards in the station?'

'No, from my observations there did not.'

The lawyer then brought Courtney through the premise for bringing the four men to Trim garda station, and whether there were other leads that would have sent the investigation in a different direction. Boyd pointed out that eight different witnesses who were in and around Porterstown Lane had given evidence which would have excluded the possibility that Donnelly's Zephyr would have been in the lane, as Una was walking home, around 7 p.m. that evening.

'Had you been aware, or had anybody in charge of this operation been aware of the evidence of these various witnesses, you would have known it was a physical impossibility, provided all these witnesses were not telling lies?'

'Yes.'

'For Richard Donnelly and Martin Conmey to have been driving down Porterstown Lane towards the Navan Road at seven o'clock?'

'No, I do not be guided by all everybody tells you. You have to weigh up the whole situation.'

The lawyer then referenced the crucial evidence obtained from Sean Reilly and Martin Madden about seeing the Zephyr heading for the Navan Road.

'And because you had two witnesses who said they had seen Richard Donnelly around seven o'clock driving down the lane towards the Navan Road you would have considered that sufficient to justify your bringing four young men into the station to assist in the investigation of a missing person and keep them there for approximately forty-eight hours?'

'That and other parts of the investigation, other inquiries we made.'

'Inspector, at this time, when you had these four men in the station, were you aware that a number of witnesses had identified a man in a Zephyr car, between the ages of forty-five and fifty, with grey hair, a beard, reddish face and stout?'

'There was mention of some gentleman and about a car coming out at Fairyhouse Road and that it was a middle-aged man driving.'

'Two witnesses so far have given evidence of seeing such a man around Porterstown during the hearing of this case?'

Courtney didn't answer the question.

'You have heard the question?'

'Yes.'

'Was that investigated?'

'Everything that came up was thoroughly investigated.'

'Was that man discovered?'

'No, he was not.'

'Have you any clue as to who he was?'

'No, I do not.'

The next witness of note in the *voir dire* was Garda Brian Gildea. According to the young men who were detained in Trim, Gildea was the garda who was most prone to violence and intimidation. The garda version is that Gildea was simply a member who was called in from his station in Balbriggan to give assistance. In cross-examination by Sorohan, Gildea said that he was forty-seven years of age and was summoned to Porterstown Lane on 16 October, two days after the Murder Squad arrived and four days after Una disappeared.

'You regard yourself, I suppose, you are still a young man – were you a bit of an athlete?'

'No, nothing in particular, hurling and football.'

'Any weightlifting?'

'No.'

'I suppose you would agree . . . what was your role in the plans? Would you regard yourself as generalissimo in charge?'

'No, in charge would be Technical [Bureau], Inspector Dan Murphy.'

'You were not, in your view, assigned to this, as a strong-armed man – forgive me using the term – to give such assistance as you might be called upon to give to Mr Conmey?'

'No, certainly not.'

Then the lawyer brought him through the hours after Martin Conmey was taken to Trim.

'At any time up to the time Inspector Reynolds came in, at or about 2 a.m., did you lose your temper with Conmey?'

'Certainly not, My Lord.'

'Was it an accident you banged the table?'

'It is a possibility I tapped it a bit; it was certainly nothing to put fear into him.'

'Is it a habit of yours to bang the table? We all have our idiosyncrasies: is it one of yours to bang the table?'

'I may have in that way.'

'Do you address public meetings?'

'An odd time.'

'Do you bang the table during your orations?'

'Occasionally I may do to emphasize a point.'

'On that night, apart from anything else, did you bang the table or did you tap on the table?'

'I did not bang it.'

'What word would you use yourself?'

'Well, tap it.'

'A light tap or a heavy tap or a medium tap?'

'It wasn't a heavy one.'

'Tell me what purpose was it when you banged the table, might it be because you were angry?'

'Certainly not through anger.'

'Was the last thing you wished to do to put any fear into him or intimidate him in any way?'

'Certainly.'

'At any time up to 2 a.m. did he appear to you to be frightened?'

'No, because as a matter of fact we had a friendly discussion.'

'I have to put it to you that in your state of mind, that you were going to break Martin Conmey in the sense that you would persuade, to use a neutral term, Martin Conmey into making a statement and if possible signing it?'

'No, My Lord, that would be incorrect.'

The lawyer then moved on to the period in the early hours of the Tuesday morning in Trim, after Gildea and Courtney left Martin Conmey and Inspector Hubert Reynolds replaced them. Following a brief discussion, Reynolds then exited and the two detectives returned.

'I have to put it to you that after Mr Reynolds had left and before Martin Conmey started to make a written statement you dragged him up from where he was sitting in the middle of the floor?'

'That is incorrect, My Lord.'

'And that you stood, to use an American term, eyeball to eyeball, and said, "Are you going to tell us now?", or words to that effect?'

'No, My Lord.'

'And that he said to you something to the effect that [he was] telling the truth or something like that?'

'He said that on several occasions during the night.'

'You gave him a blow?'

'Certainly no blow was struck, My Lord.'

'And then you repeated yourself: "Are you going to tell us?"?'

'No, My Lord.'

'And that you then gave him a slightly heavier blow that felled him to the ground?'

'That is incorrect, My Lord.'

'And that as he lay on the ground showing no sign of making any attempt to get up you lifted him up by the hair of the head?'

'That is incorrect, My Lord.'

'And that as he was rising you grabbed him by one of the side locks and tore out a bit of hair?'

'That is incorrect.'

'On several occasions, I don't know whether I asked you this before, had Mr Courtney to intervene to say to you "He will be all right and leave him alone" or words like this when you were shouting and banging the table?'

'No, My Lord, there was no necessity for Sergeant Courtney to intervene.'

The lawyer then asked him about one period during Conmey's detention during which just he and the suspect were in the interview room. The pair of them were sitting by the open fire, warming themselves. Sorohan asked him what passed between them at that stage. Gildea said the young man spoke about girlfriends.

'Then he gave me the impression that he had something to get off his mind,' the witness said. 'I asked him again did he wish to tell the truth. He looked at me for a couple of minutes and then he said, "Fair enough, I will tell you what I know."'

While Garda Gildea was projecting the image of him and young Conmey shooting the breeze and developing a relationship, the lawyer had a different scenario that he wanted to suggest.

'I have to put it to you that while you were in the room alone with young Conmey you took off your jacket and you opened your sleeves and you slowly rolled them up, looking at young Conmey and saying nothing, do you remember that?'

'I couldn't. It didn't happen, My Lord.'

Gildea stated that the following day Conmey had given a statement in front of his parents, and soon after that Gildea was leaving the station to go home for a break. He told the court that he asked Martin Conmey how he felt about coming clean and Conmey had replied: 'I feel much better. Will Dick and Kerrigan know what I said?'

Gildea was then asked about his role in interviewing Martin Conmey in Rathfarnham garda station on the day after Marty Kerrigan was killed. Gildea denied knowing anything about Conmey being shown photos of his dead friend and he denied that there was any plan to rough up Conmey in order to 'break his spirit'.

When Sorohan completed his cross-examination, Dick Donnelly's lawyer, Boyd, got to his feet. He told Gildea that Donnelly had sustained a number of bruises from his time in Trim.

'He will say, Guard, that on Wednesday about four o'clock that you hit him violently across the back with what appeared to be a poker?'

'Certainly not, My Lord, it is a complete make up.'

'And there will be evidence that he had marks on his back consistent with being hit with an implement of that sort?'

'No, My Lord, I am not even aware of any such thing happening.'

'If you didn't inflict those injuries as you say you didn't, have you any idea who might have?'

'Certainly not.'

'Did you hear anything about him being injured?'

'I heard some rumours circulating after Trim among a good number of people that there was ill treatment, tortures, every conceivable form of violence used against him. They were so beaten up as to be barely recognizable. Those rumours were circulating freely and despite the rumours I saw both of them and they showed no signs whatsoever.'

Inspector Hubert Reynolds, the head of the Murder Squad, also gave evidence of what occurred in Trim. He was asked about the period he was alone with Conmey, around four hours after the interrogation began, when Courtney and Gildea went out for a break.

'I asked him to tell the truth and not any more lies,' Reynolds told Lovatt-Dolan.

'And what did he say?'

'He said, "I want to tell the truth but I can't, I can't."'

'What did you then see Martin Conmey do?'

'He put his hands into his hair and he started pulling at his hair.'

'Did you then say something more to him?'

'I did. I asked him what happened after that, and he said she was trying to get out of the car, and Kerrigan caught her hand, and she fell over on her face against the glass.'

He was cross-examined by Dick Donnelly's junior counsel Harry Whelehan.

'And those various facts discovered in the course of the investigations by the members of the gardaí, including yourself, could have been theories about what happened on 12 October?'

'I would not like to use the word "theories",' Reynolds replied. 'It is dangerous to theorize in a case like this.'

The evidence of these three gardaí in the *voir dire* went to the heart of the case against Conmey and, to a lesser extent, Donnelly. If the gardaí are to be believed, everything was conducted properly and with due respect for the suspects. Issues like the injuries to Dick Donnelly were not sustained through any garda assaulting him. The damage done to Martin Conmey's hair could be explained by Inspector Reynolds's account of Conmey pulling out his own hair as a form of self-flagellation as he grappled with his conscience.

If Courtney, Gildea and Reynolds, the three main police-men involved in the case, were telling lies, a terrible vista opens up. Gardaí committing perjury, particularly in the Ireland of the times, would be one thing. But in this case any such perjury would have to be organized and agreed between the individuals. Doing so would amount to a con-spiracy to pervert the course of justice, to try to secure murder convictions against two young men based on false evidence.

Other witnesses were also called during the *voir dire*, most prominently Winnie Lynskey. She was asked about her interactions with Conmey in Trim. Ultimately, her evi-dence was deemed inadmissible as she had offered inducements to Martin Conmey to, as she saw it, tell the truth – these inducements were her assurances to him that she would protect him.

In the end Judge Henchy ruled that the only admissible admissions in Trim were those made by Conmey to Inspector Reynolds at 2 a.m. on the Tuesday, and the interaction between Conmey and Marty Kerrigan when both were put in a room together on that evening. He rejected Conmey's first statement because there had been the suggestion of violence. He also rejected the statement made in front of his parents as it was too long into the interrogation.

The judge also allowed what were alleged verbal admis-sions by Conmey when he was brought to Rathfarnham station on the day that Marty Kerrigan was killed. Overall, the judge appeared to have found a middle ground as far as the admissions were concerned. He was allowing some and not others. It could well be suggested, however, that if he accepted at all the threat and exercise of violence against Martin Conmey in custody, he shouldn't have admitted any of it.

The *voir dire* completed, the full trial resumed. Much of the remainder of the evidence was from gardaí, including the main three witnesses who had testified in the *voir dire*. The most dramatic, and crucial, witness in the latter stages of the trial was Thomas Mangan, the young man who claimed that Martin Conmey had made a number of admissions to him in their digs. He was brought through his statement by Lovatt-Dolan to the point where he said that Conmey, after a few drinks, had related his role on the evening in question.

'Did he describe what happened to Una Lynskey?'

'He says she was walking out on the verge of the road and that the front of the car struck her, and they lifted her in to the back of the car, and they drove along and they left her inside a fence and they came back home then.'

'Did he say where they left Una inside?'

'He says just inside a ditch.'

'Did he say where this ditch was?'

'It was near a mountain.'

'Did he say how many were in the car?'

'He says there were only two of them in it.'

'Did he say who the two were?'

'Martin Conmey and Dick Donnelly.'

Cross-examining the witness, Sorohan asked him whether Martin Conmey had ever talked about his time in Trim garda station. 'Did he ever discuss that?' the lawyer asked.

'He says he was brought in,' Mangan replied.

'Would I be right in saying – like most of us – you have a

normal kind of curiosity? Were you curious as to what might have happened to Una Lynskey?'

'No, I wasn't.'

'You never asked Martin Conmey any questions about it?'

'Just, she was killed by the car.'

'Who brought up the subject?'

'Conmey.'

'He brought it up?'

'Yes.'

'He just brought it up out of the blue?'

'Yes.'

'Were you plying him with questions about the matter when he mentioned it?'

'No, I hadn't.'

Sorohan then asked him about the circumstances in which he made the statement to the gardaí. Judge Henchy ruled that they couldn't go into that as nothing about it was contained in the statement. Mangan did admit he went into the station sometime after 4 p.m. and left after 11 p.m.

'Was it during that seven-hour session in the garda station you made a statement to the gardaí telling them about—'

The judge stopped the questioning.

'What was going on for the seven and a half hours in the station. Tell us in your own words. Give a description?'

Judge Henchy again intervened. 'No, he must not, it is irrelevant.'

'Were you well treated or badly treated in the station?'

Judge: 'It is irrelevant, you are attempting to get around my ruling.'

That was the end of any inquiry into the circumstances in which Thomas Mangan made his statement.

When the prosecution completed its case, Seamus

Sorohan announced that the defence would not be going into evidence. Then he, and his colleague Pádraig Boyd, both made applications to the judge to dismiss the case on the basis that the evidence had not reached a threshold that could be presented to the jury. After listening to the applications, and John Lovatt-Dolan's objections to them, the judge decided that the case would go ahead. It would be up to the jury to decide on guilt or innocence.

After the prosecution and defence summed up their respective cases, the focus turned on Judge Henchy's charge. In a case where the facts are highly contested, the charge is a vital piece of the jigsaw which the jury must assemble. They can take the judge's words as neutral. He or she is there to see that everything is done fairly. That does not imply that the charge is infallible. But it would be reasonable to assume that the judge is attempting to navigate a middle path in the context of the evidence. The judge's word on the law and how it must be applied is also final, irrespective of what the prosecution or defence has told the jury.

Judge Henchy, in a long charge, went through all the evidence. He dealt with the state of Una Lynskey's body when it was found and what that might say about how she died.

'We know from the pathologist that most of the skin and flesh covering the body was decomposed so it wasn't possible to establish the cause of death. Such remains as were left of the structures of the neck showed no fractures such as would indicate strangulation, and there were no fractures of the long bones of the body, or of the skull, so it would not seem that Una Lynskey was killed by impact in a traffic accident. You would expect a fracture of the skull, broken bones and so on, and you would also expect damage to the spine following it.

'If she was injured inside the car, if she had slipped, fallen against the door and died from that you would expect a fracture of the skull. There were no skull fractures from an accident. Whether this version given to the guards is a correct one, a totally false one or partly true, you would have to consider that.'

He dealt with the evidence of Martin Madden and Sean Reilly, whether they had seen a car and whether it could have been Dick Donnelly's. He dealt first with Madden.

'It is a crucial piece of evidence. I do not suggest that you should act upon it or not act upon it: it is a matter entirely for you. The witness had admitted to two versions: one in which he thought it was Donnelly's car, and the version here in which he could not be sure. Of course, the other witness in the car, Sean Reilly, is also evasive.

'These two pieces of evidence are much relied on by the prosecution as proving that Richard Donnelly, Martin Conmey and the late Martin Kerrigan were in the car that went from Barrons' shop up Porterstown Lane; met Una Lynskey; something happened which had fatal results; that the car turned back and came down Porterstown Lane towards the Navan Road. If that is not proved to your satisfaction, much of the prosecution case goes. It is essential for the prosecution case to show that Richard Donnelly's car met Una Lynskey and took Una Lynskey into the car and that something fatal happened.'

Then he turned to the evidence of Thomas Mangan.

'Now I would be very slow, I would suggest, to act on anything said by a man when he has taken drink . . . It does not seem correct that this girl was killed by a traffic accident or injured or knocked unconscious and picked up and dumped, and unless the evidence were that she was dumped while there was some life, this wouldn't tally with the cries in the field.'

Another vital strand of the evidence was what transpired in Trim garda station. Here Judge Henchy put some emphasis on the interaction that was arranged between Conmey and Marty Kerrigan, in which Kerrigan said in front of the gardaí, 'Do you remember the evening we were in the fields searching for her? Do you remember that Donnelly told us that he put her under a bridge near Lucan and not to say anything about it?'

The judge asked the jury to consider the context in which this conversation took place in Trim.

'There is something false about it if it is the case that such a conversation took place while they were searching in the fields for Una Lynskey. If it did take place, then Donnelly was telling the other two that he had dumped the body of Una Lynskey. That is not something that either of them would subsequently forget. If he told them that, presumably they knew that Una Lynskey was dead at that time, and if they knew that Una Lynskey was dead at that time, they were carrying out a bogus search, and if they knew she was dead, how did they get their knowledge?

'In any case it was a strange question for Conmey to put to Kerrigan – do you remember Donnelly telling us this? – and remember that in reply Kerrigan said, "I don't remember" . . . so there is this strange piece of evidence, that is supported by two guards, Detective Sergeant Courtney and Detective Inspector Reynolds, to the effect that this had taken place.

'This, now, is evidence, solely in the Conmey case – it can't be evidence against Donnelly. If it did take place, and its authenticity has been questioned by counsel for Mr

Conmey, it would suggest a guilty knowledge on the part of Conmey at least at the time of the search, that he had known that the body had been dumped. Of course, what you have to consider and establish is whether or not Conmey was a party to the killing, as distinct from having guilty knowledge.'

Then he dealt with the main thrust of the case against Dick Donnelly.

'As far as Richard Donnelly is concerned, the case hinges very largely on the prosecution establishing that his car went up Porterstown Lane towards Fairyhouse and turned and came back again, and that rests to a large degree, virtually entirely, on the evidence of Martin [Madden] . . . the man who was sitting in the car outside Reilly's and young Reilly and on the several pieces of evidence which you think might add up to the final recipe. If in regard to that you think that it could have happened but you are not satisfied with the proof, then the verdict should be not guilty. If, after all that, at the very end of your conclusions you think that the finger of suspicion points strongly in the direction of the accused, if you think that they are implicated but you are left with a doubt as to whether they were implicated to the extent of being party to the killing of Una Lynskey, then the verdict should be not guilty. I don't think I can put the matter any further, other than that the prosecution has to prove the case beyond reasonable doubt.'

The judge's charge complete, the jury filed out to consider their verdict at 2.58 p.m. on 14 July.

18. Legal Closure

An air of suspense fills the vacuum after a jury is sent out in a murder trial. The fate of the accused now rests in their hands and in the jury's absence lives are on pause. The accused will be aware that he or she or they may be enjoying their last hours of freedom for a very long time. Loved ones of the deceased will have justice dominating their thoughts. Just as they accompanied the body through the funeral rites and to its final resting place, so now are they accompanying the spirit to a point where closure on the circumstances of death can be achieved.

After Judge Henchy sent out the jury, there was further to and fro between the prosecuting and defending barristers. This is standard in a criminal trial. Generally it involves exchanges of opinion on whether or not the judge's charge was correct and fair. On occasion, a judge will decide that it would be better to recall the jury to clarify any matters that have arisen. In this instance, Judge Henchy decided to let the jury at it.

In 1972, in the era before mobile phones, everyone interested in the case had to stay close by the court to be on hand should the jury return. And the jury could return at any time – there was no predicting how long a jury could take. In the late afternoon, Tony Conmey and his cousin went home to milk the cows.

At 5.15 p.m. the jury was recalled. Judge Henchy asked would they like to eat. The reply from the foreman was, 'My

Lord, we would wish to have tea.' They were escorted out for food and resumed the deliberations once that was done. As the evening wore on, people from the Ratoath and Porterstown Lane area began arriving to offer support.

At 9 p.m. the judge once more called them in. This time he asked if they required any assistance on the legal front. The foreman said they would like assistance with the definition of murder and serious injury. Judge Henchy brought them through the definitions and explained the concepts to them in laypersons' language. They retired once more. As the evening wore on, most of the men repaired to a nearby pub. Eileen Conmey and a few friends whiled away the time in the foyer of a hotel.

The hours dragged on. At 2 a.m. on 15 July, the judge felt it was time to push things along. Once the jury was recalled, everybody took up their positions in the courtroom once more.

'You have now retired for eleven hours, Mr Foreman. Do you require any further assistance?'

The foreman asked would the judge define manslaughter.

'Manslaughter is proved by the prosecution when they establish that the deceased person was killed by the accused person though the injury inflicted was not with the intention to cause death or serious injury but with the intention of causing an injury less than serious,' the judge said. 'A person is also guilty of manslaughter if he didn't himself inflict the injury but was party to a common purpose or design which led to, or was intended to lead to, the infliction of such an injury.'

Soon after the jury retired again Mary Conmey went outside for some air. The quays were quiet at this hour of the morning. She crossed the road and looked down on to the waters of the Liffey. 'Padraic [Gaughan] came along. I was crying, I told him they wanted to know the definition of manslaughter and we knew that was not good. He put his arm around me. We were friendly at that stage, but not together.'

Within twenty minutes word filtered around the Four Courts that they were coming back. A verdict had been reached.

Asked for the verdict in the case of Dick Donnelly, the reply was 'Guilty of manslaughter.' And in the case of Martin Conmey: 'Guilty of manslaughter.'

Mary Conmey was sitting in the public gallery when the verdict was announced. 'My dad was standing against a wall and the Lynskeys came in the other side of the courtroom. What I remember mostly was that they looked to be very pleased with it. I couldn't get my head around that. Then I heard a commotion behind me and I looked around, and my dad, who was a tall man, his legs just went from under him. Because there were so many people around him he didn't fall over, and then a guard moved towards him to help, but Padraic, who was standing beside my dad, just elbowed the guard away.'

It was, by any stretch, a strange conclusion to the trial. Manslaughter is an option usually used when the basic facts are largely uncontested. If, for instance in this case, it had been broadly accepted that Dick Donnelly's Zephyr had encountered Una on the lane and something happened thereafter along the lines of the admissions made in Trim, then manslaughter would be a perfectly reasonable option for the jury. But the defendants were adamant that they hadn't even seen Una that evening. Their whole defence was predicated on that basis. So if the jury believed beyond a reasonable doubt that they were lying about that element, and taking into account the location of the body, surely the verdict should have veered towards murder. Yet they appeared to have settled on some form of compromise, which was highly irregular. This was touched on in the exchanges that followed delivery of the verdict.

The judge, Sorohan, Boyd and Lovatt-Dolan exchanged a few words on a date for sentencing. Then, Dick Donnelly's counsel Pádraig Boyd said: 'I am totally disinterested in such a ludicrous verdict.'

'Mr Boyd, you're premature,' the judge replied.

Boyd wanted to make an application despite the late hour. 'I'm going to apply for it now, My Lord, because I have no interest in any further proceedings in the case.'

'I can't hear you in this case,' the judge said.

'I am entitled to be heard now.'

'Sorry, after the sentence, not before.'

The lawyer's intemperate reaction to the verdict was highly unusual, practically never heard of in a serious criminal case. It might on one level be attributed to the very late hour, following a long day and a stressful trial. However, it was also a reflection of a sense of disbelief that the jury could have arrived at such a verdict based solely on the evidence they had heard over the course of the trial.

As with the Lynskey–Gaughan trial, the possibility arises that the jury allowed life beyond their room to seep into their deliberations. They would all have known the background to the case, the death of Marty Kerrigan and the outcome of the trial that had taken place two months previously. It seems obvious that the jury didn't feel that the evidence was sufficient for a verdict of murder. But if they were to acquit, what would that say? Would it imply that the Lynskey brothers and John Gaughan had killed an innocent man? Did the jury in this trial think that was possible? Two young people were dead in a close-knit community where it appeared something had gone tragically wrong. Is it plausible that some on the jury thought that the best thing would be to convict of manslaughter, the same crime for which the other three had been convicted, and leave it at that? Delving into the collective mind of a jury is hazardous, but the verdict reached was so unusual the possibility that they did or could not isolate the evidence heard in the trial from everything they knew seems plausible.

Following the verdict, the two convicted men were remanded in custody.

The sentencing hearing took place on 19 July. The character of the hearing bore a remarkable similarity to that for the two Lynskeys and John Gaughan a few months previously. There was evidence of the background to the two men from Superintendent Michael Flynn. The only previous altercation either of the two convicted men had been involved in was a charge of larceny against Dick Donnelly, dating from 1967 when he was a teenager. He and two others had entered the home of the parish priest, John Cogan, and taken £40. The money had ultimately been returned and the probation act applied when the matter came up in the district court.

Fr Cogan, who gave evidence at the sentencing hearing, said that the matter had been forgotten about as far as he was concerned. The priest also testified that both men were from good families, were good workers and good sons.

David and Eileen Conmey also gave evidence, as did Dick's father, John.

Making a plea for leniency on behalf of Martin Conmey, Sorohan told the judge that his instructions had always been that his client was never in the car that picked up Una Lynskey.

'From a number of points of view then, if there is anybody in the case and including the late Martin Kerrigan – and I won't say if they picked up Miss Lynskey but accept by the jury's verdict that Miss Lynskey was picked up in the car – then the least guilty person in my humble submission and the person of the three young men deserving the least and the most lenient and the lightest punishment is young Conmey.'

Making the plea for Dick Donnelly, Boyd said that there was 'an awful lot of suspicion around the evidence' with regard to the fact that what occurred did so around 7 p.m. He went on to describe his client as a young man with a largely blameless record. 'He is a Catholic and he has a reference from both his parish priest and his father, both of which I think your lordship will readily accept.'

He ended his address with reference to the wider fall-out in Porterstown Lane. 'This case cannot be dissociated with the other case. This is an incident which we cannot avoid, and I suggest to your lordship with respect that the penalties imposed in the other case must have a bearing on penalties imposed in this case.'

After further submission from John Lovatt-Dolan for the prosecution, Judge Henchy gave his ruling.

'This is a case with tragic connotations, and a young girl, Una Lynskey, disappeared suddenly and her body is found a long time afterwards. The jury, after very full

considerations of the facts of this case, found the two
accused guilty of manslaughter rather than murder. I have
to give respect to their judgement. The less I say about the
facts of the case the better, because it has emerged that two
young people have lost their lives – Martin Kerrigan, who is
said to have been involved with the two men before me
today, in the death of Una Lynskey, was killed in circumstances which led to a verdict of manslaughter in which
three people were sentenced, and out of these two deaths a
number of lives have been blighted. In all the circumstances
I am unable to define between the guilt of the two accused,
but giving the fullest weight to what has so forcibly been
said on their behalf by their respective counsel, I consider
that the sentence I am imposing on these two accused is
less than I would otherwise impose because I am giving
effect to their previous good record, to the words of com-
mendation that have been spoken on their behalf by their
parents, by the parish priest and also what has been urged
by counsel. I sentence each to three years' penal servitude.'

The sentence was exactly the same as that handed down
to John Gaughan and Sean Lynskey (James Lynskey got
two years in a juvenile institution due to his age). An application for bail was made two weeks later, on 30 July, and
they were set free pending the appeal.

It was a year before the appeal was heard. During that time
the two men tried to get on with their lives. They would
have had reasonable grounds to hope that an appeal would
be successful. The appeal opened on 20 June 1973 and sat
for two days. The grounds for the appeal were that the trial
judge was wrong in law in refusing an application for a direction to dismiss the case. This was a reference to the

application both counsels had made when the prosecution case was completed. The defendants were claiming that the evidence did not meet a standard required to convict, that the trial was unsatisfactory and the judge did not direct the jury fully on the defence case.

Pádraig Boyd addressed the three-judge court on behalf of Donnelly. He gave the background to the case, said it had been alleged that his client picked up Conmey and another man and that they took Una Lynskey into the car. The next thing that was known was that some considerable time later a body was found in the Dublin Mountains, approximately thirty miles away. The body was so decomposed that it was impossible for the state pathologist to give any evidence as to how Ms Lynskey had died.

As the case stood, Boyd said, there was not a shred of evidence of how she died. There was some evidence to suggest that his client was on the road, but it was very weak.

As far as his client was concerned, the strength of evidence against him was that his car might have been on the road at the relevant time. The lawyer pointed out that the direction to the jury was murder or nothing, but they had returned a verdict of manslaughter.

Seamus Sorohan spoke on behalf of Martin Conmey. He said he had eight grounds for appeal in total.

At the end of the two-day hearing the court accepted Dick Donnelly's application, ruling that the evidence to convict him had been unsafe. They reserved judgement on Martin Conmey. Just over a month later, on 30 July the court announced that it was rejecting Conmey's application. The evidence used to convict him, the court found, had been greater than that in Dick Donnelly's case. Principally, this came down to the admissions made to Thomas Mangan and, of far greater significance, the admissions made in Trim garda station. The judgement noted that what had occurred in Trim had not been entirely satisfactory from the court's point of view.

'There is no doubt that the applicant was subjected to very intensive and persistent interrogation, the necessity for which is not at all apparent from the evidence. It should have been possible for the gardaí, in carrying out their investigations at that time, to have treated the applicant with respect and reasonable consideration to which every person supposed to be innocent of any criminal offence is entitled. Nevertheless, though the treatment of the applicant may have been harsh and oppressive, the statements made by him were held by the learned trial judge to have been admissible.'

As a result, the court found that the evidence used to convict him was not unsafe and the verdict was not perverse. Martin Conmey was taken away to serve his three-year sentence for manslaughter.

19. Doing Time

Porterstown
Ratoath
Co Meath

17ᵗʰ July 1972

Dear Mr. O'Malley,

This is a plea on behalf of the undersigned, and indeed on behalf of 99% of the people in this small community, to ask you to please intervene in a case which is growing more tragic every day. You will probably recognise the above address as it has been a place of heartbreak since last October. It started off with the murder of Una Lynskey, which was tragic; however, the murder of Martin Kerrigan, which followed, was more tragic because he was murdered for something he never did. We now have two more men jailed for manslaughter and, again, they are innocent. Unfortunately, these are facts, but facts which cannot be ignored any longer.

From the start of this case, we can say, that the guards were partially to blame for the tragic happenings in this, once happy, village. Is it right to take three lads from their place of employment, without cautioning them, and keep them in a barracks in Trim for 48 hours, without food or sleep, and torture them both mentally and physically? (A certificate of health can be obtained from a doctor, whose name can be supplied if required.) Is it right to say to these three lads when released from Trim at a very late hour, not to look for protection from them (the guards) if they were attacked by the Lynskeys on their way home? (words to that effect). Can a guard come into a house and say there will be another murder before Christmas, and yes, Martin Kerrigan was murdered almost a month after he spoke those words. (The name & address of this particular guard can be supplied if required.) And is it right for a member of law to discuss proceedings of the day with the members of a household? Is this what we call 'justice' in Ireland?

We now come to the court case, which lasted thirteen days, with five days absence of jury. Why were the five days proceedings not put before the jury and the public? Was this to conceal the fact that the guards, <u>the law of the country</u>, acted so brutally and savagely to these three lads? That is how it looked to us and the people of this community. If you have been following up this case, you would have read where an unknown and strange car with a detailed description of the unknown occupant, was stressed so often in this case. It was seen by, at least, five people on the evening that Una Lynskey was reported missing, and traveling in her direction. It was also stressed that Dick Donnelly's car was seen by several people at approximately the same time Una Lynskey was taken, but several miles from that area. We cannot understand why the guards did not follow up this car, as the information on the car was available a few days after Una Lynskey was missing. Surely, they had enough information to do something concrete – they had the make & colour of the car and a detailed description of the driver, which coincided with several people's statements. But the guards thought it would be less trouble to take in Dick Donnelly & his two friends, because he was driving a somewhat similar car as to that as seen by a few people that evening, even though it could be [said], time-wise, that they were not near the area where Una Lynskey was taken. And now, we have an innocent man murdered and two innocent lads in jail.

Unfortunately, it would take a book to go into all the details, but from those few points you will understand why we plead with you to intervene. This is a small community with many young people growing up, and when they see one of their friends murdered and two more jailed for a murder they never committed, you can appreciate how they feel and that our trouble is not ending, but beginning, if justice is not done.

Yours faithfully
Anthony and Mary Gaughan
Pat and Mary Reilly
Anthony and Anne King
Michael and B. McIntyre
Mary and Mick Mahon
Christoper and Vera Ennis
Roderick and Molly O'Neill

The handwritten letter sent to the Minister for Justice, Des O'Malley, by the above signed was dispatched two days after the verdict. It didn't elicit any response. O'Malley would not have been able to intervene in the decision of the courts. He could have investigated the allegations of garda maltreatment in custody. There is no indication that he did so. He may well have made informal inquiries from garda management, but all the indications are that the government had absolutely no interest in following up on allegations of assault and intimidation by gardaí.

David Conmey, Martin's father, subsequently wrote another letter to the minister. 'You can see for yourself that there was something wrong from the beginning of this case,' he wrote. 'Please, Mr Minister, do help us, the parents of three boys, not to have a crime put on us that those boys never did.'

Again, the plea went unheard. The murder trial had heard allegations of mistreatment in custody. The judges in the Court of Appeal described the interrogation of Martin Conmey as 'very intensive and persistent' without elaborating on what exactly they meant. There was no interest in examining whether gardaí had broken the law in an investigation, one outcome of which was the violent killing of Marty Kerrigan. It was as if the whole affair was a distasteful episode which was best forgotten about.

During the murder trial, Superintendent P. J. Keane, the district officer in charge at Trim, was asked by Dick Donnelly's barrister about the allegations, and whether he had done anything about it.

'Superintendent, you are aware that very serious allegations have been made and you were privy to the fact that evidence is going to be adduced that will be consistent with that Richard Donnelly was very severely beaten in the station. You heard these allegations before now?'

'At the application for bail, My Lord, made for both of them, there was a general allegation. There was a general allegation,' the garda replied.

'And it was brought to the notice of the court on that occasion that that was the first time the gardaí became aware of this?'

'No complaint or allegation, My Lord, was made to me, or came to me through anyone.'

Keane's response ignored that the fathers of Donnelly, Conmey and Kerrigan had, in the days after Trim, all gone to garda stations and complained of how their sons had been treated.

Superintendent Keane added: 'After the bail application,

My Lord, I made an investigation in the matter and have found no evidence tending to sustain the allegations.'

He was asked if he had interviewed gardaí who were in the stations – Trim and Rathfarnham were the two the allegations centred on – at the time in question.

'Yes, they denied it.'

'Did you make any investigations outside the station or with the people primarily concerned?'

'No, My Lord, I didn't.'

'Or did you make any enquiries as to whether any of them had gone to doctors or anything of that nature?'

'No, My Lord, I didn't. However, My Lord, on 22 of December, I called to the Conmeys' house at the instigation of Mr Conmey concerning another matter and I was speaking to Mr and Mrs Conmey and no allegation or no inkling of this arose at that time.'

The alleged investigation into garda conduct was a bad joke. The superintendent in charge asked the gardaí who were present and got a denial. Did he expect anything else? He didn't bother to ask the young men concerned or their families. Was he afraid of what they might say? Neither did he bother checking on any medical evidence, some of which was sworn in the court. Clearly the so-called investigation of gardaí by gardaí was a box-ticking exercise that was not designed to find out what had happened. This would be a recurring theme when it came to similar allegations in the years to come, many of these in cases featuring gardaí who were involved in the Lynskey investigation.

Once Martin Conmey's appeal was rejected, he was taken to Mountjoy Prison immediately to begin his sentence. Sean Lynskey and John Gaughan were also in Mountjoy, but their paths never crossed in the prison, presumably by design. Martin once got a message through a prison officer that John Gaughan wanted to talk to him. He had no way of knowing whether this was a genuine emissary from Gaughan. He replied that he had no interest in talking to him.

Life in Mountjoy in the 1970s was primitive. The old Victorian jail didn't have in-cell sanitation so Martin's day began with 'slopping out' his cell – carrying any human waste from overnight in a container to be emptied into the communal toilets. Prisoners then filed into the eatery to collect breakfast. Contrary to what is portrayed on TV, there is no communal dining in Irish prisons. Following breakfast, the prisoners were given ten minutes to clean their cells and bring down the breakfast trays. Then it was the long grind of boredom. A very small number of prisoners had workshops to attend, but for the vast majority the day was spent in the exercise yard or recreation halls.

Some spent a good portion of their time simply walking in laps in the yard. In the recreation hall the main attraction was the pool tables, but there was about one table for every fifty prisoners. The lucky prisoners might be kept on the landing to do cleaning, a job that at least would assist in whiling away the day.

'My cell was on B wing,' Martin remembers. 'I got on with a fella who was there, a man from Wexford. I think he was in for bank fraud, and he didn't want anything to do with most of the other prisoners. We were a comfort to each other, I suppose. We didn't get a hard time.

'I was working in the printing room in there at one stage, and then I ended up helping the priest. It wasn't that I was mad religious, but it was something to do. Then I got a job in the kitchen. I just wanted to keep myself busy, to feel like I wasn't in prison. I would do things like make a drawing of one of the sheds back home, anything to take your mind off where you were. But there was a lot of walking around the yard too.'

The weekly visit was a small oasis of relief. Each prisoner was entitled to a half-hour visit, but time limits were strictly applied to ensure that the system kept ticking over.

One constant throughout his whole time in prison was the appearance of his parents, and particularly his mother, Eileen. The human contact was a boost for Martin, but it came with a price.

'My mother used to come in on a Tuesday,' he remembered. 'She would be smiling and all, trying to give me a lift. At the end of the visit she'd be going out the door. I'd wave goodbye and she'd turn and I'd see the tears in her eyes. I used to feel desperate going back in.'

Dinner time, which was in the middle of the day, was often tense. If violence was going to break out, if there were any tensions bubbling between individuals and factions, this was when it was going to reach a conclusion. Martin avoided any hassle. He kept his head down and nobody bothered him. He sensed a general acceptance among the other prisoners that he was not meant to be in there. It was a small mercy in an existence that was impacting hugely on his mental health.

'I used to hear people outside on the street going by, obviously young people out enjoying themselves and life,' he says. 'And I was in there for something I didn't do, locked up, kept away from everybody. It used to really get to me. A part of me blamed myself. If I hadn't told them what they wanted to hear in Trim they wouldn't have had anything on me. I used to beat myself up about it. It was a long time after before I came to accept that it wasn't my fault.'

After dinner, it was back to the workshops for the minority, and further whiling away the hours for most prisoners. Then it was time for the evening meal and a while after that the long lockdown for the evening and night all the way to the following morning. That was the routine, seven days a week, fifty-two weeks of the year. Prison is sometimes seen as less than a proper punishment for crimes, particularly crimes of violence. Yet that view takes no account of the long grind of nothingness that informs so much of prisoners' daily existence, a form of wasting away behind high walls. However difficult such a regime might be for someone who had done the crime, it has to be even bleaker for someone who has the added psychological torment of being locked up for something they didn't do.

In late 1972, the Lynskey family moved out of Porterstown Lane. There was a sense of inevitability about the move. What had been broken within the community would never be fixed again. So much had been lost in a brief, savage period when despair descended into violence and hatred. The priority now was to attempt to keep everybody safe. What, for instance, would happen when Sean and James and John Gaughan were released? They had been locked up since hours after they returned from the Dublin Mountains on the night they killed Marty Kerrigan. Would it be possible for them to resume life as before? Would it be safe?

The Lynskeys moved to Barrowhouse in Co Laois, where Pat Lynskey bought a 120-acre farm. John Gaughan and his family moved nearby. His parents and siblings also moved. The move could not have been easy for any of them. Their families, along with most of those in Porterstown Lane, had been displaced from the Erris Peninsula, where they had deep roots. In that regard, Porterstown Lane was, like other similar communities in Meath, a satellite outpost from their own place in the west. Despite the kind of petty rivalries and minor disputes that are part of any community, the bonds had run deep. Now they were sundered.

Marita Lynskey, who was just nine years old at the time, has a vague memory of the move. 'I remember coming to Barrowhouse outside Athy,' she says. 'We were all excited in a way; it was going to be a new life. I remember going to school there. We moved later to Carlow [town] and I suppose all the moving around in childhood didn't do me any good, going to new schools and that and making new friends, but I got used to it.'

The following year, at dawn on a cold November morning, some of the family returned to their old home area, this time not to the lane but the cemetery in Ratoath where Una was buried. James Lynskey, the youngest of the three convicted of killing Marty Kerrigan, had been released weeks earlier. The family had decided that they were going to exhume Una's body and take her with them across the province to their new home in Co Carlow. An application to the Department of Local Government to move the body had been accepted on compassionate grounds. On the morning in question, a council official was present at the graveside, along with a garda and family members. Even the local clergy, including parish priest Fr John Cogan, who had done much to assist everybody in the autumn of 1971, were unaware of the exhumation.

Members of the Lynskey family unearthed the coffin themselves, and it was taken away by an undertaker's firm from Co Kildare. The body was taken directly to Barrow-house church, where a Mass was said before it was reburied in a local cemetery.

Patrick Lynskey spoke to a reporter about the move at the time.

'We have started a new life here, and we wanted to have Una near us and away from Ratoath. My son John is due out for Christmas, and we will all be together again.

'I lost a daughter and two sons, but life is much better now. We have settled in well here and are part of a very nice community. While we want to forget the past, we wanted to have Una near us, and that is why we have had her buried beside us.'

Mary Conmey suggests that the Lynskeys moved because those in the community did not row in behind their belief that the three local men had been responsible for killing Una.

'I think the Lynskeys expected people to turn against Martin and Dick Donnelly, but they didn't,' she says. 'The rest of the community didn't judge us, they didn't judge the two lads. Not that it was easy. My mother hated going out for a while, but soon she saw that nobody was judging her either. You know that expression about somebody walking across the road to avoid a person they wouldn't want to be seen with? My mother had an experience one day in Ratoath where a woman saw her and made a point of coming across the road to talk to her, and it was obvious that she was in her own small way of showing a little support.'

While locally there was acceptance about what the families had gone through – as well as the loss suffered by the Lynskeys – elsewhere there was general ignorance around what had been a high-profile episode. Mary noticed it particularly in work.

'You'd be sitting around at tea break, and if there was another murder somebody would bring up what had happened and, to be fair, they wouldn't have known how close to it I was. Once at a wedding this woman was chatting and Ratoath came up in the conversation, and she said, "Sure they're all savages up there." We weren't able to talk about it at the time, but it really upset me, even though the woman was a really nice person. The following week at work I went up to her and explained and she was nearly in tears. People just didn't know what had gone on.'

The family tried everything possible to right what they saw as a horrible wrong. David Conmey approached Seán MacBride, a lawyer and politician, son of the legendary revolutionary figures Maud Gonne and Major John MacBride, one of those executed after the Easter Rising in 1916. Seán MacBride was also one of the founders of Amnesty International. He was receptive and offered some advice, but ultimately there was little he could do.

In October 1974, David Conmey, through his solicitor, served notice to bring a motion to the Supreme Court questioning the validity of the Court of Criminal Appeal, which had dismissed his son's appeal of the manslaughter conviction. One of the grounds for the motion was that the appeal court was not mentioned or provided for in the constitution. In October 1975, the Supreme Court ruled that the case had raised several major points of law, but it did not find in Conmey's favour. The whole exercise had been a long shot, but it demonstrated the desperation of Martin Conmey's family to clear his name and get him out of prison.

While the Conmey family, their relatives and the wider Porterstown Lane community attempted to come to terms with what had happened, those who had been central to everything got on with their own work. The Lynskey case had been very high profile, but the questions around the garda's role in what unfolded were largely buried. As the 1970s wore on, and other cases came to the fore, those same questions would keep arising until they could no longer be ignored.

PART III
The Heavy Gang

20. 'There is only one way these fellas understand'

John Courtney, Hubert Reynolds and the Murder Squad were very busy in the years after the Lynskey case. The main issue affecting their in-tray through the 1970s was the ongoing violence in Northern Ireland. The Provisional IRA was very active in the Republic during these years, mainly with fundraising through bank robberies and kidnappings. And there was a pervasive fear, at official level and among citizens, that the violence might spill over into the south, destabilizing the state.

In 1973 a Fine Gael–Labour government took office. Fine Gael could trace its origins back to the first administration of the newly independent state that governed from 1922 to 1932. Its early days were dominated by a civil war in which forces opposed to the Anglo-Irish Treaty attempted to overthrow the state and continue fighting the British. The response from the government led by W. T. Cosgrave was at times highly oppressive. Seventy-seven prisoners (some reports put the total figure at eighty-one) were executed. Other prisoners were tortured, and the rule of law repeatedly came under attack. Following the end of the civil war, several allegations of state-sponsored violence were pursued. Three of these centred on allegations – subsequently confirmed – that state forces had in Co Kerry tied prisoners around mines and blown them up as an act of reprisal. Despite a mounting body of evidence, the government of the new state refused to investigate these allegations and examine whether criminal charges should apply. The whole thing was brushed under the carpet.

Fifty years later, the state was potentially under attack once more. While the situation was nothing like as serious as it had been in the 1920s, there was a degree of paranoia at some levels in government. The Taoiseach Liam Cosgrave was the son of W. T. Cosgrave. Since his father's time, methods of policing had moved on. Before long, however, there would be allegations that security or police elements went way beyond the bounds of law and human rights to protect, as they saw it, the state. Instead of death squads being sent out to quell resistance, as had been the case in the 1920s, this time the protection of the state would be left largely to a group that came to be known as the Heavy Gang. While the Lynskey case had nothing to do with politics or terrorism, how the investigation was handled in 1971 can be seen as a dry run for the methods the Heavy Gang would deploy in cases throughout the seventies and into the eighties.

The term 'the heavy gang' emerged around 1975. Its first known use was during the trial for the murder of a 25-year-old man, Larry White. He had been a member of the Republican Saor Éire group, which was involved in a dispute with the Official IRA. On 10 June 1975, he was shot dead walking home from a pub in Cork city. Four men associated with the Officials, or its political wing Sinn Féin, were charged with his murder. At the subsequent trial, there were allegations that the men were beaten up in custody. All had been questioned by members of the Murder Squad, supplemented by other gardaí. Referring to the allegations and who exactly was involved, defence barrister Paddy McEntee suggested that this was the work of

'the heavy gang' within the gardaí. So came about a moni-
ker that would go on to dominate debate on policing over
decades to come.

The modus operandi of the Heavy Gang was outlined in
journalists Gene Kerrigan and Derek Dunne's book *Round
Up the Usual Suspects*. They reported how the Investigation
Section of the Technical Bureau – the Murder Squad – was
used by garda management.

'When a chief superintendent believed that his gardaí
needed expert help on a crime he formally asked for the
assistance of the Investigation Section,' they wrote. 'As time
went by the members of the Investigation Section established contacts in detective units and districts up and down
the country. They identified promising detectives who came
to be called on to assist in the investigations.'

This was exactly what had happened in the Lynskey
case. Brian Gildea and Owen Corrigan, gardaí who were
not attached to the Murder Squad, were asked to assist
the squad in the investigation. Afterwards the two men
returned to their primary duties in local stations, though
they remained on call for the squad any time it was felt that
their talents might be required. The allegations of assault
and intimidation made by the young men in Trim centred
on these two gardaí. The obvious conclusion is that the
Murder Squad knew colleagues, like Gildea and Corrigan,
who were prepared to use their fists, and practised at it.

The authors went on: 'According to garda sources, it was
among these detectives that the loose, unofficial grouping
that came to be known as the Heavy Gang came together.
Four detectives were named as the originators of the group
or were certainly among its most active members at the
beginning.' During various media investigations dating from

this time, John Courtney's name emerged consistently as one of the four originators of the group.

In April 1976, the *Sunday Independent* published an interview with an anonymous person whom the newspaper said was a member of the Heavy Gang. 'There is nothing sinister in what we do,' he told the newspaper. 'We know they are guilty. We also know that evidence must be produced for the court and often evidence is not there. Our job is to find out the truth. There is only one way these fellas understand. There is no use treating them with kid gloves. We never use instruments. We are doing a job for law-abiding citizens.'

Again, the resonance with what occurred in Trim garda station is obvious. As far as the gardaí present were concerned, they knew who the guilty men were. Their task was to produce evidence that could be used in court, and this was assembled by going back to witnesses again and again to get them to change statements so they could prove 'the truth', as they saw it. Kid gloves certainly weren't used in Trim. And at the end of it all, the gardaí genuinely believed that what they were doing was for the common good.

On the face of it, the Heavy Gang faced one major obstacle. The laws governing arrest and detention at the time were restrictive. The men detained in Trim could have refused to go there, or they could have left at any time. The gardaí were not empowered to detain them. Subsequently, the members who were in Trim claimed that Marty Kerrigan, Martin Conmey and Dick Donnelly had remained there voluntarily. But the reality was that those being held were young country lads who had never had reason to think about the ins and outs of their rights or the law, and the gardaí knew that and took advantage of it. This sort of 'misapprehension' among those who were asked to attend garda stations to help with inquiries was highlighted in Judge Ó Briain's report into issues around garda custody in 1977.

In contrast to those involved in what might be referred to as 'ordinary' crime, when it came to crime associated with paramilitary activity, those being detained knew their rights. But the gardaí had another arrow in their quiver. Under emergency powers, first enacted in 1939 and reactivated in 1972, gardaí could detain a person for twenty-four hours based on nothing more than a suspicion that they posed a threat to the security of the state. This provision was contained in Section 30 of the Offences Against the State Act. In effect, a garda just had to form a suspicion about an individual associated with security matters and that individual could be hauled in and questioned for the specified period. How the suspicion was formed was a matter for the garda and his conscience.

Allegations about the Heavy Gang featured in a variety of court cases and newspaper reports in the 1970s. One case involved a man from Cahir, Co Tipperary, named Thomas O'Connor. He and three others were arrested under Section 30 and detained in the local garda station. O'Connor later alleged that detectives arrived down from Dublin and told him that they had dealt with all sorts of criminals, and they would have no problem getting him to talk. After hours of interrogation, O'Connor leaped from a second-floor window in the station. He claimed that he was trying to escape the beating. He suffered a broken nose, a fractured pelvis and various lacerations to his arms, legs and face. He was never charged with anything. The gardaí involved denied the allegations and there was no more about it.

The general garda response to these allegations was that
it was all Republican propaganda. For many among the
public it would be easy to believe that that was the case.
After all, the Provos were, nominally at least, intent on
overthrowing the state. They and their political allies were
in constant battle with the gardaí. Painting the state police
force as one that used the kind of brutality more associated
with a totalitarian regime fitted neatly into the Provo narrative of oppression and resistance. But the evidence kept
mounting to an extent that it became increasingly difficult
to dismiss the allegations as propaganda. And then there
occurred the most notorious case of all, the Sallins mail
train robbery.

On the night of 30 March 1976, the Cork–Dublin mail train
was robbed. The train was stopped under a false pretext
outside Sallins in Co Kildare. Armed men boarded and took
away the registered mail. The exact size of the haul was
unknown but later estimated to be in the region of
£300,000,* an enormous sum for the times.

It didn't take much detective work to figure out that one
of the paramilitary groups had been responsible. The operation required the kind of planning that was, at that stage,
beyond any so-called 'ordinary decent criminal'. Gangland
crime was still a distant prospect in Ireland.

Early on, the consensus among investigating gardaí was
that this was the work of the Irish National Liberation Army,
a breakaway group from the Official IRA. Just as the IRA
had a political wing in Sinn Féin (both Provisional and

---

* The conversion from Irish pounds in 1976 comes to over €2.6 million
today.

Official), so also the INLA's equivalent was the Irish Republican Socialist Party (IRSP). Nearly two dozen members of the party were rounded up in the aftermath of the robbery. Among them were Nicky Kelly, Osgur Breatnach, Brian McNally, Mick Plunkett, Michael Barrett and John Fitzpatrick.

The interrogation of the suspects was carried out by the loose group centred on the Murder Squad. It included John Courtney, by then an inspector. All except Barrett signed confessions of involvement in the robbery. They all subsequently claimed that they affixed their names to prepared statements following hours of intimidation and assaults. Some said they had been in fear for their lives while in custody.

Kelly, for instance, said that his head was slammed against a locker and that he was spreadeagled against a wall next to a door, having the feet kicked from under him, and then somebody opened the door, ramming it into his face. At another point during his detention, he said, he was put lying on the floor with two legs of a chair on his open palms and a garda sat on the chair and spat at him.

Elements of the men's ordeal echoed the experience of the young suspects in the Lynskey case five years previously. Gardaí, including Courtney, would subsequently claim that Kelly had said in custody he wanted to tell the truth, but he was afraid of Seamus Costello, the leading figure in the IRSP. Back in Trim, Courtney had claimed that Martin Conmey said he wanted to tell the truth but was afraid of his friends Dick Donnelly and Marty Kerrigan.

Some of the suspects in the train robbery case were put in the same cell, against best practice. It would later be claimed that any injuries sustained by the men had been inflicted by each other. In Trim, Martin Conmey and Marty Kerrigan were inexplicably put in the same cell after both had, by their account, been beaten up by gardaí.

At one point in the Sallins investigation, Nicky Kelly was taken from the Bridewell Station and driven to Co Kildare. This was allegedly on the basis that he had said he would show the gardaí where they had left the money stolen from the train. It turned out to be a wild-goose chase, just like the excursion with Marty Kerrigan to Wilkinstown Wood in search of Una Lynskey's body.

Three of the six IRSP members were prosecuted: Kelly, Breatnach and McNally. The allegations of garda brutality were aired at the non-jury Special Criminal Court but given little weight by the three judges. In total, forty-seven gardaí swore under oath that they had not participated in, witnessed nor heard anything that could be described as violence during the detention of the men. All three of the accused were convicted, but by then Kelly had gone on the run as he believed that the trial had been completely biased. Breatnach and McNally were released in 1980 following a successful appeal, and after a protracted and high-profile imprisonment Nicky Kelly was released on compassionate grounds in 1984. All three took civil actions against the state, which settled the case with the award of damages. No investigation was ever conducted into how such a flagrant miscarriage of justice had come about.

The allegations of garda brutality kept mounting. In February 1977, the *Irish Times* published a series of articles on the issue. The first article began: 'Brutal interrogation methods are being used by a special group of gardaí, as a routine practice in the questioning of suspects about serious crimes.

This group uses physical beatings and psychological techniques similar to some used in Northern Ireland to obtain information and secure incriminating statements.'

The piece went on to describe whom this group were.

'The nucleus of the "Heavy Gang" comprises plain-clothes detectives drawn from the Investigation Section of the Garda Technical Bureau. They are assisted at times by members of the Special Branch and the other units of the force, directed by some officers of C4, the official title of the Technical Bureau. They operate from a base at the Technical Bureau headquarters in St John's Road, Kingsbridge, Dublin, and act as a flying squad travelling to all parts of the country. Local uniformed gardaí rarely participate in the interrogations.'

The reaction to the journalism was dismissive. The Garda press office issued a statement saying there was no section or unit in the force 'which as a matter of practice or policy inflicts physical violence on persons in custody ... brutal interrogation methods are not a routine practice at the moment, they have never been.' All of which was entirely accurate. The Heavy Gang was not a specific unit, although its nucleus was in the Murder Squad. And of course, it was not official policy to beat up detainees. That would be against the law.

In his 1996 memoir, John Courtney dismissed the media reports about garda brutality from twenty years earlier. He said he had never engaged in nor witnessed any ill-treatment in garda stations.

'One of the things I learned from my work over the years is that while the public read the newspapers and listen to the news, they make up their own minds at the end of the day about any particular issue. Time and again, people came up to me to say they were fully supportive of our work, and that was very reassuring, both for myself and my colleagues. I never really worried about adverse publicity because I was satisfied in my own mind we were doing our best.'

He didn't explain whether he was suggesting that the public didn't believe the media reports or whether they didn't care if the reports were accurate.

Not all gardaí were comfortable with the activities of the Heavy Gang. Some believed that it was tarnishing the reputation of the force. Others considered it just beyond the pale. For the most part, these members simply looked the other way, as the idea of grassing on colleagues was inconceivable; they were not willing to put their careers on the line and quite possibly destroy their whole lives.

Some senior gardaí made a point of ensuring that the Heavy Gang would not be working on their patch. *Magill* magazine reported the discomfort felt by these elements in the force. 'When they needed expert assistance, they began calling senior gardaí in Dublin, such as Dan Murphy, head of the Technical Bureau, whom they knew personally, and asking for specific detectives from the Technical Bureau to be sent, and not the assortment of physical merchants.'

Word about the activities of the Heavy Gang also reached government. In 1975 Tiede Herrema, a Dutch national who ran a factory in Limerick, was abducted by IRA members seeking the release of three Republican prisoners. The case caused consternation and fear in government and beyond, not least because of the nationality of the victim at a time when desperate attempts were being made to attract inward investment into the country. An unprecedented manhunt was launched, and the kidnappers, Eddie Gallagher and Marion Coyle, and their victim were eventually traced to

Monasterevin, Co Kildare, where Herrema was released after a two-week siege.

Years later, in his memoir *My Life and Themes*, Conor Cruise O'Brien, a minister in the Cosgrave coalition, wrote about encountering one of the gardaí close to the kidnapping investigation who told him how they had arrested a suspect they believed knew where Herrema was being held.

'The escort started asking him questions and when at first he refused to answer, they beat the shit out of him. Then he told them where Herrema was.' O'Brien went on to write that despite such an admission, he didn't, as a government minister, even contemplate sharing the story with his fellow ministers. 'I refrained from telling this story to Garret [FitzGerald]* or Justin [Keating]† because I thought it would worry them. It didn't worry me.'

Not everybody was as blasé about what, if true, amounted to state-sponsored violence and the undermining of the rule of law. Two detectives who were uncomfortable about what was going on approached Garret FitzGerald, O'Brien's colleague at the cabinet table. Like Liam Cosgrave, Garret FitzGerald's father had served in the state's first administration, but FitzGerald was widely perceived to be a liberal rather than conservative figure. The visit from the gardaí came at a time when the government was considering enacting a law which would extend the time in custody that suspects could be held. In his 1991 autobiography *All in a Life*, FitzGerald outlined what occurred.

'I was distressed by these reports, which appeared to me

---

* Garret FitzGerald went on to become Fine Gael leader in 1977 and served as Taoiseach for two periods in the 1980s.
† A Labour Party minister and therefore a party colleague of Cruise O'Brien.

to warrant investigation,' he wrote. 'Several of my colleagues shared my anxiety. Having reflected on the matter, I
decided to raise it in the government and, if necessary to
force the issue to a conclusion by threatening resignation.
In the event I was deflected from my purpose by the consensus in the government that we would be sending very
conflicting signals to public opinion if at the same time as
enacting legislation that, among other things, extended to
seven days the maximum period under which suspects
could be held under the Offences Against the State Act, we
instituted an inquiry into interrogation of suspects being
held by the gardaí. I allowed myself to be persuaded to leave
this sensitive issue for several months, and my recollection
is that I raised it again in November and/or January, but to
no effect. I have no record of this, however.'

FitzGerald's attitude speaks volumes. Despite being of a
liberal bent, he was content to allow the matter to be
brushed under the carpet for, as he saw it, the greater good.
This attitude pertained also in the opposition. When the
allegations about the Heavy Gang were aired, Fianna Fáil
was adamant that when it got into government a full investigation would be conducted. Following an election in 1977,
Fianna Fáil got a huge Dáil majority. Once in government,
the urgency over the Heavy Gang's activities dissipated and
there was no investigation.

Courtney, in his memoir, was dismissive of the approach
of the two guards who went to FitzGerald. 'Dr FitzGerald
claims he wrote a letter to the Taoiseach, Liam Cosgrave,
outlining his concerns but the 1977 general election intervened. In any event Liam Cosgrave never met the gardaí
concerned, neither should he have. Those officers should not
have gone over the commissioner's head. Dr FitzGerald

should have first asked them if the visit had been approved by the commissioner or by their chief superintendent. I believe he should have just ignored them altogether.'

Word of the Heavy Gang reached beyond these shores. Amnesty International sent a delegation to the Republic in mid-1977 to investigate. They did so, and reported back that 'maltreatment appears to have been systemically carried out by detectives who appear to specialise in the use of oppressive methods of extracting statements from persons suspected of involvement in serious politically motivated crime'.

So it was that the Heavy Gang continued to do its bidding in plain sight. There was no political will to take them on and within the force there was no question of garda management instigating an investigation. Those who participated in heavy-handed policing, or supported such an approach, justified their position on the basis that they were doing the dirty work on behalf of the state and its citizens.

Among the general population the media reports elicited, at most, transient concern. The only elements interested in highlighting what was blatant law-breaking were in the media and among a small human rights lobby. Of course, Republican activists constantly mentioned the mistreatment of suspects, but the Provos' campaign of violence meant that most of the public was sceptical of anything they had to say. Many would share the view that even if suspects were not guilty of the crime about which they were being aggressively questioned, they were likely responsible for other undetected crimes. Of course, this ignores the basic tenets of a democracy in which the rule of law is paramount, all citizens have equal rights and justice must be dispensed without fear or favour. Arguably, any public ambivalence about this reflects the corrosive effect of para-militarism in a democracy – it blurs the lines of what people regard as acceptable.

Within the force, what the prevailing attitudes towards the Heavy Gang also engendered was a feeling of impunity. If the normal rule of law was perceived as not applying when it came to tackling terrorist-related crime, why shouldn't the same approach be applied in dealing with ordinary crime? So it came about that even when crimes arose that had absolutely nothing to do with the security of the state, the Heavy Gang moved in and did their business. Two extraordinary murder cases from the period highlighted how exactly this was done.

21. Ordinary Decent Confessions

Christy Lynch was doing a nixer in a house in Sandymount in Dublin. He was a soldier but did a little house painting on the side. When he arrived at the house around noon on Sunday, 19 September 1976, he found the body of Vera Cooney. She rented a flat in the house and had been stabbed and strangled with a scarf. He reported the murder to the gardaí on the house phone and at 4 p.m. he went to Irishtown garda station to make a statement about what he had found. By then, the Murder Squad were on the job and somebody quickly came to the conclusion that Lynch was the murderer.

Over twenty-two hours he was subjected to interrogation, initially in Irishtown and subsequently in Donnybrook station. The main interrogator was Detective Inspector John Courtney. Lynch would later claim that Courtney and another garda had subjected him to continual physical and psychological pressure. During the period of detention he saw nobody other than the gardaí; no solicitor, no family member. He claimed that he was continually told that his original statement was a lie and he should come clean.

'When I replied to Inspector Courtney's accusation that I was a murdering bastard, he gave me a dig in the side because I said a man is innocent until proven guilty,' Lynch related. An Inspector Finlay entered the interview room at one point and then left. 'After Inspector Finlay left they had stripped me off down to my vest and underpants and they made me

273

stand to attention just off from the wall – and I couldn't lean back against it and they stood on each side and I was like that for about two hours. And when I swayed, they punched me to the left and I would go across, and they would punch me back to the right, and they pushed me back and forth between the pair of them all night,' Lynch swore.

He claimed they also made comments on his sex life and about his body. The gardaí denied any such activity, particularly any violence. At 2 p.m. on 20 September, twenty-two hours after he first entered a garda station, he signed a statement admitting to Vera Cooney's murder.

'There were discrepancies in his confession,' Gene Kerrigan subsequently reported in *Magill* magazine. 'He said he killed Vera Cooney at 2.30 p.m. on Saturday. But the gardaí had witnesses who saw her alive at 4 p.m. He said he strangled her with "a bit of cable", soon after he saw an *Irish Independent* left in the interrogation room, which said she had been strangled with a length of cord. She was strangled with a scarf. There were other discrepancies, but who could believe that someone would admit to a murder he didn't commit? A jury found him guilty. An appeal court ordered a retrial. He was found guilty again.'

While the only evidence against him was the statement Lynch made in the garda station, two trials did not accept that he was subjected to intimidation and violence. In 1980, after Lynch had spent three years in prison, the Supreme Court heard an appeal on the matter. The three-judge court found that Lynch had been subjected to 'harassment and oppression' which made it unjust and unfair to accept his confession. Two of the judges on the court pointed to discrepancies between the confession and the known facts. His conviction was overturned.

There was a notable contrast in the outcome of this case with that of Martin Conmey some seven years previously. On that occasion, the appeal court had accepted that Conmey had been subjected to 'very intensive and persistent interrogation the necessity of which is not at all apparent from the evidence'. Despite that, the court did not rule that the admissions made by Conmey should be discounted on the basis of such methods and the fact that his interrogation had persisted for forty-four hours. Instead, the appeal court simply said that 'the statements made by him were held by the learned trial judge to have been admissible'.

There is an inconsistency here between the two cases. One possible reason is that by 1980 there had been a succession of reports about the Heavy Gang and the oppressive, violent and illegal methods allegedly deployed by some gardaí. Were judges belatedly coming around to the conclusion that this was a systemic tactic to elicit confessions which rendered the contents of the confessions highly dubious?

While the Supreme Court in the Lynch case saw that 'harassment and oppression' were used, the court did not lay out the kind of conditions that might be acceptable for interrogation in garda stations. Neither did the judges express any view on whether such methods required deeper investigation. Instead, they merely dealt with the specific case before them, leaving anything systemic for somebody else to consider. Four years later another case would arise in which the state was not allowed to simply turn away.

On the evening of Saturday, 18 April 1984, a farmer from Cahirciveen, Co Kerry, was running along a local beach known as the White Strand. Jack Griffin was leaving the beach when he thought he spotted something lodged in the nearby rocks. Closer inspection revealed that it was the body of a baby. A post-mortem determined that the baby had a broken neck and had been stabbed twenty-eight times. A murder investigation was launched.

The previous evening, 70 kilometres away in a farmhouse outside the village of Abbeydorney, Joanne Hayes had given birth to a baby. Joanne was twenty-five and single. She, her two brothers and sister, their mother and an aunt all lived between two homes on the family farm. Joanne already had a daughter, fathered by a married man, Jeremiah Locke, with whom she was having an affair. The relationship petered out when she became pregnant for a second time, but she was determined to have her baby.

The baby did not live long. A few hours after birth, Joanne brought the body out into the family farm and lodged it in a bag in a water-filled hole. The baby's death had been a tragedy, but no blame attached to its mother, who was devastated. There was absolutely no connection between the death of Joanne's baby and the killing of the baby in Cahirciveen.

A few days later the Murder Squad were called in to the case of the Cahirciveen baby. By then it was headed by John Courtney, who had been promoted to Detective Superintendent. Courtney was from Kerry and through various connections plugged into local intelligence in the Tralee area. Word got back to them about the young woman in Abbeydorney, a village 6 miles north of Tralee, who had clearly given birth, but there was no sign of a baby. Courtney and his men put two and two together. Abbeydorney was on a different peninsula to Cahirciveen, but that was a mere detail. A narrative, or theory, was formed within the squad, just as it had been in the Lynskey case. Joanne Hayes, most likely with the collusion of members of her family, had stabbed her baby to death and thrown the baby in the sea, from where it was carried across by currents to the other peninsula and washed up in the Cahirciveen area. All that was required was some confessions to confirm the theory.

On 1 May, the Hayes family was brought in for questioning. They were not under arrest, but the family had no idea they were free to leave at any time. The Murder Squad got to work. By 1984, the squad had plenty of experience in dealing with terrorists, so a family of farmers was unlikely to present any difficulties.

Later, all the family would claim they were intimidated by the gardaí. Joanne's brothers, Mike and Ned, claimed they were assaulted. A judge-led tribunal would reject those allegations.

Joanne told the gardaí that her baby had died and was buried on the farm. They did not believe her. A garda was dispatched to the farm, where a cursory search was conducted. Nothing was found.

Within twenty-four hours of having been brought into the station, Joanne had signed a confession. She admitted stabbing her baby to death. Her confession stated that she had then driven to Slea Head on the Dingle Peninsula and thrown the body in the sea. This would fit with the body being washed up on the opposite Iveragh Peninsula near Cahirciveen. In theory, at least. Joanne's siblings all signed statements supporting this story to one extent or another.

Having suffered the trauma of losing her baby, and twenty-four hours of questioning about having killed it, Joanne was now subjected to incarceration. She was remanded in custody to Limerick Prison, while her siblings were bailed. Her family visited her, and she gave precise details of the location of her baby's body. They contacted the family solicitor, who got in touch with the gardaí. The body was located exactly where Joanne said she had left it.

Now the gardaí had a problem. They had confessions that a baby was stabbed and thrown into the sea, but they also had a baby's body located on the Hayes farm.

Further tests were carried out. It was discovered that Joanne and Jeremiah Locke were blood group O. The Cahirciveen baby was blood group A. Any baby Joanne and Jeremiah would conceive together could not be blood group A, and the Cahirciveen baby could not be theirs.

Pretty soon, the murder charges were dropped. An internal report into the matter was compiled by one of the detectives who had been involved, P. J. Browne. In the report, he departed from the stiff prose normally deployed in such official reports.

'Within the covers of this Garda report and file is told a sad tale. It occurred because a young woman in her mid-twenties was scorned by a married man she loved, had children for and wanted for herself. Hell hath no fury like a woman scorned.'

The lapse into the language of pulp fiction completely ignored what was at issue. Joanne Hayes's emotional and intimate life had nothing to do with what had arisen. The issue was that a law-abiding, quiet family had collectively confessed to a murder they could not have participated in or colluded with. Why would they ever do such a thing?

And there was the terrifying possibility that had Joanne or Jeremiah shared a blood group with the Cahirciveen baby, murder charges might have proceeded on the basis of the confessions obtained by the Murder Squad. As it was, and despite the apparently definitive blood group evidence and the dropping of charges against Joanne, the investigators could not let it go and were cooking up a new theory about what had happened, a theory that kept her in the frame as the Cahirciveen baby's mother.

Following extensive media and political comment, the government set up a tribunal of inquiry in November 1984 to examine how such a juncture was arrived at. Now, following nearly fifteen years of allegations about the conduct of some gardaí, their methods were going to be subjected to rigorous scrutiny.

While the tribunal was ostensibly set up to examine how a family could confess to participation in or collusion with a murder they could not have committed, it morphed into something else entirely. Joanne Hayes was effectively put in the dock. She was cross-examined about the most intimate details of her life for five days. At one point journalist Nell McCafferty counted forty-three men in the room, plus the frail figure of Joanne. But while there was growing outrage about how she was being treated – neighbours from Abbeydorney protested outside, alongside women from all over Ireland – that did not deflect the trajectory of the tribunal.

At the tribunal, gardaí shared their new hypothesis about the parentage of the Cahirciveen baby. To explain the anomaly over the blood group they posited the theory that 'superfecundation' had occurred. This is a phenomenon in which a woman has sex with two different men in a short time span and gives birth to two babies of different blood groups. Reaction to this veered from mirth, to disgust that Joanne Hayes was being subjected to such ridiculous speculation in order to justify the actions of others.

The chair of the tribunal Judge Kevin Lynch issued a report in which he accused the Hayes family of lying. He said the gardaí, by contrast, had been 'gilding the lily'. He didn't accept the claims of intimidation and assault in custody. In effect, when it came to deciding between claims of citizens who had been detained, including some supporting evidence, and the testimony of gardaí, a judge had once again gone with the latter.

There was little political reaction to what for those who had observed closely was something of a travesty. Elements of the media called out what was obvious to some. In *Magill* magazine, Gene Kerrigan wrote a detailed analysis of where the tribunal report conflicted with the known facts. An editorial in the magazine summed up the frustration at the outcome.

> Judge Lynch's report has made a number of things worse. It represents the largest commitment of time and money which parliament and the judiciary can make to examining, supposedly, the methodology of the gardaí.
>
> It has manifestly failed to do so satisfactorily. Our fears of garda misbehaviour must now be compounded by the fear that one of the few checks against it, a full-scale judicial tribunal, has proved impotent. By failing to answer the central question which it was established to answer, Judge Lynch's tribunal has resulted in three areas of legitimate concern; for Joanne Hayes and her family, who have been branded on evidence which we believe we have shown to be unreliable; for the gardaí as a whole, over whom the shadow of the case will continue to hang; and for the citizens at large whose right to a proper accounting of the activities of those whom they employ has not been

vindicated. In addition, it has raised serious questions about the suitability of this type of tribunal for investigating the behaviour of the garda.

Despite the media comment, there was no getting away from the outcome of the report. The first official investigation into alleged garda misbehaviour, following nearly fifteen years of detailed and recurring allegations, came up with the result that there was nothing to see here. Yet, though the gardaí got what largely amounted to a clean bill of health, a decision was taken to disband the Murder Squad. Four of the gardaí who had been centrally involved in the case were assigned to desk duty.

John Courtney, looking back on the affair in his memoir a decade later, had no regrets about how he had handled the case.

'I never lost a night's sleep over the case because I did not set out to do an injustice to Joanne Hayes or anyone else. Why should I pick on that family above anyone else? Some people appeared to believe that the gardaí wanted to charge the Hayes family but that is totally wrong.'

His justification was not unusual, but by accident or design it missed the point, the difficulty at the heart of many cases in which Courtney was involved: at the outset of an investigation gardaí came up with a theory and were then single-minded and tunnel-visioned about constructing a case around that theory, and determined to ignore anything that might contradict it. In the case of the Cahirciveen baby, it was decided that the Hayes family had killed him. The interrogations were designed to extract the truth as Courtney saw it.

Following the tribunal, Joanne Hayes cooperated with a

book, *My Story*, telling what had happened through her eyes. The publisher, Brandon Books, was sued for libel by four of the gardaí involved in the case and ended up paying substantial damages, which nearly put it out of business.

It would take thirty-four years before the Hayes family would begin to receive justice. In 2018, DNA tests conclusively proved that Joanne could not have been the mother of the Cahirciveen baby.* The gardaí commissioner apologized to her on behalf of the force, though it was not clear what exactly he was apologizing for.

The Hayes family initiated a legal action against the state and, within three years, the state settled and awarded compensation to Joanne and her family. The tribunal report was officially repudiated with all the findings of wrongdoing on the part of the family found to be incorrect.

The case of the murdered Cahirciveen baby was reopened. The baby, christened Baby John, was disinterred

---

* Notable among those who had advanced the superfecundation theory, and for decades insisted there was a basis for it, was Detective Inspector Gerry O'Carroll, a prominent member of the Heavy Gang (and a Kerryman, like his boss, John Courtney). O'Carroll and a colleague had elicited Joanne's false confession in 1984. In 2004 he told RTÉ Radio 1's Liveline that he had treated Hayes 'like my own daughter . . . I was kindness and patience personified'. After his retirement from the force in 2000, O'Carroll had a busy media career and published a memoir, *The Sheriff*, in 2007. O'Carroll robustly defended his good name and sued or threatened to sue anyone who hinted that his behaviour had been anything but exemplary in the matter of the Kerry Babies investigation, to the extent that coverage of the case over the years often studiously avoided mentioning his name. O'Carroll only finally publicly accepted the findings of the 2018 DNA tests in 2023, saying that it was 'finite proof' that Joanne Hayes could not be the mother of the Cahirciveen baby. He did not, however, offer an apology to Joanne or the Hayes family. 'I have only sympathy for two creatures on this, the babies—and that's my final word on that.' Gerry O'Carroll died in January 2024.

and a DNA sample retrieved. This proved to be the basis for the new investigation, which was primarily conducted around Cahirciveen. In March 2023, forty years after the baby was found on the White Strand, a couple were arrested in mid-Kerry. The woman had originally been from the Cahirciveen area.

Among the newspapers to cover the Kerry Babies scandal extensively was the *Sunday Tribune*. As part of its coverage, two reporters, Derek Dunne and Mark Brennock, wrote a story looking at other allegations of garda misconduct. On Porterstown Lane, Mary Gaughan (née Conmey) was, like much of the country, transfixed with what was tumbling out into the public domain. She took pen to paper and wrote to the reporters.

The Sunday Tribune
8–11 Lower Baggot St.
Dublin 2

5/2/1985

Dear Mr Brennock and Mr Dunne,

Having listened to the reports in the media and read your report on 'garda irregularities' as you call them in the Sunday Tribune on the 21ˢᵗ October 1984, I felt that I must write, not just to tell you our story but also to get the whole thing out of my system and to beg people like you in the media to have this disgusting and disgraceful behaviour exposed, because victims of this brutality have no one else to fight for them, not unless they have money or 'pull' and we have neither.

The case I wish to tell you about took place 14 years ago in 1971. It involved the murder of Una Lynskey of Porterstown, Ratoath, Co Meath. Watching the 'Today Tonight' on the Joanne Hayes case brought it all back to me. In their own way the two cases are so similar . . .

The letter went into detail about the circumstances around Una's death, the killing of Marty Kerrigan and the imprisoning of Mary's brother Martin. She concluded:

There is so much more to tell but what is the point. The dirty work is coming out now in other cases and that is the main thing. By the way, John Courtney was one of the head men in this case also . . . the level of investigative work in this case was appalling. The guards have decided they knew who did it and disregarded everything that did not fit. I feel the chances of finding the real killer were very good if they had tried. They carried out a lot of work from the Lynskey household where drink and sandwiches were provided.

I think that the man or men who killed Una may have struck again, as there has been one case anyway of a girl in Kildare that was murdered, and the circumstances are so similar. But because Una's murder was supposed to have been solved they were probably never compared. Not all of Una's family believed that these three lads had killed Una. Her cousins and next-door neighbours did not believe it, mainly because two members of this family saw this other car on the road that night. Also, Una's uncle and aunt saw the lads on the night that they were released from custody. I am now married to a member of this family. It was with their help and support and that of neighbours that got us through it all, though not everyone has got through unmarked.

Yours Sincerely
Mary Gaughan

THE SUNDAY TRIBUNE

17/5/85

Dear Mary,

First of all, I want to thank you for your letter addressed to myself and Mark Brennock of 5/2/85. On reading it, it is quite obvious that it took courage to write at this stage. Your strong feelings relating to the garda handling of the Una Lynskey case and Kerry Babies case came through.

I have refrained from writing to you until now because I thought that Detective Courtney would be questioned rather closely about his past career in the witness box. I tried to dial a telephone number – [redacted] – think it was yours, but it appears to be out of order. In any case, John Courtney has been cross-examined and very little has emerged. He may or may not be reprimanded for his conduct. He is still in charge of 25 men in the elite Murder Squad at the time of writing. He may or may not continue to hold this position.

The main reason I am writing to you is to ask if you would be willing to give me assistance in doing a story of the arrest/ charge/conviction of those who were accused of the Una Linskey [sic] killing. There is not very much point in going over old ground again I know. But the effects of the way in which this case, and others like it, were dealt with by the gardaí lives on. The fact that the primary source of solving crimes are statements, and the fact that there is no real police work done as such, leaves case after case where there is no clear evidence who commits a crime. The effects of a wrong conviction live on, and I think the most appropriate thing I could do would be to show the effects such an investigation has on everyone concerned.

If you would be amenable to this idea, I would prefer to do it for Magill Magazine, as it would allow the length necessary to explain properly what exactly went on. If you are averse to the entire idea I would understand. In any case, I would appreciate if you might let me know one way or the other. I can be contacted through the above address/telephone number.

Once again thank you for writing to me,

Yours etc.
Derek Dunne

Mary Gaughan met with Derek Dunne, but little came of it. 'I talked to him, but it just wasn't possible for anything to happen at the time,' she says. 'At that stage we hadn't even talked to each other, nobody was ready. It was all still really raw. I would have loved to have had them report on it, but there was a whole range of families involved and you didn't want to upset them. You would have been taking on an awful lot and I didn't feel I had the right to do it.'

Within a few years, however, things would finally change, after Mary's brother Martin Conmey had a moment of epiphany.

22. Calling to a Stranger

On 19 October 1989, Gerry Conlon walked free from the Old Bailey. Conlon had been one of the Guildford Four, who had been framed for the 1974 bombings of two pubs in Guildford, Surrey, in England. Five people died in the explosions and sixty-five were injured. The IRA was believed to be responsible, but the four young people who were arrested had nothing to do with it. Conlon, his friend Paul Hill, Paddy Armstrong and Carole Richardson were living in a squat, engaged in being young, experimenting with drugs and fooling around.

Following a lengthy campaign, the four were freed by the British appeal court in 1989. Conlon demurred the offer to leave the Old Bailey by a side entrance. He came through the front door into the glare of the media. With his two sisters holding an arm each he made an emotional victory march down the street, waving his fist. Supporters cheered him on. Irish construction workers on nearby buildings roared their approval, adding to what was to become an iconic scene, with TV cameras beaming his vindication around the world.

Then he stepped forward to the microphones. 'I was in prison for fifteen years for something I didn't do,' he roared. 'Something I didn't know anything about. I'm an innocent man.'

Sitting in the living room at home in Porterstown Lane, Martin Conmey watched the scene unfold. As Conlon proclaimed his innocence Martin broke down.

He had lived for eighteen years with the stain of something he hadn't done. After serving his prison sentence he arrived back in the community from which he was sprung. He attempted to get on with life. His friends gathered in around him. The stray glances, however, wouldn't go away. He might be walking down through Ratoath and somebody whom he might know vaguely or not at all would look at him for those two seconds longer than would be normal. He was *the fella who did time for the Una Lynskey killing. The others got off, but sure, they must have done it when the court decided it.*

'When I was going for a job or some work I used to pronounce my name differently because I was conscious that people might be talking and mightn't give me a job. That was with me for years. After I got out of prison I worked with Dick [Donnelly] for a while and then I went over to England to work there before coming home. It was always with me.'

In 1982, on a night out in the County Club, he met Ann Mooney, a native of Ashbourne. They married and built a house on a site near the home where he had grown up. In 1989, their son, Raymond, was born on their sixth wedding anniversary. The new responsibilities of parenthood prompted Martin to think differently about what he had been through. It was the sight of Gerry Conlon, proclaiming to the world that he was an innocent man, which set things in motion.

Martin went to Mary Wallace, a Fianna Fáil county councillor from Ratoath who was related to one of his friends. Wallace suggested retaining Tallons Solicitors, a firm in Ashbourne. Martin Conmey also went to his local TD, John Bruton, who was then serving in opposition.

'He brought it up in the Dáil,' Martin remembers. 'But the response to him from the Minister for Justice was that the whole thing had been through the courts and there was nothing more that could be done.'

That was a correct assessment at the time. However, the weight of scandals reaching back through the decades would soon change that.

The Guildford Four case was one of several high-profile miscarriages of justice that emerged in the 1970s and 1980s. Most, but not all, were linked to the ongoing conflict in Northern Ireland. Gerry Conlon and his friends always maintained that false confessions were beaten out of them. The same applied to the Birmingham Six: Irishmen who were framed for IRA pub bombings in the English city in 1974. They were eventually released in 1991.

The Republic of Ireland had its own miscarriages of justice, the most notorious being the Sallins mail train case, personified by Nicky Kelly. Unlike in the UK, the process in Ireland did not reach a conclusion when an original verdict or miscarriage was overturned. Kelly was pardoned on compassionate grounds, but his conviction stood. There was no inquiry into whether he and the others had been viciously assaulted in custody, as they had credibly claimed. Through it all there was a dawning realization that the quality of justice being dispensed sometimes fell far short of what should be expected in a progressive democracy.

In 1989, the Dublin government set up a committee to examine how the state should deal with miscarriages of justice. The committee was headed up by an experienced circuit court judge, Frank Martin. Its report was published in March 1990 and made three key recommendations. First, that allegations of miscarriage of justice should be examined by a statutory body, such as a tribunal. Second, if a miscarriage was proved, or accepted, there should be a statutory provision to award compensation. Finally, to minimize the chances of any miscarriage of justice, the questioning of suspects in custody should be recorded and videoed.

The last recommendation must have produced a wry, or more likely bitter, smile from dozens of people who had alleged over the years to have been abused in custody. How different would their detention have been had it all been recorded and available for inspection.

The government accepted the recommendations with a few caveats. The provision to videotape interviews was already in law, having been included in the 1984 Criminal Justice Act. It just wasn't being implemented. Once again, Irish ways ensured that Irish laws were elastic when it was expedient. The gardaí, including representative bodies, had been lukewarm on the idea. There was also the issue of cost; equipping all major garda stations in the country with videotaping equipment in the straitened 1980s seemed a big outlay. By 1990, a pilot scheme was in place to check how best to advance the concept, so, as far as the government was concerned, plans were advancing nicely and no more was needed.

The recommendation from Martin on compensation for the victims of a miscarriage of justice was fully accepted. However, the recommendation on setting up a tribunal-like body was not. Instead, the government decided that potential miscarriages should be referred to the Court of Criminal Appeal. This led to claims among some opposition politicians that the government was being led by the judiciary. Eamon Gilmore, a TD for the Democratic Left party, claimed that judges had opposed the measure on the basis that they didn't accept the premise that a miscarriage of justice could happen in the Irish courts. Other concerns were expressed that the gardaí would retain a central role when the matter was processed once more through the court system. A case could well be made that the courts in the Sallins mail train robbery case had facilitated the unjust outcome through neglect and self-interest. (Having represented some of the men involved in the Sallins case, Gilmore's Dáil colleague, solicitor Pat McCartan, was deeply familiar with it.)

The government rejected the criticism and made plans to bring a new bill through the Oireachtas, although there didn't appear to be any great political will attached to the project. As is so often the case, work on progressing the bill was disrupted by the ending of the government's term in 1992. Following a general election, a Fianna Fáil–Labour coalition was formed for the first time in the history of the state. The 'programme for partnership' of the new government made provision 'to provide for review of alleged cases of miscarriage of justice and to give a statutory right to compensation for such miscarriage'.

Introducing the bill to the Dáil the following year, the Minister for Justice Máire Geoghegan-Quinn set out the kind of scenarios it was designed to address. 'Clearly the circumstances where it would become necessary to reopen cases would be exceptional, but we must face that possibility and provide for it,' she said. 'It is possible, for example, to envisage an important witness coming forward after the hearing of an appeal who, for a genuine reason, was unavailable for the appeal or the original trial. Another possibility might be where a new development in forensic science enables evidence which led to the conviction and its affirmation in the Court of Criminal Appeal to be seen in a different light.'

So came into being the Criminal Justice Procedures Act 1993, the mechanism by which Martin Conmey could attempt to right the wrong done to him.

There was another wrong that hadn't been righted and maybe never would. While Martin Conmey had suffered greatly, he had at least had a life. No such privilege was afforded Marty Kerrigan, his life having come to a savage end at the age of nineteen. During the years after his death, as those he had grown up with matured and settled down, his sisters continued to carry his flame. Ann, Katie and Eileen all remained in the Ratoath area. Katie ran a fast-food outlet in the village, and Ann also worked there. They remained close, and Ann's marriage to Dick Donnelly ensured that Marty's memory would always have a height-ened presence in their home.

One day in the chipper in the late 1990s, Katie got talking to somebody who was singing the praises of a private inves-tigator, Billy Flynn, who lived in another part of the county but was known in the Ratoath area. Katie liked what she heard about the man. He sounded like somebody who was interested in pursuing justice and had an independent spirit. Through a friend, she acquired his contact details. She and Ann got an appointment and set off to meet him. They had great hopes for this new development but were full of nerves.

On the way across the county to Flynn's house, Katie's husband rang her to let them know a friend had passed away. 'When we got down there, Billy was busy and he led us into this room to wait,' Katie remembers. 'Anyway, we used the bathroom. And in there we prayed to the chap who had passed away that Billy would believe us. We were still at a stage where we just didn't know who would believe us.'

Flynn heard their story and told them that he would investigate it. 'He said anything he found, whether we liked it or not, would be coming out. He said he'd highlight it and try to find the car and the driver that were seen. Just him coming on board was like a huge win, or even more a relief to us. Now we had somebody who might be able to do something.'

If Billy Flynn didn't exist, a novelist would have had to invent him. Billy was no Philip Marlowe, patrolling mean streets. Neither was he the standard television PI, an ex-cop with a drink problem, salving his guilt by pursuing justice for all. Billy Flynn was a family man, a father of eight who had made a bit of money through insolvencies and various other business ventures before turning his talents to private investigation. He lived in a large house he called Thistle-waite House a few miles from Enfield, yet in the heart of rural Ireland. When his children grew up. most of them remained in the area, usually within a mile or two.

He was a low-sized man with curious eyes and a pair of glasses habitually perched on his balding head. He rarely left his office, preferring to direct operations therein on one of three telephones. The centrepiece of his office was a snooker table littered with files of the cases he was working on. Typically, he would in an average day walk miles around that table, a phone pinned to his left ear, the fingers of his right hand clasping a Rothmans cigarette. A photograph of Pope John Paul II hung on one wall. A few feet away there was a large portrait of the Magnificent Seven on horseback, led by Yul Brynner. Billy had a soft spot for some cowboys. When he wasn't on the phone he would keep walking, dictating his latest – usually excoriating – missive to some centre of power, while his daughter Jackie sat typing under the image of the smiling pontiff.

Flynn's first big case was investigating a fugitive financier from Cork, Finbarr Ross. Ross had fled to the USA in 1983 after the collapse of his Gibraltar-based company, International Investments. It crashed with debts of over £17 million, and 1,400 investors, mainly pensioners, were left high and dry.

Flynn pieced together a case against Ross and tracked him down to a religious community in Oklahoma. The private investigator found that Ross had managed to do such extensive damage because Irish company law was weak, he was well connected and there was no political will to investigate him properly. By contrast, authorities in Northern Ireland had attempted to bring him to justice. Some unionist politicians who took an interest in the case were highly complimentary about Flynn's work. He got a particular kick out of that as he considered himself a life-long Republican. Eventually, Ross was extradited to the North and stood trial on forty charges. He was convicted of four and served nearly two years in prison before being released on appeal.

Billy Flynn wrote a book about the whole affair with the inevitable title *Gibgate*. The self-published book was at one stage withdrawn from shops because a senior counsel who featured in it threatened a libel action. Yet the book found its way around the world. Indeed, a unionist politician, Roy Beggs, presented a copy to President Bill Clinton at a White House reception. Despite the restrictions on distribution,

Gibgate somehow got out, and for many in Ireland it was their introduction to Billy Flynn.

In the book Flynn made no attempt to make himself out to be any kind of angel. 'I am stubborn by nature and have a natural distrust of the establishment. I also loathe injustice. Especially when its victims are in no position to fight back. Don't get me wrong – I was no crusader. I entered this profession purely and simply to make money.'

Another case Flynn took on was that of hundreds of Irish immigrants in the UK who had been shortchanged by solicitors in Ireland in the processing of wills. The exiles, the vast majority of whom hadn't even completed second-level education, had been easy pickings. Flynn doggedly pursued the issue and managed to retrieve a considerable amount of money, winning praise from people like Ireland's ambassador to the UK at the time, Noel Dorr.

The campaign attracted media comment in the London-based *Irish Post* newspaper. Columnist Frank Dolan related the story of what Flynn had done, ending his column with the line: 'You will, I am sure, join me in lifting your hat to William Flynn in Enfield, Co Meath. He is a rare species in Ireland – a truly decent man.'

One day in the mid-nineties, Flynn opened his front door to be met by a man who was effectively cold-calling. Tom Coffey was a native of Galway, had a beard and a barrel chest and a smile that was warm and mischievous. He was going door to door selling televisions. *Would you, sir, have any interest in viewing the merchandise?* Flynn looked him up and down. If somebody calls with that kind of an offer you need to check the cut of his jib. Flynn liked what he saw and invited him in.

Once in the sprawling office, Coffey noticed the piled-high copies of *Gibgate*. He had read the book on the urging of his brother and had been highly impressed with the drama, the pursuit, the burning desire to right a wrong. Seeing the stack, he suddenly copped that he was in the presence of the book's author.

'We got talking and Billy said to me you look like a shrewd kind of a fella. He handed me two sheets of paper which were about a case he was on and asked me what I would do. I went into the next room, read the thing and came back to him with my opinion. Something clicked there and he asked would I be interested in working with him. I didn't have too many better offers at the time. Seriously, though, after reading *Gibgate*, I was thrilled to be on board.'

So began a working partnership that produced results. The pair of them were unconventional, even disarming on first viewing. But they were also serious men, driven in their pursuit of a result, fortified by the knowledge that they believed right to be on their side. Around the time that the Kerrigan sisters approached Flynn, he and Coffey were engaged in a major case of garda corruption which would in some ways close a circle that had been opened twenty-five years earlier in the Una Lynskey investigation.

Early in the morning of 14 October 1996, Richie Barron, a cattle dealer from Raphoe in Co Donegal, headed for home on foot after an evening's drinking in local pubs. At 12.55 a.m., his body was spotted on the side of the road, on the outskirts of the town. He had last been seen a half-hour earlier. Initially, gardaí assumed that he was the victim of a hit-and-run accident. Within forty-eight hours they had upgraded their investigation to murder.

There had been bad blood between Richie Barron and a family of local publicans, the McBreartys, so somebody in the gardaí latched on to this and put two and two together and made five. A tribunal chairman would later describe what then unfolded as 'the ability of hatred to transform myth into fact'.

The guards decided that Frank McBrearty Jr and his first cousin Mark McConnell had a case to answer for the murder of Richie Barron and arrested them. Mark McConnell later gave an interview to reporter Gerard Cunningham about what happened when the guards called to his home, where he lived with his family.

'I went to the front door and met Garda John O'Dowd. He put his hand on my shoulder and told me he was arresting me for the murder of Richie Barron. I went weak at the knees. I was standing just in my night clothes, the child standing behind me as this was all happening.'

While in custody, McConnell says, he was verbally and physically abused. He was called a 'big fat murdering bastard' and 'pushed and hauled'. At one stage a detective told him to look at post-mortem photographs of the late Richie Barron. McConnell refused.

'Eventually he [the detective] got frustrated with me. He reached for my hair and pulled my head towards the photographs. I still tried to keep away from them, but he kept pushing my head down into the photographs and telling me to "fucking look at what you've done".'

Then a senior officer came in. He 'slapped down a four- or five-page document in front of me with a smirk on his face,' McConnell recalled.

'He said, "That's a confession there to the murder of Richie Barron from Frank McBrearty Jr and he's implicating you."'

The detective then read the 'confession' out to McConnell.

'I remember vividly the opening line, it was "I Frank McBrearty Jr am showing remorse for what I have done." I remember thinking there's no way Frank would ever use them kind of words. That wasn't his vocabulary.'

'At the end of it, after four or five pages, was a signature. I know for a fact it wasn't young Frank's signature at the bottom of the bit of paper, he had a funny way of signing his name. Young Frank was released shortly after me. They'd done the exact same thing with him; they came in with a statement supposedly from myself. Young Frank came out and said to me, "Mark, don't believe anything them bastards said to you in there," and he stormed off.'

Frank McBrearty Jnr had a similar tale of abuse in custody. A tribunal would later accept that both men had been ill-treated in the garda station.

Over the following months the McBrearty family were subjected to continual harassment from gardaí. At some point, Frank Snr decided to seek help and came across the name Billy Flynn. He travelled to Flynn's home with his wife Rosalind and poured out the literal tale of woe to which their family had been subjected. A family being persecuted by the state was the kind of case that was right up Billy's street. He took it on. While Flynn travelled to Donegal several times thereafter, Tom Coffey led the investigation on the ground.

Coffey interviewed everybody associated with the case. The McBreartys filled him in on all possible connections and a history of bad feeling between various families in the area that had never really subsided. On calling to one house in an isolated rural area, Coffey was assaulted and had three ribs broken. 'At that point I was going full-out up there,' he remembers. 'I hadn't been home to my family in

Galway for seventeen days. It was a job chasing some people for interviews.'

Word began to drift back to Coffey that he was attracting attention. 'I was in one of the pubs in Raphoe having a pint one evening when this fella told me that the guards were going around talking to people who I had interviewed. I checked it out and it was true.' Then on one of Flynn's excursions up to Donegal the pair of them were sitting in a car in the diamond in the centre of the town.

'They blocked Billy in,' Coffey says, referring to gardaí in an unmarked car. 'Pulled the car out in front of him and just stared at him. They were letting him know that they were on to us.' Quite obviously, the operation of the police in the county was unorthodox, to say the least. Much of what Flynn and Coffey say they experienced would subsequently be endorsed by a tribunal of inquiry set up to examine the whole affair.

Coffey wasn't one to be easily intimidated. On one occasion he noticed that he was being followed. He was heading to the border, and as he drew near a flashing light appeared on the roof of the car behind, while a siren began wailing. Coffey didn't let up but flew right across the border into the neighbouring jurisdiction. 'About a hundred yards in I stopped the car and got out and lit a cigarette. The boys didn't cross over; they weren't going to take that chance with an active garda car. So I gave them the two fingers from the safety of the North. One of them then pulled a gun and pointed it at me. I said to myself, *There's brave and there's stupid.* And I had been stupid there.'

Ultimately, the two investigators cracked the case. Key to the McBrearty complaints was that elements in the gardaí were harassing them. If that could be proved it would inevitably lead to a full investigation into the gardaí's activities. One of the forms of harassment was threatening late-night phone calls to members of the McBrearty family. These purported to be from local people who believed the family to be guilty of murdering Richie Barron, but Frank Snr, and subsequently Billy Flynn, believed they were coming from somebody associated with the gardaí.

Flynn had a contact in Telecom Éireann, the state telephone company. He organized for his contact to track one of the calls that had been made to the McBreartys. This, of course, was illegal. Once he got word that the information he wanted was available, he dispatched Coffey to get the goods.

'I was to meet this man in a car park in Sligo,' Coffey says. 'He had the number of my car. He approached me and we swapped envelopes. There was no conversation and he just took off again.'

Flynn related to the subsequent Morris Tribunal that he knew exactly what he was doing.

'What I did was an unlawful act and I could face charges on it,' he told Judge Frederick Morris. 'But I considered my clients were facing murder charges, their pub was being harassed, McBrearty Snr was being accused of bribery and I was prepared to take the risk.'

The information he uncovered forced garda management to investigate. That turned out to be unsatisfactory and ultimately led to a tribunal of inquiry that was conducted in public. Several gardaí were identified as being central to what had gone on and the McBrearty family received large sums in compensation.

The tribunal, which recommended the setting up of an independent oversight body for the gardaí for the first time, acknowledged Flynn's and Coffey's role in uncovering the corruption. And one of the letters that Flynn dispatched in the course of his investigation got to the source of the rot.

'It was believed that Mr Barron was the victim of a hit and run and, as I understand from Mr McBrearty, the circumstances of Mr Barron's death took a twist which has resulted in what he has described as a horror story or a nightmare experience where Frank Sr and Frank Jr are the gardaí's prime suspects for the alleged murder of Mr Barron, and where the McBrearty family are the subject of garda harassment consistent with what was known in the past as "the Heavy Gang".'

The Heavy Gang had nothing to do with Donegal. The Murder Squad on which it was centred had long been disbanded by then. But the pernicious legacy left by its activities remained. Beginning with the Lynskey case, and persisting for at least fifteen years, members of the Murder Squad had gone about their business with impunity. Some gardaí had looked on askance, disturbed at the methods that had been deployed. Others saw what some of their colleagues got away with and decided to emulate them. The sense of impunity ensured that a virus infected elements of the force. Finally, as a result of this Donegal case, there was a reckoning.

Once they'd done all they could in the Donegal case, Billy Flynn and his confederate Coffey turned their full attention to uncovering what had gone so catastrophically wrong in the investigation into Una Lynskey's death.

23. Investigation

Tom Coffey pulled up outside the house in a village in the midlands. He spoke briefly with his passenger, Padraic Gaughan, got out of the car and approached a house on the street. Coffey was well advanced in the investigation into the death of Una Lynskey that his colleague Billy Flynn had started. Padraic Gaughan was with him now to try and identify a possible suspect for the killing. Over twenty-five years previously, on the evening of Una Lynskey's disappearance, Gaughan was one of those who had caught a fleeting glance of the man in the Zephyr car seen on Porterstown Lane. What unfolded immediately afterwards ensured that the man's face remained frozen in Gaughan's mind. Now, the investigators Flynn and Coffey had reason to believe that they might have located this suspect.

The man answered Coffey's knock. In the car Padraic Gaughan strained to get a good look at him, but it wasn't possible. He got out of the car and walked up to the front door, where Coffey and the man had engaged in a brief chat. Gaughan asked would it be OK to use the bathroom.

No problem, came the reply, and Padraic went into the house, to emerge a few minutes later. The brief exchange had been enough for him. The years rolled back and he was on the lane again, coming home from work, living through the last hours before his community would be irreparably damaged. He knew that face. It was twenty-five years ago, but the face was burned into his consciousness down all the years.

'I got a good look at him,' Padraic says. 'And everything about him was what I saw in the car that day.'

It was early 1999. The cold-case murder investigation by the private investigators was well under way by then. If justice was to be attained for the two Martins, Conmey and Kerrigan, then the real killer would have to be located. Flynn and Coffey had set about their task using basic police methods. The starting point was to interview everybody. The Kerrigan sisters were obviously eager to assist, as was Martin Conmey and Dick Donnelly. Digging up the past was as painful for them as for anybody else, probably more so, but they had a purpose.

Word was passed to other family and friends. Most local people who were approached willingly helped in any way they could. Flynn applied to the courts for the files from the original trial. Pretty soon, it became obvious to them that timing was a crucial factor in the case. They did a few tests of the run from Coyles' farm to where the Kerrigans had lived in The Bush and on to Porterstown Lane.

'I interviewed Mr Tayto Park,' Tom Coffey says, referring to Ray Coyle. 'He was perfectly satisfied that the men had been telling the truth. He was at the time, and he remained so, and he told me that.

'The thing is that, apart from anything else, the three lads simply could not have done what the guards said they did in that timeframe. It just wouldn't have been possible.'

Not everybody was willing to cooperate with this new investigation. Flynn wrote to all the Lynskey family whom he could locate. He received no replies. He found out that some of Una's siblings were living in Carlow and he travelled to see if they would cooperate. He was given short shrift. When he persisted, he received letters from solicitors, telling him to desist from approaching individuals. Their reluctance to cooperate with somebody who was effectively representing the relatives of Marty Kerrigan is understandable. Every indication is that the Lynskey family continued to believe that the gardaí had identified the correct suspects for Una's murder.

The two men approached the gardaí who had been involved in the original investigation. 'None of the guards would talk to me,' Coffey says. 'I approached Courtney, but he didn't want to talk. Some of the others may have been dead at the time. I know that Billy tried to locate as many as he could, but they didn't want to know.'

The investigators also tried to contact Thomas Mangan, the young man who had shared digs with Martin Conmey and subsequently claimed that Martin had confessed his involvement in Una's disappearance. Mangan's evidence had been central to the garda case. Years later, he didn't want to talk about it. He too had a solicitor send a legal letter in response to approaches from the two men.

Flynn didn't confine his inquiries to only those who had been directly involved in the case. He was aware that the community in Porterstown Lane had been very closely bonded, through both blood and the connection with the Erris Peninsula. To get a rounded picture he sought out others whose memories and voices might be independent. One such person was a woman who had grown up in the general area but removed from the immediate community in Porterstown. The letter of introduction he sent her is typical of his disarming style, something that often allayed any suspicions people might have had about a private investigator.

Dear Helen,

I am retained to investigate the true circumstances of Una Lynskey's disappearance and death and attempt to identify those responsible for same and to have them brought to justice. I have been a private detective for 20 years and this is perhaps the most tragic case I have ever come across.

I have read all the trial documents and to get a feel or picture for the case my staff and I have now commenced interviewing all the residents who resided around Porterstown Lane about that time and to seek everyone's assistance in my task and I note that you and your family lived on the main road i.e. the Dublin/Navan Road.

You have been described to me by a mutual friend as a most sincere and genuine person. I trust you will appreciate from my end that most of the families in Porterstown Lane are nearly all inter-related and we would like the views of independent families living in the area at that time.

I would stress there is no obligation on you whatsoever to meet with my representative and I have given my representative Christine your phone number and she will contact you for an appointment and I hope you will find time to meet with Christine and any help you can give us would be very deeply appreciated.

I have the pleasure of enclosing a complimentary copy of my book 'Gibgate – The Untold Story' and I trust you enjoy same in common with other readers to include Bill and Hillary Clinton.

Yours Faithfully
William G Flynn

The investigators also took statements from people who had been around at the time yet didn't feature in the garda investigation. Men such as Gerry Monahan, who was a contemporary and friend of the three men the gardaí had fingered as suspects. After their questioning in Trim garda station, Monahan had met the men individually. 'I saw each of them as friends of mine and I wanted to reassure myself of their innocence and them of my friendship,' he told Tom Coffey.

Dick Donnelly showed Monahan his injuries the day after he was released from Trim. 'His arms were bruised and there was one dreadful-looking wound on his left arm. Dick told me this was done by a red-hot poker being shoved into his arm. He told me he was punched and kicked. The lash marks on his back was done by a poker. This, I think, was told to me at Kerrigan's house.'

Marty Kerrigan in turn told Monahan that he was stripped naked in the station. 'He got kicked in the bollocks. When he got kicked the garda that did this said, "That is what you stuck into Una Lynskey," Marty told me the cops threatened to bring in the Lynskeys, put him in a cell with them and they would kill him. They continuously asked the same questions and did not believe his answers.

'After speaking to Marty and Dick following their release, my reaction was one of shock and horror. I was fucking mad. I decided there and then to call the *Irish Press*.'

He got in touch with a reporter from the *Irish Press* newspaper, then Ireland's leading daily. He met a *Press* reporter in Ratoath and brought him to Marty Kerrigan's house.

'He had a camera. He took photographs of Dick's injuries. I asked the reporter would he print an article. He said he would. I dictated the article to him in the company of Dick and Marty. They confirmed what I said to be correct before this reporter wrote it down. The reason the article was not permitted was because he refused to include the names of the offending gardaí and he stated that the article would be edited. Neither article nor photography was ever published. I never had any contact with this man again.'

Gerry Monahan died in 2022. His statement to Coffey would suggest that the media was alerted to what had gone on in Trim but declined to publish. There could have been many reasons for not doing so, but fear of libel would have featured prominently.

Another strand of Flynn's investigation involved attempting to trace the Zephyr or Zodiac seen in the lane on the day Una disappeared. Flynn had a number of contacts in the motor trade, and he set about documenting the extent to which each model was on the road at the time in question. As so many years had passed, the task proved extremely difficult. How much easier it would have been had a serious effort been made by the gardaí to do so in 1971.

In the original garda investigation, an artist had been deployed to make a photofit of the man seen in the Zephyr on the lane. Padraic Gaughan had been visited in his home by several gardaí and the artist. He assisted as best he could, though he had been puzzled that they asked him if the emerging face in the picture wasn't Dick Donnelly's, not only because he knew Dick but because the man he had seen in the Zephyr was quite obviously middle-aged.

Now, over two decades later, Padraic was being asked to complete a photofit once again. Could he still, all those years later, see that face? 'I met Billy a couple of times and he asked me to come down to his house, and we went over some statements and he had brochures with the car in them. I wasn't into cars, all I knew was it was a Zephyr or Zodiac, but I was impressed with Billy. He always reminded me of Columbo.*

'When Billy asked me to do the photofit, I could remember it exactly,' Padraic Gaughan says. 'I can still today. It's burned in my memory because of everything that happened after it.'

Flynn organized for an artist to put together the photofit in Padraic's home. Like many others who had grown up in the area, Padraic hadn't strayed too far in adulthood. He had grown up on the cul-de-sac off the lane and now he lived on the lane, married to Martin Conmey's sister, Mary.

Martin Conmey's first cousin, Michael McIntyre, was asked to come over to Padraic's to help with the photofit, as he too had seen the car on the day in question when driving to Ratoath to pick up his brother Tony and their friend, Sean Reilly. On his way up he had met the car going in the opposite direction and remembered it because the driver had been too far out on the road. He had described the car and driver in his statement to the gardaí, but the information seemed to have fallen on fallow ground.

Padraic's wife, Mary, looked on as the process got going. 'I couldn't believe it, the way that both of them had retained such detail. It was so long ago. But when the artist drew a particular part of it they would come in, sometimes one of them, others both, and point out, no, it wasn't exactly like that. At one point Padraic said stop to the artist, you have him now. And then Padraic got quite emotional.'

Flynn had a copy made of the finished product and sent it back to the two men. Gaughan looked at it, but he wasn't entirely satisfied, so they made a few minor adjustments.

* The rumpled but shrewd TV detective in the eponymous series.

When it was completed, there was a shock. Billy Flynn pulled his glasses from his forehead down on to his eyes and examined the artist's work. He pulled up the glasses and effected the kind of dramatic pause to which he was often given. 'Jesus, I think I know that fella,' he said.

In fact, he knew a few people who might plausibly match the artist's impression. The principal figure lived in a town in the midlands. Two other possible matches were farmers.

'There were three individuals that Tom brought me to see, two farmers and that other man,' says Padraic Gaughan. 'I ruled out the two farmers straight away once I saw them. The other man, though, I got a good look at him and everything about him was what I saw in the car that evening.'

Tom Coffey remembers it slightly differently. 'I got out of the car and this fella didn't want to talk to us. Padraic got a good look at him in the end, but he said it could be him, that there was a good chance, but he didn't say it definitely was. This was twenty-five years after it happened too; you have to take that into account.' The sightings were followed up by Flynn and Coffey but ultimately they were unable to assemble a body of evidence that might have made a reasonable case against any of the men in question.

There were other suspects. One was a garda who had lived locally and had since died. Old newspaper clippings featuring his photograph were located and opinion canvassed among those who saw the strange car that evening. Again, nothing conclusive emerged. The private investigators kept digging, but operating as they were, without the kind of power vested in a state agency like the gardaí, and attempting to piece together events from over two decades earlier, they were fighting an uphill battle.

*

Locating the killer was one strand of the investigation. The other was dismantling the case that had been made by the gardaí in the original probe. In pursuit of this, Flynn and Coffey obtained the transcript for the trial in 1972 and did a detailed analysis of the evidence. They identified many weaknesses, including the failure of counsel to explore some avenues of inquiry. One of these was the original photofit that Padraic Gaughan had given to the guards in his house in the days after Una's disappearance. If he had been asked about this, it would have raised serious questions as to why the man in the strange car did not receive greater attention.

Some of their analysis of the evidence was speculative. For instance, Coffey went over in detail the testimony of Winnie Lynskey during the *voir dire*, conducted to determine what evidence should be put before the jury. 'There are a large number of queries with regard to the evidence of Mrs Winifred Lynskey and it is understandable why Mr Lovatt-Dolan (the prosecuting barrister) readily accepted the judge's ruling to not allow her evidence in court,' Coffey wrote in a report he compiled as part of the investigation.

He gave a few examples of some of the terms and language she had used in the witness box, describing one of the gardaí as 'a Technical Bureau man', and saying at one stage, 'I didn't pursue it any longer,' and referencing at another point 'some members of the force'. In Coffey's estimation this use of language suggested that she had been coached.

'It is obvious from her evidence that this was a well-schooled, well-coached and easily manipulated witness,' Coffey reported. 'She uses terminology that one would not associate with her background (i.e. rural West of Ireland people). Being one myself, a West of Ireland person, I would argue that all of Mrs Lynskey's evidence was scripted by the gardaí to further their case and to frame the defendant Martin Conmey.' The analysis certainly raises some valid questions, but it may be unfair to Winnie Lynskey.

One element of the transcript proved to be vital – the evidence of Sean Reilly, his hesitancy in the witness box and his refusal to confirm the statement he had signed in Trim garda station. Coffey interviewed Reilly a few times, and Reilly was more than happy to cooperate. He related all that had occurred in Trim and the kind of pressure he and his late friend Martin Madden had been put under. The changed statements were key to the garda case at the time. And the investigation by Flynn and Coffey uncovered that the earliest statements from Reilly and Madden had not been made available to the defence in the trial. If the defence lawyers had access to these statements, it would raise the question as to why they were changed, particularly as no reasons were provided for the changes. On 1 April 1998, Reilly gave a statement to Tom Coffey that would form the bones of an affidavit that was to prove vital to the whole case. In it, he related for the first time on paper what exactly had happened to him in Trim when he and Martin Madden were brought in.

> If I was slow in giving answers, I would get punched on the shoulders and chest, they did not hit me in the car on the way to Trim. They fucked and blinded, the language was very violent and abusive.
> They told me I would be blamed for Una Lynskey's disappearance unless I told them what they wanted to know. I was very afraid. They kept telling me that I was hiding

something. They were of the opinion that I knew something and to get me to agree with them, they hit me,
threatened me and eventually got me to say what they
wanted me to say. They frightened me into saying what
they wanted me to say.

I was sick and sore after my period in Trim garda station. I believe the first time when Donnelly's car was
mentioned was while I was in Trim garda station. I have no
memory of saying anything about Donnelly's car in my
original statement. Neither do I recall saying anything
about Martin Kerrigan in that statement.

I now say that while the car may have sounded like Donnelly's I believe it could not be his and I don't know who
owned the car. I cannot identify the occupants of that car,
it was nearly dark and I don't know what colour it was. The
gardaí in Trim persisted that I knew the car, that I knew the
occupants, that I knew the colour and eventually through
fear, having been threatened with being implicated in the
disappearance of Una Lynskey and having been beaten I
signed what they wanted me to sign. I believe everything in
this statement to be true and would swear an affidavit to
this effect.

A grounding affidavit on which the case was to be brought
was sworn by one of the solicitors, Deirdre Moran. In it she
outlined the background to the case and the basis for
making the appeal.

The applicant has instructed this firm of solicitors to act
on his behalf. He wishes to have his case reopened and
reinvestigated. The applicant has never before or since this

case been convicted of a criminal offence. He was and but for this conviction would be in a position to still describe himself as being of impeccable character. He is now a married man and has a nine years of age child. His concern was that his child was of an age when he would ask questions about his father and he instructed us that he did not wish his child to think that he was responsible for killing Una Lynskey.

The affidavit was filed in 1999. If Conmey and his representatives thought that they would receive a prompt response from the state, they were badly mistaken. Already, they had experienced the snail's pace that was going to be deployed by the state. Their experience was not unique. Frequently, when the gardaí, or other agents of the state, have faced legal action, locating and collating files has presented difficulties. This usually happens when the case at issue dates back a number of years. It often emerges that there are problems locating files that would present a full picture to the court. Naturally, those who are taking on the state will assume that this is a cover-up, and there are often good grounds for believing so. It is also the case that simple incompetence sometimes means that files are not kept.

In October 1997, Conmey's solicitor had been told by the chief state solicitor that the documents were stored in both the National Archives and garda headquarters. Three months later, the state's agent changed tack. Conmey was informed that the DPP was 'constrained by law not to release the documentation sought'. This forced Conmey to go to the High Court for an order to discover the documents. The court complied, but the slow turn of the wheels of justice meant that it was another four years before the state finally provided what it said were the relevant documents. By then, a large portion of the overall file had been lost.

Some of the file was in garda headquarters, and this was handed over to Conmey. However, much of it had been retained in Dunshaughlin station. At some point, these documents were transferred to Drogheda station, where they were retained in the women's toilet in the building in a plastic rubbish bag. A superintendent who had been charged with retrieving the file told the court that quite possibly between November 1997, when the documents were taken to Drogheda, and 2001, 'the materials may have been mistaken for rubbish and disposed of.' The room in which the bag was stored was rat-infested (which was a grim insight into the women's toilet at Drogheda station).

Originally, the file had consisted of 371 statements. All that was ultimately recovered were statements from 105 people, so a total of 266 statements had gone missing since Conmey first applied for the material. In that, some will see conspiracy and others incompetence or wilful neglect.

The portion of the file retained in the National Archive didn't fare a whole lot better. After Conmey requested the material it was forwarded to the DPP's office in 1998. Thereafter it got 'mislaid'. Eleven years later a file was produced through a body called the Government Supplies Agency. A court was later told that the file mislaid and the file retrieved in 2009 'may be one and the same'. The file retrieved from the agency did not have some crucial documents, specifically depositions taken from Sean Reilly and Martin Madden in the district court in 1972.

Two issues arise from the long road of retrieval of documents which the state had a duty to retain. First, in both the files retained by the gardaí and those taken possession of by the DPP, portions went missing after Conmey first applied for sight of them. Second, the state's position when, eventually, Martin Conmey got his case into court – the state claimed it should be thrown out because it had taken too long.

The court gave that application short shrift. The reason it had taken so long was that various arms of the state were so slow in producing documents that, by right, a man who was fighting to clear his name was entitled to.

Despite the delays, the apparent prevarication, the long slog, the wheel of justice was grinding slowly to a conclusion. Martin Conmey would have his day in court, and this time it would be in an entirely different country from the one in which he was convicted of killing his neighbour.

24. Justice Beckons

John Courtney walked forward to the witness box. His erect posture and alertness belied his advanced years. Now in his eighties, Courtney had been hauled out of his retirement to account for his actions when he had been in the prime of life. He had the look of a man who was completely unflustered to be coming in for what was effectively a review of how he had gone about his work nearly forty years previously. Giving evidence in court had been a routine part of his job. On this day he was back at it again, but this time one of the central issues would be whether or not he had told organized lies in the trial of two men for the murder of Una Lynskey.

The road to Martin Conmey's appeal hearing was long and tortuous. Nearly twenty years after he set things in motion, he was finally having his day in court. The hearing, which began on 27 April 2010, was taking place in the Criminal Courts of Justice, just across the Liffey from Heuston Station. The modern new building was mainly for criminal trials, leaving the Four Courts to hear civil matters.

Conmey was surrounded by friends and supporters – his sister Mary Gaughan and her husband Padraic, his mother Eileen, his friend of forty years Dick Donnelly, Dick's wife Ann, and her sisters Katie and Eileen, there to bear witness on behalf of their deceased brother, Marty Kerrigan.

The court consisted of three judges: Adrian Hardiman, Declan Budd and Éamon de Valera. Two of the country's top criminal law barristers, Hugh Hartnett and Michael

O'Higgins, were representing Conmey, while another leading barrister, Brendan Grehan, appeared for the state. On
opening the case, Hartnett told the court that there were
'newly discovered facts', which included the existence of
earlier, contradictory statements from key witnesses and a
previously unknown allegation of violence and 'oppression' by gardaí against one of these witnesses.

A number of witnesses were asked to recall events from
thirty-nine years previously.

Mary Gaughan, née Conmey, told of the day her brother
Martin came home from Trim garda station. Mary read out
a letter she had sent to a friend about how Martin was
beaten up by two guards who had 'rolled up their sleeves'
and punched him in the face. Her voice broke as she read
how their house had become 'like a nightmare that Tuesday'. None of them had slept and her father had heard
'awful shouts' as he left the garda station.

'I couldn't believe it when I saw my brother – one side of his
face was all swollen and I could see where his hair was pulled
out,' she said. She broke down as she left the witness box.

Martin Conmey gave evidence of what he had been subjected to in Trim garda station. He had given similar evidence
in the *voir dire*, in the absence of the jury, in his murder trial
in 1972. He related what had occurred in Trim: the shouting, intimidation and violence. Then he was asked about his
experience in Rathfarnham station on the day that Marty
Kerrigan was killed.

Conmey told the court he was shown photos of Marty's
body that day and told, 'You'll be next up there.'

On day two the key evidence in the trial was given by
Sean Reilly. The statements he and Martin Madden made in
Trim were the basis for bringing in Martin Conmey, Dick

Donnelly, Marty Kerrigan and Christo Ennis. If there was an issue about those statements, or how they were obtained, then admissions that Conmey subsequently made in Trim could be regarded as null and void. Reilly told of making a statement to the gardaí in which he said he saw a car but couldn't identify either it or its occupants.

'So, just so I'm clear about this, are you saying you didn't know whose car it was?' he was asked by Grehan.

'I didn't know whose car it was. I couldn't know whose car it was because the way Martin Madden's car was facing my back was to the road.'

One of the judges then intervened: 'Is that account given in the first statement? That the car was facing in?'

'Yes,' counsel replied.

'The car was always facing in, yes,' Reilly said.

He went on to give details of what occurred in Trim when he was brought in. He told them that he had related once again the contents of his original statement. 'They were not satisfied with this,' he said. 'I was punched on the outside of the shoulder and on the cheek.' He said that a few different detectives were interviewing him at different times, up to six of them. He said he was punched three or four times, the table was banged, gardaí swore at him.

The worst, he said, was Garda Brian Gildea. 'I can tell you he was frothing at the mouth with temper. They tried to tell me that I knew it was Dick Donnelly's car that passed while I was sitting with Martin Madden. But as I say again, there was no chance of me knowing that because I wasn't turned out towards the road, but to tell them fellows, they weren't listening to me.'

Courtney then gave evidence. He was brought through

various aspects of the investigation into the disappearance of Una Lynskey. He was asked about the status of detention of the three men in Trim.

'They were not suspects,' he said. 'They came voluntarily to the station, they were not in custody.' It is factually accurate that they had come to the station voluntarily and therefore were not officially in custody. It is not credible that Courtney and his colleagues did not consider them suspects at that point. The whole legality of their custody, and particularly the intervention of gardaí to stop Martin Conmey going home with his parents on the second night of his detention, have always been highly contested.

Hartnett cross-examined Courtney on the allegations of violence.

'You were the nice guy, Gildea the bad guy?'

'Nothing untoward happened,' Courtney replied.

He was asked about the hair that was missing from Martin Conmey's head. Conmey had claimed that Gildea pulled it out as he lifted Conmey from the floor, having delivered him a blow. The gardaí, including the head of the Murder Squad at the time, Hubert Reynolds, claimed that it was self-inflicted. How did Courtney recall it?

'I can't remember anything about it,' he said. 'I used no violence on him whatsoever.'

What about the lack of sleep endured by the three men over the forty-four hours they were in Trim station?

'I'd be very concerned if somebody didn't get a reasonable amount of sleep.'

Then there was the nub of the case being brought by Martin Conmey – the ever-changing statements from crucial witnesses. Why did the gardaí go back to witnesses again and again and emerge each time with different details, which usually enhanced the case being made by the gardaí that the three young local men were culpable?

'It often happens that we had to go back to witnesses four or five times to get the full facts from them,' he said.

The only other surviving garda who was in Trim during those days was Michael Fanning, who had been based in Drogheda at the time. He was asked about the difference in the statements from Reilly. He agreed there was a 'total difference' between both statements but said that didn't strike him at the time.

He said he was not involved in taking the first statement from Sean Reilly. He also said neither he nor Garda Brian Gildea had used violence or coercion against Mr Reilly. Garda Fanning said he never saw his garda colleague lose his temper, and denied any colleague was 'frothing at the mouth'.

Barrister Harry Whelehan, who had been a junior counsel for Donnelly in the original trial,* was called to give evidence. He was asked whether he could remember if the earlier statement given by Reilly was seen by him or his colleagues. His answer was comprehensive.

'While I have no recollection, I don't believe those statements were furnished to us. If they had been furnished to

---

* By the time of this hearing in 2010 Harry Whelehan's name was famous. In 1992 he had been the Attorney General in the case of *Attorney General v. X*, one of the most contentious and consequential cases ever to come before the Irish courts. The X case – the X in question being a pregnant 14-year-old rape victim seeking an abortion in the UK – ignited a decades-long campaign to liberalize abortion law in Ireland, something that finally happened in 2018. A further controversy in 1994, relating to the bungled handling of an extradition case by his office, and Whelehan's appointment to the High Court while the controversy was still raging in the media, resulted in the collapse of the government. Days after taking his oath of office, Whelehan had to resign from the bench and return to the bar.

us, on my reading of the papers, I would have expected to find that the existence of any additional statements by these witnesses, which were not entirely consistent with one another, would have been used to challenge their credibility and their reliability. And furthermore I am firmly of the view, and I know that hindsight is a wonderful thing, but in this case I have no doubt that it is correct, that if we had been able to establish that these witnesses in the case, who are not implicated, had been brought a number of times to the garda station and further and additional statements required from them, that we would have been able to explore how they came to be brought back several times to the garda station; the nature of the interrogation or questioning to which they were subjected; and to establish a possible consistency between the allegations made by Mr Conmey relating to his treatment in custody, and indeed Mr Donnelly, concerning his treatment while in custody, and the treatment of the witnesses who are not in any way implicated in the investigation except for the purpose of putting together a sequence of events.'

Marie Teehan, who had been Conmey's solicitor in 1972, also gave evidence. 'I have no recollection of seeing them,' she said of the earlier statements. 'It is as simple as that. I did not see – I cannot recollect ever seeing them. No, and I can't understand, but that if we were made aware of them and we had seen them that we would have had to take them into account and had to do something with them.'

After five days of hearing the court rose to consider its verdict.

Judgement in the case was scheduled for delivery on 22 November. One of the key people who had got the case this far was not in attendance for the big day. On Sunday, 31 October, Billy Flynn was working at home. He had for some years been threatening to retire, constantly declaring, 'This will be my last case.' At the end of the Conmey hearing the previous May, he had told Padraic Gaughan that he would find out who had killed Una Lynskey before he retired. His latest case was to chase down subprime lenders who he believed were defrauding borrowers. During the afternoon he went for a lie down and never woke up. Billy Flynn was sixty-four when he died of a suspected heart attack.

Another absentee was Eileen Conmey, Martin's mother. She was still alive, but not in good health. Everybody else was there though. The ruling was to be delivered in the Hugh Kennedy Courtroom in the Four Courts, where the Supreme Court usually sits. The room is just a stone's throw from the Round Hall, where the original murder trials took place in 1972. At 10.05 a.m., Martin Conmey entered the room. He went and sat beside his friend Dick Donnelly, just as they had thirty-nine years earlier in the same building when they sat accused of murder. Around them were Dick's wife, Ann, and her sisters, again there for Martin, but also for their brother Marty. Martin's sister Mary and her husband, Padraic Gaughan, were in attendance also. At the other side of the room were two women who grew up in Porterstown Lane, two of the Lynskey sisters, also there to bear witness.

At 10.10 a.m. the ruling was delivered. Judge Hardiman didn't read it out in full but said that the court had ruled Mr Conmey's 1972 conviction to be quashed. There were audible gasps in the court, most likely of disbelief, and then people got to their feet and began clapping. Martin Conmey looked dazed. 'Even when he said the words, I didn't know that the conviction was quashed. I turned to Stephen

[Cooney, his solicitor]. I was in shock. I couldn't believe it. I didn't let myself believe it. Then I just began crying.'

At fifty-nine years of age, Martin Conmey was shedding an awkward, horrible skin that he had acquired on the cusp of adulthood. He had lived most of his life with the stain of having been declared a killer. Not just that, but a man who had killed a woman, a young neighbour with whom he had practically grown up. His tears flowed. He was not alone. For Ann Donnelly, and her sisters Katie and Eileen, this was also for their brother who had never had the chance to live past the age of nineteen, who had died with the same stain that his friend Martin Conmey was now free of. Martin's wife Ann and son Ray rushed to embrace him. Then the others came in around the family, a community huddling together in joy and relief, the families who had borne this for nearly forty years, who had seen nearly all their parents go to their grave with the whole thing unresolved.

The two Lynskeys looked on in silence and quickly got up to leave. They did not comment, but from their demeanour it was obvious that they didn't believe justice had been done.

Outside the court, Conmey told the media that the years since his conviction had been 'hell'.

'I'm just so delighted that the court has come to this decision, and they've seen justice at last and seen that there was a wrong done to me,' he said. 'I've been innocent, and I've suffered all these years.'

Standing next to him, Padraic Gaughan was sobbing openly. Padraic mentioned the role of the gardaí in what had occurred.

'They didn't investigate the case properly, and they destroyed families over this,' he said. 'They hounded three young men for years.'

323

On Martin's other side, his sister Mary, Padraic's wife, remembered Una Lynskey, who, she said, had not been given justice, as her real killer had never been found. Mary held up the photofit that Padraic and Michael McIntyre had assembled for Billy Flynn's investigation. 'This man could have been found within a week,' she said.

'It made me bitter,' Conmey told the *Irish Examiner* days after the ruling. 'It destroyed me in some ways, having taken away so many years of my life, but at least the result restored some of my faith in the justice system. I'm just sorry my father didn't live to see my name cleared. And Billy Flynn. He worked tirelessly on the case. It's terrible unfortunate that Marty Kerrigan never had the opportunity to walk into a court to clear his name.'

The basis for overturning the original conviction was the changing statements of Sean Reilly in particular, but also those of Martin Madden and John Shevlin, the 13-year-old boy who had given four statements to the gardaí. Madden and Shevlin were both deceased by 2010, so Reilly was the only one of the three available to give evidence.

The court found that after Reilly and Madden had given their original statement, 'they were again interviewed, a process which produced dramatically different, quite contradictory statements.' This, Judge Hardiman said in his ruling, 'led to the applicant [Conmey] and his friends being taken to Trim garda station'. At the station, Conmey was 'told that Madden and Reilly had made statements putting your car in the opposite direction at a different time'.

'In other words,' the judges ruled, 'he was confronted with the later, unfavourable statements of the men named, but not with their earlier, favourable accounts. On the hearing of this application there was evidence that a large Zephyr or Zodiac car had been seen on Porterstown Lane about the relevant time, but the description of the occupants was inconsistent with any of the three suspects.'

The ruling went on to point out that the gardaí came back to Reilly, Madden and Shevlin for further statements.

'Why they did this and why, and how the statements changed, are all unexplained, except in the case of Mr Reilly.' This was a reference to Reilly's evidence of having been intimidated and assaulted while in Trim garda station.

The eleven-page judgment went on to conclude:

In those circumstances the existence of the original statements and the questions which must necessarily arise as soon as these originals are considered, about how the witnesses' account came to change, appear to be highly relevant both to the question of the applicant's movements at the relevant time, and quite separately, to the question of the veracity and reliability of the garda account of the legality of his lengthy retention (to use a neutral term) in Trim Garda Station. On this, in turn, depends the admissibility of the statements attributed to the applicant while in Trim Garda Station. It is quite impossible, especially after so many years, even to approach certainty as to what the effect of this non-disclosure was. However, the task of the Court on an application such as this is not to attempt the fruitless task of achieving certainty about a hypothetical change in the evidence in a trial that took place more than thirty years ago. It is instead to resolve the question whether this is a case '. . . where facts came to light for the first time after the appeal which showed that there might have been a miscarriage of justice' [this was a quote from a previous judgment]. The Court is of the opinion that it is such a case. On this basis the Court will quash the conviction of the applicant.

In 2014, the Court of Criminal Appeal issued a certificate of Miscarriage of Justice to Martin Conmey. That opened the way for him to take a legal action against the state for the way he had been treated. Two years later, the High Court was told that a settlement had been reached between the parties, which was to include the payment of a substantial sum of compensation. As part of the settlement, the state issued a public apology to Martin Conmey.

> The Minister for Justice and Equality, on behalf of the State, wishes to formally acknowledge that Mr Martin Conmey, who was convicted of certain offences in 1973 and served a term of imprisonment in consequence, was a victim of a miscarriage of justice. This has been certified by the Court of Criminal Appeal.
>
> The State apologises unreservedly to Mr Conmey. The State regrets the pain and loss experienced by Mr Conmey as a result of his imprisonment and has taken steps to pay appropriate compensation to him in accordance with the provisions of the Criminal Procedure Act 1993.

At the age of sixty-five, Martin Conmey could feel that he had fully retrieved the good name that had been taken from him forty-five years earlier.

25. Anniversaries

Una Lynskey
Late of Porterstown Lane, Ratoath.

October comes with sad regret,
Those dark days we will never forget.
Little did we know what was in sight,
When you walked down Porterstown Lane that night.

Deeply missed and always in our thoughts by your sisters, brothers,
aunts, cousins, sisters-in-law, brothers-in-law, nieces, nephews,
grand-nieces and grand-nephews.

 – Memorial for Una Lynskey in a newspaper
notice on the fortieth anniversary of her death.

Detective Superintendent Des McTiernan entered the conference room at 11 a.m. on 12 October 2023, the fifty-second anniversary of the disappearance of Una Lynskey. The room is on the ground floor of Walter Scott House on Military Road near Heuston Station, home to some of the specialist units of An Garda Siochána, including McTiernan's Serious Crime Review Team. It is the building where the Murder Squad were based in 1971, but it has been totally renovated. McTiernan sat before a bank of TV cameras and reporters on the far side of the long conference table. He took out his glasses and began reading from a prepared statement.

The Serious Crime Review Team examines what are known as cold cases, mainly crimes of violent death that have remained unsolved. The team has had some successes. Earlier in 2023, Noel Long of Maulbawn, Passage West, in Cork had been convicted of the 1981 murder of 54-year-old Nora Sheehan. That followed a painstaking investigation. Also in 2023, thirty-nine years after Joanne Hayes had been falsely accused of murder, two arrests had been made in the Cahirciveen baby case. Now the team was turning its attention to the coldest case it had ever tackled.

McTiernan read out the background facts to the Lynskey case. 'The murder of Una Lynskey on 12 October 1971 and the subsequent murder of Martin Kerrigan on 19 December 1971 has devastated the Lynskey, Kerrigan, Donnelly and Conmey families,' he said. 'Both murders still have an impact on the community in Ratoath.' His classification of Martin Kerrigan's death as murder was technically inaccurate, as three men had been convicted of manslaughter rather than murder in that case.

'The family of Una Lynskey are seeking clarity on matters relevant to the murder of their sibling,' he said. 'The subsequent prosecutions taken against Dick Donnelly and Martin Conmey have had a significant impact on them and their families.

'Martin Conmey and the families of Dick Donnelly and Martin Kerrigan have questions as to the garda investigation that took place in 1971. I, as the reviewing officer, have been appointed to carry out a full review of the investigation into the murders of Una Lynskey and Martin Kerrigan. A full review involves the independent examination of all material gathered in the course of all relevant current and past investigations,' he said.

'My intent is that this full review will hopefully answer all questions highlighted by the Lynskey, Kerrigan, Donnelly and Conmey families and bring the events at the end of 1971 to some conclusion for those involved.'

The superintendent took a few questions from the media but little that added anything to the statement. Asked what matters the Lynskey family were seeking clarity on, he said he wouldn't comment on that. Normally, the primary matter of concern to the family of a murder victim is identification and prosecution of the perpetrator. If that was the case in this instance it is difficult to understand why the detective superintendent wouldn't say so. If, on the other hand, the Lynskey family continued to believe that the three local men were responsible for Una's disappearance, there is nothing that the gardaí could do about that. Conmey and Donnelly had been cleared of any involvement in her killing. Considering that, it is impossible to envisage a scenario where Marty Kerrigan would have been found guilty, had he lived.

McTiernan also refused to say whether anything new had come to light all these years later which had prompted the full review. He was asked by the author of this book was he prepared for uncovering a scenario where the Murder Squad in 1971 had identified the wrong suspects and then tried to build a case around them by intimidation, assault and, ultimately, organized perjury.

'That's a hypothetical situation, but I understand why you are asking it,' he replied. 'Any review worth its salt has to be independent and impartial and, rest assured, that this review will be that.'

There was no getting away from the reality of what he and his team were facing. A full review of the case would have to examine why the three local men were identified and pursued to the exclusion of any other leads. The most obvious lead at the time was the strange car sighted in the area in the time before and after 7 p.m. on 12 October 1971. McTiernan told the press conference that there had been up to ten sightings of cars in this period. This is factually correct, but most of the sightings pointed towards a particular car and some of those had descriptions of the driver.

A full review would have to explore how so many original statements were subsequently changed, particularly in relation to Sean Reilly, Martin Madden, Mary Collins and John Shevlin. Was it a coincidence that each change honed in further on the three local men? Why, in all the sequence of statements, was there no explanation whatsoever as to why the witness was providing a different account in their latest version? And in the case of Reilly and Madden, was their treatment in Trim garda station a contributory factor to their changed statements? Reilly told the Court of Appeal in 2010 that the changes he made were the result of sustained intimidation, some violence and prompting from the gardaí interviewing him.

A review would also have to examine the treatment of the three men in custody, for which there is substantial evidence that they were assaulted. It would have to find out whether the Lynskey family were informed about the gardaí theory, whether they were encouraged in their belief that their neighbours had murdered their loved one. If all of that was found to have a basis, then the ultimate conclusion is that a whole range of gardaí were complicit in assault of the men in custody and committed organized perjury in the murder trial of Martin Conmey and Dick Donnelly and bore some culpability in heightening a grief-induced rage in the Lynskey family.

The road to the review was curious. The case had attracted intermittent attention over the previous two decades or so. In November 2000, the author of this book reported in the *Sunday Tribune* on the investigation by Billy Flynn and Tom Coffey. It went quiet after that until the 2010 Court of Criminal Appeal hearing and ultimate ruling. In 2014, Conmey's receipt of a miscarriage of justice certificate attracted further media attention.

In 2018, TG4 broadcast a programme on the case, including interviews with Conmey and others. The Irish-language station has a record of excellent programming but has a narrow reach. Then, in January 2022, RTÉ One television broadcast a three-part series, *Crimes and Confessions*. The programme, made by award-winning reporter Mick Peelo and producer John Downes, examined three stories involving the Heavy Gang: the Lynskey case, the Sallins mail train robbery case and the Kerry Babies case. The first programme was to be the Lynskey case, scheduled to broadcast on Monday, 10 January 2022.

The previous Friday afternoon, Martin Conmey answered a call to his home on Porterstown Lane. He opened the front door to the sight of a garda sergeant, who asked him to confirm that he was Martin Conmey. The sergeant then handed him an envelope and made off. The envelope contained a letter from the garda commissioner, Drew Harris. The commissioner was offering an apology for any pain and suffering felt by Martin Conmey as a result of the garda investigation in 1971. Curiously, the letter didn't say what exact actions the commissioner was apologizing for. The courts had determined that Martin had been the victim of a miscarriage of justice and the state had apologized for what he had been put through. But no court or inquiry had ever determined that the gardaí had behaved in a manner for which there should be an apology. Yet the commissioner, who was only in the job since September 2018, was telling Martin Conmey that, on behalf of his organization, he was sorry for anything that had been done wrong against him.

Drew Harris is regarded as a compassionate man, in the best tradition of police, and cognisant of the plight of victims of crime. Yet a sceptic might view his gesture as little more than a public relations exercise before the broadcast of what was expected to be a damning exposé about the conduct of the Heavy Gang and its influence on garda culture, something that would attract a lot of critical public attention.

Some months later, the commissioner met with members of Marty Kerrigan's family, including his sister and Dick Donnelly's widow, Ann. The family told him that they wanted some acknowledgement or apology from the gardaí for what had happened to Marty. While Dick and Martin Conmey had been exonerated in the courts, Marty did not have a chance to defend himself. He was killed precisely because his killers believed him to be responsible for Una's death. The commissioner was receptive to their request and said that he would attempt to meet their requests by the end of the year.

In September 2022, the family were told that the case was now the subject of a cold-case review, which would include circumstances around Marty's death. As a result of this development there would be no apology for the

Kerrigan and Donnelly families until the review was completed. The review, at the time of publication of this book, is ongoing.

The first forty-eight hours are vital in any police investigation. If a suspect is identified in that timeframe, there is a greater chance of a successful outcome. Similarly, the evidence collected in those early days is the most important and is most likely to identify a suspect. Once the days push on, the trail can go cold. When, as has happened often in miscarriages of justice cases, a suspect is identified early who turns out to be innocent, all other avenues tend to be closed off. In such a vacuum it will be very difficult to restart an investigation and find a culprit.

In the recent cold cases where the gardaí have been able to progress the investigation, nearly all have had DNA as a central plank of evidence. There does not appear to be any possibility of DNA evidence in the Lynskey case. Una's body had been through just shy of ten weeks of decomposition when discovered and there were no notable traces of any forensic evidence that could be attributed to another person. This means that any new leads depend on the faint possibility that somebody might come forward with information half a century after the fact. Obviously, the strange car, a Ford Zephyr or Zodiac, which was seen in the area is a clue. As is the sighting by at least three witnesses of a middle-aged man driving it.

Inevitably, rumours have filled the vacuum. Some locally suggested that Una's killer was known to her. Others speculated that the killer could have been associated with Una's work in the Land Commission, either a colleague or somebody who engaged with her through her work. Again, this may have been an avenue worth exploring at the time, but it wasn't. There has even been speculation that the arrival of the Murder Squad in Porterstown Lane within forty-eight hours was curious. Were they dispatched to ensure the investigation would go in a particular direction? There is no factual basis for such a conspiracy theory, but that hasn't stopped it being disseminated. While major questions arise as to how the Murder Squad went about its task, there is nothing to suggest they were, initially at least, acting in anything other than good faith in the Lynskey case.

Billy Flynn's and Tom Coffey's investigation threw up some clues, but they couldn't identify a prime suspect. There was of course the photofit picture Padraic Gaughan and Michael McIntyre came up with for Flynn, the one Martin Conmey's sister Mary held up outside the court when her brother's conviction was finally quashed, suggesting there was a possible suspect out there gardaí should look into. Based on the photofit, Flynn had identified three possible candidates, and on meeting one of them Padraic thought he bore a close resemblance to the man he saw in the Ford Zephyr or Zodiac on Porterstown Lane that night. However, this was always likely to be regarded as a flimsy lead, as the photofit had been created so long after the events of October 1971. The man Tom Coffey brought Padraic to check out is now dead. To have cracked the case over twenty-five years after the event, and without access to the powers and resources vested in a law enforcement agency, would have been a gargantuan task.

In 2012, the case was raised in a totally unconnected tribunal of inquiry. At the time a tribunal was investigating whether there had been any garda collusion in the murder of two RUC officers in Northern Ireland in 1989. The pair

had been returning to Belfast following a meeting with
gardaí when they were killed by the IRA. One of the gardaí
who was suspected of colluding with the IRA was Detective Owen Corrigan. This was the same Owen Corrigan who
had been in Trim garda station interviewing Dick Donnelly
in October 1971. Donnelly had alleged that he, along with
Brian Gildea, was the most aggressive garda that Donnelly
had encountered.

At the tribunal in 2012 Corrigan gave evidence about his
work, including his history of being picked for involvement
in murder investigations. 'I had been part of hand-picked
teams, investigated murders all over the country,' he told
the chair of the inquiry, Judge Peter Smithwick. 'I have been
working with the heads of [every head of] the Murder
Squad since 1969, and when I was in Drogheda I was – it
was the murder of a girl called Una Lynskey and then . . . It
was [a] more relaxed atmosphere.'

Five months earlier, the *Sunday Independent* had reported
that the tribunal was examining whether there might be a
connection between the Lynskey case and the IRA.

'Sources close to the tribunal said lawyers are looking
into the possibility that Una Lynskey was murdered by a
member of the IRA who was either living in the area near
her home or was in the area when the teenager got off the
bus. The possibility that a garda acted to protect an IRA
figure who may have carried out the murder "is not being
ruled out" by the tribunal,' the report stated.

'Lawyers acting for the Smithwick tribunal have requested
papers from the Court of Criminal Appeal and from the
gardaí about the quashing of the case.'

The obvious connection was Corrigan. Nothing came
of it. John Courtney was asked about it at the time but

dismissed it out of hand. Again, in a vacuum, conspiracy theories flourish. Owen Corrigan died in 2022.

During the course of researching this book, the author was contacted by a woman who said she had information about Una Lynskey's murder. This woman was based in the south-east. She claimed that she had always suspected her brother-in-law of being involved. This suspicion had arisen in the days after Una disappeared, but then it was discounted when Donnelly and Conmey were charged. In recent years, with publicity again focused on the case, she thought about it again.

Her brother-in-law, referred to here as Mr X, used to drive around to race meetings with a friend, a man who owned a large car, either a Zephyr or Zodiac. The Fairyhouse Race-course is literally around the corner from Porterstown Lane. The car owner was a middle-aged man, while Mr X was in his late twenties. The woman was often in the car, as she used to get a lift to Dublin with them when she was a teenager. She claims that in the days after 12 October 1971, an aunt of hers claimed that Mr X was responsible.

Mr X had a record of violence and robbery. On 30 October 1971, he was remanded in custody on robbery and assault charges. Subsequently he was sentenced to five years in prison for the offences. As best can be established, the car owner was never convicted of any serious offence. The records also show that there was no race meeting in Fairy-house on 12 October or the week preceding or following that date. Further inquiries have not led to establishing any other links. Mr X died in the late 1980s.

Again the question arises: who knows what might have emerged if gardaí had done the painstaking work of tracking down all owners of Ford Zodiacs and Zephyrs in 1971? Mr X might have turned up for consideration and been looked into further or eliminated. Either way, it would have been a lead. Tracing the owners of Zephyr or Zodiac cars at the time would not have been an impossible task. Police work can be grindingly slow, frustrating, and more often than not leads down redundant alleys. But all of that work is undertaken with the aim of eventually arriving at and establishing the facts. Once the decision was taken to focus entirely on the three local lads, every other possible lead was discounted or ignored.

Finding the killer today is a mammoth task, though there may be somebody who has knowledge of what occurred, or, like the woman from the south-east, harbour a strong suspicions. The gardaí may eventually be able to identify a prime suspect. But acquiring enough solid facts to the point that naming such a person could be justified remains a long shot. The chances of ever identifying who killed Una Lynskey remain remote. And after all this time, it is likely that the culprit or culprits are dead, having, literally, got away with murder.

26. All Their Tomorrows

In 1971 Porterstown Lane was a small, tight, rural community of displaced westerners, farmers for the greater part, bedding in as first-generation Co Meath people. Today the lane is a desirable long-reach suburb of Dublin. There were eighteen homes on the lane, including down the cul-de-sac, in the year Una Lynskey and Marty Kerrigan died. Today there are seventy-seven.

On the lonely stretch of the lane from the Fairyhouse Road, where Una met her killer, there were no houses. Today there are fifteen. All along the lane the houses are big and the families generally small. Back in 1971, the young people on the cusp of adulthood had grown up with anything from five to ten siblings. Today, in houses, some of which are a multiple of the size of those at the time, typical families might have two or three children. A brochure in 2023 advertising one of the houses on the lane went like this:

> Located on this popular road on the outskirts of Ratoath village. Ratoath offers a multitude of facilities, including supermarkets, restaurants, the Venue Theatre, music school, not to mention rugby, soccer, pitch and putt, etc. Excellent choice of junior schools and a secondary school are all within minutes' drive. Commuters are well catered for as Porterstown Lane is equal distance from both the M2 & M3. Dublin Bus provides an hourly bus service

between Ratoath/Dunshaughlin and many locations in Dublin including City Centre and Dublin Airport. The property benefits from a bus stop at the bottom of Porterstown Lane – a mere five-minute walk.

This new world has been superimposed on the one that existed in 1971. Many who grew up there still live in and around Porterstown Lane. Martin Conmey and his wife, Ann, live within a stone's throw from where Martin grew up. Further along the lane, Martin's sister and her husband, Padraic Gaughan, live close to where they both came of age. Sean Reilly is still there. So is Christo Ennis, still married to Vera.

Ann Donnelly lives between the lane and Ratoath in the home where she and her husband, Dick, reared their children. Dick died in 2020. He and Martin Conmey remained firm friends all their lives. Katie Kerrigan also stayed local. She married Brian O'Neill, from whom Dick acquired the new body for his Ford Zephyr earlier in 1971. Eileen Kerrigan also remained, living in the home in The Bush where the family were all reared. Every year the sisters make a point of visiting Billy Flynn's grave, as a gesture of gratitude for what the private investigator did for their family.

The wounds opened up in the autumn of 1971 didn't heal. The Lynskeys or the Fairyhouse Road Gaughans never came back. Neither was there any reconciliation with the other Gaughan family who had stood by the accused men.

Padraic Gaughan had some brief encounters with his estranged cousins over the years. 'We did meet at funerals along the way,' he says. 'A few of them turned up at my father's funeral, and we met at a few others. Michael Gaughan came back to the house after my mother's funeral and we had a good chat. Me and Michael would have been friends before it all started. I think he was at Dick Donnelly's funeral too, but we were all wearing masks then, during Covid. There was another time also when my brother Anthony was home from America, we went down the country. We decided to call into Michael's pub in Durrow, and we met and chatted. We didn't talk about those times. Me and Danny went down to a few funerals too. That's as much as there was, really.'

There was one major change as the decades rolled on. Martin Conmey's successful Court of Criminal Appeal hearing and all that flowed from it made a huge difference to his life and that of his family. Both his family of origin and those who had been his friends in 1971 all shared in the sense of vindication. 'The Gaughans [Padraic Gaughan's family] in standing by us back then meant so much to me and my parents,' Conmey says. 'It was a big decision for them to make.'

Still, though having his name cleared and receiving some compensation brought some relief to Martin and his family, the past never really went away. A few years after his conviction was overturned, Martin was set to holiday in the USA with his wife, Ann. He didn't reveal his conviction when applying for the holiday visa, simply because it had been wiped. Yet that wasn't how the Americans saw it, and his plans to visit were thwarted at the last minute.

'The night before we were due to fly, I got word that the visa was cancelled,' he said. 'We lost four thousand euro on the holiday. Later, when we were going again, I had to go to the American embassy and apply in person, disclose everything about what had happened. That got it sorted, but it was a reminder.' The couple have since also been to

Australia for a holiday, enjoying the sense of freedom that Martin had been denied for so long.

As for John Courtney and the Murder Squad, after completing the investigations in Porterstown Lane they had moved on, leaving devastation behind them rather than resolution. Courtney would go on to feature prominently in the work of An Garda Siochána over the following two decades. His 1996 memoir, *It Was Murder*, recounted his work on some of the most high-profile cases seen in the country.

Included, for instance, was the investigation into the deaths of Bridie Gargan and Donal Dunne, who had been murdered by upper-crust killer Malcolm Macarthur in 1982, which set off a major political controversy after Macarthur was discovered hiding out in the apartment of the government's Attorney General. Courtney was much praised for his role in identifying and arresting Macarthur. He also mentioned the Kerry Babies case, which he oversaw.

There was no mention in his book about what was one of the most high-profile cases to feature in his career, the investigation into the deaths of Una Lynskey and Marty Kerrigan. The omission was notable. By 1996 there was no question of the case being revisited, as it eventually was fourteen years later. Why didn't he include it in his long record of cracking serious crime? Was it something he thought best forgotten? If so, why?

Courtney died in 2017. He had been regarded as a top cop, albeit one who, due to the many rumours and allegations about various investigations on which he had worked, often had the word 'controversial' affixed to his name. In an interview the year before his death, he looked back on his career.

'It could be hard at times,' he told the *Kerryman* newspaper. 'You see a lot of tragedy, and looking at dead bodies is never nice. You can't think about it too much. You just do your job and try to do the best for people. You work away, plug through and try to solve the problem.'

Within An Garda Siochána he was highly regarded. In journalist Harry McGee's book about the Macarthur case, *The Murderer and the Taoiseach*, a detective who worked under him, Brian Sherry, described Courtney to McGee as tough but fair.

'You didn't bullshit Courtney. You daren't bring in a statement that was only half done, or where you had failed to ask all the relevant questions.

'If you prepared a statement, you made sure you asked everything. You drained the witness of every scrap of information they had in their head, you bore into them to try and get it.

'Courtney would be there at the table at six o'clock in the morning reading statements. And if your statement was not up to scratch, when the conference started, he would tear ribbons off you.'

Undoubtedly, Courtney did the state some service over the course of his career. He solved many crimes, brought solace to victims. He was, for the greater part, a highly efficient cop. He was in a crucial role at a time when some in politics believed the state to be under threat and gardaí like Courtney vital cogs in defending it. Yet there is also copious evidence that he misused his power at various points, and in doing so not only broke the law in solving crimes but targeted and destroyed innocent people.

In 2012, when the theory about an IRA link to the Lynskey case was raised, Courtney was interviewed by the

Sunday Independent. He dismissed the theory. Just below the interview the report continued as follows: 'Other sources told the *Sunday Independent* that gardaí were satisfied that two men had attempted to abduct Ms Lynskey with the intention of raping her but that she had suffocated. One of these suspects was Martin Kerrigan, a young local man who is believed to have been one of the two men who abducted Ms Lynskey and after she died partially buried her body in the Dublin Mountains.'

The source is unnamed, but it may well be the case that Courtney related this element to the reporter on an 'off the record' basis. This is standard practice – and entirely legitimate – in reporting. By 2012, Martin Conmey had been cleared. So, the story now being related was that Marty Kerrigan had been in the car with one other. This couldn't but have been Dick Donnelly, who had been cleared back in 1972.

Immediately after Marty Kerrigan's death, when it suited the garda theory, it had been thrown around that Conmey and Donnelly were the two in the car. Now it was expedient to imply it had been Kerrigan and Donnelly. Throwing in that rape had been the objective was a despicable detail. Courtney may not have been the source for this nugget, but it is difficult to see who else it might have been in 2012. If he was the source, it reflected very badly on his character. It also illustrated that even so late in the day, despite copious evidence, he simply could not bring himself to accept that he had targeted the wrong men. Perhaps in doing so he would have had to allow into his conscience the possibility that he bore some responsibility for the chain of events that led to Marty Kerrigan's violent death.

*

A number of attempts were made in the course of writing this book to make contact with the Lynskey family and John Gaughan, who was convicted of Marty Kerrigan's manslaughter. Most approaches were ignored. Marita Lynskey agreed to meet the author, and she spoke briefly about her memories from 1971. She was just eight at that time but her cooperation was highly valued and appreciated.

For the greater part, the family has maintained total silence about Una's disappearance and the fall-out. Their pain and bereavement are obviously deep. By all accounts, the large family has remained close. It appears that most, if not all, the family continues to believe that the three local men were responsible for Una's death. There have, over recent decades, been a few social media posts to that effect. On the fiftieth anniversary of Una's disappearance and presumed death, her sister Sally Kirwin posted the following on a social media platform.

> On this day 50 years ago our beautiful sister was taken from us. She went to work in Dublin, went to see our sister Cathy, who was expecting the first baby in the family during her lunch break. Travelled home with her cousin Ann and said there [*sic*] goodbyes at the top of the road. She walked down the road home. A road she had walked many times since childhood. But as she approached a slight turn in the road at the bridge evil awaited her. She was taken by 3 evil animals. How scared and terrified she must have felt when they passed the cup de sac [*sic*] to her home where she was safe in the love of her parents, Granddad and siblings. For weeks they searched but to no avail. Our parents and Granddad were from Co Mayo and on the 8th December they travelled to Knock to pray that her body be found.

A few days later a lovely man made the grim discovery. Our worst fears came through [*sic*]. Una was gone. Robbed of her life at the hands of evil. Never again would we see her beautiful smile or feel her love and kindness. And so today we meet to have her 50th Anniversary in Knock Co Mayo. RIP Dearest sister we will never forget you. Forever young Xxxx.

Following publicity about the case in 2022, in response to a social media post about what an 'interesting' case it was, Una Lynskey's niece, Una Curran, posted the following:

This may be an interesting story to you & your subscribers but please remember this is not a story to her family. This was a hugely traumatic event at a time with no counselling or support available for the family. The media have published many different reports over the years with no awareness of the trauma it causes to her parents & family. Please consider how you would feel if a stranger was telling a story of a murder of one of your family members. After 51 years Una's beautiful soul deserves to be allowed to rest in peace & the trauma of her family acknowledged.

The pain that has reverberated down through generations is obvious. However, like the gardaí who were involved, the apparent collective view of the Lynskey family has to be seen in light of the killing of Marty Kerrigan. If Kerrigan was innocent, then Sean and James Lynskey and John Gaughan would have to face up to an appalling vista. Everything around Una's disappearance would have to be seen in a different light – the reality that their family was not the only one to lose a member violently in an act of extreme injustice. In the absence of a new prime suspect in the case, it is understandable that the Lynskeys hold firm in their belief about the guilt of the men the gardaí told them were responsible for Una's murder. As outlined in the previous chapter, the prospects of the cold-case review positively identifying a new suspect are slight. What the review can do is scrutinize how the 1971 garda investigation was conducted. It has some chance of accessing the truth about how Dick Donnelly, Martin Conmey and Marty Kerrigan came to be the gardaí's sole focus. But even if the cold-case review's conclusions about the 1971 investigation are damning, without a credible new suspect it is hard to see the Lynskeys accepting the three men's innocence.

After all this time, the cold-case review's priority must be to address the injustice that is the stain on Marty Kerrigan's character. When Marty Kerrigan died, he was suspected of committing murder, and that was why he was killed. He never had the chance to clear his name. Arguably, if he hadn't been killed, charges may never have been preferred against him or his two friends. Had things not come to such a violent head, there's a slim possibility that the Lynskey family might have come to accept that their neighbours had nothing to do with Una's death.

Marty Kerrigan's five siblings have carried his torch all their adult lives into their autumn years. Their one remaining wish is that the record shows that their brother was an innocent man whose status as a murder suspect was based on lies.

'It has been there for a lifetime,' Ann Donnelly says of the fight to clear Marty's name. 'Our whole lifetime has been taken up with trying to clear all their names and the stain that they were left with. Our dad never recovered. The night he was dying he mentioned James Lynskey, who was Una's grandfather, the head of the family that brought them all here from Mayo. That man had nothing to do with what happened to Marty, but it was as if he was thinking if any of it would have happened if the Lynskeys hadn't come over with the rest of us.

'And he was saying, "Don't let Katie get into the car with them." He was reliving the whole thing with Marty. It had stayed with him always, how it had happened, how he lost his son.'

Ann says that her husband, Dick, before he died in 2020, would have loved if some way could have been found to clear his friend's name. 'We were all thrilled for Martin Conmey when he won in court, we were all there with him. And he and Dick were there together, but Marty never made it.'

'Justice is what we want,' Ann's sister, Katie, says. 'We want justice, and we deserve it. We want to clear his name. We want an apology from the gardaí and the state. I'd like to think we are closer to getting an apology, but I don't know. After everything, surely it's not too much to ask?'

Acknowledgements

The writing of a book about recent historic events requires assistance from a whole range of people, from those who were around at the time to guardians of public record and historians. Many of the scenes depicted in this book, including those in garda stations, are reproduced from accounts given by those who were present.

People who lived in the general Porterstown Lane area in 1971 were extremely helpful. Ann Donnelly and Katie O'Neill, Marty Kerrigan's sisters, and Marty's niece Michelle Donnelly, were always open and welcoming, as were Martin and Ann Conmey and Padraic and Mary Gaughan. All these families also provided me with invaluable records. The late Dick Donnolly was always very helpful down through the years when I had reported on this case.

The recollections of Sean Reilly, Christo and Vera Ennis, Danny Gaughan and Marita Lynskey were also invaluable.

Tom Coffey was gracious with his time, and Billy Flynn's son and daughter, Patrick and Jackie, provided assistance and gave me access to Billy's files. Billy Flynn introduced me to this case over twenty years ago and I am extremely grateful for that. I still miss his friendship and sense of drama and fun. Martin O'Halloran's time and his book on the Land Commission were also helpful, as was Gerry Moloney. Journalist Mick Peelo was generous with insights and information. Others to thank are Gerry Curran and David McLoughlin from the Courts Service and Catriona Crowe.

ACKNOWLEDGEMENTS

The role of some gardaí in this story reflected badly on their organization. However, it would be wrong to paint all members then or now with the same brush. Both serving and retired gardaí, all of whom would prefer to remain anonymous, provided background information and insight.

The *Irish Examiner* has always given me time and the opportunity to follow stories such as this one and for that I am grateful to various editorial executives past and present, including Tim Vaughan, Allan Prosser, Tom Fitzpatrick and John O'Mahony.

Ronnie Bellew and Maureen Gillespie read drafts of early chapters and Gary Murphy, Shane Colemen and Una Clifford provided encouragement.

Luke and Tom Clifford separately assisted with survey work for the price of lunches in Ratoath.

Pauline Sweeney held the fort while I disappeared to South Kerry at various points to make progress with the writing. Her love and support have always been key to getting through a big project such as this one.

Thanks as always to my agent, Faith O'Grady. At Penguin, Michael McLoughlin and Patricia Deevy were supportive and professional. Thanks also to copy-editor Sarah Day.

This book is dedicated to my mother, Aideen Clifford, a writer and teacher, who like many of her generation suppressed her own talents to concentrate on raising a family. She read early chapters and offered the same tenor of advice as she did fifty years ago reading my first school compositions.

It is also dedicated to the people who lived in and around Porterstown Lane at the time of the two killings.